PENGUIN BOOKS
SRIKANTA

SARATCHANDRA CHATTOPADHYAY (1876–1938) was born in Devanandapur, an obscure village of Bengal. His childhood and youth were spent in dire poverty as his father, Motilal Chattopadhyay, was an idler and dreamer and gave little security to his five children. Saratchandra received very little formal education but inherited something valuable from his father—his imagination and love of literature. He started writing in his early teens and two stories written then have survived—'Korel' and 'Kashinath'.

Saratchandra came to maturity at a time when the national movement was gaining momentum together with an awakening of social consciousness. Much of his writing bears the mark of the resultant turbulence of society. A prolific writer, he found the novel an apt medium for depicting this and, in his hands, it became a powerful weapon of social and political reform. Sensitive and daring, his novels captivated the hearts and minds of thousands of readers not only in Bengal but all over India.

Some of his best known novels are *Palli Samaj* (1916), *Charitraheen* (1917), *Devdas* (1917), *Nishkriti* (1917), *Srikanta* in four parts (1917, 1918, 1927 and 1933), *Griha Daha* (1920), *Sesh Prasna* (1929) and *Sesher Parichay* published posthumously (1939).

ARUNA CHAKRAVARTI took her master's and PhD degrees in English literature from Delhi University. Her academic record has been a distinguished one, her doctoral dissertation on Ruth Prawer Jhabvala being described as a 'valuable contribution to Anglo-Indian studies', by one of her examiners. She taught in Delhi University for many years and retired as the principal of Janki Devi Memorial College.

Aruna Chakravarti's translation of *Srikanta* fetched her the prestigious Sahitya Akademi Award. *Those Days*, a translation of Sunil Gangopadhyay's *Sei Samai*, published by Penguin Books India in 1997, received rave reviews and became a best-seller. This was followed in 2001 by *First Light*, a sequel to *Those Days*. She has also written a novel, *The Inheritors* (2004), and has edited a volume of Bengali short stories, *The Way Home* (2006).

SARATCHANDRA CHATTOPADHYAY

Srikanta

Translated, with an Introduction, by
Aruna Chakravarti

PENGUIN BOOKS

An imprint of Penguin Random House

PENGUIN BOOKS

USA | Canada | UK | Ireland | Australia
New Zealand | India | South Africa | China | Singapore

Penguin Books is part of the Penguin Random House group of companies
whose addresses can be found at global.penguinrandomhouse.com

Published by Penguin Random House India Pvt. Ltd
4th Floor, Capital Tower 1, MG Road,
Gurugram 122 002, Haryana, India

Penguin
Random House
India

First published by Penguin Books India 1993
This edition published by Penguin Books India 2009

This translation copyright © Aruna Chakravarti 1993

All rights reserved

10 9 8 7 6 5 4 3 2

ISBN 9780143066477

Typeset in Palatino by Digital Technologies and Printing Solutions, New Delhi

Printed at Manipal Technologies Limited, India

www.penguin.co.in

MIX
Paper | Supporting
responsible forestry
FSC® C043100

This is a legitimate digitally printed version of the book and therefore might not
have certain extra finishing on the cover.

To K. P. C.

in undimmed remembrance

Contents

Introduction   ix

The River   1

Exile   105

Forbidden Fruit   223

Journey's End   331

Glossary   487

Introduction

A CONSCIENTIOUS TRANSLATOR TAKES ON THE FORMIDABLE TASK of bridging gaps between cultures and traditions of the world through the medium of a chosen author and language. The Italian proverb *Traduttore tradure* (a translator is a traitor) may warn him about the pitfalls that lie in his path but does not ask him to abandon his task. When the translation is of a work as immense in range and depth as the one undertaken in this volume, the difficulties of communication become almost insurmountable.

'Why then,' the reader may ask, 'did you take it up?' 'For that reason, precisely,' would be my answer. 'The more hazardous the task—the greater the challenge.' But that, of course, is not all.

Srikanta is, without doubt, one of the most significant novels of our age and time—a novel that defies translation. This is not to say that it has eluded translation so far. A number of translation projects have been taken up and successfully concluded in the regional languages of India. But *Srikanta* is a national masterpiece that deserves international status. Hence the need for a translation in a link language such as English which can ensure an extension of its boundaries from a minority of Indian readers to a plurality of receiving minds from all over the world. That its author, Saratchandra Chattopadhyaya, recognized this is evident from his oft expressed wish that *Srikanta* be translated into English.

In 1935, his young friend, Dilip Kumar Roy, published an English translation of his novel, *Nishkriti*. The work was conducted under the supervision of Aurobindo Ghose and an introduction was provided by Rabindranath Tagore. Many eminent scholars, European and Indian, took an interest in the project. But the choice of the novel did not meet with Saratchandra's approval. He thought *Srikanta* more suitable than *Nishkriti* for projection to a Western readership, and urged Dilip Roy to take it up. 'Why do you hesitate to translate *Srikanta*?' he wrote in a letter dated 21 May 1935 and two months before that, Take up *Srikanta* this time. I wish to see its English rendering before I die.' (21 March 1935, *Awara Masiha*, by Vishnu Prabhakar, 1974). His wish was not fulfilled. Dilip Kumar Roy did not translate *Srikanta*.

Saratchandra's desire to see the novel's inclusion in the literature of the West was based on a conviction of its universal validity. *Srikanta* is more than a simple work of fiction. It offers a penetrating analysis of the life and culture of Bengal—itself a microcosm of India—in the century preceding our own. Yet it is no mere sociological document. The social attitudes depicted in the novel are far from obsolete and still exist, in some form or other, all over the country. The devaluation of the female—the prop and support of nineteenth century Indian society—is still a conditioning factor in everyday life. The bride burnings and dowry deaths that are reported in the newspapers every day; the treatment meted out to widows and abandoned women and the double standards that determine man-woman relationships, provide ample testimony to a woman's low worth even in this last decade of the twentieth century.

But the last thirty years or so have also seen a shifting of values in certain sections of society. Contact with the West on a basis of equality has sensitized the educated Indian's perception of women. A novel like *Srikanta* is particularly relevant in the present milieu, for the world it depicts is recognized as still existing in some places, and one that needs to be drastically changed. The enlightened of today's India find themselves identifying with Saratchandra's position with regard to women in a powerfully motivated manner. Saratchandra is, undoubtedly, our first and most fiery feminist writer. It was this recognition that he sought from the rest of the world.

Was the Bengali novel ready to contain a work like *Srikanta*? Was there any precedent in the writings of Saratchandra's predecessors for his sensitive analysis and ruthless criticism of the pressures exerted on women? At one level, we discern a breadth of vision and a bold dismissal of tradition that point to a greater affinity with European writers of the present century than with his predecessors of the Bengali novel. Yet, woven into the fabric of his startlingly original interpretation of everyday life is a streak of preconditioning that unites him unmistakably with his forebears and foster a sense of continuity. Saratchandra's contribution to the Bengali novel lies, therefore, not in a breaking away from the literary tradition he inherited but in an extension and development of it.

A survey of this tradition reveals three phases. The first is dominated by Bankimchandra Chattopadhyaya with his historical romance (*Raj Singha*), novels of social and domestic life (*Visha Vriksha, Krishna Kanter Will*) and novels that are a combination of the two (*Durgesh Nandini, Kapala Kundala, Mrinalini*). The concern is less with social and historical authenticity than with depicting a glamorous world of princes and warriors, ascetics and astrologers, dacoits and a decadent feudalism. His characters are flat, for the most part, as he avoids analysis. His heroes are male stereotypes of the times, and his heroines paragons of beauty and virtue. Bhramar, Prafulla and Suryamukhi live out the traditional ideal of chaste womanhood, reflecting their creator's deep-rooted faith in the Hindu moral order. Romance is the keynote of Bankim's world. All is colour and light, unmarred by shades of grey.

The death of Bankim saw a fading out of this world and an emergence of a new world—a real one peopled by living, breathing human beings. The earliest writing of Rabindranath Tagore, the dominant writer of this second phase, show traces of Bankim's influence. *Rajarshi* and *Bou Thakuranir Haat* are historical romances up to a point. *Nouka Dubi* is strongly biased in favour of traditional morality. With *Chokher Bali*, however, Rabindranath makes a bold deviation from the course charted by Bankim. He creates the child-widow Binodini—universally acknowledged as a landmark character in the growth of feminist consciousness in Bengali fiction. Yet the reader gets the distinct impression that Rabindranath was not sure of how far he wanted to go along with Binodini's rebellion. Rabindranath tears apart the cloud of romance and sentiment that clung to the image of the woman but not with a ruthless hand.

There is recognition and acceptance of Binodini's sexual aspirations but no sympathy. Binodini's rebellion gets her nowhere. Her behaviour grows stranger and more bizarre as the novel advances and at its conclusion she is presented as an image of destruction.

Yet Saratchandra, the lion of the last phase, owed a great deal to *Chokher Bali*. He inherited Rabindranath's realism and his perception of suffering in a society hedged in by traditional norms. But if Rabindranath was satisfied with depiction and analysis, Saratchandra was not. He was an angry rebel who defended human failings and abberations with passionate logic. His relentless questioning in *Srikanta* of the worth of religion and society that only oppress and destroy, brings the novel within the mainstream of serious world literature. Society, in *Srikanta*, wields power in two ways. It is an external force that seeks to crush individual aspirations through established institutions and venerated traditions.

But it also dwells within and has to be struggled against. The characters of *Srikanta* are ruled by the norms they have inherited and imbibed over generations. But some among them—the finest and the most sensitive—have feelings and perceptions that are at variance with these norms. The first, the collective consciousness, is very strong, particularly in women, and so inextricably blended with the second, the individual consciousness, that they are often indistinguishable. Only in cases of extreme provocation do the two separate and are perceived in a state of conflict. The pain and suffering that follows is rarely resolved in death. Death glorifies the protagonist in European tragedy but in Saratchandra's world there is no glory. Death is incidental and tragedy is seen in terms of a slow crushing out of beauty and greatness. Man is robbed of his glory and therein lies his tragedy. A sense of waste pervades the world of *Srikanta*.

The two central characters, Rajlakshmi and Srikanta, whose lives and fortunes provide the connecting link in the series of episodes that make up the novel, epitomize this conflict and the resulting loss. Rajlakshmi's conflict is the more overt for it derives from the dual personality she has been forced to assume over the years. Wedded as a child to an elderly Kulin[*] and abandoned immediately afterwards, she is sold into prostitution by her own mother and becomes the notorious Pyari Bai of Patna—famed for

---

[*] This and all other castes mentioned in the book are explained in the Glossary.

her beauty and her skill in seducing men. Then, one day, in a prince's retinue, she meets her childhood sweetheart, Srikanta, and the little Rajlakshmi she had cherished and nurtured within herself through the stormy years, quivers into life. But Pyari does not die altogether. She lives on—in silence, in secret, rearing her head in flashes. And thus the eternal battle goes on—between a reaching out for happiness and fulfilment and submission to a faith that robs her of all fulfilment. She questions this faith in bitter, stinging words but cannot root it out. She takes Srikanta by the force of her personality—fighting his feeble resistance with every weapon in her possession. But, having won him, has no use for him as he has not been given to her through the holy mantra of wedlock. This mantra, which means nothing to Srikanta, is so important to Rajlakshmi that she puts herself through a strenuous round of purificatory rites so as to be enabled to claim Srikanta as her true husband in the life hereafter. She drives herself towards her goal relentlessly and pitilessly but the peace that comes from such self-denial eludes her. Her prayers and pilgrimages, her hours of meditation and moral instruction are marred by the consciousness of what she is doing to the man she loves. This swaying between two extremes becomes more and more painful. She tries to resolve it by deserting Srikanta and practising the rigid austerities laid down by the Shastras for the life of a widow. Then, becoming aware of the sterility of it all, she returns to her lover. But there is no triumph in the reunion. Srikanta's health is broken and he has learned to find security in a withdrawal from reality. And the bitter battle that Rajlakshmi has fought with herself over so many years has taken its toll— destroying all that was bright, beautiful and divergent in her. At the end of the novel she stands considerably reduced. She has become an automaton engaged from morning till night in soulless service.

Srikanta's conflict is pitched at a much lower key for he lacks Rajlakshmi's strength. Hence his fight is usually lost even before it has begun. Srikanta is less of a hero than any other hero of Saratchandra's novels. An aimless drifter and passive spectator, he has hardly any ties with the world around him yet, like some strange and beautiful parasite, he cannot survive without the support of some other, stronger, form of life. As a young boy he idealized Annada Didi and her unswerving loyalty to the husband who, having raped and murdered her own sister, was a fugitive from justice. In his child's vision she appeared larger than life. She assumed the dimensions of a goddess, of a Sita, a Savitri—chaste women of the epics and legends on which he was reared. This idealization coloured his view of women for many years. Then it faded as he came under the influence of others. From Abhaya he learns to challenge the very basis of the Shastras which exacts unquestioning obedience and unflawed chastity from the wife but leaves the husband free to follow his own inclinations. He understands that moral tradition is geared to the well-being of a dominant class and becomes a powerful weapon in its hands. The Brahmin used it to dominate the Shudra; the male uses it to subjugate the female. It is from Abhaya that Srikanta derives the strength to acknowledge Rajlakshmi as his wife at the end of the second book. But the effect is transitory. Before long his collective consciousness takes over and, though he loves Rajlakshmi, he feels trapped by her love. He has learned from Abhaya that to sacrifice happiness because a cruel world demands it, is a foolish waste—yet he cannot rise to the level of his own aspirations. Like Hamlet he cannot act.

The character of Abhaya is generally believed to be modelled on that of a battered wife of Saratchandra's acquaintance in the mistri *palli* (a locality in which the majority of the inhabitants are mechanics or artisans) of Rangoon. This woman had a lover who was willing to rescue her from her brute of a husband. Such slavish chastity must have appalled the novelist and made him realize that it was far from being a virtue. It was a waste of human potential and an affront to human dignity. What is more, it encouraged men in their evil ways. So he makes his fictitious character leave her husband and live openly with her lover. Srikanta tries to build up a case in favour of traditional morality but it cannot stand the test of Abhaya's intelligent cross-questioning. Abhaya's fiery logic pulls it to pieces, for Saratchandra evolves the brilliant, new technique of making the woman demand her rights in her own voice. He ensures a complete victory for Abhaya's rebel-consciousness over that of her inherited one. There is a struggle but it is brief. Abhaya is the only character in the novel who refuses to accept alienation as a way of life and boldly carves out her own destiny.

Most of the other characters are also based on real people. Rajlakshmi is generally believed to be Dhiru—Saratchandra's childhood playmate from his ancestral village of Devanandapur. The dare-devil Indranath with whom Srikanta goes off on midnight adventures is either Satish Chandra Bhattacharya of Devanandapur or Rajendranath Majumdar of Bhagalpur. Some biographers back one view, some the other. A third point of view—the most credible one—is that the fictitious character is a combination of the two.

Annada Didi is another character located in biography. As a child Saratchandra and his friend often visited a Muslim woman who lived with her snake-charmer husband in a little hut in Malirpur village across the Saraswati river. It is a fact that, after her husband's death, she sold her earrings to the grocer at Devanandapur and left five rupees with him with the instructions that they should be handed over to Saratchandra. She disappeared from the village soon afterwards.

Gahar is another character taken from real life. Three or four miles away from Devanandapur, across the Saraswati river, stood Sri Sri Raghunath Goswami's *akhra* (a place where Vaishnavs assemble for religious worship). A Muslim couple, who had partially assimilated Hindu customs and beliefs, lived near the *akhra* and their son—Gahar—was Sarat's playmate. The only important character for whom no counterpart can be found in real life is the Vaishnavi, Kamal Lata.

And Srikanta himself? Is he and Saratchandra one and the same and do they share a single view of the world? By the novelist's own admission they have a great deal in common. In a conversation with Kalidas Roy, he said that many of his experiences have been depicted as Srikanta's.

'But,' he added, 'they do not follow a common course. Fragments of experience, at different times of my life, have been presented as complete experiences ... with the aid of the imagination.'

Saratchandra evolves an interesting blend of the subjective and the objective for his treatment of this most famous of his characters. With no other character, in his huge gallery, is his attunement more perfect and yet he is Srikanta's bitterest critic. Rigorous and ruthless self-analysis goes hand in hand with intimate self-revelation.

The form of the novel reflects this contradiction. It is a fictional autobiography—a story of the growth of an artist's consciousness. But there is no movement towards a predetermined conclusion. The overall impression is one of structural disruptions and indirect presentation. Though not a travelogue, *Srikanta* is built around many journeys—physical and spiritual. It has the noise and confusion of a departure, the weariness and monotony of a lengthy journey and the fatigue of a midnight arrival. A sense of ceaseless travel leading nowhere pervades the air. Its prevailing atmosphere is analogous to a nightmarish journey of the soul.

Asked once about what he considered *Srikanta* to be—a travelogue, an autobiography or a novel—Saratchandra replied, 'A collection of scattered memories—nothing else.' (*Sarat Samiksha* by Shudhwasatwa Basu, 1975.)

The River

One

As I SIT DOWN TO TELL MY STORY IN THIS FADING AFTERNOON OF my wandering life, I am flooded with memories.

From childhood onwards I have carried the mark of shame branded on me by friends and strangers alike, so that I can no longer view my life as anything other than a prolonged stretch of ignominy. Yet, looking back, it seems to me that the cross I carry is undeserved. It seems to me that only some chosen ones are pulled by invisible strings to the centre of God's amazingly diverse creation and exposed to all its nuances. He who is thus chosen is not the proverbial *good* boy who fares well in examinations and succeeds in life. He is a compulsive rover but is not among those who travel in luxury in the company of friends, and write romantic travelogues. He is intelligent but impractical and eccentric. Since his passion for experience overwhelms all norms of accepted conduct he is unloved and ignored by those around him and gradually driven to a state of exile within the very society that reared him. Then, knocked about and defenceless, he disappears one day carrying a burden of guilt that grows heavier with each passing year.

But let me just tell my story—even if that is easier said than done, for though two legs may be all that one needs to go from place to place, a hand that can hold a pen is not the sole requisite for writing a travelogue. And I am singularly unfortunate in this that God has not blessed me with the faintest trace of a romantic imagination. I see with these eyes only what there is to see. Where there are trees and mountains I see trees and mountains. Where there is water I see nothing but water. I may look up at clouds till my head spins but not a strand of those dark tresses that unfailingly appear to the eyes of poets is visible to me. I have stared at the moon till my eyes were glazed but seen no semblance of a beautiful face. It is not, therefore, for me to tell a romantic story. I can only describe the events of my life as they actually happened and that is what I shall do.

But first let me tell you about him who, in my early youth, aroused the wanderlust that must have lain dormant within me. His name is Indranath. I say *is* though I do not know if he is alive or dead. One morning, many years ago, he walked out of our lives and never returned. How the memory of that day still haunts me!

I met him for the first time at a soccer match played between Hindu and Mussalman boys in our school compound. It was almost evening. I was watching enthralled, when a sudden commotion accompanied by the sounds of slaps and cries of 'Catch the scoundrel' and 'Break his legs' took me completely by surprise. Within seconds the crowd had dispersed but I stood dazed and stupid till a sharp blow on my head with the butt of an umbrella brought me back to a sense of my surroundings. By then I was already enclosed in a ring of Mussalman boys, armed with umbrellas, that advanced menacingly.

All of a sudden someone hurled himself at the ring and, penetrating it with lightning speed, stood in front of me. He was a boy of about my height with a hawk-like nose, a high forehead, a sprinkling of pock-marks on a dark face and arms that hung down to his knees. He could swing those arms with surprising agility (as I got to know later) and deliver enormous punches on the noses of his adversaries. (His name, I discovered, was Indranath.) 'Don't be afraid. Just follow me,' he hissed in my ear. I pressed my body behind his and within two minutes we were out of the ring.

'Get away,' he shouted.

I started running, then stopped short and asked, 'What about you?'

'Get away, you fool,' he thundered.

But, fool or no, I would not escape alone. I stood my ground and said firmly, 'No.'

Indra said, 'Then get beaten. See that?'

He pointed with his finger at another gang of advancing boys, then suddenly changing his mind he yelled, 'Let's run as fast as we can.'

I was a village boy who had been sent to my aunt's house in the city to be educated. If I could do anything well it was to run, and now I ran for my life. It was dark by the time we reached the main road and there were lights in the shops. There was no chance now of being overtaken. I was panting and my throat was dry. But Indranath spoke in a normal voice—just as though he hadn't got into a fight and run over a mile.

'What's your name?'

'Sri—kan—ta.'

'Srikanta? Oh!' Indra fished in his pocket and brought out a handful of dry leaves. Cramming some into his mouth he shoved the rest into my hand.

'I gave the rascals a proper licking,' he said, his jaws working.

'What leaves are these?' I asked timidly.

'Shiddhi.*'

'Shiddhi? I don't touch shiddhi.'

But if I was shocked so was Indranath.

'You don't?' he exclaimed. 'What sort of an ass are you? Come on—eat them. You'll have a good trip.'

But unfamiliar with trips, good or otherwise, I shook my head and returned the shiddhi leaves which Indranath promptly put in his own mouth.

'Have a cigarette, then.' Indranath took two cigarettes out of his pocket, lit them and put one into my hand; then shaping his own like a funnel, drew upon the other so long and deep that it was reduced to half its length in a single pull. Scared out of my wits, I whispered, 'If someone sees you . . . .'

'Everyone knows,' Indranath said, then puffing nonchalantly he turned the street corner and disappeared from view.

My first meeting with Indranath is etched in my memory in bold, clear strokes. Yet, to this day, I cannot say if the feelings aroused in me that day by that strange boy who defied social norms

---

*   A plant similar to Indian hemp.

with such supreme confidence were of liking or aversion.

*

A month later. It was a summer night, hot and dark without a breath of wind. We lay on the terrace, restless and unable to sleep though it was well past midnight. Suddenly the sweet strains of a flute floated up from below, from the dense forest that lay to the south-east of the house. Originally a mango and jackfruit orchard, it had been neglected over many years and had turned wild and well-nigh impenetrable. Pishima (my paternal aunt) sat up on her string-cot and asked her eldest son, 'Who could that be, Nabin? Could it be Indra?'

'Who else would enter that jungle at this hour? And who can play the flute like that?' Barda (the eldest brother) answered.

'*Durga! Durga!*[*] Is he coming through *Gosain Bagan*?' Pishima glanced at the dense black mass below and shivered. 'So many people have died of snakebites in that jungle. What is the boy doing there? Why doesn't his mother keep him at home?'

'He is taking a short cut,' Barda smiled. 'Why should he walk miles on the main road when there is a shorter route. The jungle may be swarming with lions and tigers for all that the dare-devil cares.'

'Bless the boy,' Pishima sighed. The strains of the flute—a sweet Ramprasadi[**] hymn—came closer, then faded away.

This was Indranath. On our first meeting I had admired his strength and courage. Tonight, I kept wishing, over and over again till I fell asleep, that I could play the flute like him.

I wanted to make friends with Indranath but got no opportunity. He didn't go to school anymore. I was told that the Sanskrit pandit had once been very unjust to him—had wanted to make him wear a dunce-cap, as a matter of fact. Deeply hurt, Indranath had done something unspeakable, then vaulting over the school wall, had gone home never to return. Indranath told me later that what he had done was nothing much. He had merely cut

---

[*]   An exclamation common among Bengalis, usually used to ward off evil.
[**] Devotional songs composed by Ram Prasad Sen—a great devotee of Kali.

off the small tuft of hair that sprang from the pandit's otherwise shaven head as he sat dozing in his chair. And although, on his return home, Panditji had found his hair safe and sound in his coat pocket, he had been very angry and had complained to the headmaster. Consequently, Indra abandoned the pen in favour of the oar. From the time he left school he was continually seen on the Ganga, sailing his small dinghy from dawn to dusk, through wind and rain and storm and sun. Sometimes, he would let the current carry him as far out as it would. Drifting aimlessly, he would disappear for a week, even a fortnight. It was on one of these escapades that I renewed my acquaintance with him.

It had been a day of incessant rain—the sky heavily overcast with clouds. Darkness had come on well before the evening was over and the rain still fell in torrents. My cousins and I had had an early supper and now sat with our books on the floor of the living-room trying to do our lessons by the light of an oil lamp. At one end of the veranda Pishemoshai (my paternal aunt's husband) lay snoring on his canvas cot. At the other, old Ramkamal Bhattacharya sat puffing at his hookah—eyes glazed with his daily dose of opium. The servants congregated on the porch as someone recited Tulsidas in a nasal voice. Inside, the three of us squirmed under the iron discipline that Mejda (the second brother) thought fit to impose on us. Jatinda and I were in Class VI, Chhorda* in Class VII and Mejda, after failing a couple of times, was gravely preparing to appear once again for the Entrance. We were supposed to study from 7.30 to 9 p.m. To prevent us from talking and wasting his valuable time, Mejda had devised certain safeguards for himself. As soon as the study hour commenced, he took up a pair of scissors and began cutting out some twenty to thirty slips of paper. On each slip he wrote out a caption such as: TO SPIT, TO BLOW NOSE, TO DRINK WATER, etc. These slips were then distributed amongst the three of us.

The system worked somewhat like this: Jatinda goes up to Mejda with a TO BLOW NOSE ticket. Mejda signs it and writes *From 8.33 to 8.34-5* just below his signature. The moment Jatinda leaves the room, Chhorda presents his TO SPIT ticket. Mejda returns it

---

* The brother just preceding oneself.

unsigned. Chhorda sits glumly for thirty seconds, then presents his TO DRINK WATER ticket. This time Mejda signs it and writes *From 8.41 to 8.47.* Chhorda goes out with a gleam in his eye and Jatinda comes in. He hands his TO BLOW NOSE ticket to Mejda who checks the time, then sticks it in a register he keeps for the purpose. Thanks to this system not a minute of our study hour was wasted and I am convinced that the Goddess Saraswati herself came half way with us when we retired for the night. But Mejda's examiners were so shortsighted that they never recognized his passion for scholarship and his immense respect for time. Like blundering fools they failed him year after year. But that, unfortunately, is the way the world goes and there is no point regretting it.

That evening was no different from any other. After Chhorda's return I went up with my TO DRINK WATER ticket. Mejda had just opened his register to apprise himself of the number of times I had expressed a similar desire in the last two days, when I heard a loud roar behind my back followed by a series of frantic screams from my three cousins. I spun around but before I could see anything Mejda had knocked down the lamp and lay writhing and groaning in the dark. Pandemonium broke loose. Pushing my way out of the room I found a rudely awakened Pishemoshai clinging to his two younger sons and screaming at the top of his voice, 'Beat the rascal. Beat the life out of him.' Within a few minutes, servants, lights, and people from the neighbourhood filled the yard and the guards at the gate dragged in the escaping thief. But when the lamplight fell on the culprit's face we were petrified with horror for it was old Ramkamal Bhattacharya—half dead with fear and the thrashing he had received at the hands of the guards. Then, while one dashed water on his face another fanned him vigorously, Pishemoshai asked him, 'What made you run, Ramkamal Babu?'

Trembling violently the old man quavered, 'It wasn't a tiger! It was a bear. A great big bear. It came rushing out of the living-room.'

'It wasn't a bear, it was a wolf,' Chhorda and Jatinda clamoured in unison. 'It was sitting on the doormat with its tail tucked in.'

It was at this point that Mejda, recovering from his fit, opened his eyes and murmured, 'The Royal Bengal tiger,' and passed out again.

But tiger or wolf or bear, whatever it was, where was it? Several people took up lanterns and began looking for the animal. Suddenly Kishori Singh, the chowkidar, bellowed, 'There! There!' and leaped on the veranda. A mad scramble followed. Everyone had to be on the veranda and be there first. At one corner of the yard stood a pomegranate bush and it was in the bush that the animal crouched. Within seconds the people in the veranda had pushed their way into the living-room and locked the door, Pishemoshai calling out wildly over and over again, 'Bring guns, bring spears!' But even if there were guns and spears in the vicinity, who was going to risk his life trying to cross the yard?

At this juncture Indra made an appearance. He had been walking past the house when he heard the commotion and decided to investigate. Instantly, a hundred voices cried out to him, 'Tiger! Tiger! Run for your life.' Nonplussed, Indra dashed into the house, then having heard the story, went out again. He picked up a lantern and started peering into the pomegranate bush. The women of the house, watching from an upstairs window, nearly fainted at the sight and Pishima began sobbing and chanting the 108 names of Durga. The guards stood at a safe distance egging him on and assuring him that they would have joined him if they had had weapons. Indra had a good look and announced, 'I don't think it is a tiger.' Before he could finish his sentence the Royal Bengal tiger emerged, brought his front paws together and began sobbing in a human voice.

'No, Babu *moshai*,[*] it pleaded in perfect Bengali, 'I am not a tiger. I'm Chhinath Bouroopee.'

Indra gave a delighted laugh. Ramkamal Bhattacharya ran out, wooden clog in hand. In his excitement he let out a torrent of abuse in broken Hindustani. 'Haramzada!' he screamed crashing the clog on the tiger's back. 'Because of your tomfoolery I was beaten to a pulp by these *khottas*.[**] How dare you come here and frighten us like this?'

Chhinath alias Srinath went on sobbing and pleading his case.

---

[*] A term of courtesy used for men.
[**] A term of contempt used by Bengalis for the people of Bihar.

He lived in Barasat, he said, and earned his living as a Bohurupee.[*]
Every year, around this time, he came up to town to earn a few
rupees. Only a day earlier he had come dressed as Narad muni
and had sung to the ladies of the house. If the little boys hadn't
panicked and knocked the lamp over he would have announced
himself. But in the commotion that followed he had lost his nerve
and had hidden himself in the pomegranate bush. Pishemoshai
continued to rant and threaten the poor creature cringing at his
feet till Pishima took matters in her own hands. 'Thank your stars
it was not a real tiger,' she called out to her husband, 'and let the
poor man go. As for your valour and that of your guards—the less
said the better. A little boy showed more courage than all of you
put together.'

Pishemoshai glared about him with an expression that said,
'Had I wished, I could have squashed this impertinence but it is
beneath my dignity to argue with a woman.' Completely ignoring
his wife he thundered, 'Cut off the rascal's tail.' Delighted at the
command the guards pounced on the hapless Srinath and within
seconds the long tail of straw and velvet was severed from the
tiger's body.

'Keep the tail,' Pishima called out in disgust. 'It may come in
useful someday.'

Indra asked, 'Do you live in this house, Srikanta?'

'Yes, where are you off to so late at night?'

'Late at night? It is barely evening. I'm going out fishing in
my dinghy. Want to come?'

'But it is already dark. Won't you be scared on the river?'

'No,' Indra laughed. 'It's wonderful! And the darker it is, the
better the fish bite. Do you swim?'

'Very well.'

'Then come.' He caught me by the hand. 'I find it difficult to
pull against the current by myself. I'm looking for someone who
isn't afraid of the river.'

Till that moment the possibility of violating the rules of the
house in which I was a guest and of walking out into the night
with a total stranger had never presented itself. I should have had

---

[*]   An itinerant showman who entertains people by assuming different guises.

doubts but I didn't. I followed him without a word. Looking back I realize that I could never have resisted Indra's call. The vision of riding high on the crest of a wave on that dark rainy night was so alluring that when I came to the edge of *Gosain Bagan* I did not falter for an instant. Like one possessed I walked through that dense jungle to where the Ganga swirled and foamed between steep banks of rock under a leaden sky. An ancient ashwatha tree stood on the bank looking like a massive black knot. About fifty feet below it Indra's tiny row-boat tossed about like a nutshell in the rushing water. I was not a coward but when Indra pointed to the rope which held the boat and said, 'Hold it tight and go down carefully. If you slip no one will ever find you again,' my heart missed a beat. Nevertheless, I asked, 'What about you?'

'I'll untie the knot as soon as you reach the dinghy. Don't worry about me. There are plenty of grasses and roots that I can use as footholds.'

I gripped the rope with both hands and started inching my way down the slippery rocks. It seemed to take ages but I was in the boat at last. Then Indra released the rope and swung himself down the cliff. I shut my eyes in horror. My heart beat violently. For a minute or two the roar of rushing water filled my ears. Then a light laugh made me look up. It was Indranath. Giving the boat a shove he leapt in. The little dinghy took a sharp spin, then shot off like a comet over the dim expanse.

Two

WITHIN SECONDS WE ENTERED A CAVERN OF IMPENETRABLE darkness. The world was wiped out. Only a vast body of water—violent and indomitable—stretched as far as the eye could see. And on its heaving breast a frail bark, carrying two children, tossed about in a weird dance. The night, like a gigantic Kali, swirled her ink-black hair winding Heaven and Earth in its strands and her sharp teeth gleamed out of the frothing peaks in a cruel smile. We were too young then to comprehend the magnificence of the sight but I have never forgotten it. All around us the turbulent waters eddied and whirled, exploding into sprays of jewels or leaping forward with a deafening crash in a mad race towards the sea.

I was aware that the dinghy was moving in a slanting line across the Ganga. What I couldn't fathom was towards which point, in the darkness ahead, was Indra steering. Indra broke the silence with the question: 'Are you scared, Srikanta?'

'No.'

'That's good! If you can swim you have nothing to fear.'

I suppressed a sigh. What difference did it make? Would I ever be able to swim across this infinite stretch of water against such a strong current? We floated on in silence. After a long time a series of thuds reached our ears—they were muffled at first, then increased in volume.

'What are these sounds, Indra?'

'That's the surf pounding on the bank. Did you hear that crash? The land is breaking under the weight of the water.'

'Is the tide very strong, then?'

'Terribly strong. That reminds me. It rained last night. We'd better not sail too close to the bank. If the boat gets hit we'll be ground to pulp. Will you take the oars, Srikanta?'

Putting them in my hand Indra pointed with his finger. 'Do you see that dark patch there? That's a sand-bar. There's a sort of creek winding through it which we must enter. But be very careful. If the fishermen catch us they'll crack our skulls with their poles and bury us in the bog.'

'Then let's not go through the creek,' I said, very scared.

Indra laughed. 'But there's no other way. We can't go by the big bank. Our little boat would get buried in the sand. Even a ship won't be safe tonight.'

'Then let's forget about the fishing,' I said lifting the oars. The boat spun violently and went back several yards.

'Coward!' Indra hissed angrily. 'Why did you come, then?'

I was fifteen years old at that time and the word 'coward' stung. I dropped the oars into the water and recommenced straining and pulling in the direction he had indicated.

'That's the spirit.' Indra smiled. 'But we must be very careful. I'll take the boat past the tamarisks and through the corn fields so cleverly that they'll never guess. And even if they see us they won't catch us. Listen, Srikanta, if they get too close when they're chasing us in their dinghies—just jump out and swim underwater as far as you can get. They won't be able to see you in the dark. We can spend the night at Satwa then swim across in the morning and go back the way we came.'

'Satwa? Isn't that a great way off?'

'No, it isn't,' Indranath answered. 'Not more than twelve or thirteen miles. When you get tired just keep floating. There'll be plenty of driftwood on the water. You'll see!'

I dared not voice an opinion but my heart sank at the prospect. To swim so many miles across these swollen waters on a night when visibility was practically nil, then spend hours waiting for the dawn in an unknown place was not as easy as Indra made it sound. On the other hand, landing anywhere else was ruled out. On this side of the river the surf rose twenty feet high.

I plied the oars in silence for a while, then asked, 'What about the dinghy?'

'The other night I did just as I said. Next morning I went and brought back my dinghy. I told the fishermen that someone had stolen it and brought it here.'

As we approached the mouth of the creek a row of fishing-boats with flickering lights came into view. Wedged between two sandbanks the creek stretched out like a wide canal. We sailed in a curve to the other end where the eroding soil had created innumerable shallow lagoons concealed from each other by forests of tamarisk and casuarina. Guiding the dinghy gently through one of these we entered the creek. From this point the fishing-boats looked like dark clumps in the distance. A hundred yards up the creek and we reached our destination—the fishermen's *mayajal* which, while keeping a vigilant eye on the mouth of the creek, they had left unguarded. In the summer, when the creek runs dry, fishermen drive strong poles of bamboo firmly into the ground from one end to another and hang their nets on the outer side. This is called a *mayajal*. When the rains come and the water rises, shoals of large fish come swimming into the creek then, hitting the fence, leap beyond it and get trapped in the nets. Indra lifted out five or six king-sized *rui* and *katla* weighing from ten to twenty seers each and threw them into the dinghy in the twinkling of an eye.

'That's enough. Let's go,' he said picking up the oars. The boat, still rocking with the struggling fish, sped like an arrow over the dark water.

We sailed in silence for the next two minutes and then, with a violent jerk, the boat swerved and entered the field on the left.

'Why! What's the matter?' I called out in alarm.

'Shh!' Indra pushed the boat a little further and said, 'The fishermen have seen us. They are coming in their dinghies. Look there!'

It was true. Ploughing the water with ferocious strokes, four dinghies, like four black ogres, were rapidly advancing up the creek. There was no escape now, for the nets were behind us, the fishermen in front of us and the cornfield would not provide adequate cover.

'What shall we do, Indra?' A sob stuck in my throat as visions of being hacked to pieces and being buried in quicksand rose before my eyes.

'Don't be scared,' Indranath said bravely but his voice quivered a little. He continued to push the boat with desperate strokes further and further into the field. The land lay submerged in water—breast high in places, knee deep in others—and over the water the dripping maize rose to a height of fifteen feet. Above our heads the sky was as black as pitch and all around us impenetrable forests of tamarisk and bamboo stretched away as far as the eye could see. The fishermen's voices came wafting on the air, suspicious and angry. We crept along inch by inch, the oars getting stuck in the slime. Suddenly the boat tilted and I found myself alone.

'Indra,' I whispered.

'I'm in the water,' he whispered back. 'I'm towing the boat. I have a rope tied around my middle.'

'Where are you taking it to?' I asked.

'To the big river. It is just a little ahead.' I breathed more easily now and the boat moved painfully on. Suddenly a loud clanging on tins, accompanied by a crackling of bamboo stems, burst in on us.

'What is that?' I asked, startled.

'Farmers on a machan are shooing away a wild pig.'

'A wild pig? Where is it?'

'How can I say? Can I see in the dark?'

I sat silent, cursing the impulse that had made me come out on this crazy adventure. Yet I was sitting in the boat while Indra, neck deep in mud and slime, was struggling against the dense foliage. From time to time a violent swaying of the maize stems filled me with horrifying visions of the wild pig crouching among them. I communicated my fears to Indranath but he laughed them away: 'Those are snakes rustling among the leaves,' he said.

'Snakes!' I gasped, 'What kind of snakes?'

'Oh! All kinds. Adders and kraits and cobras. They get flushed out of their holes when it rains and climb up the stems. Don't you see that there's not a speck of dry land anywhere?'

I could see that well enough. What I could not see was how Indra took it all so calmly.

'They don't bite,' he continued, 'they're dead scared themselves. Two or three huge ones just glided past me. They must be water-snakes. And even if they bite—well, one has to die one day.'

Indranath said all this in a normal, everyday voice while I sat frozen—in mortal terror that a snake would swing itself down from a maize stalk and fall with a thud into the dinghy.

But what was Indranath? Was he a man, a god or a demon? If he was a man, what was he made of? If he had a human heart why did it know no fear? On the day of our first meeting he had risked his life for me—a complete stranger. That night, even as he confronted a terrible death, over and over again, the smile never left his lips. Many years have passed since. I have travelled far and wide and seen many kinds of men. Yet I can solemnly swear that, to this day, I have not seen one like Indranath.

But to get back to my story. After sometime the sound of rushing water reached my ears. I realized that we were approaching the edge of the forest beyond which the river churned and foamed with its deadly currents. Indra came up and sat in the dinghy, his face relaxed and smiling.

'We've reached the river,' he announced. 'We are safe.'

Even as he said these words a terrible shudder passed over the dinghy as the current sucked it out of the lagoon and flung it across the water in a magnificent arc. The wind rushed into my face—the blood into my head. I shut my eyes. When I opened them again the dinghy was shooting like a meteor over the breast of the Ganga and the moon, rising behind massed clouds, was pouring out a stream of opalescent light that, on touching the river, turned it into a sheet of silver.

Three

'$\mathscr{I}$ AM DREADFULLY SLEEPY, INDRA. CAN'T WE GO HOME?'

'Of course you're sleepy,' Indra smiled as tenderly as a woman, 'but we can't go home just yet. I have a lot of work tonight, Srikanta. Why don't you lie down on that plank and sleep for a while?'

I obeyed him but sleep wouldn't come. Gazing up at the sky I watched the moon weaving in and out of the clouds while the roar of the water filled my ears. I've often wondered about that night. I was not old enough to spend hours watching the play of moonbeams on clouds, yet that is just what I did. Perhaps, after the fearful events of the night, my soul sought a tranquil and beautiful world in which I could rest myself. Time slid slowly by. Then, all of a sudden, the moon dipped behind the clouds and swimming across in a curve, rose again in the eastern sky. I lifted my head. The dinghy had changed direction. I wanted to ask where we were going but a strange lassitude crept over my senses. My head fell back and I passed into a kind of trance.

Crash! The dinghy's keel scraped against a sandy shore. I sat up. What place was this? Before I could ask, Indra said: 'You wait in the boat, Srikanta. I'll be back in a minute. Don't be scared. There are fishermen's huts a little way up the bank.'

My courage had been put to the test over and over again that night. I could not fail. I was young then and youth knows no logic but its own. I have often thought that behind the contradictions that characterized the love of the young Radha and Krishna of Vrindavan, some youthful logic was at work. The wise try to explain this logic, the pious to moralize—but comprehension eludes one and all. Only those who, spurning analysis and comment, submerge themselves body and soul in bhakti, are rewarded with a bliss that is akin to madness. Joyous with song and ecstatic with prayer, they drink at the fount of a divine passion which, to this day, is shrouded in mystery. Some such logic, incomprehensible even to me, prompted my answer. With a sinking heart and quivering lip I said: 'Why should I be scared? Go wherever you like.'

Indranath walked away, then, as if remembering something, rushed back to the dinghy.

'Listen, Srikanta,' he said urgently, 'if people come to you asking for fish don't give them any. Even if one of them looks exactly like me. Tell him to pick what he wants with his own hands, but don't you go near him. Not on your life. Understand?'

'Why, Indranath?'

'I'll tell you later.' Indra ran in the direction of the fishermen's huts.

All the hair on my body stood on end. I knew what he meant and the knowledge made the blood freeze in my veins. Many terrors had beset me that night but they paled in comparison with this one. As I sat in the dinghy the air around me grew thick with muffled whispers. I dared not look up for there were figures in white peeping slyly from behind the trees. Would Indranath never come? The voices swelled—grew louder. There was a swimming in my brain, a dark mist swirled in front of my eyes. Shutting them tight I grabbed my *poité* (the sacred thread worn by Brahmins) and began winding it feverishly around my thumb.

After aeons, as it seemed, human voices and footsteps reached out to me as if from a vast distance—Indranath's voice talking in Hindustani to two fishermen. But was it really Indranath? I remembered something I had been told as a child—that spirits may take on the semblance of mortal beings but can leave no shadows. I opened my eyes, warily, to apply this supreme test. Yes, there they were—three shadows, dim but unmistakable, gliding towards the dinghy. Nearly fainting with relief I watched the two men come up, lift the fish with practised hands and drop them into a net. Then, pressing something into Indra's hand (whose faint tinkle suggested money) they walked away as rapidly as they had come.

We set sail once more, this time along the bank. I sat silent, my breast heaving with many emotions among which disgust and a sort of self-pity were uppermost. So Indra stole the fish to make money! And he did not hesitate to involve me in the crime. For stealing of, or for, money *was* a crime. Village boys like us stole fruit from people's orchards and fish from their ponds as a matter of course. That, though wrong, was not stealing as I saw it. Until the moment of that little clink in the dark, the fish-stealing had been a wonderful adventure. Now it lay heavy on my heart.

Indra broke the silence. 'You weren't scared even a little bit, were you, Srikanta?'

'No,' I answered shortly.

'No one but you could have sat alone in the dark,' Indra said enthusiastically. 'I don't have another friend like you, Srikanta. I do love you. Whenever I come out in my dinghy I'll call for you. Shall I?'

I sat in sullen silence. Indranath did not seem to notice. Suddenly the clouds parted and moonbeams rained down on my companion's face. In that face I saw something—I can't say what—that wiped out all my grosser feelings. I turned to him asking eagerly, 'Have you ever seen them, Indra?'

'Seen whom?'

'Those—people—who ask for fish.'

'No I haven't seen them. I've only heard of them.'

'Can you come here alone?'

'I always come alone.'

'Don't you feel scared?'

'No, I chant "Ram Ram" as I go along. Then they dare not come near me. There's tremendous power in Ram's name. You can chant "Ram Ram" and walk right past a snake. But not if you're scared. They always know if you're only pretending. They can see right through you.'

The sandbank gave way to a pebbly shore. The tide was much lower on this side of the river. 'Do you see that jungle there?' Indranath lifted an oar and pointed with it. 'We'll be going through it. I'll stop the boat there and leave you for a few minutes. You don't mind, do you, Srikanta?'

I could not say that I did mind—not now that Indranath had

complimented me on my courage. The old fears returned despite his assurances of the power that Ram's name invests on its chanter. I was in no mood to test their truth—not if it meant sitting alone in the dinghy under some ancient banyan tree in the middle of the forest. There was one saving grace, however. There was no fish left in the dinghy. So the fish-lovers would probably leave me alone. But there would be others, I thought—those who love nothing better than a drink of warm blood and a bite of a boy's tasty flesh.

As the dinghy approached the forest the wild tamarisks and tussocks stared as if in horror at the foolhardiness of two children of men. Some even shook their heads in warning. Had I been alone I would have heeded them but my helmsman rowed rapidly past the waving branches towards an inlet that had enlarged itself into a sort of lake with only one opening northwards.

'There's no bank here. Where will you moor the boat, Indra?' I asked.

'There's a little bank further up beyond that banyan tree.'

An unpleasant odour hanging on the air grew sickeningly strong with every gust of wind. I covered my nose with the edge of my dhoti. I said uneasily, 'There's something rotting here, Indra.'

'Corpses!' he announced. 'There's a lot of cholera about. The poorer villagers can't afford to burn their dead. They just touch the bodies with a flaming tussock and throw them in the water.'

'Where, Indranath?'

'Right from that end to this. This is a burning-ghat. *Aré aré*, don't look so scared. Those are only jackals fighting amongst themselves. Come and sit by me.'

I shut my eyes and crept up to where he sat. He put an arm around my shoulders and said, 'There's nothing to be afraid of, Srikanta. I come to this ghat quite often all by myself. If you take Ram's name thrice no one can come near you.'

'Indranath,' I begged, 'let's not stop here. Let's go home.'

'No, Srikanta,' he said firmly, 'I can't go home—not before I give this money to someone I know. I'm three days late as it is. They'll be waiting for me.'

'Give it to them tomorrow.'

'No, Srikanta, don't ask me to do that. Come with me if you like but don't breathe a word about it to anyone.'

The dinghy crept out of the shadows and the bank where we

were to alight, came in view. Looking on it, bathed as it was in moonlight, I felt a momentary joy dispelling the terrors of the night. But, even before the keel could touch the pebbles, Indra had leaped out with a startled exclamation and in that moment I too saw what he had seen. The body of a boy, six or seven years old, lay in the water. The head rested on the bank. He could not have been dead for more than three or four hours for the wave-washed limbs were as smooth and firm as sculpted marble and the face, turned up to the moon, gleamed like a flower. Looking on that face in the hushed silence of the night, broken by an occasional nightbird's call or the scream of a jackal, I had a strange vision. I saw the pain-tortured boy leap into Mother Ganga's lap. I saw her clasping him to her breast, nursing him tenderly and washing his limbs with her tears. Then, with infinite love, she laid her soothed and sleeping child on this watery bed.

I glanced at Indranath. Tears were pouring down his cheeks. 'Move aside, Srikanta,' he said hoarsely, 'I'll put him in the dinghy and row him out to the river where the jackals can't get at him.'

Tears had come to my eyes too on seeing Indranath's. Yet I was dismayed by the suggestion. It is one thing to weep over a person's distress—it is quite another to get involved with it. Besides, born as I was in a conservative Hindu family which carried in its veins the purest of pure Brahmin blood, the idea of touching a corpse was repugnant to me. The weight of a whole tradition was upon me in an instant and I felt hedged in by many taboos. I did not know what disease the boy had died of, what his caste was, what his lineage. I wasn't even sure if the necessary rites had been performed over his body before it was thrown into the water. I expressed my doubts to Indranath. 'We don't know his caste. We can't touch the body,' I said.

Indranath slid one arm under the boy's head and the other below his knees and, lifting him as easily as he would a knot of grass, placed him tenderly on the plank on which I had lain. Giving the dinghy a push he seated himself and said, 'Corpses don't have castes.'

'Of course they do,' I answered with some heat.

'No, Srikanta. Look at our dinghy. At one time it may have lived as a mango or a rose-apple tree. But now it is dead wood. It is nothing but a dinghy.'

I realize now that Indranath's argument was a childish one.

Yet it must have contained a sharp grain of truth which pricked me at that time and does so to this day. Indranath often said things like that. Wild and indisciplined as he was, with little or no formal education, his view of the universe was original and dynamic. Speculating on the source of this philosophy, so many years later, I am convinced that it sprang from his basic honesty—the truth within him that recognized the all-pervasive truth beyond and became one with it. Deception, after all, does not exist in nature. It is confined in the minds of men alone. Brass, when it is passed off as gold, will remain brass though the buyer and the seller are both caught in a web of falsehood. The universe admits nothing but the truth—this Indranath saw as clearly as if it was reflected in a mirror within him. That is why his responses were always instinctive and sure.

Reflecting on this aspect of Indranath's character I recall an incident that took place ten or twelve years later. One evening, the town buzzed with a rumour that the body of an old Brahmin lady was lying uncremated in a house in the next mohalla. On making enquiries I found out that she had been on a pilgrimage to Kashi but, having fallen ill on her way back to Calcutta, had alighted at our station and had taken shelter with a distant relative. She had passed two days and nights in terrible anguish and had died that morning. This relative had been to England many years ago and was, for that reason, treated as an outcaste. Consequently, no caste-Hindu would defile himself by touching the body of the dead woman. For, though a staunch Hindu herself and just returned from a pilgrimage, she had committed the unforgivable offence of dying in the house of one who had upon him the stigma of excommunication. Some of us got together and cremated the body but on returning from the burning-ghat we found our own doors locked against us. We heard that the leaders of the community had approached every Hindu family in our absence with the decree that unless we shaved our heads, ate cow-dung and begged forgiveness we were to be denied entry into the house. Not knowing how to deal with the situation we went to Doctor Babu for advice. A skilled physician with a large practice, Doctor Babu had made himself indispensable to the local Bengalis by not charging them his professional fees. On hearing our story he was livid with anger. He announced that from that day onwards he would not treat the families of those self-styled leaders—even if they lay at the point of death. No one knows how the threat got conveyed but by evening the elders had come up with a fresh verdict. The shaving of the head was waived. All we were required to do was to apologize and to partake of the holy matter already mentioned. On our rejecting the verdict the second half of it was deleted. An apology would be enough. When even that was denied them the leaders announced that, this being our first offence, they had forgiven us unconditionally. At this point Doctor Babu stepped in. He declared that things would only come back to normal if an apology was forthcoming from their side. In consequence, many a grey head was seen entering the doctor's residence that evening. What passed between them I do not know but by morning the doctor's anger had cooled and we were permitted to enter our homes without performing any penitential rites.

But I am digressing wildly. My sole intention in recording this incident is to stress the gap between the two philosophies of death—the ignorant child Indra's and that of these men, so far ahead of him in years and experience. And I am convinced that had Doctor Babu not given their moral conditioning such bitter medication they would never have been cured of their malady.

To return to the events of the night. By the time we had reached the river and had lowered the body into the water the night was nearly spent. A pearl-grey mist was creeping over the eastern sky as we watched the child floating away, past the dripping tamarisks and wild reeds, weaving in and out of patches of light and shadow.

'Let's go, Indra,' I said.

'Where?' He lifted a face contorted with pain and compassion.

'You said you had to go somewhere.'

'No. We'll leave that for another day.'

'Very good,' I cried joyfully, 'then let's go home.'

Indra stared at me for a few seconds, then asked, 'Do you know where the dead go, Srikanta?'

'No, I don't. They go to heaven. Let's go home please.'

'Everyone can't go to heaven. Some stay on the earth—at least for a while. As I was laying him in the water he whispered in my ear. I heard him clearly. He said "Bhaiya".'

'You are frightening me, Indra,' my voice trembled and tears sprang to my eyes. 'I think I'm going to faint.'

Without a word Indra picked up the oars and started propelling the boat towards the middle of the river. Suddenly he spoke in a sombre voice: 'Ram Ram, Ram Ram. He's in the boat, Srikanta, sitting just behind me.'

Sky, river and Indranath blacked out in an instant and I fell, face forward, on the floor of the dinghy. When I came to I was lying on the plank and Indranath was sitting at my feet. The sky was streaked with dawn and the dinghy rested by a bank.

'Get up, Srikanta,' Indranath said, 'we'll have to walk the rest of the way.'

Four

$\mathcal{T}$HE SUN HAD JUST RISEN OVER THE RIVER WHEN I ENTERED THE house dragging my feet. Joyful cries of 'He's here' and 'Srikanta is back' rushed out at me from all directions. Jatinda, who was about my age, got so excited that he ran from room to room announcing my return; then, clutching my hand, dragged me to where Mejda was sitting solemnly over his books.

'Here he is, here's Srikanta,' he announced. Mejda glanced up at me, then lowered his eyes in the manner of a tiger who, having secured his prey, can take his time over the eating. This was the same cousin under whose supervision we were studying last night and whose blood-curdling screams had chased the Royal Bengal Tiger out of the house into the pomegranate bush.

'Satish,' Pishima's voice called from within the house. 'Just look into the almanac and see if it is all right to eat brinjal this morning.' Pushing open the door she entered the room, then catching sight of my pale face and bloodshot eyes she exclaimed: 'Why? Where were you all this time, you good-for-nothing boy? Worrying me to death! I couldn't sleep a wink the whole night. Why are your eyes so red? You haven't caught a fever, have you?' Coming closer she laid a hand on my forehead and cried out to the others in the room. 'Just as I said. He's burning all over. Never in my seven lives have I seen a boy like this one. You deserve to be tied down and stung with nettles, you rascal. Now come upstairs and go straight to bed.' And totally forgetting her earlier preoccupation with brinjals she drew me along with her.

'Srikanta! Don't leave the room,' Mejda commanded in a terrible voice.

'Why not?' Pishima asked but before Mejda could answer she was shaking her head vigorously. 'No. No lessons now. He must eat first and get some sleep.' She took me by the hand and led me to the door. This was too much for Mejda. Forgetting himself he shouted, 'Stay where you are, Srikanta. Don't you dare leave the room.'

Even Pishima was startled for a moment, then collecting herself gave Mejda a long and level look. 'Satish,' she said in a voice like thunder. 'I know that you often beat and bully the little ones. I haven't said anything till now but, after today, if I ever catch you touching one of them I'll have you tied to a pillar and whipped by the servants. It is no concern of yours if they study or do not study. Pass your own exams first.' Saying this she took me away with her leaving Mejda sitting in gloomy silence. Upstairs, in her room, she helped me change my clothes, then stuffing me with an enormous quantity of milk and hot jalebis, put me to bed scolding me heartily all the while. Then, informing me that it was only with my death that her bones would get a rest, she went out of the room. I heard her lift the catch and walk away.

Five minutes later there was a little click at the door and Chhorda came running in, laughing and out of breath. Throwing himself on the bed he whispered: 'Ma has ordered Mejda to keep away from us. He is to study in a separate room. Barda will help us with our studies. We needn't be afraid of Mejda anymore.' Bringing his thumbs together he wiggled them gleefully. Jatinda, who had followed Chhorda, was determined to take the credit for what had happened. 'It is I,' he announced, slapping his chest like a doughty warrior. 'It is I who brought this about. Had I not taken Srikanta to Mejda, Ma would never have given such an order. You should both be grateful to me. You must give me your new top, Chhorda.'

'Take it from my desk,' said Chhorda who, till that moment, had valued his top above everything else in the world.

I realized then how much more precious to him was his independence! Adults are often unaware that children value their freedom and yearn for their fundamental rights in exactly the same measure as they themselves. Mejda, exploiting his position as the elder brother, had denied us our legitimate rights as human beings. We were like slaves to his whims and moods. Every Sunday he would make us walk miles in the hot sun to call his friends over for a game of cards. On summer afternoons we had to take turns in fanning him as he slept and in winter, while he lay reading a book in the cosy comfort of his quilt, one of us had to be on hand to turn the pages. Whenever the fancy took him he would call out in a terrible voice, 'Keshav, take out your geography book. Jatin, go and cut a strong switch from the casuarina tree and bring it to me,' which meant that a flogging was inevitable. That protest was possible, never occurred to us. No wonder, then, that our joy at his degradation knew no bounds.

My fever rose that night and I was confined to bed for a week. Ten days elapsed before I was allowed to go to school and another month before I met Indranath again. It was Saturday—I remember that distinctly. The rains were over and the river had begun to shrink. I sat, fishing-rod in hand, at one of the streams that meandered away from the Ganga trying to catch the catfish that swarmed in the shallow waters. Among the other boys who sat at different points along the bank I noticed one catching an incredible number in rapid succession. His face was hidden from view by a clump of reeds. Only the swift dipping and jerking of his line was visible from where I sat and that was enough to tell me that he was an expert fisherman. I decided to sit next to him. As I approached the clump a familiar voice spoke: 'Come and sit on my right side, Srikanta.'

On hearing that voice a tremor passed through me and the blood leaped up in my veins. I was speechless with the many emotions that warred within me. I am aware that terms like these are worn clichés that come nowhere near expressing my feelings of that moment. But, with my limited powers of self-expression, what alternative do I have but to fall back on them? Where can I find words that will truly mirror the strange complex of emotions that I struggled with in that moment of reunion with Indranath— the delight, the yearning and the dread. I sat next to him but could not speak.

Indra broke the silence with a question. 'Did you get a thrashing that morning, Srikanta?' I shook my head. His face lit up.

'I knew you wouldn't. I prayed very hard to Ma Kali. "Don't let Srikanta get beaten," I begged and begged. She's a very benign goddess—is Ma Kali. If you have true faith in your heart she will always grant your prayer. Then no one can beat you.' Saying this he put down his line, brought his hands together and touched his forehead in reverence.

Hooking some bait onto his line he dropped it in the water and said, 'Had I known you were going to get fever I could have prevented that too.'

'How?' I asked.

'I would have plucked lots of *jaba*[*] and thrown them at Ma Kali's feet. She loves *jaba*. She'll give a boy whatever he prays for if he brings her blood-red *jaba*. Everyone knows that. Don't you?'

'Didn't *you* get fever after that night?' I asked.

'Me?' Indranath was amazed. 'I never get fever. I never fall ill. If you pray to all the gods and goddesses twice everyday they'll come and stand before you. You'll see them clearly. Then you'll never fall ill. No one can touch a hair of your head. You can go where you like, do what you like, exactly like me.'

I nodded, then dropping my line in the water, asked softly: 'Whom do you take with you in the dinghy?'

'Where?'

'To the other bank. To catch fish?'

'I don't go anymore.' He put down his rod and tackle on the grass.

'Why?' I asked.

'She made me swear—' Indranath left the sentence in mid air and clammed up as though alerted.

But I had not forgotten that exchange of money in the dark. 'Who made you swear? Your mother?' I probed.

'No, not my mother.' Twining the tackle around the rod he asked suddenly, 'You didn't tell anyone where we went that night? Did you, Srikanta?'

'No,' I answered, 'but everyone knows I went with you.'

He sat silent for a while, frowning a little. Once he opened his mouth as if to say something, then changing his mind shut it again. Breaking off a reed he circled it slowly in the water, his face turning

---

[*]   The hibiscus flower.

a rich red as he stared at the breaking ripples. Suddenly he blurted out: 'Do you have any money, Srikanta?'

'How much?'

'Say—about five rupees.'

'Yes.'

I had the money and I was delighted to give it to him. But Indranath didn't seem to share my joy. He hung his head and said glumly: 'I can't repay it.'

'I don't want you to repay it,' I announced with some spirit.

I tried to search his face but he wouldn't meet my eyes. He went on staring into the water for a long time. At last he spoke.

'I don't want it for myself. I want to give it to someone I know. They are very poor, Srikanta. They don't get enough to eat. Will you come with me and give the money yourself?'

Something stirred in my memory.

'Is it the same person? The one you wanted to visit that night?'

'Yes,' Indranath murmured absently. 'Didi won't touch my money anymore. If you don't come with me she won't take your money either. She'll think I've stolen it from my mother's trunk.'

'Is she your *bon* (sister)?'

'No, she's not my sister but I call her Didi. Will you come, Srikanta?' Then, seeing me hesitate, he added hastily, 'We'll go during the day. Tomorrow is a Sunday. If we start at noon we'll be back by the evening. We'll meet here tomorrow at twelve o'clock.'

His pleading eyes left me powerless to refuse. With the promise that I would accompany him the following day I went home.

I spent the whole evening in an agony of anticipation—the memory of that terrible night rousing a whole range of discordant emotions. All night I tossed and turned in my bed waiting for the dawn but when it came my first thought was: 'Do I have to go? What if I don't keep my word?' Nevertheless, I reached the clump of reeds at the appointed hour with the five rupees in my pocket. Indranath was already there sitting in his dinghy. On seeing me his face broke into a smile. I took my place beside him without a word and we set sail once again.

Reliving that memory now, when the shadows of death are already darkening around me, I thank my Maker in all humility for helping me overcome my fears and hesitations. For what followed was an experience I have never forgotten. That afternoon I discovered a presence that has remained with me to this hour. It was out of this encounter, in the most impressionable years of my life, that my life-long vision of woman has been formed. I have argued and reasoned with myself but none of it could ever shake the conviction that a woman is essentially noble, chaste and loving. If there is evil surrounding her she can, I am convinced, shed it like a worn garment at any given moment and take her place among the purest and brightest of spirits. My friends tell me that this is a foolish preconception unsupported by logic and reason. I do not protest for it is true that I have no convincing arguments to counter theirs. All I have are primary instincts that have swelled and strengthened with the passing years.

When we reached the burning-ghat the sun still blazed, high over the horizon. We tied the boat to the exposed roots of a gigantic banyan tree that stood just beyond it, and started walking through the forest. A hundred yards away from the bank we came upon a goat track winding away to the right. Indranath took it and I followed. Ten minutes later a dilapidated hut fenced in with wattles came into view. Indranath untied the rope with which the fence was fastened, pushed it open and went in beckoning me to follow. Then he secured the fence once again retying the rope with care. I stared around me for I had never seen such a dwelling-place in all my life. Set in the heart of the forest, the hut was overshadowed by two huge trees—an enormous fig whose branches towered up to the sky and a great shaggy tamarind—so that even in mid-afternoon there was a sense of impending dusk. A flock of hens came cackling out at the sound of our footsteps and a couple of goats, tied to the tamarind tree, bleated dolefully. As we approached the hut the sight of a huge python coiling and uncoiling in the yard sent me scrambling up the wattle fence to the utter panic of the hens who scratched and fluttered wildly. Indra gave a merry laugh and, picking up the python by the neck, threw it on one side. 'He is quite harmless, Srikanta,' he said. 'His name is Rahim.'

Still seated on the fence I looked around me. On the threshold of the hut, on a pile of filthy sacking and rags, lay a man as thin and brittle as a bamboo. He was racked with a violent fit of coughing. He had long tangled hair wound up in a knot high on his head and rows of beads round his neck. He wore saffron robes which were torn and dirty and his long beard was tied to his matted locks with a filthy turban. I recognized him instantly by his garb. He was a snake-charmer whom I had often seen wandering about our town with his gourd flute and basket of snakes. Five or six months earlier he had performed in our own courtyard. This man, whom Indra addressed as Shahji, motioned to us to sit down, then pointed to the hookah, chillum and pile of ganja that lay in one corner. Indra got up instantly and, preparing the ganja, brought it to him without a word. Shahji paused in his coughing and took a deep draught covering his nose and mouth with his left hand so that not a whiff of the precious smoke was wasted. Then, giving his head a violent shake, he passed the hookah to Indra saying, '*Piyo* (Smoke).'

Indra pushed it away and shook his head. Shahji threw him a look of surprise as if to ask, 'Why not?' But before Indra could enlighten him he had gripped the hookah with both hands and recommenced sucking at it with greedy lips. Pull after pull he took of the noxious substance in between fits of a rasping cough that threatened to shatter his emaciated chest. Finally, when all the drug was consumed, he put down the hookah and proceeded to converse with Indra in a low voice. I could hear little of what was being said and I understood still less but I noticed one thing—Shahji was speaking in Hindi and Indranath in Bengali.

As the afternoon waned Shahji's voice rose higher and higher and became increasingly hysterical. A stream of filthy abuses issued from his lips. Had I known then, as I do now, to whom they were addressed, I would have grabbed the old man by his beard and shaken the life out of him. Suddenly his voice trailed away and his body crumpled up like a bundle of orange rags and became still. Indra and I sat silently watching the scene. Then, bored with the long conversation and its aftermath, I said, 'It will soon be dark, Indra. Let's go to your Didi.'

'I'm waiting for Didi. This is her home.'

'But these people are snake-charmers. They are Mussalmans,' I said, shocked beyond belief.

Indra's face paled and his eyes reflected some inner pain. 'That's not the whole truth,' he said at last. 'I'll tell you about it someday.' Then, equally swiftly, his mood changed. With a merry gleam in his eye he said, 'I can charm snakes, Srikanta. Do you want to see me try?' Dashing into the hut he brought out Shahji's flute and basket of snakes. Lifting the lid of the basket just a little, Indra put the flute to his lips.

'Don't open the basket, please, Indra,' I begged. 'What if a cobra comes out?'

Indra did not bother to reply. Swaying his head to the strains of his flute in the manner of snake-charmers, he uncovered the basket. I watched in horror as an immense cobra shot up three feet high and, darting a wicked-looking forked tongue from its fanned out hood, stung viciously at the basket lid. Then, lashing out at the gourd flute in Indra's hand, it slithered out of the basket and crawled inside the hut. Indra leaped into the yard with a startled exclamation and I ran to the safety of the wattle fence with shaking legs.

'It's a different snake,' Indra's voice trembled with shock. 'It's not the one I know. This one is absolutely wild.'

Fear, helplessness and anger brought tears to my eyes. 'Why did you do such a thing? What if it comes out and bites Shahji?' I asked.

Indra looked guilty and ashamed, 'Shall I close the door of the hut? But perhaps it is hiding just behind the door.' Then suddenly losing his temper, he shouted, 'Serves the old rascal right if he gets bitten. Stuffing himself with ganja and keeping wild snakes in the basket. Ah! Here is Didi. Don't come near. Stay just where you are.'

I turned around and looked at Indra's Didi. 'Fire smouldering beneath ashes,' I thought. There was an expression in her eyes that I could not fathom. It conveyed a sense, dimly—for I was little more than a child then—of unswaying devotion to something held dear over centuries and aeons, through many cycles of human life. She was wearing a yellow sari and lac bangles in the manner of Mussalman women of Bihar but in the parting of her hair the vermilion mark of Hindu wifehood burned like a flame. Against her left hip she held a stack of firewood and a small basket filled with greens and vegetables dangled from her right hand.

'What is it?' she asked as, putting down her wood, she proceeded to untie the rope that secured the fence.

'Don't come in,' Indra called out excitedly. 'A huge snake has escaped from the basket and is crawling about the hut.'

She smiled up at me and spoke in Bengali. 'It is strange, is it not, that a snake should be found in a snake-charmer's hut? What do you say, Srikanta?' Then, turning to Indranath she asked, 'How did it escape?'

'It crawled out of the basket. It is a wild snake. Shahji has had a lot of ganja and is fast asleep. He won't wake now even if we scream our lungs out. What shall we do?'

Didi smiled and said, 'So you took the opportunity of showing off your snake-charming skills to Srikanta. But never mind. I'll catch it for you.'

'No, Didi, no!' Indranath pleaded, 'I won't let you touch it. It will kill you.'

Didi's eyes misted as they gazed at Indranath. 'Silly boy,' she said in a voice of infinite tenderness. 'Nothing will happen to your Didi. I'll catch it in a minute.'

Picking up a lamp that hung from the bamboo machan she lit it and entered the hut. Within seconds she was back, the snake dangling from her right fist. Without a word she shoved it into the basket and shut the lid. Indra ran to her and touched her feet. She stroked his face lovingly and touched her fingertips to her lips.

Five

ON HEARING INDRA'S ACCOUNT OF THE EVENING'S EVENTS DIDI shuddered and said, 'It was very wrong of you to play with danger like that. What if the snake's fangs had touched your hand instead of the flute? Promise me you'll never do such a thing again.'

Indranath beamed at her. 'I'm not such a fool, Didi, that I did not protect myself first. See what I've got?' Untying a knot in the corner of his dhoti he brought out a tiny dried up root tied with a thread. 'If I hadn't had this with me I could never have escaped. I begged and begged Shahji and at last he gave it to me.' He thought for a few moments and added, 'And even if the snake had bitten me, so what? I would have woken Shahji up and got him to apply the poison stone. How long does it take the stone to suck out the poison? Half an hour? One hour? No, it doesn't take that long, does it, Didi?'

Didi's eyes were on him but she did not speak. Indra went on excitedly, 'You have so many poison stones, Didi. Why don't you give me one? I've been asking you for ages.' His voice changed— became sullen and resentful. 'I do everything I can to please you and you keep putting me off. If you don't want to give it to me why don't you say so straight out and I'll stop coming.'

Indranath was too full of his own grievances to see anything around him but I noticed the shame and anguish that crept into Didi's face. Forcing a smile on her wan lips she asked Indranath, 'So you come to your Didi's house only for poison stones and snake-charms, Indra?'

'What else?' Indra said bluntly and, glancing at the sleeping Shahji, he muttered, 'He doesn't teach me anything. He only takes my money. But I'm not going to depend on him anymore. I know, from the way you caught the snake, that you are no less than Shahji. I'm going to learn all the mantras from you.' Glancing once again at the pile of rags in the corner he said reverently, 'Shahji smokes ganja and all that but he is a genius, Srikanta. He can put life into a corpse three days old. Can you do that, Didi?'

A peal of laughter burst from Didi's lips and died in the air in a few moments. An unnatural calm descended. But Indra neither saw nor heard. 'You can't fool me,' he went on, 'you've learned everything from Shahji. I know that. Just teach me all you know and I'll be your slave for the rest of my life. How many corpses have you raised, Didi?'

'I can't put life into the dead, Indranath,' Didi said quietly.

'Shahji hasn't taught you that? Then it must be very very difficult. But he has surely taught you to fly cowries?'

'I haven't even heard of flying cowries.'

Indra looked at her with disbelief in his eyes. 'Don't pretend. Of course you know all about it.' Then turning to me, he asked: 'Have you ever seen flying cowries, Srikanta? You take two cowries, murmur some mantras and throw them out of the window. They fly through the air till they spot a snake. Then they stick fast to the snake's hood and fly back to you dragging the snake behind them.'

Turning to Didi he continued, 'Even if you haven't learned to fly cowries you must have learned all the other arts. Like sealing the body, sealing the house, throwing dust and all that. And if you haven't, how did you catch the snake?'

Didi sat silent for a while. Then raising her head, she said, 'I have no knowledge of such things, Indra, even though I am a snake-charmer's wife. The reason for that—well, it is a long story. I would like to tell it to you and Srikanta. It will be a load off my chest. I have carried it for a long time. Too long.' Her voice trailed away and her eyes resumed their old expression. She caught our gaze and added, 'Will you believe me?'

I spoke up for the first time that evening, 'I'll believe every word you say, Didi.'

She turned to me with a smile. 'I know you will. Only mean

and base people shut their eyes to the truth and take pleasure in thinking ill of others.'

Another stretch of silence. The shadows of twilight faded away and darkness set in. A sliver-thin moon rose high above the fig tree and its beams, filtering through the leaves, etched a pattern of light on the dim earth below. Suddenly her voice came out of the darkness, 'I thought I would unburden myself tonight but I see that the time has not yet come. But I have something to say to you, Indra. Take my advice. Don't run after Shahji anymore and don't give him money. We have nothing to give you in return—neither charms nor mantras. We cannot raise the dead or send cowries flying through the air. I don't know if anyone can. We certainly cannot.'

I believed every word she said but Indranath, despite his long association with her, did not. He said angrily, 'How did you catch the snake then?'

'That was just a trick of the hand, Indra.'

'It means you have cheated me all these months.' Indra stood up and his voice trembled with fury. 'Both of you have cheated me. You have taken my money and stuffed me up with lies and false promises. Cheats! Tricksters! Scoundrels! I'll show you what's what.'

By the light of the kerosene lamp that burned dimly in a corner I saw Didi's face turn as white as a sheet as she answered fearfully—hesitantly, 'We are snake-charmers, Indra. Deceiving is our profession.'

'I'll take care of your profession. Just you wait.' Indra dragged me away by the hand. 'Let's go, Srikanta. They're both the same—liars and cheats. We won't stay here a minute longer.'

I could not blame Indranath, for his hopes had been cruelly dashed, but I could not take my eyes off Didi's anguished face. I pulled my hand from Indra's grip and taking the five rupees out of my pocket put them down where she sat. 'I brought this for you. It is my own money,' I said.

Before Didi could say a word Indra pounced on the coins and picked them up. 'You don't have to give her anything, Srikanta. They've had enough from me. I don't care now if they die of starvation.'

'But I brought the money for Didi,' I protested.

'Don't call her Didi. She's no one of ours.' Indra grabbed me by the shoulder and pushed me towards the fence.

It was at this moment that Shahji woke up. Disturbed by the commotion and Indra's loud voice he sat up and blinked. '*Kya hua? Kya hua?* (What's the matter?)' he asked looking from one face to another. Indra let go of me and rushed up to where he sat.

'You old scoundrel!' he shouted. 'Stuffing me with lies! I'll skin you alive and bury you in lime. Then we'll see who comes to raise you from the dead.'

Shahji sat like a statue—his eyes blank. We had reached the fence once more when his voice came out to us from the dark. For the first time that evening I heard him speak in Bengali. 'Come here, Indranath. Tell me what has happened.'

'You are frauds and tricksters,' Indra said going back to the veranda. 'You don't know any mantras. Why did you lie to me? Why did you make me serve you like a slave and bring you money?'

'Who told you I don't know any mantras?'

Indra pointed to the silent, bowed figure without any hesitation. 'She did. She told me that deceiving is your profession.'

On hearing these words Shahji's eyes burned like live coals. Looking at them my blood froze. I watched in mute horror as he staggered up to where she sat and pushing away the matted locks from his face, asked in a terrible voice, 'What did you tell Indranath?'

Indra gave me a push and said, 'Come on. Let's go home. Can't you see how late it is?'

It was late but my feet would not move. I stood rooted to the ground till Indra grabbed my arm and dragged me to the fence.

'Why did you tell him that?' Shahji's harsh tones floated out from behind us. There was no reply and we pressed on.

We had hardly gone thirty yards when a blood-curdling cry shattered the silence of the night. Indra let go of my arm and ran in the direction of the hut. I followed but in my haste I was flung headlong into a vast bush of thorn berries that stood by the path. Extricating myself with difficulty, for I was pricked and scratched all over, it was some time before I reached the hut. Stepping into the yard I nearly stumbled over Didi's unconscious form lying on the ground.

At the other end, guru and disciple were engaged in a deadly combat. A murderous looking spear lay on the ground where they wrestled. Shahji had a wiry strength despite his thinness. But he was no match for Indranath. Within a few minutes Indra had flung him down and, sitting on his chest, had gripped his throat with both hands. I ran and pulled Indra away. Had I not done so, Shahji's snake-charming career might have ended that night.

When I managed to separate the two, after a lot of pulling and pushing, I noticed something that made me whimper in terror. Indra's clothes were drenched with blood that flowed from a three-inch cut on his forearm. Tearing a strip from his dhoti he handed it to me and said, 'Don't cry, Srikanta. Tie this tightly round my arm. The drug-eating bastard threw the spear at me.' Then, turning to Shahji, he said, 'If you dare move an inch I'll step on your throat and pull your tongue out. You don't know me.'

Shahji sat still, looking at him with the eyes of one of his own venomous snakes.

'I don't trust you,' Indra continued, 'you're a murdering swine. I'm going to tie your hands.' Yanking the snake-charmer's turban off Shahji's head Indra tied his wrists with strong knots. Shahji did not protest or try to stop him. He submitted to everything without a word.

Indra picked up the heavy stick with which Shahji had struck Didi and threw it to one side. 'Ungrateful wretch,' he muttered. 'I've given him so much money. I've even stolen for him. And he didn't think twice before throwing the spear at me. Keep an eye on him, Srikanta. I must take care of Didi.'

Sprinkling water on her face and fanning her vigorously Indra continued, 'Ever since Didi told me not to give him money he has beaten her everyday. She said to me, "If you had earned it, Indra, I would have taken it from you but I can't let you do what you are doing." She made me swear that I would never bring Shahji any money again. He couldn't take that. He beat her mercilessly. Didi earns a few rupees by selling dung cakes and wood. She feeds him out of that and even buys him ganja. But it isn't enough for the dirty scoundrel. I'll set the police after him or he'll kill Didi some day. He's a murderer. I know it.'

I thought I saw a look of alarm spring into the man's eyes. A shudder passed over his frame and he lowered his eyes. It was only for a moment but I'm convinced that the shaft had gone home. Indra's words had awoken a memory as shameful as it was vile.

It was well past midnight when Didi opened her eyes. Another hour passed before she recovered fully. Then, after hearing the full story from my lips, she stood up. Walking over to Shahji she released him from his bonds. 'Go back to sleep,' she said.

After Shahji went into the hut she called Indra to her side and taking his right hand in hers she placed it on her head. 'Swear on my head, Indra, that you'll never come to this house again. Leave us to our fate. Stay away and forget that we ever existed.'

Indra stared blankly at her for a few moments. Then, bursting like a bomb, he shouted, 'You don't blame him even though he tried to kill me. But because I tied him up I'm being asked to leave the house. You are both the same. Selfish and ungrateful. Come, Srikanta. Not a moment more in this house.'

Didi stood like a figure of stone. Why she did not utter a word of protest or explanation was incomprehensible to me then. Later, much later, I understood the meaning of her silence. I left the five rupees on the floor of the veranda and followed Indranath out of the hut.

Stepping into the yard Indra delivered his final shot, 'What else can you expect from a high-born Hindu girl who elopes with a low-class Mussalman? Depraved, immoral creatures! To hell with the pair of you! I have nothing to do with you from this moment onwards.' Saying this he rushed out of the yard, and crossing the jungle, came to where the boat was moored.

As it moved rapidly away from the bank I saw Indranath lift his arm and dash the tears away from his eyes. The dinghy floated on past the tamarisks and tussocks. The burning-ghat came into view but tonight it held no fear. I sat, dazed and silent, unaware of time and its passing. When the dinghy reached our bank the night was almost over.

As I climbed out of the boat Indra said, 'Go home, Srikanta, and keep away from me in future. You've brought me bad luck everytime. I'll never take you out in my dinghy again.'

He rowed rapidly away towards the deeper waters and in a few minutes, became a fleck on the horizon.

Six

I DID NOT EVEN TRY TO CHECK THE SOBS THAT SHOOK MY CHEST AS I stood on the bank looking at the fast disappearing dinghy. I loved Indranath. For his sake I had risked expulsion from the house in which I was being educated. But he had no use for my love. He had accused me of bringing him bad luck and had left me alone to find my way back home through the dense forest at that time of the night.

His harsh words had wounded me so deeply that for months after that I turned my face away if I encountered him in the streets. The breakdown of our friendship was, to me, a source of pain which welled afresh with every glimpse of him. But he seemed not to care. He had so many friends and followers. He was the hero of the cricket and football clubs. In the gymnasium his performance was unparalleled. Why he had singled me out in the first place and then abandoned me was a mystery I could not fathom. I suffered but did not attempt to resume our old relationship. When I heard the other boys talk of Indranath as if they owned him I sat in silence. Not by a word did I betray the fact that I knew him intimately and that he had said I was his best friend. I had understood, as early as then, that lasting friendships were not possible except between equals. This understanding served me well in later years when the chance of friendship with many 'superior' people came my way. I learned not to take them too seriously, for unequal friendships do not last. At some stage or the other one friend becomes the master and the other his slave.

*

Three or four months passed before I spoke to Indranath again. It was during Kali Puja which the Datta family celebrated every year with a good deal of fanfare. Among the cultural events organized that year was a performance of *Meghnath Badh*. I was very excited, for though I had seen many *jatras* in my native village, this was to be my introduction to the theatre. I rushed around helping to set up the stage and felt very important when the man who was to act the part of Ramchandra that evening asked me to hold a rope. On the strength of this acquaintance I had pleasurable visions of being invited to the green room, before the play commenced, to the chagrin of the other boys who were sure to be kept out. But alas! I stood outside the torn curtain that served as the door to the green-room for hours. Ramchandra went in and out time and again but did not deign to throw a glance at me.

When the first bell rang at ten o'clock I abandoned all hopes of entering the green-room and came and sat in the audience. The play began. I watched spellbound as Meghnath, seven feet tall and five feet around the girth, raved and ranted on the stage. The curtain fell and rose again. It was Lakshman's cue. He had barely begun his speech when Meghnath suddenly leaped in from nowhere causing the boards to totter and creak horribly. Four of the five footlights toppled over. Worse followed. Meghnath's golden cummerbund gave way with a loud snap. Pandemonium broke loose among the audience. Some yelled at Meghnath to sit down. Others shouted for the drop of the curtain. But brave Meghnath did not falter in the face of duty. Dropping his bow he held his slipping dhoti with one hand and, with the other, flung arrows at his enemy with undiminished vigour. Who had ever seen such a battle? Or a hero of this stature? Bowless and with one hand out of action he fought on till Lakshman was put to flight and the

---

*   "The vanquishing of Meghnath"—an epic drama.
**   A rustic opera.

scene was over. I was watching entranced when I felt a tap on my back It was Indranath.

'Didi has sent for you, Srikanta,' he whispered.

I stood up. 'Where is she?'

'Come with me,' he said.

He walked away and I followed him till we reached the bank where his dinghy was moored. We took our places in silence and Indra set the boat adrift. The night was already waning by the time we reached the hut. By the dim light of a kerosene lamp I saw Didi sitting on the threshold with Shahji's head in her lap. A dead cobra, stretched out to its full length, lay at his feet. Didi told us what had happened quite calmly. Shahji had been sent for by a rich man of the locality to catch a snake that had been observed in his house. Shahji had succeeded in drawing out the snake and, flushed with triumph, had spent all the money he had been given on toddy. He had come home roaring drunk and, ignoring Didi's warnings, had proceeded to charm the snake he had caught. It was only afterwards, just before putting the snake away in the basket, that he had become careless. Bringing the snake's mouth close to his own he had made kissing sounds at it. The snake had responded by stinging him viciously in the neck.

Wiping her eyes with the edge of her faded sari Didi said, 'Even as he was dying he knew he had to kill the snake first. "Come, let's die together," he said and, pressing his foot on the snake's head, he stretched its body out to that length with both hands.' She pointed to the dead snake and added, 'They died together.'

Removing the covering from Shahji's face she kissed the lips, rapidly blueing with snake venom, with great tenderness and said, 'What had to happen has happened. I bear no grudge to God.' After a moment of silence she continued, 'I have no one but you two in the world. So, young as you are, you must bear my burdens. There is an open space in the jungle behind the hut. I thought I would lie there after my death but Fate willed otherwise. When morning comes you must help me to carry him there. He has suffered untold misery in this life. Now, God willing, he will find some peace.'

'Are you going to bury Shahji?' Indra asked.

'Yes. He was a Mussalman.'

'Are you one too?'

'Yes,' she replied without hesitation.

Indranath looked at her with uncomprehending eyes. It was obvious that he had not expected this reply. It seemed to me that, despite his knowledge of Shahji's faith, Indra had hoped that Didi had retained her own religion and was still one of us. As for me I would not think of her as anything other than a high-born Hindu woman.

With the first glimmerings of dawn, Indra went out into the jungle to dig a grave for Shahji. Then the three of us carried the body out and placed it in the grave and covered it with earth. Twenty feet below the little clearing where Shahji lay, the Ganga flowed tempestuous and strong. Around the grave were tall trees festooned with creepers. A chill breeze blew and birds sang out of the leafy branches. We sat around the grave, the roar of the river in our ears, waiting for the sun to break out of the eastern sky.

Suddenly, Didi flung herself on the mound of earth with a piercing cry, 'Where shall I go? To whom shall I turn?'

Indra lifted Didi's head from where it lay on the earth and placed it tenderly on his lap. 'Come home with me, Didi,' he said. 'My mother will look after you. You are no Mussalmani! You are a Hindu like us.'

Didi lay as if in a swoon. At last she arose and climbing down the bank waded out into the river. We followed her. She took off the iron hoop that encircled her wrist and threw it in the water. Then, breaking her lac bangles against a rock, she scooped up a handful of earth. With this she scoured out the sindoor from the parting of her hair. Then, dipping her head thrice in the Ganga, she bathed. As she walked back through the jungle, the rising sun irradiating her dripping form, she looked the image of a newly widowed Hindu woman of high birth and lineage.

Back in the hut, as we sat together, Didi told us that Shahji was her husband. Indra asked in disbelief, 'Are you not a Hindu, then?'

'Yes,' she answered. 'My father was a Brahmin. So was my husband.'

'Why did he change his religion?' Indra probed.

'That I cannot say for certain. But when he did I was obliged to do the same, for a woman must embrace her husband's faith. I did not give up the faith of my ancestors of my own accord. Nor have I ever done anything to tarnish it.'

'That I know,' Indra said in a voice thick with emotion. 'That is why—forgive me, Didi—I have often wondered why you were here; how you could so forget your birth and upbringing. But I won't listen to another word. You must come home with me to my mother.'

Didi sat in silence for a while. Then, raising her head, she said decidedly, 'I can't go anywhere, Indranath.'

'Why not, Didi?'

'I know my husband has left some debts. I cannot leave without repaying them.'

Indra lost his temper. 'Yes, he owes money in the toddy and ganja shops,' he said. 'But what is that to you? Who will dare ask you for money? You come with me and I'll see who tries to stop you.'

Didi smiled at him. 'Crazy boy! No one and nothing can stop me except my own conscience. My husband's debts are my debts. How can I run away from them? Go home today, and take Srikanta with you. Come back again after two or three days.'

I had been listening quietly all this while. Now I spoke. 'I have another five rupees at home. Shall I fetch them?'

Before I could complete the sentence Didi came up to me and, taking me in her arms, pressed my head against her breast. Then, kissing my forehead very tenderly, she said, 'No, Srikanta. That will not be necessary. But I shall remember your offer to my dying day. May God dwell in your breast and make your heart weep for the afflicted through all the years of your life.' Tears flooded her eyes and rolled down her cheeks.

Around eight o'clock we got ready to leave. Didi walked part of the way with us. Before turning back she took Indra's hand in hers and said, 'I will not take the liberty of giving you my blessing, Indranath, for you are far above it. God follows you like a shadow and will make you his own.'

Indra touched Didi's feet and said in a tearful voice, 'I can't leave you alone in this jungle, Didi. Something tells me I'll never see you again.'

Didi did not reply. Turning, she walked rapidly away wiping her eyes with the edge of her sari. We stood and watched her weaving her way through the path till the forest swallowed her up. She didn't look back and we both knew why.

Three days later I found Indranath waiting for me outside the school gate. His face was pale, his feet bare, and dust coated his legs right up to the knees. I had never seen him like that for he came from a rich family and was always neat and well-dressed. He came up to me and whispered urgently, 'Didi has gone away. I don't know where. I've been looking for her since yesterday. She left a note for you in the hut. Here.' He handed me a piece of rough paper and walked away without a backward glance. I sat down right where I was and opened the note. Though many years have passed since then, I can more or less remember what she had written:

Srikanta,

I am leaving you but my blessings are with you and will ever remain so. Don't grieve because I'm gone. I know that Indranath will wear himself out looking for me. Try to stop him if you can. You are both too young to understand fully what I am about to write in this letter. Yet, in the hope that you will do so when you are older, I am tempted to unburden myself. You may wonder why, instead of telling you about these events in my life, I am putting them down on paper. I wanted to tell you once. But I couldn't for my story is also my husband's and that is a painful record of guilt and depravity. I do not know what sins I have committed in this life. But I know, without a doubt, that the sins of my previous birth are grievous and innumerable. I did not wish to add to them by lowering my husband in your eyes. It is not that I can do so now because he is dead. Yet I cannot go away either, without sharing my lifelong anguish with you and Indra.

Srikanta, your unfortunate sister's name is Annada. My father was a wealthy man and a Brahmin of high lineage. We were two sisters. To take the place of the son he never had, he brought home a poor Brahmin boy and married him to me. He wanted to educate him and make a man of him. But though he succeeded in the first endeavour he failed miserably in the second. My widowed elder sister lived with us. My husband murdered her one day and disappeared from the house. He was never traced so it is possible that he left the country. You will wonder why he did this terrible thing. I cannot enlighten you for you are children and have no knowledge of such things. But someday, when you are older, you will understand. Then you will also sense the shame and humiliation which this deed heaped on my head. That fire burns in my breast to this day!

Seven years passed before I saw my husband again. He was wearing the garb in which you have seen him, charming snakes before a crowd in front of our house. He was unrecognizable—but not to me. He told me that he had undertaken this dangerous venture for my sake but that was a lie. Nevertheless, at dead of night, I left my father's house. I went away with my husband but everyone knew that I—a Hindu wife—had eloped with a Mussalman snake-charmer. I have carried this stigma all these years and will do so till the day of my death. While my husband was alive I could not reveal the truth. I knew my father. He would never forgive the killer of his flesh and blood. Now that my husband is dead I could go back. But who will believe my story after all these years? There is no place for me in my father's home. Besides, now I am a Mussalmani!

I had a pair of earrings hidden away which I sold to pay my husband's debts. I have not spent the five rupees you left with me that first day. They are lying with the owner of a dry goods shop that stands at the corner of the path from my hut. He has instructions to hand them over to you. Go to him and reclaim the money. Don't be disappointed because I return it. I take with me something far more precious—your tender little heart locked away in my breast. Don't grieve for me, Srikanta. Suffering doesn't frighten me and pain cannot torture me anymore. My sweet little brothers! If the wishes of a chaste wife have any value in God's eyes may your friendship never die.

your loving sister,

Annada

Seven

$\mathcal{I}$ WENT TO THE SHOP AND STOOD BEFORE THE OWNER. UNTYING
A tiny rag bundle he took out a pair of earrings and five silver
rupees. He handed me the coins with the words, 'Bahu sold me
her earrings for twenty-one rupees and paid off Shahji's debts.
Then she went away—I don't know where.' Making a mental
estimate of what Shahji had owed he added, 'She had only five
annas and one pice with her when she left.'

So twenty-two pice were all that Didi had when she started
out on her long and arduous journey into the world! Tears rushed
to my eyes at the thought. To hide them from the old man I turned
and walked away. My ego was hurt because she had returned
my money. 'She took from Indra but not from me,' I thought
resentfully. I was a child then and did not realize that Indra and I
were not the same in Didi's eyes. She could accept his charity but
not mine for Indra was Indra and I was far beneath him.

I have travelled far and wide in my later life but I never set
eyes on Didi again. Through my youth and manhood, whenever I
thought of her and her stoic adherence to her ideals, I was filled
with resentment against God and Man. In a country like ours,
where Sita and Savitri are deified for their chastity, why was Didi
made to suffer such shame and humiliation? Why was her brow,
pure and shining as that of any goddess in heaven, blackened with
the stain of a false faithlessness? I would rave against God, 'You
took from her everything she had. Her father, sister, friends and

relations. You even robbed her of her faith. But what did you give her in return? She, who should have taken her place with the brightest beings of your creation, has had to live out her life bowed down by the condemnation of the world. What justice is in this?' I would ask in despair. I longed to go to her father and reveal the truth. I wanted to proclaim to the world that Annada was no wanton but a shining example of chaste wifehood—a woman whose devotion to her husband had been like a bright and unwavering flame.

For many days after he gave me the letter there was no sign of Indra. But whenever I walked by the river I saw his dinghy tossing about in the water under the open sky. Only once, after our trip to the hut on the night of Shahji's death, did we sit in the boat again. That was the last time for both Indra and me. I remember it well not only because it was our last boat ride together but because, on that trip, I came across the most perfect embodiment of selfish self-centredness that I have yet to see.

It had been a bitterly cold day and, by dusk, the wind was blowing needles of ice on our hands and faces. It had rained the day before and the sky shone clear and frosty. A full moon, swimming in the sky, bathed the earth in liquid silver. I was poring over my school texts when Indra walked in.

'There's a play being performed in — village,' he said. 'Want to come?'

I was crazy about the theatre so I jumped at the offer.

'Get ready and come to our house in five minutes,' he said and vanished.

I dashed upstairs, pulled a wrapper around me, and ran after him. The place he had mentioned was some distance away and could only be reached by train. But when I got to his house Indra informed me that he proposed to take the dinghy. I was disappointed, for going by the river meant hard work at the oars and a long stretch of exposure to the cold night air. Besides, it was much slower than the train and we might not reach in time.

'The boat will go like an arrow in this gale. We won't be late,' Indra said encouragingly. 'A cousin of mine is here from Calcutta and he wants to go by the Ganga.'

We got the boat ready and took our places in it. But time went by and there was no sign of Indra's cousin. I waited with mounting impatience, tortured by thoughts of the scenes I would surely miss.

At last a dim figure appeared on the bank. I got a bit of a shock for I had never seen anyone dressed quite like that. A heavy woollen overcoat was buttoned right down to his knees. His head and neck were wrapped in layers of cap and muffler. Gloves on his hands and silk stockings and pumps on his feet completed the ensemble. It was obvious that this Calcutta babu had taken every possible precaution against the inclement winter of the west. Making a face at our beloved dinghy he stepped into it in the manner of a potentate, one hand resting heavily on Indra's shoulder and the other gripping mine like a vice. Then, comfortably ensconced in the best seat, he glared at me and asked, 'What is your name, boy?'

'Srikanta.'

'Srikanta!' He gave a contemptuous laugh. 'What is the Sri for? Kanta is a good enough name for you. Come, don't go on sitting there like a dummy. Prepare a hookah for me. Indra—give the boy the hookah and tobacco. Let him make himself useful.'

'I'll prepare your hookah, Natunda,' Indra said in an embarrassed voice. 'You take the oars, Srikanta.'

I did not reply. Neither did I move from my place. I prepared the hookah but my rapturous mood of a few minutes ago changed to one of deepest gloom. I had never been spoken to in that tone of voice. I had never even seen a servant being spoken to like that. But he was a babu from Calcutta with an LA degree and Indra's cousin as well, so I was forced to swallow his insults.

After a few puffs Indra's Natunda asked, 'Where do you live, boy? What is that on your shoulders? A wrapper? What a filthy rag it is! It stinks from a hundred yards away. Take it off and spread it on the plank. Something is poking me.'

'Take mine,' Indra said quickly. 'I'm not cold,' and removing his woollen shawl he flung it towards his Natunda who folded it neatly over the plank and sat on it without a moment's hesitation.

We crossed the river within half an hour for it had shrunk considerably with the onset of winter. But no sooner did we touch the opposite bank than the wind dropped. The sail sagged and the boat came to a halt.

'What do we do now?' Indra asked Natunda.

'Give the boy the oars. Let him pull the boat.'

Indra laughed at the ignorance of his city cousin. 'That would be quite useless. It's impossible to row in still water like this. We'll have to go back.'

'Then why did you bring me in the dinghy, you fool?' Natunda gnashed his teeth at Indra. 'You'll have to get me there tonight. I don't care how. I've been invited to play the harmonium.'

'There are others who can take your place.'

'Hmph,' Natunda grimaced. 'Others who can take my place! As if one could find a decent harmonium player in these backwaters. I don't want to listen to any of your nonsense. You promised to take me there and you will. How you do it is your business.'

Sensing Indra's predicament I volunteered a suggestion, 'Maybe we could tow the boat, Indra?'

Even before the words left my mouth his cousin snarled viciously at me, 'Why don't you do so then instead of sitting here hunched up like an animal?'

Indra and I looked at each other. There was no way of reaching our destination other than towing the boat. The water was as cold as ice as we stepped into it and our hands and feet, cut to pieces on shell and rock, grew numb and blue. But the man for whom we were suffering these torments was as indifferent and unconcerned as the plank he sat on. From time to time he barked out a word of command at which we had to stop the boat and minister to his needs—which mainly involved the preparation of a fresh hookah. Then, as we strained and pulled at the heavy boat with all our childish strength, he smoked his hookah with comfortable sucking sounds. Once when Indra requested him to take the helm, he refused point-blank declaring that he had no intention of removing his gloves and catching his death.

'You can keep them on...' began Indra but he was cut short.

'Yes and ruin them on your dirty rudder. Don't be stupid. Just carry on with whatever you are doing.'

I can say, in all honesty, that never before or after this encounter did I set eyes on a person as unadulteratedly selfish and mean as Indra's Natunda. Through our nightmarish journey he sat as stiff as a board afraid to move lest a drop of water fall on his precious clothes and spoil them. Worse followed. The fresh air over the Ganga acted as a tonic and gave him an appetite that increased with each passing hour. Around eleven o'clock he could bear the pangs no longer.

'Are there no shops nearby, Indra?' he called, 'Can't you get me something to eat?'

'There's a village just ahead, Natunda. I'm sure we can buy some food.'

'Then hurry up and get me there. You, boy! Can't you pull harder? Don't you get enough to eat?'

After some time we arrived at the village. Here the bank was wide with a long shelf of sand stretching far into the river. We dragged the boat onto shallow water with a mighty effort and heaved a sigh of relief. The babu from Calcutta stood up. 'I'm cramped from sitting in this nasty boat,' he declared. 'I must stretch my legs.'

There being no question of his wetting his feet Indra lifted him out of the boat and carried him far out where the sand gleamed dry and white in the moonlight.

As the two of us set out for the bazaar Indra said, 'Why don't you come too, Natunda? You'll be frightened here all by yourself. People around here are honest. No one will steal the dinghy.'

'Frightened?' Indra's cousin snarled at him. 'What do you think of me? I am Calcutta born and bred—not a Bihari rat like you. I fear nobody and nothing—not even Death. If you think I'm going to walk through your dirty villages you're mistaken. The natives stink so—they make me puke.'

The solution, as he saw it, was that Indra should proceed to the village to buy food and that I should stay behind to prepare his hookah as and when he needed it. Indra was not averse to the idea but I rebelled outright. No force on earth was going to make me stay here alone with this man! I shook off Indra's restraining hand and walked with him, away from the vicinity of his cousin. From behind us came the sounds of a nasal chant accompanied by a vigorous clapping of hands. '*Tinkle, tinkle teacup*,' sang the Calcutta born and bred aristocrat as he walked up and down the bank.

I could see that Indra was acutely embarrassed by his cousin's behaviour. 'Calcutta folk,' he murmured. 'They are not used to our kind of climate.' He glanced at me out of the corner of his eye.

'Hmph!' I grunted.

Indra then proceeded to give me an account of his cousin's outstanding academic achievements. 'He'll pass his LA in a couple of years and become a deputy,' Indra prophesied in a desperate bid to wipe out my annoyance and kindle a spark of admiration for his cousin.

Many years have passed since that night. I have no knowledge of what became of Indra's cousin—whether he rose to the eminence of a deputy or not. But it is possible that he did. For, if what I hear is true, his was the stuff that Bengali deputies are made of. Indra's Natunda was in the first flush of manhood at the time I'm writing about. It is generally believed that during this period the heart is at its largest and the mind at its most expansive. Yet, in the few hours that we were together, he managed to dispel this view totally and completely. Fortunately there are not many like him in the world, else it would be difficult to live in. But I digress again. Let me get on with what happened for it is more important that I give my readers the conclusion to the night's adventure.

Indra and I reached the grocer's shop in a few minutes. As we had anticipated, the shop was shut and the owner, with his doors and windows locked securely against the cold, was sunk in a slumber so profound that not all the clamour of the world could wake him. Indra and I banged on the door and yelled with all our might but to no avail. We were dealing not with a gentleman of leisure for whom sleep is a luxury, but with a hardy yokel who worked like a machine from dawn to dusk and, having assumed the horizontal position, was lost to the world. After half an hour of trying we had to give up and return to the bank empty-handed.

The dinghy bobbed up and down where we had left it but where was Natunda? The beach stretched stark and white as far as the eye could see. Not a shadow of the Calcutta cousin marred its gleaming surface.

'Natunda! Natunda!' Indra and I shouted till our lungs were fit to burst but nothing save the reverberations of our own voices came back to us. We stared at one another as a terrible thought took possession of us. For a man to be attacked and killed by a wolf was not an uncommon occurrence in these parts. In winter, packs of wolves frequently descended on unsuspecting villagers and dragged babies out of huts and goats from their pens.

'It—it—couldn't be a wolf—could it, Srikanta?' Indra's voice shook. At this voicing of my fears a trickle of ice water ran down my spine and goose bumps broke out all over my body. I didn't like Indra's Natunda but I hadn't wished him such a terrible fate.

As we strained our eyes scanning that vast expanse of sand, an object, gleaming in the moonlight, caught our attention. Going towards it we discovered that it was one of Natunda's much prized pumps. Indra broke down completely. Flinging himself on the wet sand he howled like a child. 'What shall I do? How can I face my aunt, Srikanta? I won't go home. I just can't go home anymore.'

As I stood watching him, jumbled thoughts in my head took shape and acquired a focus. I remembered that when we were rapping on the grocer's door and shouting his name, a loud chorus of barking dogs had reached out to us from the bank. Intent on our purpose we hadn't given it a thought. But now it was obvious that the dogs had seen the wolves attacking Natunda and had set up an alarm—which we had foolishly ignored. I could still hear faint sounds of barking from a distance which left no doubt in my mind that somewhere, further up the bank, a pack of wolves was feasting on Indra's cousin and that the pye-dogs of the village were looking on and barking with all their might. Indra sat up suddenly, grim determination on his face.

'I must go to Natunda,' he said.

'Oh no.' I laid a hand on his arm. 'You can't do that. Have you gone mad?'

Indra shook me off and walked to the dinghy. Picking up an oar he threw it over his right shoulder. Then, taking a large knife out of his pocket, he held it, blade upwards in his left hand. With eyes blazing out of a face that was pale and drawn with anxiety, he said, 'You stay here, Srikanta. If I don't return send word to my parents.'

I knew that his mind was made up and I made no further protestations. Picking up a length of bamboo from the dinghy I followed him as he strode purposefully up the bank. Indra turned around and, snatching the bamboo away, flung it into the water.

'Why should you risk your life, Srikanta?' he said. 'What has happened is through no fault of yours.'

'It isn't your fault either,' I replied.

'That is true,' he admitted, 'I told Natunda not to come by the river. He wouldn't listen. But I can't return home without him. I have to go.'

I knew that. I also knew that I could never let him go alone. I retrieved my weapon from the river and the two of us walked in the direction of the barking dogs. As we went along Indra warned me, 'Don't try to run on the sand. Jump into the water if they attack.'

After walking about half a mile we came to a sand dune. As we climbed to the top we saw some five or six pye-dogs, a little distance up the bank, apparently guarding some object immersed in the water. From time to time they set up a chorus of barks. As far as we could see there was no trace of any other animal—not even a jackal.

'Natunda!' Indra shouted.

'Here I am,' the object called out sobbing loudly, in a voice surprisingly like that of the brave babu from Calcutta. The dogs yelped and ran as Indra and I rushed forward and pulled the near fainting Natunda out of the water. Torrents of water ran from his overcoat, muffler, cap and gloves and the shining pump on one stockinged foot was bloated like a drum. We understood, without being told, that the canine population of the village had been so charmed by his melodious rendering of *Tinkle, tinkle teacup* that they had rushed towards him in appreciation. Later, his nervous bid for escape had startled them into giving him a chase. Slipping and scrambling over the sand he had lost a shoe. Then, in a desperate attempt to elude his pursuers, he had jumped into the freezing water and had been standing neck-deep in it for the past half hour. But wonder of wonders! The first words that came out from between his chattering teeth, as we dragged him out of the water, were, 'My other pump?'

Then, one by one, he mourned the fate of his greatcoat, his cap, his muffler and his gloves—alternating his lamentations with curses on the pair of us for setting him on the shore instead of carrying him to the boat where he could have removed his wet clothing without messing them up with sand. All through the journey homeward he raved and bemoaned the fate that had cast him in the company of savages like us who hadn't even seen such things as an overcoat, pumps, a muffler and gloves and therefore, had no idea of their value. What filled us with a kind of awed admiration was that his body, which he had hitherto jealously protected from the smallest drop of water, did not feature in his lamentations.

It was past two o'clock at night when the dinghy touched our bank. With my wrapper tucked around his middle—the same wrapper whose stink had made him swoon earlier in the evening—and Indra's shawl around his shoulders, he allowed himself to be led home, grumbling all the while at being forced to touch to his body rags too filthy for him to wipe his feet on. However, all this abuse fell on our ears as sweetly as raindrops on a yam leaf. Our relief at being able to bring him home alive glowed within us so warmly that even the penetrating cold of that winter night meant nothing to us. Wrapping the edge of my thin dhoti around my bare chest and back I walked home, my heart singing with happiness.

Eight

I OFTEN WONDER, WHEN SITTING DOWN TO WRITE, HOW IT IS THAT certain events in one's life are remembered as clearly as if they had occurred just the day before while others are clean forgotten. Wise men tell us that the memory is like a mesh through which the unimportant sinks beneath the weight of the important and is lost. I do not agree for, in my memory, many trivial incidents stand out bright and clear while others, which should have been preserved and cherished, have rusted and been reduced to dust.

One such remembrance had lain dormant in my consciousness till a chance meeting brought it to light. It happened many years later—at a period of time when even the memory of Didi had been misted over. I had been invited to a hunting expedition by a prince who had been a class fellow of mine at school. I had done his sums for him time and again and in consequence, though princes ordinarily have short memories, he had kept in touch. We had exchanged letters even after we had both passed the Entrance examination and gone our own ways.

One day, quite by accident, I ran into him. His father had died in the intervening years and he had inherited the estate. He was organizing a hunting party which he invited me to join. He had heard, he said, that there was no one who could beat me with a rifle in these parts. He had also heard of certain other talents I had acquired as I stepped into manhood—talents that entitled me to a friendship with a prince who had money to burn.

But I must confess, in all modesty, that what he had heard were exaggerated reports from kind relatives and friends. However, let that pass. The Shastras tell us not to turn down the appeals of princes. So, being a Hindu and a Brahmin, I decided to follow the doctrines of our illustrious forefathers and accept his invitation.

On reaching the camp, after a twenty-mile elephant ride from the station, I found that the hunting expedition had all the trappings of a luxurious safari. Five tents had been set up. One, exquisitely fitted up and furnished, was for His Highness exclusively. One was set up as a kitchen. Of the other three, one housed his retinue of friends, one his servants, and the last—set a little apart from the others—had a couple of dancing girls in it. These, with their attendant musicians, had been brought along to entertain the prince and his party after each day's hunt.

Twilight had set in by the time I announced my arrival. As I approached His Highness' tent I could hear strains of music coming from within. The entertainment had clearly been going on for some hours, for my host had reached such a stage of inebriation that his happiness on seeing me made him fall back with a thud on the silken cushions. The other occupants of the tent gave me a thunderous, if somewhat confused, welcome for not one of them knew me. The singing girl stopped her song and sat, eyes downcast, on the velvet rug. This young woman had been procured at great expense from Patna. I was impressed by His Highness' taste, for she was beautiful as well as a skilled singer with an extremely melodious voice.

On my host's recommendation I asked Pyari—for that was her name—to resume her singing. She smiled and looked pleased. I could see that she was relieved to find among her audience one man sober enough to appreciate her singing. For the rest of the evening, till late into the night, it seemed as though she sang for me alone. I had the strangest feeling that she was trying to drown the drunken revelry around the two of us with all the beauty of her person and the sweetest of her songs. I was so transported that when the singing came to an end I could find no adequate words of appreciation. I mumbled a conventional word of thanks at which Pyari smiled and lowered her eyes. Then, bringing her hands together in a namaskar—not a salaam—she prepared to depart.

I looked at the sleeping, semi-conscious forms around me and suddenly found my voice. 'Baiji,' I said in Hindustani, 'I bless the fate that has brought me here. I am looking forward to the privilege of hearing you every evening for the next fortnight.'

She stood still for a few seconds, then coming up to me said softly in Bengali, 'His Highness has paid me handsomely to entertain him and his friends. So sing I must. But why should you waste your time toadying for a prince's favours? Leave this place. Go home tomorrow morning as early as you can.'

I was so startled by her words that I stood and stared dumbly at her retreating back as, with a swish of her silken garments, she swept out of the tent.

The first hunt was scheduled for the following morning. We were eleven hunters in all with fifteen guns between us of which six were rifles. Innumerable hampers of food and wine borne by servants accompanied us as we rode out to our destination. The place selected was a huge dried up carcass of a river with enormous silk-cotton trees stretching for miles along one bank. Opposite was a beach of white sand dotted with catkins and wild grass. I could see no signs of game except some doves cooing contentedly from the branches of the silk-cotton trees and a few curlews and herons flitting over the stagnant water.

Baiji's words rang in my ears as I watched my fellow hunters regaling themselves with whisky in between an animated discussion on the strategy of the hunt. I threw down my gun. His Highness noticed the action.

'You are not yourself, Srikanta. Is anything wrong?'

'I don't shoot birds,' I answered shortly.

'Why not?' he asked, amazed.

'I haven't used grape-shot since I grew a moustache,' I answered. 'I'm out of touch.'

My host laughed till tears ran down his cheeks, his unrestrained delight at my witty remark was reinforced, I am convinced, by the golden liquid he had been imbibing so freely.

But the rest of the company was not amused. One of them—a Bihari named Sarayu—glowered at me. 'Is there anything shameful about shooting birds?' he asked testily.

'Not for everyone,' I replied. 'There are always exceptions.' Then, turning to my host I said, 'If you'll excuse me I'll return to the camp. I don't feel too well.'

Entering my tent I first ordered a cup of tea, then lighting a cigarette, lay back against the silk cushions. I had barely taken a couple of puffs when a servant appeared and, salaaming respectfully, requested me to accompany him to Baiji's tent as she had expressed a desire to see me. I had been half hoping for, half dreading, such a call.

'Why does she wish to see me?' I asked.

'I can't say.'

'Who are you?'

'I am Baiji's khansama.'

'Are you a Bengali?'

'Yes, I am a barber by caste. My name is Ratan.'

'Is Baiji a Hindu?'

'Yes.' Ratan laughed. 'Would I work for a Mussalmani?'

Leading me to the door of his mistress' tent Ratan disappeared. I lifted the silken curtain and walked in. Last night, dressed as she was in baggy trousers and a veil, I had thought her a Mussalman prostitute from the north. Now, seeing her as she sat alone waiting for me, I realized that she was a Bengali and a high-caste Hindu. A milk-white *garad* (a kind of silk fabric) sari was draped around her slim body and long wet hair streamed down her back. She had a tray in front of her with betel leaves, nuts, catechu and lime in little compartments. A highly ornamented pipe and bowl with tobacco in it stood on one side.

She rose smiling as I entered and pointing to the velvet rug beside her, invited me to sit. 'I would rather not smoke in your presence,' she said in the voice of an old acquaintance. 'Ratan! Take the pipe away.' Then, as Ratan removed it, she said apologetically, 'I can't offer you my pipe. But I will send for some cigarettes.'

'You don't have to,' I answered shortly. 'I have some in my pocket.'

'That's good,' she said rather naïvely and went on, 'Make yourself comfortable. We have a lot to tell each other. Strange are the ways of God. I never dreamed that I would meet you here of all places. You went with His Highness to the hunt. What made you come back?'

'I was disgusted with the hunt.'

'So you should be. How cruel men are! Taking innocent lives for pleasure. Is your father well?'

'Father is dead.'

'Dead!' she exclaimed. 'And your mother?'

'She went before Father.'

'So—that's why—' She bit her lip and her eyes swam. I thought I had imagined it but when she spoke I knew I hadn't for her voice was soft and had a hint of tears in it. 'You have no one, then, to care for you. I can see that you are not married. Are you still with Pishima? What about your studies? Have you given them up with everything else that was good in your life?'

Till this moment I had patiently answered her questions, satisfying her unaccountable curiosity regarding the intimate details of my life. Now I lost my temper. 'Who are you?' I asked roughly. 'I don't think I have seen you before. Why do you ask me so many questions?'

'Who am I?' She smiled. 'I am Pyari. But if my face means nothing to you the name my parents gave me won't either. Besides I am not from your village.'

'Where are you from?'

'That I won't tell.'

'What is your father's name?'

Pyari bit her tongue and shook her head. 'He's dead and gone to heaven. I can't soil his name with my impure lips.'

'Well,' I said with mounting impatience. 'At least tell me how you know me. You can do that, can't you?'

'Yes,' Pyari dimpled back, not offended in the least. 'But will you believe what I say?'

'Try me.'

'I know you from the moment I knew myself. It is stupid of me but that's how it is. You have made me weep so often and so long that, had the sun not dried my tears, I would have been standing in a pool. Do you believe that?'

I did not. I thought this another bit of vivacious flattery that women of easy virtue employ to captivate men. I realized, later, that the mistake was mine. I had forgotten that her lips had always been formed like that—as if a mocking smile lurked at the corners of the twin arches. I made no answer.

She studied my face for a few moments and gave a delighted laugh. 'You are not as stupid as I thought. You know that such words mean nothing—that they are the tricks of my trade. But let me tell you something. Men far cleverer than you have been duped by words like these. And if you are so clever why can't you find yourself a better job than that of a professional toady? You are no good at it anyway. Why don't you quit and go home?'

Anger surged through me and hot words rose to my lips. Curbing them I said quietly, 'A job is a job even if I'm no good at it. But it's time I took my leave. People will talk about us if I stay too long.'

'You should feel flattered if people talk about us. Why should you regret an acquaintance with me in your present circumstances?'

I turned away from her and moved towards the door. From behind me came peal after peal of shameless laughter. 'Dear friend,' she mocked. 'Don't forget me and my pool of tears. Repeat the story to His Highness and his friends and it may be the making of you.'

I walked out without a word, her taunting words stinging my back like a cluster of scorpions. Back in my tent I drank my tea and lit a cigarette with trembling fingers. Forcing my confused brain into some semblance of order I asked myself, 'Who is this woman and why did she behave so strangely?' But however hard I tried to recapitulate, nothing in my past reminded me, even vaguely, of Pyari. Yet she obviously knew me and all about me. She knew my background and character. She had as good as told me that being a prince's toady was not my natural vocation. She had even enquired after Pishima. She had said many other things that made little sense to me. But one thing was clear. For some reason, known only to herself, she wanted me out of the way. Puzzling over this I tossed about on my bed unable to sleep. When the hunters returned in the evening I pleaded a headache and kept to my room. From where I lay I could hear Pyari's singing and the drunken cheers of her audience far into the night.

In the next few days I noticed a change in the mood of the hunting party. The fiery enthusiasm of the first day seemed to have waned and the hunters were loath to leave the camp. Things being as they were, I expressed a desire to leave. Not that I was particularly unhappy or uncomfortable where I was. It was the presence of Baiji that put a severe constraint on me. The moment she entered the room I had the strongest urge to get up and walk away. When

I couldn't do that I would turn my face away and pretend an absorption in something or someone else. The fact that she was desperately trying to meet my eyes was not lost on me.

It being decided that I would leave on Saturday afternoon, His Highness had arranged a special session of music after breakfast. After the singing was over the men sat on, chatting idly on various topics. Somehow the conversation veered around to the subject of ghosts and one of the company—an elderly Bihari gentleman and a resident of the village in which we were camping—had an interesting contribution to make. He announced that if anyone of us doubted the existence of spirits, he should visit the village burning-ghat that night for, it being a Saturday and a new moon night in conjunction, the spirits would be abroad for people to see and hear. I remembered my childhood fears and laughed aloud.

The old gentleman threw me a sharp look and asked, 'You don't believe me?'

'No.'

'Why not? Any special reason?'

'No.'

'Then you *should* believe me. You Bengalis sneer at the supernatural because you've read a few pages of English. Bengalis are godless and unclean—un-Hindu.'

I was shocked at the man's rancour and his offensive generalizations. But I spoke quite calmly, 'I don't wish to argue with you. If not believing in ghosts makes me unclean and un-Hindu, so be it. But one thing is certain. If anyone claims to have seen a ghost he is either deceived or deceiving. That is my considered opinion.'

The old man looked at me with blazing eyes and clutched my arm. 'Can you go to the burning-ghat tonight?' he asked in a tone of challenge.

'I certainly can,' I answered. 'I've often done so in my childhood.'

'Don't make false claims, Babu,' he snarled. Then he proceeded to tell his audience a series of hair-raising tales about the burning-ghat which was no ordinary burning-ghat but a *mahasamsan* (a vast cremation ground). He told us of people who had seen Kali and her demons playing a ball game with a hundred human skulls; of others who had heard demoniac laughter. He talked of white foreigners who had lost their lives in their attempts to test the truth of his assertions. He told these stories well and with conviction and I could see that many of my co-hunters were paralysed with fear.

Suddenly I became aware of Pyari. She had crept up to where I sat and was listening open-mouthed. Her shoulder rested against mine and I felt her tremble. Noting the effect his words had on his audience the old Bihari turned around and looked triumphantly at me. 'So, Babu saheb,' he asked with a sneer. 'You will go tonight?'

'Yes,' I said.

'As you wish. If you lose your life—'

'If I lose my life I won't blame you. But I won't go unarmed. I'll take my gun.'

At these words a torrent of invective burst from the company—not against me alone. My entire community came under censure. Bengalis were Anglicized and atheistic. They did not follow the Hindu way of life. They ate meat and other unclean food. They hesitated when it came to killing birds but thought they could shoot down ghosts and demons. And, for all their brave words, they were cowardly at heart. All this and much more my fellow-toadies poured into the willing ears of the prince till, unable to bear it any longer, I got up and walked away.

Just before dusk a young man named Purushottam accosted me outside my tent. I knew him slightly and liked him for, though a Bihari, he was not as much of a Bengali-hater as the others. He also talked and drank much less and had admitted that he was no hunter.

'Srikanta babu,' he said. 'Take me with you tonight. I've never seen a ghost in my life and I shouldn't miss this fine opportunity.'

'You don't believe in the supernatural?' I asked, laughing.

'Not a bit.'

'Why not?'

'Because it doesn't exist.'

He proceeded to give me many rational arguments in support of his claim. I was not particularly impressed by his arguments for I knew that fears of this kind are not resolved by arguments. I didn't want to take him along but he wouldn't take no for an answer. Strapping his dhoti tightly between his legs he picked up a length of oiled bamboo. 'Srikanta babu,' he said, 'you may carry a gun if you like. But I am confident that I can keep all ghosts and demons at bay with my stick.'

'Will the stick be in your hand when the time comes?'

'Rest assured it will. The burning-ghat is two miles away. We should leave the camp by eleven o'clock.'

An hour or so before we were to start I was pacing outside my tent speculating on what the supernatural was all about. It was not that I feared the coming ordeal for my terror of the dead had passed with my childhood. I did not believe that spirits exist. Even Indra, who did, never claimed to have seen any. Yet, my thoughts repeatedly went back to an experience that I had had on just such a dark and moonless night five or six years ago. That day had also been a Saturday. I remember that distinctly.

Nirupama, whom I called Nirudidi, was a virgin widow who lived in the town in which I had been reared. Large hearted, self-sacrificing and devout, she was loved and looked up to as a model of Indian womanhood by her family and neighbours alike. Then, one day, she was thirty years old at the time, it was discovered that she was carrying a child. The shock and horror of the Hindu community knew no bounds. Its guardians were of such immaculate character themselves and so zealous of the community's moral welfare that they were forced to advocate a policy of ruthless ostracism. She was compelled to leave her home and take refuge in a hut at the edge of the forest. When she lay dying of puerperal fever after six months of intense suffering, not one of her family or friends were at her side. I was young and couldn't do much for her. But I sat by her watching her die.

It was a dark and stormy night. After twelve o'clock the wind increased in velocity and rain fell in torrents. I sat half dozing in a broken chair by Nirudidi's bedside when I heard her voice, strong and clear, 'Srikanta.'

I started up and went to her.

'Srikanta—go home,' she whispered.

'In this pouring rain?' I asked, amazed.

'Yes. Go quickly before they get you.' I touched her forehead. It was burning. 'She's in a delirium,' I thought. To appease her I said, 'I'll go in a few minutes. As soon as the rain stops.'

'No! No!' She sat up excitedly. 'Don't wait another moment. Go now.'

'Why Nirudidi?' I was frightened by the passion in her face and voice.

She clutched my arm and pointed to the closed window. 'Can't you see them?' she whispered. 'Those soldiers with dark faces peeping into the room? They've come to take me away. They'll kill you if you stay.'

Then, for the rest of the night, she tossed and turned, screaming all the while, 'There, there—at the window—under the bed. They are coming. They'll kill you. Run, Srikanta, run.'

I was so terrified that I would have run out into the storm and rain if it wasn't for those 'soldiers with dark faces' who stood just outside. Nirudidi's passionate conviction that I was in danger was dispelled only with her death—just as dawn was breaking over a storm-tossed sky. Thinking of that night brought on the dull ache that crept into my heart whenever I remembered Nirudidi.

'Babu,' a voice broke in on my thoughts. It was Ratan's. 'Baiji sends her regards and requests you to meet her in her tent.'

I was astonished at this intrusion and extremely displeased. To send for me at this time of the night was a liberty Pyari had no right to take—particularly after her offensive behaviour the last time we were together. I looked sharply at Ratan but on his face was the bland incomprehension of the well-trained servant.

'That is quite impossible,' I said, controlling myself with an effort. 'I must leave in a few minutes. Tell your mistress that I'll see her tomorrow.'

'She wishes to see you tonight, Babu.' Ratan's voice was firm but respectful. 'If you can't go to her tent she will come to yours.'

'I'm sorry, Ratan,' I said with all the patience I could muster. 'I can't see her tonight. I'll see her tomorrow. I promise.'

'Then she will come to you. In the five years that I've worked for her I have never known her to change her mind.'

My blood boiled at these words. Was there no limit to the woman's audacity and irrational demands? I felt trapped. I had no intention of gratifying her whims but if she really came to my tent, as she threatened to do, my already worn reputation would be in shreds.

'Wait a minute, Ratan,' I said, and entering my tent I pulled on my boots and picked up my rifle. Then, in a militant mood, I walked over to Baiji's tent.

She stood by the entrance, waiting. Looking me up and down she said without preamble, 'You are not going to any burning-ghat. Is that clear?'

I was startled enough to stammer foolishly, 'Why, why?'

'Because even if *you* don't believe in ghosts—they exist. If you go tonight you'll never come back,' and suddenly, incomprehensibly, her face crumpled and she burst into tears. This was something so unexpected that I stared at her, speechless with astonishment.

'All your life you have been the same—stubborn and rash,' she continued between sobs. 'Will you never grow up? I won't let you go alone. That's certain. If you insist on going I'll come with you.'

'Fine. Come along,' I said.

My sarcasm was not lost on her. Her eyes dried—turned hard and jewel bright.

'What do you think of yourself?' she cried passionately. 'Don't you have a family and a society to go back to? What will people say when they hear that you went on a ghost-hunt accompanied by a prostitute? Who ever dreamed that you could sink so low—could degrade yourself like this?'

She bit her lip and fresh tears welled up in her eyes. Suddenly my anger melted away. I thought I recognized Pyari.

'Does public opinion really matter?' I asked gently. 'Did anyone dream that you would degrade yourself the way you've done?'

At my words a smile, like a faint ray of autumn sunshine, flickered over her face. But it was only for a moment. Then her eyes clouded once more and she asked in a frightened voice, 'What do you know of me? Can you tell who I am?'

'You are Pyari.'

'Everyone knows that.'

'Do you want me to admit that I know more about you than anyone else here? If you really wished that, you could have revealed your true identity on the very first day. But you didn't and neither will I. I must go now. It is getting late.'

Swift as a flash of lightning Pyari stood in front of me. 'I won't let you go,' she said.

'Why won't you let me go?'

'Because real ghosts exist and confronting them is dangerous. I swear I shall scream if you insist on going.'

I burst out laughing. 'I have never seen a real ghost,' I said, 'but I admit to having seen fakes. They laugh and cry and block one's path. And sometimes they even devour human flesh.'

Pyari's face went white. 'So you do recognize me,' she said at last, 'but what you said about fakes is incorrect. They do not devour human flesh—at least not of those they love. They have their near and dear ones just as you do.'

'You are speaking of yourself,' I said with a smile. 'Are you a ghost?'

'What is a ghost? One who inhabits the earth even after death. That is what you meant, didn't you, when you spoke of fakes? It is true that in a sense I'm dead too. But I didn't die of my own accord nor did I announce my death. My mother did that for me.'

The moment she said that all my doubts vanished. She was Rajlakshmi—a young Brahmin widow of our village. She had accompanied her mother on a pilgrimage and never returned. She had died of cholera in Kashi—so her mother had announced after coming back alone. Pyari's face and form had not struck a bell but I had been intrigued, from the moment I saw her, by a habit she had of biting her underlip whenever she was agitated or angry. The vaguest of feelings nagged me that somewhere, in the distant past, someone had done just that. Now I knew that the prostitute, Pyari, was the Kulin widow, Rajlakshmi. I stared at her in mute horror.

About ten years ago, when I was still with my parents, a Brahmin lady came to live with her brother in our ancestral village. Her Kulin husband had driven her away after taking another wife and she had nowhere else to go. She had two daughters—Suralakshmi and Rajlakshmi. Rajlakshmi was eight years old at the time and Suralakshmi—twelve. Rajlakshmi was very fair but no beauty. Her skin was pale and waxy from years of untreated malaria. Her abdomen was distended due to an enlarged spleen and stuck out from her thin frame like a drum. Her arms and legs were like sticks and only the faintest copper coloured down covered her head. She used to come to the village pathshala where I was the head boy. I was a great bully and so great was Rajlakshmi's fear of me that she would roam the forest everyday in search of ripe *bainchis* (a wild berry) which she would string into a garland and offer to me as a bribe for leaving her alone. If the garland was not long enough for my liking I would take her up on her lessons and slap her hard if she couldn't answer my questions. She never rebelled or expressed any grievance. After the beating she would sit quietly in a corner biting her lip gloomily.

Then a marriage was arranged for the two girls. Her uncle was on the point of being excommunicated by the village elders for his inability to find grooms for his nieces when he discovered that the old cook in the house of the Dattas, was a Kulin Brahmin and therefore, an eligible parti for his elder niece. Offering fifty-one rupees as dowry, he started the negotiations. But the prospective bridegroom, though he looked fat and foolish, was self-interested enough to drive a shrewd bargain.

'Impossible!' he exclaimed, shaking his head vigorously. 'You have no idea of current prices. You can't get a pair of healthy rams for fifty-one rupees and you're looking for a son-in-law. Make it hundred-and-one and I'll marry both the girls. Nothing can be fairer than that. The least you can give me is the price of two bullocks.'

No one doubted the justice of his claims but the uncle was poor and had daughters of his own. After a great deal of haggling and entreaty the sum was brought down to seventy rupees and Suralakshmi and Rajlakshmi were married in a single night.

Next morning, the wily Brahmin left the village for his home town of Bankura—the seventy rupees tucked securely in the folds of his dhoti. No one ever heard of him again. Within a year and a half of the marriage, Suralakshmi died of splenetic fever and another year and a half later Rajlakshmi was sanctified by her death in Kashi.

'I can read your thoughts,' Pyari said suddenly.

'What are they?'

'You're saying to yourself, "Poor girl! How badly I treated her when we were children. I made her pick berries from thorny bushes and beat her mercilessly if she couldn't pick enough. And she never complained—never asked for anything in return—till tonight. Let me give her what she wants. I won't go to the burning-ghat if it makes her happy." That's what you were thinking, weren't you?'

I burst out laughing and Pyari joined in. 'I knew it,' she said. 'I knew that you would not spurn me once you realized who I was. The love one bears in childhood is never lost. But why are we standing outside? Come in and sit down. I have so much to tell you. What are you laughing at?'

'I'm laughing at the skill with which women like you can charm a man into submission to their will.'

'I don't deny my skills but I wouldn't try them on one who has held me in the hollow of his hand since my earliest childhood. How strange that you forgot me so completely! You should be ashamed of yourself.' Pyari laughed till her diamond ear drops trembled and twinkled in the star light.

'I was so little aware of you that forgetting you was the most natural thing in the world. In fact I'm surprised that I remember you now. But it's nearly twelve o'clock. I must go.'

Pyari's smile vanished—her face became ashen. She said in a small voice, 'Even if there are no ghosts—there are snakes and other wild creatures in the jungle. You must admit that.'

'I know that and I've taken every precaution.'

'I knew I couldn't stop you,' Pyari sighed. 'Still I tried. Well, go if you must. But remember—if anything happens to you in this God-forsaken place you'll find no one but myself at your side. Your rich and powerful friends will not spare you a glance. You boasted to my face that you were unaware of me. That was a very manly thing to do. But I, being a woman, cannot return the compliment when the time comes.'

Her words clutched at my heart but, ignoring them, I said with a sneer, 'Thank you for your kindness, Baiji. I have no one in the world. It gives me great satisfaction to know that there is one who will not disown me when I am in trouble.'

Pyari's eyes blazed. 'You knew that all along. Yet you call me Baiji and insult and humiliate me. I wish I *could* disown you. That is what you deserve. But women are disgusting creatures. If they love once, they are lost forever.'

'Very good,' I said. 'I hope some evil befalls me tonight. Then your love can be put to the test and you may come out in flying colours.'

'*Durga! Durga!*' Pyari shuddered and said, 'Don't say such things. You don't have to test my love. Doubt it by all means. Only come back alive—and well.' Her voice broke and she turned her face away. 'I was born unfortunate and will die so,' she said. 'It is not for me to look after you in health and nurse you in sickness. If I could—well, it would be the one good thing I did in this life.'

'Who knows?' I taunted her. 'God may grant you your heart's desire.'

I did not know then that my words were prophetic. As I walked out of the tent I could hear Pyari call '*Durga! Durga!*' after me. I walked rapidly across the dark expanse of the mango grove, then along the bank of the river till I stood on the bridge. My mind was in a whirl. How strange and incomprehensible was the female psyche! And how wonderfully superior to the male! Years ago, a little girl with thin arms and legs and a stomach like a drum had offered me her infant adoration in the form of *bainchi* garlands. And I had been totally unaware. I had ignored her and later forgotten her. But she, through all the bitter battles of her life and all the degradations of her profession, had kept my image burning bright and clear within her. She had professed many a false love but had cherished and preserved her true love. The more I thought of it, the more it overwhelmed me.

Ba-ap! A night bird shrieked. I came to with a start. Before me stretched a vast tract of sand with a thread-thin stream of water twisting painfully on its surface as far as the eye could see. Clumps of catkin, ten feet high, dotted the landscape. From where I stood they looked like giant men who had just walked across as I had done, to see the dance of the demons. Above my head, out of a dense velvety sky, innumerable stars and planets stared at the earth below. Not a leaf stirred. Not a sound marred the silence of the night save the beating of my heart. I turned my face westwards where the burning-ghat lay. Tall silk-cotton trees with spreading branches stood before me like sentinels guarding the dead. As I walked through them a low moaning sound came to my ears—like the soft whimpering of an exhausted child who has wept for his mother so long and so loud that he can weep no more. I recognized the sound. It was the cry of a baby vulture who had lost his mother in the dark. I looked up and found that I was right. Above my head the branches of the silk-cotton trees were hung with the dark shapeless forms of hundreds of vultures.

When I reached the burning-ghat I realized that the old man's description of a hundred human skulls was not a wild exaggeration. The ground was criss-crossed with the bones of innumerable skeletons, brittle and bleached white by a million suns. Interspersed among them the grinning skulls gleamed wickedly in the faint starlight. The balls and rackets were there but where were the players? I fitted some cartridges into my gun and sitting on a sand heap, waited for the game to begin.

Suddenly, I thought of Pyari. She had pointed out the illogicality of risking my life to see something that I knew did not exist. 'Why did I come?' I asked myself. 'To put to the test an old man's foolish assertions and prove him wrong in the eyes of the world? Or to prove my own valour before a bunch of ignorant Bihari yokels who had said Bengalis were cowards?'

All of a sudden, a gust of wind whipped up a cloud of dust and leaves and swirled them across my face. Then another and another. The forest came alive with the moaning and crackling of silk-cotton stems and the skeletons around me breathed deeply. I shivered in spite of myself. I knew that it was only the wind passing through the cavities of the skulls. But, try as I would, I could not subdue the primeval fear that, however deeply buried beneath layers of conscious reasoning, rose up now to awe and frighten the fear of life after death. I sensed that if I could not control this fear there was no knowing what would happen to me. I knew, now, that I shouldn't have come. I was no Indranath. I had neither his courage nor his faith. I yearned to see something living—even a tiger or a wolf—but nothing lived. The dead surrounded me on all sides. The air grew thick with their sighs and muffled moans. I felt, rather than saw, the skeletons arise and position themselves all around me. One of them stood close behind breathing down my ear and neck. I didn't turn my head but I saw him—a vast gaping skull with monstrous nose holes through which air gushed out as chill as death. My legs shook under me. I tried to control them but I couldn't for they were not mine. 'I must not faint,' I repeated over and over again to the beat of my thumping heart.

From the leaves of the silk-cotton tree the baby vulture whimpered on. Then others joined him and the chorus of moans surged and billowed around me like the waves of an unknown sea. Through the terrible clamour that crashed into my ears one sound acquired a focus—became distinct. *Babu-u-u-u* followed by *Babu sahe-e-e-e-b*. It roared and dipped, swelled and ebbed. Then the clamour died away.

Human voices reached out to me. Words that I understood fell on my ears as sweetly as dewdrops on flowers.

'Don't shoot. For God's sake, don't shoot. It is I—Ratan.'

I tried to call out but no sound came. With a tremendous effort I managed to turn my head. Three or four men bearing lanterns were rapidly approaching the sand heap on which I sat. As they drew near I recognized them. They were Pyari's guard, Ganesh, her tabla player, Chhotu Lal, Ratan and the village chowkidar.

'It is three o'clock, Babu,' Ratan said. 'Come back to the camp.'

I stood up.

'I envy you your courage, Babu,' Ratan said as we walked away. 'We were four together and we were frightened to death.'

'Why did you come then?'

'We have been given a month's wages for coming here tonight.' Then coming closer he whispered, 'After you left I saw Ma sitting in a corner and crying. She told me to take Ganesh and Chhotu Lal and go after you. But I hesitated. I was scared and I didn't know the way. Then Ma asked the chowkidar to go with us.' Ratan shuddered and gripped the edge of my coat. 'Did you hear a baby crying, Babu? What was that but a ghost? We would surely have lost our lives tonight if Ganesh Pande had not been with us. He is a Brahmin and ghosts are scared of Brahmins.'

I was too exhausted to protest or laugh. 'Did you see anything, Babu?' Ratan probed.

'No.'

'Are you offended because we came after you? If you had seen the way Ma cried—.'

'No, Ratan. I'm not in the least offended.'

As we approached the camp the chowkidar, tabla player and guard took their leave. Ratan said, 'Ma wanted to see you before you went to your tent.'

I hesitated. My whole being went out to Pyari. I visualized her sitting before a flickering lamp with tears in her eyes waiting anxiously for my return.

'Come,' Ratan said.

I shut my eyes and looked within myself, flashing a powerful beam in all the nooks and corners. I saw a thousand drunken devils leap up at her name. I felt them throbbing in my blood and hammering at my heart. No. I could not go to Pyari like this.

'Come, Babu,' Ratan said again.

'No, Ratan.' I was surprised at the calm of my voice. 'Not now.'

'Ma has been waiting—'

'Give her my regards and my apologies. I will see her tomorrow before I leave. I'm very sleepy. Good night, Ratan,' and leaving him staring after me in puzzled indignation, I walked away towards my tent.

Nine

$\mathcal{T}$HERE IS NO GREATER FOOL IN THE WORLD THAN THE MAN WHO attempts to analyse himself for he has taken into his own hands a task that he should have left to God. Some go even further. They attempt to draw conclusions about others—even characters out of books. 'So and so could never have acted as he did,' and, 'The reaction of such and such is most unconvincing,' they proclaim confidently and, in nine cases out of ten, win the acclaim of readers. They are successful critics and respected for their ability to pull another's created world to pieces. I am ashamed of such men. It is not that I resent their criticism. Far from it. The world is full of flaws and my books certainly are. What I do resent is their ignorance of the complexities that make up the human psyche and their proud parading of this ignorance. They have no knowledge of the many emotions that lie dormant in the consciousness, ready to erupt and explode at a spark.

Let me speak for myself. From childhood onwards I had cherished an image of womanhood and held it close to my heart. Needless to say it was that of Annada Didi. Day by day it had grown brighter and more chiselled under my jealous care. I had wept innumerable tears over it, made promises to it and dreamed dreams. I had believed in its immortality. If someone had told me, even a week ago, that my image was made of clay and could be reduced to dust by a singing girl's smiles and tears I would have called him mad. For I was as firm as a rock about one thing—that only the woman who could reach the height of stoic idealism that Annada Didi had set as a standard, could find a place in my heart. Yet, the morning after my night's vigil at the burning-ghat I woke up with a strange pain lacerating it—a pain irretrievably linked with Pyari's tear-filled eyes and trembling mouth. But how could such a thing happen? How could Pyari's memory throw a shadow on Annada Didi's? What did the two have in common? One wore a crown of thorns—the other wallowed in silk and velvet. One was the picture of renunciation—the other of erotic extravagance. I had thought that my heart, sealed as it was with Annada Didi's burnished gold, would never admit baser metal. But alas! Unworthy and despicable brass had shattered the gold and tumbled joyfully in, filling all the nooks and corners.

I am aware that my critics are getting impatient. 'Why all this beating about the bush?' they grumble at me. 'Why don't you confess the honest truth—that you were falling in love with Pyari? And since that *is* the truth don't drag your Annada Didi into it. Whatever you may say, however you may say it, one thing is certain. The image of stoic idealism that you say was stamped in your soul, must have been as insubstantial as mist. Otherwise you could never have replaced it with that of a prostitute's physical perfections.'

I will not argue my case for I know that argument will get me nowhere. People will call me a humbug and a hypocrite and I must resign myself to hearing these words. Yet, I was not a hypocrite. The only sin I was guilty of was that of omission. I had not kept track of my unconscious motivations. Today, when one—the least worthy of them—rose up and proudly claimed the highest seat I was bewildered and could not control it. My head was bowed in shame but my soul danced on a wave of ecstasy.

'Babu Saheb!'

I sat up in bed. It was the prince's servant. With a respectful salaam he bade me come to His Highness' tent as a large crowd had gathered there, anxious to hear the events of the night.

'How do they know I went?'

'His Highness' guard saw you return at dawn.' I washed the sleep out of my eyes and, changing into fresh clothes, walked over to the prince's quarters. As I entered I was welcomed by a chorus of voices clamouring all at once. The old man who had challenged me yesterday stood by the prince, his eyes burning with a fanatical light. Pyari and her musicians occupied one corner. I looked in her direction but she refused to meet my eyes. She sat in sullen silence, eyes downcast—face averted.

When the clamour subsided, His Highness spoke. 'Well done, Srikanta! You're a brave man. What time was it when you reached the burning-ghat?'

'Between twelve and one o'clock.'

The old man spoke, 'It was the most inauspicious hour. The moon had dropped its last digit by half past eleven and amavasya had set in.'

Several people spoke at once but my host's voice—anxious and frightened—rose above the others. 'What happened then? What did you see?'

'Human skulls and skeletons.'

'Were you at the edge of the burning-ghat?'

'I walked right in and sat on a sand heap.'

'Could you see anything from where you sat?'

'A vast sandy shore.'

'And—?'

'Tussocks and catkins and silk-cotton trees.'

'And—?'

'The river . . . .'

'I know all that,' His Highness broke in impatiently. 'Didn't you see anything else? Anything—you know what I mean?'

'I saw a couple of bats. They flew over my head,' I said, laughing at my host's expression. The old Bihari came forward and asked in Hindustani, 'You didn't see any spirits?'

'No.'

My reply was disappointing to a tent full of people. The old man voiced the collective indignation.

'What you are saying is nonsense,' he cried passionately. 'You haven't been to the burning-ghat.'

I smiled at this childish outburst. His Highness gripped my arm.

'Tell me truthfully, Srikanta. What did you see?'

'I told you I saw nothing.'

'How long did you stay?'

'Three hours.'

'In three hours you saw nothing and heard nothing?'

'I heard a good deal.'

At this everyone in the tent sat up. Some of them crept up close to me, their faces avid with curiosity. I told them of the night-bird that had shrieked *ba-ap*; of the baby vulture that had whimpered for his mother; of the sudden gusts of wind that had set the skulls sighing and moaning and of the skeleton that had breathed a cloud of icy vapour over my neck and ear. I think I told my story well for long after it was over my audience sat silent—as still and grave as rows of stone figures.

At last the old Bihari spoke. 'Babuji,' he said, 'you are a true Brahmin, or else you would never have come back alive. But promise this old man that you'll never take such a risk again. Blessed are the parents who gave you birth. It was their penance that saved your life.'

He then proceeded to explain the phenomena I had described in terms of the supernatural, and so strong was his language and so great his histrionic power that even I—unbeliever as I was—felt runnels of ice-water trickling down my spine. I sensed a trembling body close behind me. I turned my head and saw that it was Pyari. She had left her place and had crept up to where I sat. Her eyes were enormous in a face as white as paper and her cheeks were streaked with unwiped tears. Whenever I thought of Pyari, in later years I thought of her like that. That white-flower face, rain-drenched and drooping, was welded in a flash to the deepest sources of my being. At the conclusion of the discourse she rose quietly and bowing to the prince, begged leave to retire. Then, without a glance at anyone else, she walked out of the tent.

I was to have left the camp that morning but, overcome by a curious lethargy and depression—the result, no doubt, of my night's vigil at the burning-ghat—I decided to take His Highness' advice and postpone my departure. I returned to my tent and lay down but sleep wouldn't come. I thought of Pyari and of how she had refused to meet my eyes. In the few days that I had known her she had been deep and tender, spirited and provocative, even sharp and shrewish at times, but never cold—never aloof and withdrawn. Yet her indifference did not hurt. It gladdened and warmed my heart. I knew little of the psychology of young women but something—the minutest fragment of the collective knowledge of the world that lay unbeknown within me—told me that this was another expression of Pyari's love. Her indifference did not spring from pride or dislike but from a sense of injury. I had ignored her entreaties; had not thanked her for sending a search-party and had refused to meet her after my return. She was suffering—as only a woman can suffer—from what she believed to be a thwarted and unrequited love.

I slept fitfully through the day—the hope that Ratan would come for me making me restless. But afternoon waned into evening and still Ratan did not come. The conviction that Pyari would send for me was so strong that I felt sure Ratan had come into my tent and, seeing me asleep, had left. 'The fool!' I thought angrily. 'Why couldn't he wake me up?'

I was assailed by a sense of loss. The mellow green-gold winter afternoon could have been ours together and I had wasted it in dull, stupid sleep. There was no doubt in my mind that Ratan would come again after dark. He would leave a message or a note or an invitation to come to Pyari's tent. The sun was quite low in the west but it would take some hours for darkness to set in. What could I do to fill in the hours before Pyari sent for me? Shading my eyes with my hand I looked out on the landscape.

A vast sheet of shimmering water lay ahead, I walked towards it and sat on the crumbling bank. It was an enormous lake nearly a mile across—so old that no one knew its age or history. The locals believed that villages had once flourished around it and drawn their source of life from its waters. Then a terrible wave of cholera had devastated the land. There had been a mass exodus and the lake had been abandoned. Over the years large parts of it had been reclaimed by the forest swamp. From where I sat I could see deserted homesteads crumbling to dust and dark brooding tamarisks creeping over the lake on stealthy feet. The water was still and black except where the slanting rays of the setting sun turned it into liquid gold. Then the gold burnt out into ashes and the mauve-grey mists of twilight fell over the lake. A jackal slunk out of the jungle and stood for a moment silhouetted against the fading light.

It was time I rose and went back to the camp. But some power beyond my control willed me to stay. I thought of the many people who had inhabited the land around the lake before pestilence had stricken their ranks. Gaunt, grim-faced men passed me like figures in a shadow show. Women, long dead and gone, rose from the lake and walked away, dripping water as they went. The ghosts of little children laughed and played as they bathed in the twilight. I saw innumerable men and women in the last throes of death, staggering to the lake on unsteady feet only to drop down—their thirst unquenched.

'Babuji,' the old man had said, 'death is not the end. The unhappy soul lingers on, thirsting for the joys of the flesh long after the body is consumed to ashes.'

In the morning light that had streamed into the tent, his words had fallen on deaf ears. Now, in this desolate darkness, they took shape and form and were imbued with a deeper meaning. I understood, in a flash of intuition, that if anything truly exists in life—it is death. We nurture our joys and sorrows, loves and hates, desires and renunciations through all our living years for the supreme moment of consummation that is death. After that—what? I had never asked this question before. Today, I did.

A light footfall behind me shook me out of my reverie. I looked back but there was no one and nothing but the deep, dense gloom. I stood up and started on the walk back. What hour was it? By the look of the sky it was well past midnight. How long had I sat by the bank of a dead lake communing with creatures who had long since shed their mortal frames? Were my nerves playing tricks on me? Why else did I feel I had been walking for hours and hours? Something that looked like a gigantic bamboo clump loomed ahead of me. Had it been there when I walked to the lake? On reaching the spot I found that my eyes had deceived me. It was the shadow thrown by three immense tamarind trees which, entwined together for centuries, reared up hydra-headed to meet the sky. A thread-thin track serpentined below it. It was so dark that I could not see my own hand. A drumming sound filled my ears which I knew to be the beating of my heart. I shut my eyes and walked rapidly past the spreading tangle of trees. When I opened them again I saw something I dimly recognized—almost as if from another life—the bridge across the river on which I had stood last night. How did I get here? My legs trembled and almost gave way. But, driven by a force I did not understand, I ran till, my lungs fit to burst, I stood on the bridge viewing the *mahasamsan* at my feet. But the inexorable footsteps that had driven me from one land of the dead now led me to another. I climbed down the bridge as if in a dream, walked through the forest of silk-cotton trees till I came to the burning-ghat. Almost fainting with weariness I sank down in the dust and shut my eyes. The footsteps I had followed did not falter. They went ahead growing fainter as they entered the heart of the *mahasamsan*.

$\mathcal{T}en$

IF MY READERS EXPECT ME TO EXPLAIN THE EVENTS OF THE
NIGHT I must beg leave to cry off. Why I walked those long miles
from the lake to the burning-ghat and whose footsteps lured me
on is a mystery—even to me and I prefer to let it lie undisturbed.
This distaste for analysis does not indicate a regression in terms
of my distrust of the spiritual. Far from it. In fact, my nightmarish
journey from one dead man's land to another puts me in mind of
a strange character I had known in my boyhood.

He was an old, half-crazed peasant who begged for a living
during the day and played funny tricks on his benefactors at
night. Draping a white sheet on a ladder he would walk about
with it, to the terror of the villagers. Sometimes he covered his
face with soot and, peeping through windows, called out to the
occupants in a nasal voice. During the day he was the picture of
humble obsequiousness. At night he transformed himself into a
malicious imp—so clever that though many suspected him, no
one ever caught him. When he lay dying he confessed everything
and with his death the village was rid of its ghosts. But he never
explained why he had played these pranks and what he had
gained by them. That remained a mystery—perhaps even to him.
Some such character may have been abroad on the night of my
sojourn from the lake to the burning-ghat.

To go back to what I was saying. When I dropped down at the
edge of the burning-ghat, the footsteps I had been dogging grew

faint and were lost in the sounds of the night. As they faded on the air they said to me, 'For shame. Did you walk all these miles only to stop like a coward on the threshold? Take courage. Come all the way. Come right where our hearts beat. Become one of us.'

I don't know if I heard these words or only felt them in my blood as it pounded and pulsed in my brain. Then, for a long while, I sat motionless till my eyes glazed and the blood grew cold and heavy in my veins. But, even in that state of suspended life, a spark of consciousness urged me to turn back, to flee to the mortal world where I belonged. But I could not move. A lassitude, sweet and heavy, weighed down my limbs. I was content to sit where I was, alone with the night.

I realized then, as never before, that night had a beauty unparalleled by any other universal phenomenon. Darkness flowed out of a vast vault of sky and I floated on its waves. How exquisite was this ocean of unfathomable darkness! I wondered who the fool was who first taught man to glorify light and discredit the dark. Darkness is the first, the primeval truth that lies at the heart of Creation, I thought. It broods over all that is deep, inexplicable, eternal and infinite in the Universe. Pervading darkness shrouds the source of all light and all life— that is God. Even Death—the one inexorable truth in the life of all created things—is a journey through chasm after chasm of impenetrable darkness. Just such a wondrous, awesome darkness must have filled Radha's eyes with the love that flooded the world! My whole being quivered in ecstasy at the thought. I was in the midst of death and Death, like the eternal lover, was strange and darkly beautiful. I rose and followed Death's silent footsteps.

'Beloved,' I murmured as I went, 'release me from the pain and weariness of living. Carry me on your wings to that infinite darkness that is your domain. Give me a place with those you love.'

I walked on like a soul possessed till, reaching the heart of the crematorium, I sank down among the dust and bones. I don't know how long I sat there but after what seemed only a little while the darkness lifted from one end of the sky and Venus—star of the morning—rose, pristine and pure, from the other. Voices, low and muffled, were at hand. Gradually they grew louder and more insistent. Then someone spoke from out of the trees.

'Srikanta Babu!'

'Who is that? Ratan?' I responded instantly.

'Yes. Come away from there. Ma is waiting for you in the cart.'

'Are you going away, Ratan?'

'Yes. We left the camp before dawn.'

I walked through the forest to the bridge where the cart with its bullocks stood silhouetted against the grey sky.

Pyari pushed away the curtain that hung in front and said, 'I knew it was you the moment the cart-driver said he could see someone among the trees. Get in. I have something to say to you.'

'I can't. I have to get back to the camp.'

Pyari put out a hand and pulled me in. The cart moved on.

'Don't make a scene in front of the servants.' She almost screamed the words. 'Sit down for God's sake.'

Stunned by the passion in her face and voice I sat, quite meekly, waiting for whatever was coming.

'Why did you come here again tonight?' Her voice was sharp.

'I don't know,' I said and it was the truth.

'That's a lie.'

'It isn't. I didn't wish to come. I don't know why I did.'

'Do you mean to tell me you were blown away from your tent by the spirits?' Her voice had a sneering edge to it and her hot fingers gripped mine like a vice.

'No. I walked all the way. But why and when I cannot say.'

Pyari fell silent at these words. Her eyes, dark and frightened, stared into mine.

'Rajlakshmi,' I said gently, 'let me tell you everything.'

I described the events of the night as best as I could. As I did so I could feel the hand that still held mine grow cold and tremble like a leaf. But she didn't speak a word. After a while I said, 'I must go.'

'No! No,' Pyari murmured as if in a dream.

'But I must,' I insisted. 'Don't you see? People will think we have gone away together.'

'Does it matter what people think? They are not your guardians. I beg you, Kantada—don't go back to the camp. Another night there will kill you. Don't come with me if you don't want to. Go home or anywhere you please—but don't, for God's sake, go back to that terrible place.'

'My clothes . . . ' I began helplessly.

'Let them be. If your friends wish to, they can send them after you. If not—bear the loss. They are of little value.'

'That is true. But you forget something. Can the loss of my reputation be borne as lightly?'

As I said these words the cart turned a bend and the eastern sky came into view. I looked from one rose flushed face to another and it seemed to me that the two had something in common. Both faces—that of the morning sky and the prostitute Pyari—reflected the glow of a wondrous sphere of pure flame as it spun through darkness and chaos.

'Why are you silent, Rajlakshmi?' I asked gently.

Pyari smiled. 'You know why, Kantada?' she said lightly, 'I have signed so many false documents in my life that my hand stops at signing a true deed of gift. Go if you must. But promise me you'll leave the camp before evening.'

'I promise.'

Pyari pulled a ring from her finger and placed it on my feet. Then touching her forehead to the ground she rose and dropped it in my pocket.

'I have another favour to ask of you,' she said. 'Will you write me a letter as soon as you reach home?'

'I will.'

I climbed out of the cart and walked away. I did not look back even once but I knew, to a certainty, that the cart stood still in its tracks and a pair of dark agonized eyes gazed upon my form till it faded from view.

The sun was well above the horizon by the time I reached the camp. My eyes fell on Pyari's tent—deserted and reduced to cloth and bamboo. I felt a lump in my throat. Averting my face I walked purposefully on.

As I pushed aside the curtain that hung in front of my tent, Purushottam stirred in his sleep and said, 'You went out early, Srikanta Babu.'

I did not reply. Stretching out to my full length, I shut my burning eyes.

Eleven

AS SOON AS I REACHED HOME I WROTE MY PROMISED LETTER TO Pyari. Her reply came just as promptly. It contained no invitation to visit her in Patna but the last line of the letter was intriguing. 'Remember me in your sorrow if not in your joy,' she wrote. But, both in sorrow and in joy, her memory grew hazy and promised to fade away altogether as the days went by.

Then a strange thing happened. It was Holi night—I remember that well. Exhausted from the excitement of the festival, I lay on my bed—too lethargic even to wash the colour from my face and hair. The window by my pillow was wide open and a huge ashwatha tree that stood just outside it had a glorious full moon trapped in its branches. This I remember clearly. Then, I don't know when, I rose and walking out of the door went straight to the railway station, bought a ticket to Patna and got on to the train. When I woke up the next morning the train was standing at Badh station. Patna was only a few miles away.

Suddenly, I have no idea why, I got off the train. I stood on the platform watching it glide away, gently at first, then gathering momentum on its path towards Pyari. Putting my hand in my pocket I fished out a two anna bit and ten pice in loose coins. This will do for the present, I thought and a curious happiness welled up within me. I walked to a sweet shop and had a lavish breakfast of *chire* (flattened rice), rich curd and molasses (which took care of half my cash) after which I set out to explore the village. I wandered about for sometime realizing, quite soon, that excellent as the food was, the air and water of the village were to be condemned, for the enormous meal I had eaten got digested so soon and so thoroughly that I felt as if not a grain had passed through my lips in years. I decided to leave the place. As I stood reflecting on which direction I should take, I saw a thin column of smoke rise from a mango grove just a little distance away. Smoke indicated fire and fire meant cooking. I decided to investigate.

The most wonderful of sights met my eyes as I pushed my way through the dense undergrowth. It was a makeshift ashram with every evidence of good living. What could be a holier combination? Tea, bubbling in a huge brass pot, ejected clouds of fragrant steam. A young sanyasi was milking a goat—an older one stirring bhang in a stone pot. Hookahs for smoking ganja were scattered about. Two camels, two mules and a plump milch cow with her calf were tethered to the trees. Amidst all these riches the Baba sat, coated with ashes from head to toe, eyes closed with devotion and ganja fumes. I was so entranced by the scene that I decided to become a part of it. 'To hell with Pyari,' I thought.

I clutched the Baba's feet and said in a piteous voice, 'I am your unfortunate, errant son, Babaji. Show me the true light. Give me the privilege of serving you and so lead me to a higher state of existence.'

Babaji smiled into his ashen beard. 'Go home, son,' he said in Hindustani. 'The path of the ascetic is planted with thorns. It is not for you.'

'Babaji,' I implored, 'the *Mahabharata* tells us that the demons, Jagai and Madhai found salvation through service to a rishi. Am I even lower than them that you do not deem me worthy of serving you? Keep me as the lowliest of all your servants and I will attain moksha. I know I will.'

Babaji was pleased. 'You speak right, my son,' he said with an indulgent smile. 'As Ramji wishes!'

The elder of the two disciples now came forward with a huge glass of tea which he handed to the Baba. The Baba sipped from it and, having had his fill, distributed the dregs among the company. For, by virtue of touching the holy man's lips, the tea had become prasad. Then, it being too early for bhang, Babaji ordered me to prepare a chillum of ganja. The speed and efficiency with which I accomplished this task won his approval. 'You have many talents, my boy,' he said. 'You are fit to be my disciple.' Thrilled at the turn my life had taken, I touched his feet.

Early next morning, I bathed in the river and put on the garb of my new calling. I was given a full suit of saffron, a dozen rows of rudraksha beads and a pair of heavy brass bangles. I took up a handful of ash from the censer and rubbed it on my face and hair for greater effect.

I couldn't resist the temptation of seeing how I looked. I winked at Babaji and asked for a mirror. I could see that Babaji had a sense of humour. He smiled conspiratorially and opening a tin trunk, handed me a small mirror of the type that barbers use. I retreated with it to a safe distance and examined myself. I couldn't stop laughing at the face that looked back at me. No one could recognize me now for the elegant young man who had consorted with princes and been entertained by singing and dancing girls, only a few days ago. After an hour or so, when my mirth was under control, I returned the mirror to my guru maharaj and sought a formal initiation into my new life. My humble request pleased him exceedingly but he forebore to grant it.

'Wait a month or two, my son,' he said.

Then he proceeded to treat his disciples to a discourse on the life of the ascetic. He told us that it was based on a stoic renunciation of the joys of the flesh and a total submergence of self in the Eternal and the Infinite that was represented in the world by the guru. He spoke bitterly of charlatans who had tarnished this noblest of callings and enjoined upon us to follow his instructions to the letter, for only by so doing could we avoid the pitfalls that lay on the road to salvation.

He then proceeded to give us some practical advice. He told us that the fruits and leaves of certain bushes and shrubs contain properties that, if inhaled or partaken of orally, act as a miraculous aid to the kind of renunciation and submergence he advocated. However, along with this treatment, care must be taken to feed the body on substances that help to sublimate the mind and keep one's thoughts and actions pure and holy. The spiritually uplifting foods recommended by Babaji—roti, milk, butter, ghee, curds, chire, sugar, etc.—were all freely available in our ashram. I was an obedient disciple and followed my guru's instructions closely. The result was a blossoming in health and looks which my body had not seen in years. In a few days the faintest swell of a paunch became visible beneath my ascetic's robe.

There were only two things that irked me in my new calling. One was the mandatory begging for alms that was an integral part of the life of a sanyasi. I found it most distasteful but, it being one of the primary tasks allotted to me, I couldn't escape it. In time, however, I came to accept it and it was made endurable by the fact that Bihari women, as a rule, were more open-handed than their Bengali sisters. Unlike the latter, the women I begged from never advised me to try next door or asked point-blank why a hulking young fellow couldn't work for a living. On the contrary, the moment they saw a saffron robe they voluntarily offered a portion of what they had. The second—the mosquito menace—threatened to shake the foundations of my new found faith. During the day, life in the mango grove was idyllic. But the moment the sun set, such a buzzing and stinging was let loose that the temptation to abandon my great quest for moksha became irresistible. But the days passed and, as the thin Bengali skin I deplored grew thicker and less vulnerable, I was enabled to come to terms with this as well.

While things were in this state our guru was struck with a sudden inspiration. One morning, after a bath in the river, I came back to the mango grove in search of some spiritual refreshment, when I heard Babaji chanting some verses in praise of Bharadwaj muni—who was a great servant of Ram and the presiding deity of Prayag.

Bharadwaj muni basahi prayaga
jinhi Ram pada ati anuraga . . .

Babaji sang in a cracked nasal voice. The message was clear: pack up and begin the journey to Prayag. There was nothing to do but obey. Strapping our belongings on the backs of the camels and gathering our livestock together, we set off. After walking five miles or so we reached the outskirts of a village named Bithaura and entered a grove of wild lichees and rose-apples. The sun was setting and the green leaves were dappled with gold. It was such a charming scene that it won Babaji's instant approval. Spotting a spreading banyan tree he ordered us to unpack and set up our camp in its shade. Though I wondered how long it would take us to get to Prayag at the rate we were going, I was not disappointed for I was in no hurry.

Why I still remember this village and its name is another story and I propose to tell it here. One day, as I was doing my rounds, my eyes fell on a Bengali girl through the open door of a courtyard. I was intrigued for, in the five or six days we had spent in Bithaura, I had never seen a Bengali—male or female. I noticed that her sari was of the cheap local weave that Bihari village women wear. But the manner of wearing it was distinctly Bengali. Sanyasis enjoy privileges that other men don't. I walked in through the open door and stood face to face with her. I can never forget the eyes that stared into mine. She was a child, no more than ten or eleven, but despair and agony streamed out of every feature, and every limb of her small face and form.

'Alms for a sanyasi, beti?' I said in Bengali. Her eyes held mine for a few seconds. Then her lips began to tremble and she burst into tears. I was alarmed for, though there was no one in sight, I could hear voices within, speaking in the local dialect. If someone came out and saw us together what would they think? I stood irresolute, wondering if I should attempt to console her or rush out of the house. Before I could do either she sobbed out a string of questions in fluent Bengali.

'Where are you coming from? Do you live in Bardhaman district? Do you know a village there called Rajpur? When are you going back there? Do you know Gauri Tewari of Rajpur village?'

'Is that where you come from?' I asked.

'Yes.' The girl wiped her eyes with the back of her hand. 'My father's name is Gauri Tewari. My brother's name is Ram Lal Tewari. Do you know them? I have been married these three months but I haven't had any news from home. How are Ma, Baba, Khoka, Giribala? Do you see that house by the banyan tree? That is my sister's husband's house. Last Monday my sister hanged herself from a hook in the kitchen. Her in-laws say she died of cholera.'

'Why did she hang herself?'

'She was terribly homesick. She used to cry all the time. She wouldn't do the work she was told to do. She wouldn't eat. So they tied her by her hair to a beam and kept her hanging for a whole day and night. That's why she killed herself.'

'Are your in-laws Bihari too?'

'Yes.' Fresh tears welled up in the girl's eyes. 'I can't understand what they say. I can't eat their food. I cry all day and all night. But Baba doesn't come to take me away.'

'Why did your father marry you off to a Bihari?'

'Because we *are* Biharis. Our caste name is Tewari. My father couldn't find husbands for us in Bengal. He was forced to send us here.'

'Do your in-laws beat you?'

'Don't they? Look!' And she showed me bruises and welts on her arms, back and neck. 'I'll die too like Didi,' she sobbed bitterly, 'I'll kill myself.'

I couldn't stand there another moment. Turning my face away to hide the tears that were burning in my eyes I walked out of the house.

She came after me. 'You'll go to my father? You'll tell him to come and take me away? If not I'll—'

I nodded my head vigorously stopping her in mid-sentence. Then, with the little girl's impassioned plea ringing in my ears, I rushed out of the house.

A small grocer's shop stood at the end of the road. As I entered it, the grocer rose greeting me with the deference due to an ascetic. When I asked for a postcard and a pen and ink instead of food stuffs, he complied, though not without a surprised stare. I sat down and wrote a letter to Gauri Tewari. I described the exact circumstances in which I had found his daughter and repeated, word for word, what she had said. I did not hesitate even a little to inform him that his elder daughter had committed suicide. With the warning that the younger one would follow in her sister's footsteps if he did not come to her aid immediately, I ended the letter, signed my true name and addressed it to village—Rajpur, in District Bardhaman. I don't know if the letter reached him or, if it did, if he took any action. But the memory of the child-bride remains with me to this day. Everytime that innocent, stricken face comes before me, my heart is filled with a terrible hatred for our ancient heritage—our great Hindu culture which, under cover of its network of caste and creed, encourages and propagates the most sordid discrimination against the women of our land.

Hindu philosophers tell us that it is by virtue of our strict adherence to the levels and gradings spelled out by the caste-system that our culture has been able to survive for centuries where so many others have crumbled away to nothingness. I am well aware that, in the face of this great historical truth, the violent deaths of two tender young girls in an obscure village of Bihar may be dismissed as unimportant. But is the survival of any religion or culture the sole test of its greatness? Innumerable tribal faiths have survived for centuries in India, Africa, America and in the many archipelagos of the oceans of the world. Some of them are older than civilization itself and are governed by laws that make our flesh creep. What, then, is the worth of such survival, based as they are on the dominance of one class over another and of men over women? How did Gauri Tewari feel when he was forced between two alternatives—the loss of his daughters or the loss of his place in the Hindu order? What choice did the poor man have but to sacrifice his daughters faced by the pressures of his inherited faith? What is the worth of a structure that cannot accommodate the lives and well-being of two innocent children? Could a truly great religion be so inflexible and static?

Mercifully, our thoughts are neither seen nor heard. I left the shop—the picture of a calm, steadfast, Hindu ascetic. I found Babaji in a foul mood. He complained that the people of Bithaura were lacking in deference to sadhus and holy men. The alms they gave was insufficient and he had no desire of prolonging his stay. I welcomed his suggestion of moving, for a secret urge to visit Patna was making me restless. And I had had enough of the villages of Bihar. They didn't stand comparison with those of Bengal. Everything about them—their women, trees, rivers—was drab and uninteresting. Oh, for the lush luxuriance of rural Bengal! Had I never left it I would never have learned to value it. Our ponds choke with rotting sedge—our abdomens with diseased spleens. Our air is thick with malaria! Factions and squabbles divide every family and every clan and each village is the sworn enemy of every other. But it is my land and I remembered it with nostalgia. The urge to cast off my ascetic leanings and flee from these dull, unfamiliar surroundings became so strong at times that I could barely resist it.

The next day we left Bithaura and continued on our journey. My secret wish was not gratified for Patna was ten miles off the direct route to Prayag. I came to terms with my disappointment with the thought that, in my present state of sainthood, I should not lust in my heart for such an unworthy object as Pyari. One evening we set up camp at a little village called Chhota Bagia—about fifteen miles away from Ara station. Here I became acquainted with a Bengali gentleman whose real name I do not propose to disclose. He was middle-aged and very warm and effusive. I never learned why he had left his native Bengal and settled down in this remote village of Bihar, and how he had acquired his property. It was obvious that he was in comfortable circumstances. He had a young, second wife and three or four children. I met him once again many years later, but he did not know who I was. This did not surprise me. Benevolent men like him prefer to let their good deeds lie in the dark. Since he is about to feature in my story for a little longer and since I respect his desire to remain incognito I shall give him a pseudonym. Let us call him Ram Babu.

The morning after our halt we heard that there was a severe outbreak of smallpox in Chhota Bagia and its surrounding villages. People are apt to be more generous to the mendicant in times of stress. In consequence, Babaji was inspired to break journey and take a well-earned rest. In return for a pinch of ashes from the censer and a sprinkle of water from our holy urn, we were overwhelmed with gifts. Food, livestock and money poured into the ashram. I noticed something about the psychology of renunciation that my subsequent encounters with holy men have confirmed. The true sadhu cannot resist the goods of the world even if his life is at stake. Like the locals, Babaji believed in the principle: *Javat jeevat sukhang jeevat* (while you live, live happily). But, in his pursuit of *sukhang jeevat*, Babaji forgot that one must be alive to enjoy life. Treating the risk of catching smallpox as of little importance he encouraged us to make our rounds and collect as much as we could from the distraught villagers.

It was in these circumstances that I first met Ram Babu. One morning he burst into the ashram sobbing out a tale of woe. One of his sons was stricken with smallpox and the other lay delirious with a high fever. Seeing a fellow-Bengali in distress I went with him to see what I could do. I would like to skip over the events of the next three weeks. How the boys escaped the jaws of death and regained their health is a long story and it would tire me to tell it and the reader to hear it. I will just mention the event that changed the course of my life.

When Babaji was ready to move on, after ten days or so, Ram Babu's wife threw herself at my feet. 'Sanyasi Dada,' she wept. 'You are not a real sanyasi. You are loving and humane. If you desert me now my sons will die. I know they will.'

Ram Babu joined his pleas with those of his wife. I couldn't refuse. I told Babaji that I could not leave just yet but that I would join him either on the road to Prayag or in it. Babaji received my proposal coldly and tried to make me change my mind. Then, giving up the attempt, he advised me to join him as soon as I could and departed.

The boys recovered but the pestilence raged on, increasing in fury everyday. Soon people started leaving the village. The evening before Ram Babu and his family were to leave his wife came into my room.

'Sanyasi Dada,' she said. 'Why don't you come with us to Ara? We can catch our separate trains from there.'

'I'll do that,' I said, 'but you must give me a place in your bullock-cart.'

'Why?' she asked in genuine astonishment. 'We have only two carts and there is just enough room for our luggage and ourselves.'

'I can't walk all the way, *bon*,' I said. 'I feel very unwell. I have a high fever.'

My new sister's face paled. 'Fever? How terrible! You can't mean it,' she said and, without waiting for a reply, she walked out of the room.

A strange lassitude had been weighing down my limbs for the past few days. I had ignored it, putting it down to the sleepless nights I had spent nursing the two boys. But last night I had vomited several times and from morning onwards my body burned with fever. After my hostess left, I sank into an exhausted sleep. When I awoke it was broad daylight. The house was deserted and locks hung from every door. From the outer room, where I lay, I could see the cattle track winding its way to Ara station. At least five or six carts passed this path everyday—their owners intent on flight.

By late evening I was able to find myself a place in one of these.

The old Bihari who befriended me dropped me off outside Ara station at crack of dawn. There was a tin shed under a tree which had once been used as a waiting room for passengers. It had become so dilapidated over the years that it was no longer fit for human use. Stray cattle and dogs sheltered in it against the rain. I was dragged into this shed by a couple of coolies and a young man that the Bihari had called in from the station. This young man laid me down on some tattered bedding that must have been his own, stifling my feeble protests with the assurance that he never used it. Then, bringing me a bowl of hot milk, he asked me if I wanted to inform anyone of my condition.

I realized that I was very ill and, if such a high fever persisted, would lose consciousness in a few hours. But I couldn't come to a decision as to whom I should inform. When he visited me again in the evening carrying a bowl of water and a lantern, I called him to my side and said, 'If I pass into a coma abandon me to my fate. But before that write a postcard to Pyari Baiji of Patna. Tell her that Srikanta lies, mortally sick, in a tin shed outside Ara station.'

The young man rose saying, 'I'll send off a telegram immediately and also write a letter.'

To this day I regret the fact that I did not get to know him better. There was no time, for within a few hours of our conversation, I lost consciousness. Five or six months later, when I had regained my health, I made enquiries at Ara station and was told that he had died of smallpox a couple of months before then. All I could gather about him was that he had come from East Bengal and was a railway employee earning fifteen rupees a month.

My last thought before I crossed the twilight zone between the conscious and the unconscious states was, 'May God grant that Pyari receives the message.' After that—merciful oblivion.

The first thing I became aware of on regaining consciousness was the ice bag on my head. I was lying on a bed in the middle of a spacious room. A small table stood by my side with some medicine bottles on it. Someone in a red checked wrapper was lying on a string-cot that stood by the wall. I remembered, as if from a dream, faces passing before me; hands lifting me on to a palki; my head being shaved and medicine being poured down my throat. Then, someone spoke in a voice I recognized.

'Banku, isn't it time we changed the ice?'

A young man of eighteen or nineteen rose from the string-cot. 'I'll change it,' he said, 'but why don't you take a rest, Ma? The doctor said it isn't smallpox. Why do you worry—?'

'Goodness,' Pyari's voice cut him short. 'Can women ever stop worrying? I'm quite all right, son. You change the ice and go back to bed.'

Banku obeyed and presently faint snores came from the string-cot.

I softly called out, 'Pyari!'

Pyari's face appeared above mine instantly. 'Do you recognize me? How do you feel now?' Very tenderly she wiped the sweat off my brow with the edge of her sari.

'Better,' I said. 'When did you come? Are we in Ara?'

'Yes. We're going back home tomorrow.'

'Home?'

'Home to Patna. Where else can I take you in this state?'

'Who is the boy, Rajlakshmi?'

'My stepson. But he is no less to me than a blood son. He lives with me and studies in Patna College. Now don't talk anymore. Try and get some sleep!'

She covered my mouth with her hand. I took it in mine and turning over on my side, fell asleep.

Twelve

I WAS SUFFERING FROM SOME FEVER BUT NOT FROM SMALLPOX. IT may have had a medical name but whatever it was—it was unknown to me. I gathered that Pyari had come post-haste to Ara the moment she received the telegram. Renting a house on the very day of her arrival, she had had me shifted and had brought all the doctors of Ara—good, bad and indifferent—to my bedside. It was well that she had done so, else the readers of *Bharatvarsha** would not have been tested for their patience.

Early next morning, Pyari woke Banku up. 'Go to the station and reserve a second-class compartment to Patna. Don't delay, son. The sooner we leave this place the better.'

Banku rubbed the sleep from his eyes. 'Are you in your senses, Ma? The gentleman is too ill to be moved.'

'Get up and see him for yourself and then decide,' Pyari said with a smile.

Banku rose and, after examining my condition, he washed, changed his clothes and departed for the station. It was still quite early and we were alone in the room.

'Pyari,' I murmured.

Pyari was resting on a string-cot at the foot of my bed. She sat

---

*   See Glossary.

up with a start. 'What is it? Are you awake?' She leaned over me and ran her fingers through my hair.

'I have been awake for sometime.'

'The fever has broken. Try to rest. You will soon be well.'

'How long have I been ill?'

'Thirteen days.'

Then, assuming the voice and manner of an elderly matron, she said, 'It is better not to use that name in front of the boy. Why don't you call me Lakshmi? You have always done so.'

'I'll try to remember.'

Then I said what I had been planning to say to her ever since I came out of the coma. 'Have you not suffered enough for me? Why do you want to prolong it? Give up your plan of taking me with you.'

'What do you wish me to do?'

'I think I shall recover in three or four days. Stay with me till then. After that—go home.'

'And what about you?'

'I'll see what I can do. Don't worry. I'll manage.'

'That you will.' Pyari smiled and sat on one side of the bed. 'I know this fever will leave you—if not in three days, in ten or twelve. But who can cure you of your other malady—the real one?'

'What do you mean?'

'You think something, say something else and do yet a third. This has been your problem ever since I can remember. You know very well that I won't let you out of my sight before a month is out. Yet you advise me to go home and not suffer for you any more. If you were really so concerned about my sufferings—never mind—let me tell you what I saw when I first came to Ara. A sanyasi in a filthy saffron robe with lashings of rudraksha beads and hair caked with dirt, lying on a tattered sheet under a tin roof. I was so shocked I didn't know whether to laugh or cry.' Her eyes filled and, lifting a hand she dashed the tears away. 'What a day that was! Banku asked me who you were. I had nothing to say. Was ever a mother in such a predicament? Honestly, I rue the day I first saw you in the pathshala. I have suffered since then as no woman in the world has ever suffered. And now, when smallpox is raging in the town and I'm worried to distraction, you tell me to go away and leave you to your own fate.'

We left for Patna that very night. A young doctor accompanied us with a case full of medicines against emergencies. Within a fortnight of our arrival I felt well enough to move about. One morning I decided to explore the house. As I went from room to room I noticed something that puzzled me. I was familiar with houses of this type. Their interiors were invariably dark and ornate and crammed with love tokens from a variety of donors. Carved furniture, pictures, glass-cases, mirrors and chandeliers fought for supremacy in every existing inch of space. I always had a curious feeling, on entering one of these houses, that the battle was a vicarious one—that the inanimate objects were involved in a struggle to ensure a place for their animate masters somewhere within its walls. In contrast, the rooms in this house were light and airy and the furniture, though expensive and beautiful, was limited to the essentials. I also felt that whatever there was, was selected by the mistress herself in accordance with her own needs and tastes. There was no sign, anywhere, of trespassers encroaching on her domain. I noticed another thing that seemed odd in the house of a famous singing girl. There were no musical instruments and no audience hall.

As I walked along the upstairs gallery I came upon a room that I instantly recognized as Pyari's bedroom even though it was completely different from what I had imagined. The floor was of milky marble, the walls pure and shining white. A narrow bed with a spotless cover was placed against one wall. A wooden rack with some clothes hanging from it stood at the other. A third item of furniture was an iron safe. That was all. The stark simplicity of the room was like a blow to my unprepared senses. A strange reluctance to put down a shod foot on that polished marble made me stoop at the threshold and take my shoes off. Then I walked in and, suddenly overcome with fatigue, sank on the bed. A slight shiver of a breeze blew in from the branches of a neem tree that reared its head just outside the window. As I watched the sunlight glinting through the leaves the sound of a sweet crooning filled my ears. I turned my head. Pyari had come into the room. Her sari was dripping wet from her early morning dip in the Ganga. Without glancing in the direction of the bed she walked straight to the rack and stretched out an arm.

I said quickly, 'Why don't you take your sari to the ghat?'

Pyari gave a startled laugh. 'When did you come creeping into my room like a thief? No, no—don't go. I'll change in the other room.' Then, *garad* sari in hand, she walked away, her footsteps light as air. Within five minutes she was back—a pleased smile on her face. She sat on the bed by my side and said, 'There's nothing of value in my room except myself. What did you come to steal? Not me, I hope.'

'I'm not such an ingrate. To wish to steal you would be unforgivable. I am guilty of many sins but avarice is not one of them.'

Pyari's smile vanished and a pallor spread over the glowing face of a moment ago. I realized that my careless words had pained her. In an effort to cover up I said quickly, 'Does anyone steal what belongs to them? Why should I want to steal you?'

But she was unimpressed. 'You needn't try to please me,' she said bluntly. 'I am overwhelmed with gratitude that you deigned to send me a message when you thought you were dying.'

'Lakshmi,' I said in a genuine effort to bring back the radiance that I had robbed from that lovely face on this bright, sunny morning. 'You must know my true feelings. Had you not come for me that day my corpse would be rotting by now in the dirt and filth of the tin shed. No one would have cared to even dump me in the local hospital. It was my great good fortune that, in my delirium, your words "Remember me in your sorrow if not in your joy", came back to me. I owe my life to you.'

'You admit that?'

'I do.'

'Then I may claim what is mine whenever I like.'

'You may. But my life is of such little value that you will find it useless.'

The smile came back to Pyari's face. 'I'm glad that you've discovered your true worth after all these years,' she said and grew solemn again.

'You have recovered well enough,' she added after a pause. 'When do you propose to leave?'

I was startled for I hadn't expected such a question.

'I have nothing special to get back to,' I said. 'I would like to stay on for a while.'

'But my son might wonder about us if you stay too long.'

'Is that so important? You are his benefactress. You need not fear him. I'm very comfortable here. I'm not leaving just yet.'

Pyari's face became sullen and a little resentful. 'You don't see the practical side,' she said and, biting her lip, abruptly left the room.

The next day, as I lay in an easy chair watching the sunset from the western veranda, Banku joined me. I took kindly to the boy. There was a simplicity and innocence about him that I liked.

'What do you study, Banku?' I asked.

'I passed my Entrance last year.'

'Are you in college now?'

'Yes.'

'How many brothers and sisters are you?'

'I am the only son. But I have four sisters.'

'Are they married?'

'Yes. Ma arranged and paid for their marriages.'

'Is your own mother alive?'

'Yes. She lives in our ancestral village.'

'Has your stepmother ever been to the village?'

'Oh yes! She only returned from there six months ago.'

'Doesn't her presence create a disturbance there?'

'It does. The villagers ostracize us but I can't throw my mother out because of that. And such a gem of a mother! Who has a mother like mine?'

I wanted to ask him the reason for his excessive devotion but stopped myself just in time.

He continued enthusiastically, 'What harm has Ma ever done anyone? She sings for a living. What is wrong with that? Is it not much better than idling away one's time in gossip and scandal-mongering? Ma pays for the education of ten boys from our village. She distributes clothes and blankets to the poor every winter. Are these not to be admired?'

'Certainly they are,' I agreed.

'Only last year we fired bricks and rebuilt our house. Ma decided to enlarge the quarry and convert it into a pond because of the acute scarcity of water in our village. But the villagers are so wicked—they refused to draw water from it.'

'Good God!' I cried. 'They preferred to go without water than to . . . .'

'That's just it,' Banku interrupted with a laugh. 'How long can such senseless malice last? People started coming to the pond on the sly—first the Shudras, then the Brahmins and Kayasthas. But the villagers did not allow Ma to perform the consecration ceremony. She was deeply hurt but did not utter a word of protest.'

'This is cutting off the nose to spite the face,' I said.

'Exactly!' Banku agreed enthusiastically. 'Who wants to be part of such a community? I'm glad we are outcastes and can keep to ourselves. What do you say, Srikanta Babu?'

I smiled and nodded. I saw that the boy really loved Pyari. He went on singing her praises, with mounting enthusiasm, till he realized that he was doing all the talking and my role was reduced to that of an audience. Slightly shame-faced, he changed the subject.

'You'll be with us for a little longer, I hope.'

'No. I intend leaving tomorrow morning.'

'Why?' he asked, genuinely astonished. 'You look far from well yet. Do you feel fully recovered?'

'Till this morning I did. Now I'm not so sure. I have a slight headache.'

'Then why do you wish to leave? Is there anything that disturbs you here?'

The boy scanned my face for tell-tale marks. I watched him in silence. I saw a clean honest face—simple and childlike. I wondered if I should tell him the truth. Before I could do so a slow crimson spread over Banku's cheeks—downy with the first flush of manhood.

'Don't leave just yet,' he pleaded. 'Your presence makes Ma very happy.' Then, blushing fiercely, he rose abruptly and left the room.

I saw that the boy was simple but not unintelligent. I realized now what Pyari meant when she had said that if I prolonged my stay Banku might wonder what our relationship was. My conversation with Banku did something else for me. I understood Pyari as I had never done before. I saw that, beneath her glamorous exterior, lay maternal yearnings that tore at her heart. She was beautiful, wealthy and sought after by the highest people in the land. She was completely free to live the life she chose. Yet, from the moment that she had stepped into the role of a mother to some ordinary village children, she had bound herself with invisible chains. Her own loves and lusts, her hopes and desires paled into insignificance before her respect for her new found maternity. She could cheerfully gamble away the former for one look of love and trust on her son's face. I was filled with wonder at the thought. I imagined her exotic, passionate youth—the luxuriant days, the moon-kissed nights. Someone who had loved her deeply had given her the name of Pyari—the name with which she had assumed her new identity. Yet, she had not hesitated before abandoning both for the sake of her son.

The sun dipped and sank. Looking at it I experienced the strangest sensation. My whole being was suffused with the rose-gold hues of that magnificent sunset. I felt my heart melt and merge with that great ball of fire. I loved Pyari. I knew that without a doubt. We were drawn irresistibly to one another, linked by memories that dated from our early childhood. But Banku's mother stood between us like a colossal peak and we had to respect her presence.

'I must break all bonds with Pyari,' I thought. 'When I leave tomorrow morning, it must be forever. On no account must I yield to the temptation of leaving the slightest thread hanging between us.'

I sat, watching the twilight fade. Dusk came flowing in from the river wrapping me in a cool soft haze.

'Why are you sitting out in the cold with a headache?'

Pyari crossed the veranda, censer in hand, as she went from room to room fumigating them with incense smoke.

'It isn't cold at all, Lakshmi,' I smiled up at her.

'Well! There's a chill wind blowing.'

'You are wrong, there's no wind at all—chill or warm.'

'Everything I say and do is wrong. But your headache is a fact, isn't it? Why don't you go and lie down? Where is Ratan? Why can't he rub your temples down with eau-de-Cologne? The servants in this house are the most idle bunch of no-goods I've ever seen.' And with that Rajlakshmi went about her own business.

After a while Ratan came in with eau-de-Cologne and cool water. He looked a bit shame-faced. 'How was I to know you had a headache, Babu?' he grumbled. 'Ma becomes so unreasonable at times. When she's in a bad mood we servants get the worst of it.'

'Why is she in a bad mood?'

'How am I to know? Big people can afford to have moods . . . .'

Pyari's voice cut in from the dark, 'If working in big people's houses is so painful, Ratan, why don't you just leave? I told you an hour ago that Babu had a headache. What were you doing all this while? And now you dare to talk about me behind my back. Start looking for another job from tomorrow. I can't keep you anymore.' She departed as silently as she had come and reappeared almost immediately. 'I hear you are going home tomorrow.'

I meant to leave Patna but I had no plans of going home.

'Yes, I'm leaving tomorrow morning,' I said.

'What time is your train?'

'I'll start early and board the first train I can get.'

'I'd better send someone to the station for a time-table,' Rajlakshmi announced to the world at large and went in.

Ratan completed his ministrations and left.

The household noises died away and the world was wrapped in slumber. Only I couldn't sleep. I tossed and turned on my bed tortured with the question of what I had done to offend Pyari. Why was she so eager for my departure? I was aware of her predicament but, as we were both reasonably intelligent and self-disciplined, I failed to see what danger lay in my presence. I tried hard to stifle the pain that welled up in my heart at the thought that perhaps, after all, she did not love me as I had thought.

Sometime in the night, I do not know how late it was, I was awakened by a light footfall. Rajlakshmi entered the room. She lifted the lamp that burned at the table by my bed and stood it behind the door. Then she closed the window through which a draught of cold air was blowing straight from the river. For a moment or two she stood still. Then, coming up to my bed, she put her hand in through the mosquito net and felt my forehead and chest. After that she buttoned my shirt and, pulling the cover up to my shoulders, tucked me in as tenderly as she would a child. Her stealthy footsteps and secret ministrations were embarrassing to me till I reminded myself that she had nursed me back to health out of a deep coma. She left as silently as she had come, shutting the door gently behind her. All my tension eased away and my whole being was flooded with peace.

She had come in secretly and I let her go the same way. She never guessed how much of herself she had left behind in my heart on that night of my desolation. I awoke the next morning— my body burning with fever. My eyes smarted and my head felt as heavy as a stone. But go away I must, I thought. I couldn't trust myself a minute longer in her house. I realized that the self-control with which I had proudly encased myself was as delicate and brittle as the thinnest glass and could be shattered to fragments at the flick of a finger. I did not mind my own defeat. I minded hers. I had to leave her for her own sake. She had washed herself clean from the impurities of her past life. She had struggled with her deepest love and found the strength to reject it in return for the love and respect of her children. If I snatched her away from this bright world that was her due, I would be making a poor return for the noblest, purest love the world had ever seen.

'How do you feel this morning?' Pyari entered the room with a pale and anxious face.

'Not bad. I'm well enough for the journey.'

'Must you go? I mean—must you go today?'

'Yes, I'm afraid I must.'

'Will you write me a letter as soon as you get home? We'll be worried about you.'

I was awed by the unwavering light in her eyes. 'Certainly,' I said, making my mind up, there and then, to go home as she had wished. 'I'll write to you the moment I get home.'

'I too will write. I have something to ask of you.'

Before stepping into the palki I looked up at the house. I saw Pyari standing on an upstairs veranda—her hand on a column. Her face was as smooth and blank as polished marble. I suddenly remembered Annada Didi. Many years ago, centuries it seemed to me, she had stood with just such an expression on her face. The same look of resignation had been in the eyes that gazed at the blueing face and twisted lips of the dead Shahji. Those eyes had haunted me all these years but I had not read their meaning. Today, looking at another pair of dark unwavering eyes, a dim perception came into my own. A great love draws two hearts together with a magnetic force. But it also has the power to pull them apart with equal ruthlessness. If my love for Pyari had been formed of base metal I could never have resisted the temptation of being by her side—through eternity. I had voluntarily rejected this haven of love and peace for Pyari's ultimate good.

'Don't grieve for me, Pyari,' I murmured in my heart. 'You gave me my life. I cannot squander it away on ignoble aspirations. That would be insulting your gift. Wherever I am, whatever I do, I shall hold that life as my dearest possession.'

Exile

One

WITH MY PARTING FROM PYARI A CHANGE CAME OVER ME. IT WAS as if my life was split in two. One part of me went through the motions of living. But the other—was Pyari's. It was because of her that the sky was a brighter blue, the earth more green and the breezes of heaven gentler and more balmy. The world was mine and I was of the world. I floated on a sea of divine content.

Many years have passed since. I have lost the contentment I speak of but I have no regrets. It is enough for me that I once experienced a joy beyond compare. What fills me with an awesome wonder is the thought of the divine power that, working within me, enabled me to overcome the tensions and frets within and without, and kept my soul dancing on a wave of ecstasy. If I had only vested that great happiness in the hands that hold the world instead of Pyari's frail, vulnerable ones, I would not have lost it the way I have done.

I wrote my promised letter to Pyari immediately after my return from Patna. Her reply came several months later. She expressed her concern for my health and advised me to get married and settle down as soon as possible. Ending with the plea that, owing to her various commitments, she might not find the time to write, she requested me to drop a postcard, now and then, and apprise her of my well being.

That was all. The castle I had built in the air crumbled to dust. If a few pieces fell to the ground I did not waste my time looking for them. I may have wept a little—I don't remember. Anyhow, another six months went by.

One morning, as I was about to leave the house, the postman brought me an envelope. It bore my name in a shaky female hand. As I drew out the contents, a small piece of yellowing paper fell out of a larger folded one. It was in my mother's hand and bore her signature. It was in answer to a letter written by her *Gangajal*[*] thirteen years ago, just after the latter had had the misfortune of giving birth to a daughter. Distraught and unhappy, she had poured out her woes to my mother, hinting at her poverty and the difficulties of finding suitable husbands for daughters. My mother had written back, comforting her with the promise that if the worst came to the worst her own son would accept her *Gangajal*'s daughter as wife.

I read the letter over and over again. It was no less than a legal document. Without giving it a thought, she had bound me to her promise as surely as if she had been an experienced lawyer. Not a loophole had she left for my escape! Why her *Gangajal* had preserved the document for thirteen years without staking her claim was obvious. She had hoped that someone better than me would turn up. When no such thing happened and her daughter's physical enhancements started drawing the attention of her neighbours in a not too neighbourly way, she was forced to draw out the weapon in her possession.

If my mother had been living I would have swallowed her alive for putting me in this position. But she was so far above my reach that I couldn't touch her toenail with the mightiest leap. I decided to try my luck with her *Gangajal* and with that pious intention, I boarded the train to her village the same night. When I reached her humble cottage, travel-stained and weary, it was mid-afternoon and Gangajal Ma was taking her afternoon nap. She started up on seeing me and, though she did not recognize me at first, she shed so many tears over me and lamented my motherless state so thoroughly that I was quite alarmed. Then, assuring me that no one stood more in the place of my dead mother than she herself, she asked me innumerable questions on what money and lands my father had left me; what jewels my mother had possessed;

---

[*]   See Glossary.

why I didn't work for a living and if I did what salary I could expect. All this and much more she wormed out of me with consummate skill in a remarkably short period of time.

It did her no good, however, for it was evident, at the end of it, that her hopes had been severely dashed. In a final effort she told me, with a mournful face, that a relative of hers had made a fortune in distant Burma—a land whose cities had streets paved with gold and where Bengalis were at such a premium that they were lifted bodily from ships carrying them the moment the latter touched the shore, and carried away by Englishmen to be showered with jobs, money, power and prestige. For the first time in my conversation with Gangajal Ma I sat up, alert and interested. It was not that her description of the wealth and status enjoyed by Bengalis in Burma—a foolish misconception and one shared by many others as I later found out—enthused me particularly. My roving instinct which had lain dormant for so many years was roused by the thought of that fabled land which one could reach only after crossing an infinite stretch of wild and violent sea. I longed to go.

I had taken it for granted that Gangajal Ma had given up her idea of securing me for her daughter. I was wrong. That night, after serving my meal, she sat by me and treated me to a long monologue on happiness in marriage and how it rested on the girl's fate alone. She cited many examples (corroborating them with names and dates) of marriages arranged after careful consideration of the wealth, education and lineage of the groom, coming to naught because the girl was not fated to enjoy them. On the other hand, many marriages which were considered unfortunate during the negotiations turned out very happy and in many cases men who were both uneducated and poor miraculously attained wealth and status solely by virtue of being the husbands of their wives.

I told her, as firmly as I dared, that though I had no quarrel with wealth and status I had no intention of securing them through marriage and, in any case, there was no guarantee that her daughter was one of the lucky ones. But she brushed aside my fears and wishes. Having had me in her power for thirteen years she was loath to let me off so lightly. She spoke to me sentimentally of mother love and what a beautiful thing it was; of mothers' promises and how it was the duty of all grown-up sons to redeem them or else the mother might suffer pangs of guilt even in paradise. My fears had reached alarming proportions and my tired brain ran in circles desperately seeking a loophole of escape when Gangajal Ma suddenly announced that there was an eligible bachelor in the next village who was prepared to marry her daughter with a dowry of five hundred rupees.

I heaved a sigh of relief but it was only for a moment. Five hundred rupees! Where would I find such a sum? I tried to reason with myself. Why should I bind myself to an idle promise made by a woman long dead and gone? But, however hard I tried, I could not shake off the sense of responsibility. My mother had given her word and there was no escape. Satisfying Gangajal Ma for the present with the promise that I would return with the money in a month's time, I departed.

The only person I could think of approaching for the five hundred rupees was Pyari, but I hesitated. It was over a year now since I had seen her or even heard from her. Except for that one letter I had written after leaving Patna, and her brief reply, there had been no correspondence between us. Yet, surprisingly enough, I arrived in Patna one evening with the ostensible objective of begging Pyari to finance the marriage of a poor village girl. As I walked in through the gate the two uniformed guards who sat on either side stared at me as if they had never seen the likes of me in all their living years. I realized that unbathed, unshaven and shabbily dressed as I was, I was an anomaly in these surroundings. I wondered why Pyari had exchanged her old and courteous darwan for these arrogant strangers.

Undecided about whether I should ignore them and walk in or to seek permission to enter, I stood hesitating, when Ratan came running out of the house and, touching his forehead to the ground at my feet, asked with a beaming face, 'What are you doing outside, Babu? Why don't you come in?'

'I've just arrived, Ratan. How are you all?'

'We are well. Go right upstairs, Babu. I'm going out to buy some ice. I'll be back in a few minutes.'

'Is your mistress upstairs?'

'Yes,' and with that Ratan departed.

As I went up, snatches of conversation and sounds of gay laughter wafted down from a room at the top of the stairs. I was surprised, for that room had not been in use the last time I had been here. It had had furniture piled up at one end and only Ratan entered it, once in a while, to dust and sweep. As I walked in through the door my surprise turned to amazement. The marble floor was covered with the finest carpets over which spotless white sheets were spread. Velvet cushions and bolsters were scattered about and resting against them, half-lying, half-reclining, sat a group of men. My entrance must have startled them for they stared at me as though they were seeing a ghost. Although they wore dhotis like Bengali gentlemen, I guessed that they were Biharis from the embroidered muslin caps on their heads. A tabla player with his instrument occupied one corner and near him, a harmonium in front of her, sat Pyari Baiji herself, resplendent in silk and brocade, and flashing with jewels.

The blood drained from her face as she looked up at me. After what seemed hours (though it was only a few seconds) she forced a smile to her wan lips and said brightly, '*Aré*! It is Srikanta Babu. What a surprise! How long have you been in Patna?'

'I arrived today.'

'When? Where are you staying?'

I looked around me in a daze. I couldn't find my voice for a minute but when I did, it was steady.

'You don't know everyone in Patna,' I smiled. 'Their name would mean nothing to you.'

The gentleman who sat in the centre of the room, and was probably the chief person in it, now extended a cordial welcome. 'Come, Babuji. Take a seat,' he said, patting the cushion beside him with a smirk. Without saying a word he had conveyed to the company that he knew, to the last detail, what my relations were with Pyari. My face burned. With a word of thanks I bent down to untie my shoe laces debating furiously with myself as to what my conduct should be. In the few seconds that I had, I decided that I would not betray, by a word or glance, the hurt bewilderment that had taken hold of me. As I went in and sat in the place indicated, I knew that my face bore not a trace of the storm that was raging in my heart.

Flashing a brilliant smile at Pyari I said, 'Baiji Bibi, if I had had Sukhdev muni's address I would have dragged him here and tested his powers of resistance. What have you done? You have drowned us all in the ocean of your beauty.'

The Bihari gentleman, who was from Purnea and understood Bengali, smiled at this fulsome praise and wagged his head in appreciation. But a slow, rich red crept up from Pyari's neck and suffused her face till even her ears were flaming. That this was prompted not by pleasure but by anger and humiliation was not hidden from me.

I turned to the company and said, 'My arrival seems to have disturbed you in your merry-making. Please forgive me. Let the singing continue.'

The Bihari gentleman slapped me on the back in a gush of fellow feeling. 'By all means,' he cried, 'Pyari Bibi! Let us have another song.'

Pyari pushed away the harmonium and stood up. 'After dusk,' she said shortly and went out of the room.

After her departure the gentleman started conversing with me in a low voice. He was a zamindar from Purnea, he said, and a relative of the Maharaja of Darbhanga. He had known Pyari Baiji for seven years and admired her singing. She had performed in his ancestral home on several occasions and he himself came to Patna three or four times a year, staying up to ten days sometimes, to hear her sing. Only three months ago he had spent a week in her house. He then asked me bluntly why I had come. Before I could think of a suitable reply Pyari came into the room.

'Why don't you ask Baiji that?' I said.

Pyari threw me a sharp look but her voice, when she spoke, was gentle and subdued.

'He is from my village,' she murmured.

'Babuji,' I said in a hard bright voice glancing out of the corner of my eye at the pensive form that stood by my side. 'Where there is honey—bees will congregate, be they from the same village or otherwise.'

The Purnea zamindar didn't seem to appreciate what I said. His face darkened and grew solemn and when his servant came and announced that all had been arranged for the evening's puja he rose and left without a word. The tabla player and the other men in the room followed.

Ratan came in and asked Pyari, 'Ma, which room shall I prepare for Srikanta Babu?'

'I don't know,' Pyari said angrily. 'Can't you do any thinking for yourself? Is there a dearth of rooms in the house?' And she swept out of my sight with an arrogant swish of silk and brocade.

I realized that my unexpected arrival had thrown the domestic arrangements out of gear.

Pyari returned in a short while and, giving me a long and level look, asked quietly, 'Why this sudden visit?' and, without waiting for a reply, 'Do you intend to stay here for the night?'

'If you invite me to do so—I will.'

'Why do you talk of invitations? You are welcome to stay. Only—you may be a little uncomfortable. You see, the room you had last time . . . . '

'Is occupied by the Babu,' I said finishing the sentence for her. 'That's no problem. I'll sleep in one of the rooms downstairs.'

Pyari stared. 'Do you really mean to tell me that all this does not affect you? Since when have you become a saint?'

'You don't know me, Pyari,' I thought. Aloud I said, 'Why should it affect me? And talking of comfort, the poorest room in your house is more comfortable than the railway platform. I shall be fine. If there is a shortage of bedding—don't worry. I have a blanket with me.'

Pyari was silent for a while. Then she said spitefully, 'I'm quite sure you do. But if I were you, I would rather sleep out in the fields than endure such humiliation.'

I laughed at the passion in her voice. I knew what she wished to hear from my lips but deliberately, stubbornly, I made my voice calm and detached. 'I'm not such a fool, Pyari,' I said, 'that I do not understand your predicament. I know that, had it been in your power, you would have given me the best room in the house as you did the last time I was here. But the matter is so trivial that it is hardly worth discussing. Tell Ratan to show me my room. I'm terribly tired.'

'You are wise,' Pyari said. 'I'm relieved that you understand.' Then, suppressing a sigh, she added, 'But you haven't told me why you have come.'

'There are two reasons but I'll tell you only the second.'

'Why not the first?'

'It has become irrelevant.'

'Let us have the second then.'

'I'm going to Burma. I may never see you again—at least not for many years. I wanted to see you once before I left.'

At this point Ratan came and announced that my room was ready.

'Good,' I said. 'I must sleep for a while, Pyari. Come to my room after an hour or so if you can. I have something more to tell you.'

When Ratan led me upstairs to Pyari's bedroom I was surprised.

'Why this room, Ratan? I was supposed to sleep downstairs.'

'Downstairs? You to sleep downstairs? Are you joking, Babu?' And Ratan smiled and turned to go.

'Just a minute, Ratan,' I said. 'Where is your mistress to sleep?'

'I've made a bed for her in Banku Babu's room.'

I looked around me. There was no sign of the narrow cot and wooden rack that I had seen on my earlier visit. A vast, intricately carved four-poster stood in the middle of the room with snowy sheets spread over a high luxurious mattress. A small table stood on one side with a lamp, a few books and a bowl filled with jasmine on it. It was obvious, at one glance, that no servant's hand had done all this. The room bore, in all its details, a loved one's touch. Even the bed had been made by Pyari—I had not a doubt.

Pyari's pain and humiliation at my feigned indifference was crystal clear to me for I knew and understood every nuance of her character and temperament. My abrupt entrance had startled her into somewhat uncharacteristic behaviour, but no one knew better than I what lay in her heart. She had expected, even hoped, that I would betray a sense of grievance and jealousy. It was to that end that she had flung her childish barbs at me. But I had ignored her deepest needs. I had affected a cruel unconcern in the proud conviction that it expressed my strength and manliness. The thought filled me with guilt. I tried to sleep but sleep would not come. I waited for her footfall in eager anticipation.

I may have dozed off for a few minutes. I woke up suddenly to find Pyari sitting by me—her hand on my chest. I sat up.

She said without preamble, 'People who go to Burma never return. Do you know that?'

'No, I don't.'

'Then . . . .'

'Even if what you say is true, why should it affect me? I don't leave anyone behind for whom I must return.'

'Don't you?'

It was a simple question but it hit me in a vulnerable spot which I had not known existed. In the past I had successfully hardened my heart to all her pleas and tears. But now, to my horror, my self-control suffered a complete breakdown. Without knowing what I did, I murmured, 'There is one. I admit it. If I ever come back it will be for your sake alone.'

Pyari flung herself on me and wept without restraint. I felt her body shaking with sobs and warm tears trickling down my chest on to the sheet.

'Get up, Pyari,' I said, laying a hand on her head. She did not reply, nor did she raise her head. I held her face between my palms and forced her to look up.

'No, Pyari, no,' I said, and wiped away her tears.

'Tell me,' she said hoarsely, 'tell me truthfully—that man's presence here—you don't think ill of me?'

'No.'

'But—but you know I'm not a good woman. You know I've led an immoral life.'

I was silent. It was a paradox and I had no way of resolving it. I knew all there was to know about her. Yet I could not think of her as immoral and depraved.

Suddenly she sat up—her head held high.

'May I ask a question?' she said, her voice hard as nails. 'Why is it that a man, however degenerate, is allowed to change his ways and come back to his family and the society in which he was born while a woman, should she commit the tiniest error, finds all doors locked against her?'

I had no answer.

'I was young and innocent. People exploited me and made me what I am. Now that I seek a new identity, why won't you give it to me?'

'No one can stop you from reforming yourself. Even if society won't accept you there are other means of escape from the life you lead.'

Pyari gazed on my face long and full and there was something in her eyes I could not fathom.

'Very well,' she said, 'then you can't stop me either.'

A slight cough was heard and Ratan stood by the door.

'What is it, Ratan?' Pyari asked, sitting up.

'It is very late. The cook has dozed off in the kitchen. Isn't it time Babu had his meal?'

'Gracious!' Pyari looked guilty and shamefaced. 'I lost track of the time. You must all be hungry.'

She went down quickly and brought my meal, as she always did, with her own hands. Then, after I had eaten, she came up to my room and flung herself at the foot of the bed. It was one o'clock.

'I have passed many sleepless nights for your sake,' she said. 'I'm going to keep you awake tonight whether you like it or not. I've thought it over. I can't let you go to Burma.'

'What am I to do, then? Keep drifting as I am?'

Pyari did not condescend to reply. She asked me another question instead. 'Why do you wish to go so far away?'

'I want work. I'm not going there for my own amusement.'

Pyari sat up angrily. She fixed her eyes on my face and said in a passionate voice, 'You may fool the whole world but you can't fool me. God will never forgive you if ....'

'I know all that,' I interrupted. 'But what do you want me to do?'

Pyari looked pleased at this appeal. 'I want you to give up your wandering ways. I want you to marry, settle down and raise a family.'

'Will that really make you happy?'

She nodded so vigorously that her earrings trembled and twinkled.

'That's a relief,' I said. 'As a matter of fact that is one of the reasons I came to Patna. To tell you that I'm to be married.'

'Really? Do you really mean it? I've prayed and prayed to Ma Kali and at last she has answered my prayers. But please remember that I shall choose the girl.'

'You can't. The girl has been chosen already.'

A shadow fell over the laughing face. 'That is good news,' she said.

'I don't know if it is good news or bad. All I know is that my marriage is settled. There is no way out.'

Suddenly, Pyari lost her temper. 'All lies!' she shouted. 'Why do you always trifle with me?'

'What I have just told you is the absolute, unadulterated truth. See these.' I pulled the two letters out of my pocket and handed them to her.

She took them but said resentfully, 'I don't read other people's letters.'

'Then you needn't worry about other people's futures either.'

'I'm not worrying in the least.'

But she did not return the letters. After a while she walked up to the table and read the letters by the light of the lamp. After what seemed an incredibly long time, she returned to the bed. 'Are you asleep?' she asked softly.

'No.'

'I can't let you marry this girl. I knew her as a child. She was not a nice girl.'

'You read Ma's letter?'

'Yes, I did. There is nothing in it that can be considered binding. And even if there is, I won't let you marry her. That's final.'

'What kind of girl would you have me marry?'

'I can't answer that straight away. I must think it over and then decide.'

'If I am to wait for the girl *you* approve of I may as well resign myself to being a bachelor—in this life at least. In my next birth we shall see. So be it. I'm in no hurry. But the girl has to be married off. Five hundred rupees will do it. Her mother told me that.'

Pyari sat up in her excitement. 'I'll send the money tomorrow,' she cried joyfully. Then, sobering down, she added, 'Believe me, I object to this match only because she's not the right girl for you. Otherwise ....'

'Otherwise what?'

'Otherwise nothing. I'll find a girl worthy of you and then talk about it.'

'Your efforts will be wasted,' I said. 'You'll never find a girl worthy of me.'

She was silent for a long, long while. Then she asked suddenly, quite out of context, 'Will you take me with you to Burma?'

'Do you have the courage to come with me?'

Pyari's eyes held mine. 'Do you really believe I don't?'

'What about all these? Your house, furniture—all your possessions?'

'I'll give them all to Banku. What is my wealth to me if, in spite of it, you are forced to go to Burma to earn your living.'

I made no comment. I stared out of the window into the dark expanse outside.

'Is it necessary to go that far?' Pyari put out a feeler. 'Will my money never be of any use to you?'

'No. Never.'

'I knew that. But will you take me with you?' She placed a soft, moist palm on my foot.

I remembered the day Pyari had practically asked me to leave her house out of her consideration for Banku's feelings. I had marvelled at her strength of mind. Tonight I witnessed a total collapse of the rigid self-control that was such an integral part of her character. Her soft voice, humble with love, threatened to shatter all my powers of resistance. But I did not succumb.

'I can't take you with me,' I said. 'But I'll come back to you the moment you call. Whatever I do, wherever I am, I shall be yours and only yours.'

'Only mine?' she cried out in wonder.

'All my life.'

'Then you'll never marry? Never lead a normal life?'

'No. I will never do anything that makes you unhappy.'

Pyari's lip trembled and her eyes swam. 'You will live the life of an ascetic? For a woman like me?'

'That I will. It is not much of a sacrifice for what you have given me has fulfilled me completely. You must always remember that, Rajlakshmi.'

Her eyes held mine briefly. Then, flinging herself on the bed, she burst into a storm of passionate tears.

The house was dark and silent. Not a mouse stirred. I had a sudden vision of the night looking in through the window at her exquisite counterpart—born of the same womb, as rapturous, as passionate—performing her heart-breaking act. I felt her quiet eyes rest on Pyari. I saw a gentle smile hovering about her mouth as with a last, lingering look, she turned away and was lost in the first pearly light that streamed from the east.

Two

THERE ARE SOME MEMORIES THAT NEVER FADE NO MATTER HOW many years roll by. Pyari's last words, just before I left Patna, still ring in my ears as clearly as if they were uttered yesterday. 'I'm not an ignorant child,' she had said, weeping bitterly. 'I know I must be punished for what I have done. But what is being meted out to me is too painful to be borne. Our society is too unequal—too cruel to its women. It will suffer for this some day. A terrible punishment awaits it—as God is my witness!'

Why Pyari cursed Hindu society the way she did was known to herself and to her God. It was not totally unknown to me either but I chose to remain silent.

As I stepped into the carriage, Pyari rushed up to me. 'You are going so far away. I don't know if I'll ever see you again. I have one last request. Will you grant it?'

'I will.'

'The way you live,' she murmured. 'If anything happens, God forbid, will you send me word?'

'I will.'

Pyari wiped my feet with the end of her sari. She said hesitating, humble, 'Do you *have* to go? Don't go.'

I averted my eyes from her streaming face and trembling lips. The carriage moved on. The clamour of creaking wheels and horses' hooves exploded in my ears but through it all I heard her soft, almost inaudible sobbing all the way to the station.

Three

ONE FOGGY MORNING, A WEEK LATER, I STEPPED OFF THE TRAIN AT the Koilaghat area of Calcutta. A khaki-clad coolie swooped down on my tin trunk and bedroll like some bird of prey and vanished out of sight in the twinkling of an eye. I scanned the crowd, forcing back the tears of panic and fury that stung my eyes, but it was several hours before he reappeared. As the train was entering the station I had observed herd upon herd of motley-coloured animals packed between the road and the jetty. Coming closer I recognized them for what they were—not animals but men, women and children who had spent the night in the cold and the fog in the hope of securing some space to sit in on the boat that was to carry them across the black water. I had a reservation for the deck but my heart quaked at the thought of forcing my way through this turbulent sea of humanity to the entrance of the jetty.

There were people from the length and breadth of India— from northernmost Kabul to southernmost Kumarika. There were foreigners too. A group of Chinamen in black vests dominated the scene. Suddenly, as if at a signal, the fifteen or sixteen hundred people stood up and started forming lines, as meek and docile as a gigantic flock of sheep. I wondered why, for, as far as I could see, there was no sign of a ship, not even in the distant horizon.

I asked a man in the crowd, 'What is happening? Why has everyone stood up?'

'Dog-tori,' he mumbled.

'What?'

'Dog-tori. For the Pi-lage.'

I was no wiser for this communication. Nevertheless I decided to follow the instincts of the herd and wedge myself somewhere in the line. But, try as I would, not a chink could I discover in the solid wall before me. Finally, at the tail end of the queue, I found some Mussalmans from Khidirpur standing, not with the belligerence of the others, but rather awkwardly in scattered twos and threes. There is one characteristic that distinguishes the Bengali from the other races of India. He is more sensitive to humiliation. That being made to wait for hours like sheep and goats is an affront to human dignity was writ large on the faces of these men. I decided to join them. They worked as tailors in Rangoon, they said, and had made the trip several times. They explained to me that all the passengers were required to go through a medical examination because the authorities feared that some may be carrying the plague.

After what seemed hours a white doctor and his assistant were seen approaching and the examination began. I could not see much of what was going on for the stretch before me was formidable. However, as the line diminished, I noticed that the examination involved a stripping of the body down to the hips and a probing into all those private parts that might conceal a lump. I heard the exclamations of fear and pain as men, women and children were subjected to the insensitivity and ruthlessness that characterize the white race in its dealings with the coloured and I cursed the passivity that has been bred in the Hindu from time immemorial.

When my turn came, I shut my eyes and surrendered to the inevitable. Mercifully it lasted only a few minutes. I was declared fit to travel. The next step was to find a place in the boat.

One who has never mounted the deck of a ship has no idea of how it is done. Packed into a congealed mass of stinking bodies I was alternately pulled forward and pushed backwards in a series of jerks that bore a closer resemblance to the motion of a giant machine than to the movements of human beings. I reached the deck, almost swooning from lack of air, but there was no way I could stop there. The relentless pressure from behind propelled me on to a gaping hole through which a flight of dark steps led to the monstrous cavern of the ship's hold. The mighty stream of Punjabis, Bengalis, Madrasis, Gujaratis, Marathas, Afghans,

Chinese, Marwaris and Biharis gushed into the cavern with the force and turbulence of a mountain cataract. I may have lost consciousness for a few moments for I have no memories of the downward flight. When I came to, I found myself standing, dazed and stupid, at one end while my travelling companions were already seated and chatting with their neighbours. The floor of the hold was miraculously partitioned into thousands of segments with sheets and blankets, steel trunks and wooden crates. It was at this moment that my coolie reappeared.

'I have kept your luggage on the deck, Babu. Shall I bring it down?'

'No. On the contrary, take me out of here if you can.'

Movement was impossible without stepping on people's bedding and stumbling over their possessions for, barring the few inches of space on which my feet were planted, there was not a spot of unoccupied territory on the floor of the hold. The coolie gripped my hand and with commendable speed and efficiency, got me out of the hold without seriously disturbing the floor arrangements. Then, leading me to my tin trunk and bedroll, he took his tip and departed.

I looked around. Here too the floor space had been neatly apportioned among the travellers and there was no room for a latecomer like me to spread my bedding. There was nothing for me to do but sit on my trunk and watch the magnificent expanse of the Ganga over which the steamer was now inching along. I had been thirsty for a good while now and the terrible ordeal of the last two hours had done nothing to ease it. But I had neither a glass nor a pitcher with me. In the hope of borrowing one from a fellow-Bengali I walked gingerly towards the steps that led down to the hold. As I stood at the top a deafening clamour assailed my ears, the likes of which I had never heard in all my living years. It sounded as if a gigantic cowshed, the one owned by King Virat of the *Mahabharata* perhaps, was on fire—such a snorting, bellowing, stomping, fuming, raving, raging, came from below. With a quaking heart I peeped down the hole and what a sight met my eyes! Each member of that vast sea of humanity was engaged in singing his national or provincial anthem with a ferocity that only matched his neighbour's. It seemed as if the ship was carrying as its cargo all the musical talent to be found from Kabul to the Brahmaputra, from Kumarika to the distant borders of China.

I have heard it said that Shakespeare, the great bard of England, believed that the man who loved music was incapable of murder. But Shakespeare, possibly, hadn't heard the kind of music that drove a man to murder. While I stood rooted to the ground, I saw a man making frantic signs to me from below. I climbed down and pushed my way through the crowd, ignoring the indignant looks and exclamations that followed me till I came to where he stood. When he realized that I was a Brahmin he folded his hands with great humility and introduced himself as the 'famous' Nanda Mistri of Rangoon. Beside him sat a corpulent woman in her forties with enormous red eyes rolling in her head above which her unnaturally thick eyebrows met—as fierce and bushy as a field of tussock.

'Babu *moshai*,' Nanda Mistri said, rubbing his hands. 'This is my wi—.'

But before he could finish, the woman had lashed out at him as venomously as a hooded cobra. 'Wife!' she spat out the word. 'He dares to call me his wife! Are you my wedded husband? I warn you, Mistri—don't you dare ruin my reputation with your evil lies.'

I stared, shocked beyond belief.

Nanda Mistri went on rubbing his hands and trying to placate her. 'Why do you lose your temper, Tagar?' he asked humbly, 'What is the difference? We have lived together for twenty....'

'So what if we have lived together for twenty years? Does that make us man and wife? Since when has the daughter of a Boshtom-born been the wife of a Shudra? Have I ever let you enter my kitchen or touch my food? Not even my sworn enemy can say that of me. Tagar Boshtomi would rather die than besmirch the caste she was born into,' and Tagar rolled her eyes at me in pride and triumph at her illustrious birth.

Put in his place, so severely, Nanda Mistri mumbled angrily, 'You heard what she said, Babu? Caste! As if there is anything left of it after all these years. I am a simple man and I put up with her arrogance. Anyone else ....' and looking into the eyes of his companion of twenty years he gulped and left the sentence in mid-air.

I borrowed a glass and departed. All the way back to my tin trunk I couldn't stop laughing at the Vaishnavi's logic. But immediately afterwards I reminded myself that Tagar was, after all, a foolish illiterate woman. There were many educated and respectable men in the cities and villages of Bengal who fell back on a similar logic when faced with the prospect of losing caste. But males—no matter what they do or say—are protected from mockery in our society. We laugh at women—never at men.

Towards evening, clouds started massing in the east and after midnight strong winds, accompanied by intermittent rain, set the ship rocking drunkenly. However, the morning dawned calm and clear and the steamer resumed its staid and stately motion over the blue water. I hadn't suffered any ill effects, possibly because I had experienced the motion of a boat over and over again from my early childhood. I wondered how Nanda Mistri and Tagar had fared in the night. I went down to the hold as soon as it was light and found the pair sitting solemnly in their corner. The musicians of yesterday were sprawled all over the floor around them. It would obviously take them a little while longer to be able to sit up and resume their singing.

'How did you pass the night, Mistri?' I asked.

'Well enough,' replied Nanda with a yawn.

'Well enough!' Tagar bared her fangs at Nanda. 'Have you taken leave of your senses? It was the worst night of my life—*Ma-go-Ma!*[*] What a commotion!'

'Why? What happened?'

Nanda Mistri grinned up at me. 'Nothing much, Babu,' he said. 'Have you seen the Calcutta vendors prepare *sade batrish bhaja*? With three flicks of the thumb at the bottom of the cone they make the thirty-two-and-a-half ingredients jump and dance about till rice, beans, peas, chhola, matar, masur, arhar—all become as one. That is exactly what happened last night. We all rolled about the ship from this end to that. Fortunately, a true Boshtom-born doesn't lose caste or else my Tagar—'

'Again! You dare utter those blasphemies again.' Tagar glared at Nanda like a wounded bear ready to spring.

Nanda apologized hastily and, pulling a long face, sat staring at the roof of the hold. A few yards away from them a pair of Kabuliwalas, coated with filth and grime from head to foot, were

---

[*] 'Oh my mother!'— an exclamation common among Bengalis.

busily stuffing large pieces of roti into their tangled beards, quite oblivious of the fiery darts showered on them from Tagar's saucer-like eyes.

After a while, Nanda got restive. 'Are we never going to eat?' he asked plaintively.

I was puzzled. 'It is barely dawn,' I said, 'After a while . . . .'

'We had a fine large pot of rosogollas with us,' Nanda said tearfully. 'I had been begging Tagar to open it ever since we boarded the steamer. "Let's have some," I said. "Why do we deny ourselves." But would she listen? "I want to take it with me to Rangoon," she insisted. Now take it with you to Rangoon if you can.' (This to Tagar.)

Tagar made no answer to the charge. Snorting angrily she continued to roll her fiery eyes at the hapless Kabulis.

'What happened to the rosogollas?' I asked, unable to contain my curiosity.

Nanda glanced briefly at Tagar. 'I don't know that. All I saw in the morning was the broken pot, there,' he pointed with his finger, 'and the syrup all over the bedding—here, see. If you want more information ask those rascals,' and he glared balefully at the Kabulis.

I was dying to laugh but I controlled myself with an effort: 'Forget the rosogollas,' I said. 'Don't you have *chire* with you?'

'That we do.' Nanda brightened visibly. 'Show Babu *moshai* the *chire*, Tagar.'

Tagar kicked a small bundle viciously in my direction.

'Whatever you may say, Babu *moshai*,' Nanda said, recovering his *bonhomie* of a few minutes ago. 'Kabulis may be unholy and unclean but they are true to their salt. They ate our rosogollas but they offered us a stack of their rotis in exchange. Put them aside carefully, Tagar. They may come in handy for your *malsa bhog*.'[*]

I burst out laughing at Nanda's joke but one look at Tagar and the blood curdled in my veins. Her face was mottled with fury and her voice, coming out of her deep chest, rumbled like thunder shocking the shipful of sleepers into a rude awakening.

---

[*] Food offered to Radha and Krishna in an earthen basin—a custom among Vaishnavs.

'You dare taunt me about my caste?' she bellowed. 'You rotten worm! You dare talk of caste with your vile Shudra mouth? I warn you, Mistri….'

'No, no, Tagar,' Nanda was the picture of abject humility. 'I didn't mean to taunt you. It was a joke—I swear on my head—it was only a joke.'

'A joke?' Tagar's voice rose higher and to the thunder of her voice was added the lightning of her eyes. 'What kind of a joke? You have the gall to tell me to use a mlechha Mussalman's roti for my Govinda's *malsa bhog*? Go stuff them into your Shudra stomach! Go feed them to your pig-father's ghost.'

At this Nanda could contain himself no longer. He leapt into the air like an arrow released with a twang from a tensed string-bow. 'You filthy harlot!' he screamed grabbing her by the hair. 'You dare to utter my father's name with your foul mouth?'

'A hundred times! I'll say it a hundred times, you son of a whore, if you dare bring my caste on your evil tongue.' Tagar sprang to her feet and the two were locked in a deadly combat which threatened to shatter the very floorboards they stood upon. The battle raged on. The Hindustanis forgot their nausea and applauded enthusiastically. The Punjabis turned up their noses in disdain. The Utkals ran hither and thither squeaking like frightened mice. I stood rooted to the ground. Never in my wildest dreams had I believed such a vulgar display possible— particularly from people who belonged to my own community. I walked away from the scene, my face flaming.

As I came to the foot of the steps, the Jaunpuri darwan who had been watching enthralled, nodded approvingly at me. 'Bengali women are good fighters, Babuji. They don't give up.'

I couldn't look him in the face. I ran up the steps back to my trunk on the deck.

Four

$\mathcal{I}$ HAVE NO IDEA OF HOW LONG THE BATTLE LASTED OR HOW IT ended; what the terms of the truce were and whether they were honoured, for I did not venture into the hold again. It was clear that Tagar and Nanda had led this cat-and-dog life for twenty years and there was no reason why they should not continue to do so—for another twenty.

All day tattered wisps of clouds blew from one end of the sky to another. Then, late in the afternoon, the wind dropped. A dense blackness, appearing on the horizon, spread rapidly like a stain over half the sky. I noticed the crew glancing fearfully upwards; then darting about their tasks with feverish haste.

I called an elderly sailor to my side, '*O hé mian!*[*] Will there be another storm tonight, do you think?'

'Get down to the hold, *moshai*,' he said, by way of a reply.'The captain says a cyclone is coming.'

Within a few minutes I realized that his warning was not an idle one. The deck passengers were ordered to enter the hold. Those who resisted were forcibly dragged from their places by the second officer and pushed down the steps. My trunk and bedroll were

---

[*]   O hé: Oh you!

    Mian: A term of respect used for Muslim men.

taken down but I eluded my protectors and slipped away. I couldn't bear the thought of entering the hold for I had heard that when a severe storm or cyclone was imminent it was customary to seal the hold in the interest of the ship's safety as well as that of its cargo. But safety did not appeal to me—not just then. I had never seen a cyclone—not even on land. I hadn't an inkling of what it was like, to see, to hear, to feel—and the prospect of experiencing one at sea set me quivering with anticipation. I told myself that even if the ship broke into a million pieces and I was flung out to sea—it would be a wonderful death. Who would exchange that buoyant engulfing by the waves under the open sky for a slow squeezing out of life in a suffocating death trap in which thousands of humans dashed about like rats, cracking their skulls and drowning by inches. That was my first passage to Rangoon. I had no idea then, that monstrous sharks swarmed the waters about the king's ships and that a sea-death might well follow a terrible ripping of flesh and a crunching of bones under the waves.

Towards dusk the mild drizzle changed into a heavy downpour and the wind increased in velocity. I decided to look for shelter. As I stepped onto the deserted deck I caught a glimpse of the captain examining the sky with a telescope. Afraid of being caught and sent down to the hold I slipped away again till, in my wanderings all over the ship, I found what I thought was an excellent hideaway. Piled one on top of another, at one end of the deck, were several immense iron crates with livestock in them. I climbed up to the topmost one. I was safe. Little did I know, then, what fate had in store for me!

By now the rain had become a lashing torrent and the gale was whipping up flecks of salt foam that hit my face and settled on my lips. The sky grew darker by the minute and the ship bobbed up and down on a steadily swelling sea. This is the cyclone, I thought. I had yet to discover the real thing.

Suddenly the ship's whistle blew a blast so shrill and penetrating that a tremor ran through my frame. I looked up at the sky and was amazed to find the cloud cover gone. Before I could react to this strange phenomenon an unearthly rumble rose from the bowels of the sea and, gathering momentum, exploded against my ear drums with a deafening clap. And with that came the storm.

Nothing I had experienced in my life before or after was comparable to what I experienced then. There was a story my grandmother used to tell me often in my childhood, as I snuggled against her breast on dark winter nights, of a prince who had dived into a pond and brought up a silver box with the lives of seven hundred demons trapped in it in the form of a golden bee. And as he crushed the bee between his palms the demons, crazed with pain, had trampled the earth and rocked the sky in the last throes of death. Something of the kind was happening now but the demons numbered—not seven hundred but seven million and seventy.

The gale had become so violent that it threatened to tear the very earth from its axis. I had taken the precaution of tying myself tightly to the iron pole that rose from the deck or else I would have been blown away as lightly as a leaf. As it was, the wind strained and pulled against the wrapper which bound me, so viciously, that it threatened to snap any minute. The water around the ship's hull bubbled upwards pushed by the water beneath. Gripping the pole with all my might I looked out to sea.

And then—my eyes viewed that which made me bow my head and utter a humble prayer. 'My Maker,' I murmured, 'You gave me eyes with which to view your world. But, tonight, in your boundless bounty, you have shown me that which lay beyond my wildest dreams—that which is peerless among your creations.' For, even as I looked, a vast body of water gathered itself from the heart of the ocean, and rising like a mighty mountain peak that threatened to shatter the sky, began gliding majestically towards the ship. Its crown of glittering phosphorescents shone like rows of jewelled lamps against the blue-black sky and in their light that darkly beautiful, that awesome, wondrous face was revealed.

My body and soul quivered in ecstasy. 'Oh! Lord of the waves!' I exclaimed, 'though death at your hands be imminent let me spend my last moments feasting on your beauty.'

The ship's whistle continued to blow in trembling spurts. The terrified voices of the sailors, calling hysterically upon Allah to save them from death, rose above it. The cataclysmic wave that was to engulf us—that which had been dreaded and awaited— was now upon us.

A deafening explosion rent the air and then the heavy velvet of salt water curled and foamed around me and above and beneath me. I thought the ship had sunk and that we had all drowned and were on our way to the subterranean chambers of the Sea King's palace, there to feast and make merry as his guests. But in half a minute the ship crested the wave and the water gushed out. Wave after wave crashed against the ship, flooded the deck and ran out in a few seconds. Below me the sheep and goats bleated fearfully and the ducks and hens dashed their wings against the bars in a frantic attempt to escape a watery death. Then they fell silent. Clutching the iron pole with both hands I managed to elude death by drowning.

But now a new fear gripped me. If I had to stay here much longer, dripping water from head to foot, with the wind cutting into my flesh with blades of ice, I would certainly die of pneumonia. My teeth chattered in my head and my hands and feet turned numb with cold. I had to get out of the place and get out fast.

I thought of entering one of the pens but changed my mind. That was even more dangerous and the pen might well be my watery bier. The thing to do was to make a dash for one of the cabins in the thirty odd seconds that the ship crested the wave before it went down.

I untied the wrapper and slid down the pole but the cabins were not near enough to reach in one go. I had to crouch down on the deck thrice, as the great tidal waves threatened to sweep me out to sea, then get up and run again before I reached a second-class cabin. But the door was locked. I hammered with all my might but the iron door did not yield an inch. Once again I ran, crouched, and ran again in the direction of a first-class cabin. This time I was lucky. The door opened. It was unoccupied. Heaving a sigh of relief I dashed in and sank down on the bed.

By midnight the rain and the gale had exhausted themselves but the sea roared on and wave after wave was hurled at the ship's hull till the grey dawn glimmered over the eastern horizon.

When morning came I went down to the hold to find out how my travelling companions, particularly Nanda and Tagar, had fared in the night. Nanda had comically likened his experience of the night before last with the dancing of the ingredients in a cone of *sade batrish bhaja* and had confessed that they had returned to their original positions only a short while ago. I wondered how he would describe the events of last night.

As I descended the steps, a sickening stench of vomit and faeces rose like a cloud, assailing my nostrils so devastatingly that I could barely breathe. Before me, sprawled in unnatural shapes and positions, lay a field of bodies over which a gigantic grinder, of the kind women use to grind their spices, seemed to have rolled. The ship's doctor was attending to them while jamadars cleaned up the mess. Doctor Babu looked me up and down. It was evident that he thought me a second-class passenger. Yet he feigned great astonishment. 'You look quite fresh,' he remarked. 'Did you manage to get hold of a hammock?'

I shook my head. 'What I got hold of was a crate—an iron crate. That's why I look so fresh.' Then observing the doctor's astonishment, I added, 'I am a third-class passenger like these others but, lacking their strength of body and will, I shrank from entering this hell of hells. I spent part of the night sitting on a crate among the chickens and ducks, and the rest in an unoccupied first-class cabin. It was a clear case of trespass.'

The story of my adventures entertained Doctor Babu so much that he instantly invited me to share his cabin for the rest of the journey. On my declining the offer he insisted on lending me his deck chair, which I accepted.

Several hours later, as I lay on the borrowed chair, half dead with exhaustion and hunger, one of the Mussalman tailors from Khidirpur came up to me and said, 'Babu *moshai*, a woman from the lower deck has sent for you—a Bengali woman.' It must be Tagar, I thought, and what should she want me for except to act as an intermediary in her caste war with Nanda? But why me? I was in no mood to humour her.

'Tell her I'll come after a while,' I said.

The messenger looked crestfallen. 'She's in deep distress,' he said. 'She begs very humbly that you come to her aid at once.'

The terms 'deep distress' and 'begs very humbly' didn't quite fit in with Tagar's personality but there was no doubt in my mind that it was she who had sent for me.

'What about the man with her? What is he doing?' I asked.

'It is his illness that has upset her so. That is why she seeks your help.'

After last night anybody might well be ill! Thinking this, I got up and accompanied the man who led me—not to Tagar and

Nanda—but to the extreme end of the hold where, partially hidden by some enormous coils of rope, sat a young woman in her early twenties. On a piece of dirty matting by her side lay an emaciated young man. His eyes were closed and his breath came in gasps. I was surprised that I had not noticed them before for the woman's face had something in it that held the eye. It was not a beautiful face—at least, not of a conventional beauty. A high forehead is not generally regarded as an asset in the female physiognomy but this woman's large forehead was rendered attractive by the intelligence and force of character that was stamped on it. There was something about her that reminded me of Annada Didi. She was dressed in a cheap red-bordered cotton sari. Not a speck of gold adorned her body. Her only ornaments were a pair of conch bangles and the bright red sindoor that filled the parting of her hair. The iron hoop of wifehood hung from her wrist.

She rose at my approach and addressed me with a directness that surprised me as I was completely unknown to her. 'You are acquainted with the doctor,' she said, looking straight into my eyes. 'Would you ask him to come and examine him?' she said, pointing to the man on the mat.

'I made his acquaintance only this morning,' I answered, 'but he seems a kind man and will surely come.'

'If he expects a fee,' she said coolly, 'we cannot pay. In that case you must help me take the patient upstairs.'

'The ship's doctor's services are free, I believe,' I said. 'But what is the gentleman suffering from?'

I had thought that the man was her husband, so I got a bit of a shock when she leaned over him and asked, 'When did the stomach trouble start? Before you left home?' Then, on the man's nodding his head, she turned to me and said, 'He was suffering from dysentery even before we boarded the ship. Then he had fever. It is very high this morning.'

I bent down and touched the sick man's forehead. The fever was, indeed, very high. I left her and went upstairs to call the doctor.

After examining the patient and leaving medicines and instructions, Doctor Babu turned to me. 'Come, Srikanta Babu,' he said. 'Let's go up to my cabin and have a chat.'

'You have no objections to tea, I hope,' he asked after we had settled down.

'None at all.'

'And biscuits?'

'Even less.'

As we sat sipping our tea, Doctor Babu asked me a strange question.

'How did you manage to find your way into that set up?'

'The lady sent for me.'

Doctor Babu wagged his head with an air of wisdom. 'That's only natural,' he said. 'Are you married?'

'No.'

'Then it might not be a bad idea! Hmmm! The man is suffering from typhoid and his constitution isn't strong enough to fight it. He won't live long—that's certain. You'd better keep an eye on the woman or someone else will steal her from under your nose.'

'I don't understand a word of what you are saying,' I said sharply.

But Doctor Babu was neither embarrassed nor offended. 'What do you think, Srikanta Babu?' he went on, following his own line of thought. 'Do you think the man seduced her or was it the other way around? She's quite forward, isn't she? And very articulate.'

'What makes you so sure they aren't husband and wife?'

'Experience. There are couples like them on every boat. Last time there was a pair from Belghoria. Once you reach Burma you'll see what I mean.'

His words were confirmed, over and over again, during my years in Burma. But that was much later. At that moment, an acute depression overtook me. Taking leave of the doctor I went down to the hold to see Nanda Mistri.

Nanda and Tagar were just settling down to their mid-day meal. Nanda glanced briefly at me and asked, 'Who is the woman, Babu?'

'What is that to you?' Tagar snarled. She had a headache and had tied a piece of cloth tightly around her head. The face below the bandage was red and hot.

'Look, Babu,' Nanda appealed to me, 'have you ever seen a woman with a fouler mind? A Bengali girl with a sick husband is travelling with us and I can't even ask who she is.'

Tagar threw her bandage off and her headache along with it.

Fixing her protuberant cow-eyes on mine she said coldly, 'Babu! Men like this creature here have passed through my hands in dozens. I know them inside out. Tell him not to try any tricks with me. Is he a doctor that he goes rushing off to see the sick man the minute I go upstairs to fetch water? Who is she to him? I warn you, Mistri—if I ever catch you even looking at her I'll break your . . . .'

'Are you my keeper?' Nanda sprang up excitedly at her words. 'Am I your pet monkey that I'll dance to your tune? I'll visit the sick man whenever I like. Do what you can.'

'We'll see,' Tagar said darkly, winding her piece of cloth back on her head.

I walked away from them, back to my chair on the deck. Twenty years was a long time, I thought. Enough to make Tagar appreciate the fact that where there were no legitimate claims, only vigilance and a show of ownership kept a relationship going. She dared not relax her hold on Nanda, even infinitesimally, for the moment she did that, he would roll away from her hands as callously as her youth and beauty had. But the woman she had recognized as a potential rival, about whom Doctor Babu had made those snide remarks—who *was* she? Where did she come from? What was her history? Tagar and Doctor Babu had boasted of their experience in such matters, and claimed that they couldn't be fooled. But I, who had known Annada Didi, could not accept their assessment without question. Yet, try as I would, I could not attune myself to the complete absence of womanly modesty in her speech and manner. The doctor had called her 'forward'. She was that indeed! The fact irked me, despite myself.

I was sent for, once again, late that night. Informing me that her companion was much better, she proceeded to tell me about herself. Her name was Abhaya, and she came from a Kayastha family of the Uttar Rarhi clan from a village near Baluchar. The man with her was from the same village. His name was Rohini Sinha. Abhaya's husband had migrated to Burma eight years ago leaving her in her native village. He had kept in touch for the first two years—sending her letters and small sums of money from time to time. For the last six years, however, there had been a complete absence of communication. Her mother, her sole surviving relative, had died last month. Alone, abandoned by her husband and totally without support, she had found it impossible to stay on in her ancestral home. She had then taken the decision to journey Rangoon, look for her husband and claim maintenance. She had asked her Rohini Dada to accompany her and he had agreed. Now, in her candid, forthright manner, Abhaya extracted a promise from me to help her in her search once we set foot on Burmese soil.

I must confess that something—a faint distaste—held me back from responding whole-heartedly to Abhaya's friendly overtures. Yet, try as I would, I could not put a finger on what it was that I found distasteful. There was not a trace of coquetry in her manner nor any garrulity in her speech. Common sense, warmth and honesty, together with a deep respect for the man who had stood by her, emanated from her personality.

'Srikanta Babu,' Abhaya asked suddenly, 'Do you blame me for what I have done? Would it have been better for me to spend the rest of my life in passive acceptance of my fate instead of making an effort to reclaim what is mine? A young woman without a male protector is so vulnerable in our society. There are so many ways in which she can be exploited.'

'Do you have any idea of why your husband has ceased to communicate with you?'

'None at all.' Then, reflecting a little, she added, 'All I know is that he lives in Rangoon and works for the Burmese Railway. I have written many letters but have received no reply. Yet they must have reached him for not one came back to me.'

I knew the reason for her husband's silence. Doctor Babu had told me many stories about Burma—how Bengali men often took Burmese wives and started new families. Many never returned at all. They even died there and were buried according to Burmese rites.

Abhaya threw me a sharp glance and said, 'You believe he is dead—don't you?'

I shook my head. 'On the contrary, I'm convinced he is alive and well.'

Abhaya stooped quickly and touched my feet before I could stop her. 'I pray that you are right, Srikanta Babu. I want nothing more in life than my husband's health and happiness.' We were silent for a while and then Abhaya said, 'I know what you are thinking.'

'Do you?'

'Don't I? Am I not a woman and a wife? Do you think your suspicions have not been mine? But I am not afraid. If it comes to that—I can live quite amicably with a co-wife.'

I did not speak. But Abhaya read my thoughts as if from a book. 'You are wondering if my acceptance of her will be enough. She may not accept me.'

'If that is how it is—what will you do?' I asked, struck by her perception.

Abhaya looked frightened and her eyes grew moist. She said, 'In that case you must help me, Srikanta Babu. My Rohini Dada is too simple—too good. He won't know what to do.'

I promised to help her if I could but added that it might not be a good idea to bring in a third person to sort out marital differences. 'These things are best handled by the two persons concerned,' I said, and she agreed with a sigh.

The ship was due to reach Rangoon at noon the next day. But from sunrise onwards I detected a certain restlessness and dread among the passengers. A new word, *kerentin*, was on everybody's lips. On making enquiries I discovered that the word was quarantine. I was told that the British government, anxious to prevent the spread of the plague, had cordoned off a section of the shore, about ten miles downstream from Rangoon, and put up a row of sheds in which passengers from India were required to spend ten days before they were allowed to proceed to the city. The rule, however, was relaxed in the case of passengers with influential relatives in Burma who could obtain a sanction from the Port Health Officer on their behalf.

Doctor Babu called me into his cabin and gave me all the information. 'You should have made arrangements to avoid the quarantine before coming out, Srikanta Babu,' he said. 'These ten days are hell for the passengers. They are treated worse than animals. For one thing—no coolies are allowed to enter the quarantine sheds. Then everything is ripped open and sterilized in boiling water. What with the heat, the dust—.'

'Is there no way of getting out of it, Doctor Babu?' I asked quite alarmed.

He shook his head. 'No! But I'll have a word with the English doctor's clerk. He may be willing to vouch for you—'

Before Doctor Babu could complete his sentence a commotion,

accompanied by loud curses and screams, sent us hurrying to the deck. What we saw there shocked me beyond belief. The second officer of the ship was engaged in viciously kicking and cursing some five or six sailors who ran screaming helter-skelter in a desperate attempt to escape the heavy boots. I had observed the English youth's arrogance and domineering ways and I knew that Doctor Babu had had words with him on several occasions.

'This is highly irregular,' Doctor Babu said, his voice choking with fury. 'You'll regret it some day—I warn you.'

The Englishman turned round nonchalantly. 'Why? What have I done?'

'You have no right to kick the sailors.'

'How does one manage cattle without kicking them?'

Doctor Babu was a bit of a nationalist. He said hotly, 'They are human beings—not animals. My countrymen are gentle and meek. That is why they do not report you to the Captain. And you know they won't—so you dare heap these indignities on them.'

Suddenly the Englishman smiled—a wide smile of pure delight. Taking the doctor by the elbow he pointed a finger and said, 'Look, Doctor, they are your countrymen, you ought to be proud of them!'

Looking in the direction of the pointing finger I saw the men who had been kicked only a few moments before peeping from behind some barrels and grinning from ear to ear. The Englishman laughed again and, wagging his thumbs in front of the doctor's face, walked away swelled with triumph.

I glanced at Doctor Babu. Anger, revulsion, humiliation and despair struggled against each other on his face. He walked rapidly up to the men and said harshly, 'What are you grinning at, you rascals?'

At this a good measure of self-respect returned to our countrymen. They stopped laughing and, advancing aggressively, spoke as if in one voice, 'Who are *you* to call us rascals? Are we your servants that we have to take your permission before we laugh?'

I dragged Doctor Babu away, back to his own cabin. Holding his head between his hands he sank down on the bed. 'God,' he groaned, pulling savagely at his hair. Not another word could he utter.

At eleven o'clock the small steamer that was to carry the passengers to the dreaded quarantine docked alongside the ship.

Everyone got busy packing and getting his luggage together. I was in no hurry, for word had reached me that the doctor's clerk had agreed to sponsor me. As I stood idly on the deck watching the sailors at work, a voice spoke behind me. It was Abhaya's.

'Why haven't you packed?'

'I don't have to. I'm getting off at Rangoon.'

'You can't do that,' she said. 'You must come with me.'

'Impossible!' I exclaimed, astounded at her tone. 'I'm not going to the quarantine.'

'Then I'm not either,' she announced. 'I'd rather jump into the sea and drown. I've heard about it. It's a horrible place. I won't go there without you.'

I stood and stared at her.

'I didn't dream that you could be so cruel,' she continued, dabbing at her eyes with the edge of her sari. 'Come, get your things together. You know I have a sick man on my hands—you'll just have to come with me.'

I realized that Abhaya was involving me in her life to an extent that I had never sought. But I couldn't refuse her.

As the steamer glided away with me on board I saw Doctor Babu making frantic signs from the deck of the ship. 'You don't have to go,' he shouted waving his arms. 'Come back. You've been given permission.'

'Many thanks,' I yelled, 'but another command has come my way.'

The doctor's eyes fell on Abhaya and Rohini Babu. He smirked and added, 'Very good. But why did put me through the ordeal of getting you a sponsor?'

'I'm truly sorry. I beg forgiveness.'

'You are forgiven. Goodbye and good luck.'

And Doctor Babu waved a friendly hand in farewell.

Five

QUARANTINE, UNDER THE BRITISH REGIME, IS A FORM OF imprisonment fit only for the lowest of the low. And anyone who cannot pay more than the minimum ten rupees for a passage to Burma is automatically relegated to that category. And since such people have few or no possessions (thus the British mind analyses) it is perfectly in order that they carry their own luggage through the half-mile walk from the jetty to the encampment. Although I cannot disprove this logic, the reality of being off-loaded on the burning sands of a strange river with an alien sun raining its fiery beams on my head and the steaming air clogging my lungs, was too much for me. My fellow passengers, with the adaptability and resilience I have already admired, expertly shifted the heavier among their belongings on to the heads and backs of their women and, picking up an odd pot or a blanket, walked briskly to the encampment. Within minutes the three of us were left alone, staring at each other while our luggage, strewn in untidy piles, littered the shore.

Presently, Rohini Babu sank trembling on the sand and, leaning against a bundle, shut his eyes. Prolonged dysentery, fever and fatigue had reduced him to such a state that he could barely sit—let alone walk. Abhaya was a woman. Thus the only bridge between the encampment and the boxes and bundles that represented our worldly possessions was myself.

Although I'm quite sure that the more idealistic among my

readers will praise me to the skies for my selfless service to my fellowmen, I have to admit that anything but love and pity for Abhaya and Rohini Babu dominated my emotions of the moment. Self-disgust and self-pity were uppermost. I kept telling myself that no greater ass than myself was ever born on this planet. But what filled me with wonder was how Abhaya had unerringly picked me from a shipful of passengers to carry her loads when I looked just as human as anyone else.

A low laugh from Abhaya made me turn round and look at her. Worry, despair and extreme fatigue were marked on her countenance but her laughter rang out pure and clear. I was surprised. I had expected her to cringe before me in gratitude and humility for what was she, after all, but an ignorant village girl?

Instead she laughed again and said, 'If you think you are being shamelessly exploited you are quite wrong, Srikanta Babu. No one could have prevented you from going your own way. That you chose to come with me was owing to your own generosity. Not everyone gets an opportunity of proving their generosity to the world. You should thank me for providing you with one. But come, let's leave our things here for the present and carry Rohini Dada to the shed.'

I took the sick man on my back and proceeded to the quarantine camp. Abhaya followed, carrying what she could—a small tin box. The rest of our luggage was left where it lay but, fortunately, nothing was lost. We had it brought to us later the same day.

Looking back on the quarantine I'm forced to admit that the reality was much better than our expectations. Barring a few initial difficulties, life in the quarantine shed was not unendurable. This was almost entirely due to Abhaya's efforts and the fact that money can buy comfort even in hell. The doctor had called her 'forward' from the little he had seen of her in the boat. He had no idea of how 'forward' she could be when the need really arose. For all practical purposes my work was over the moment I deposited the sick man at the entrance of the encampment. After that she took over.

'You are tired and deserve a rest, Srikanta Babu,' she said! 'You've done your bit. Now *I'll* do what needs to be done.'

I *was* tired. My legs shook under me and the sweat ran in streams down my head and back. Nevertheless, I asked, 'What will you do?'

'Goodness! There's heaps of work. First I must send someone to fetch our luggage. Then I must get hold of a good room, get it cleaned, make the beds and cook a meal. No, no! Don't get up. I'll get everything organized in a few minutes.' Saying this she turned and walked purposefully in the direction of the quarantine office.

Within half an hour a chaprasi came and escorted us to the room in which we were to stay. I looked around and was pleasantly surprised. It was a fair-sized room, airy and well ventilated. A British lady doctor was getting it cleaned under her personal supervision. Two string-cots stood against the walls with bedding spread on them. Our luggage had arrived and was neatly stacked in one corner. Bags of rice and lentils, flour, potatoes, ghee and firewood and even new vessels for cooking, were piled in the other. Abhaya was talking energetically, in broken Hindi, to a South Indian doctor.

She turned on seeing us approach. 'Rest for a while,' she said. 'I'll have a quick bath and get a meal going. A rice and dal khichri will do for now.' She picked up her *gamchha* (indigenous towel) and sari and bowing deferentially to the lady doctor walked away with a sailor in tow.

The days of our quarantine, organized as they were by Abhaya, passed pleasantly enough. But, surprisingly, I didn't get to know her any better than I had on the boat. I noticed that her attitude to me had something contradictory in it. On the one hand she would not allow the slightest thread of intimacy to develop between us. Something about her manner stood stark and forbidding like a stone wall reminding me every moment that we were merely passengers in transit awaiting the arrival of our destinations and that, once there, we would be as nothing to one another. On the other, she looked after my creature comforts as tenderly as if I were the closest of relatives. She would take all the hardest tasks upon herself. If I offered to help, she would laugh and say, 'Let me do it. After all, I am responsible for the situation we are in. Neither you nor Rohini Dada would have been here if it weren't for me.' Her intelligence and capacity for action made me wonder at her husband. But I was certain that, once she found him, he would learn to value her. For, brute though he was, he was a man, and what man would spurn such an asset?

Then, one day, the quarantine was over. By the time we got

our permits, Rohini Babu was fully recovered and we set out together for Rangoon. It was decided that I would help them to find suitable accommodation before I went my way. I also promised Abhaya that I would try my best to seek out her husband.

The day of our arrival in Rangoon coincided with that of an important Burmese festival. The streets were thronged with votaries, dressed in bright silks, on their way to and from the temple. There was a predominance of women, for the Burmese do not confine their women to the zenana as we do in India. Old, young and middle aged were dressed alike in vibrant colours with flowers in their hair, behind their ears and around their necks. Many of them were beautiful with complexions of pale gold and luxurious hair falling well below the knees. They were all bareheaded and completely free in their movements. Laughing, chattering and singing, they surged up and down the streets like cascades of colour.

I was charmed. This is as it should be, I thought. I couldn't help comparing them to Indian women and wondering what we had gained by depriving them of the freedom that their Burmese sisters enjoyed. Were we any happier in our women than the Burmese men were in theirs? Could they spread the sweetness and light that the latter did so freely and spontaneously? 'Far from it,' I thought, with a stab of envy. 'If our women could only break their shackles and stand equal to men . . . .'

My train of thought was rudely interrupted by a commotion just behind me. I turned around. Three women had just descended from a carriage and were arguing with the coachman about the fare. The latter—an Indian Mussalman—kept repeating that he had asked for eight annas while the passengers insisted, loudly and harshly, that five annas was the fare they had settled. Within a few minutes the argument got beyond the verbal. Screaming with fury the three fair ladies darted to a barrow piled high with sugar cane and, snatching up lengths of cane, began raining blows on the hapless coachman's head and back. The poor man, unused to hitting out at women, tried to ward off the blows first with one arm then with the other while a crowd of spectators looked on interestedly. Off flew his turban as a blow descended, with a thwack, on his head. His whip clattered on the pavement and was crushed to splinters under the feet of the agitated ladies.

Finally, unable to bear it any longer, the man fled screaming, 'Police! Police!' while the crowd jeered and clapped their hands in appreciation.

Newly arrived from an obscure village of Bengal I had only heard of female emancipation—never seen it. I was amazed, for the idea that emancipation enabled women of decent families to attack a strong hulk of a man and beat him black and blue in full public view, had never entered my head. I was so shocked by what I had seen that I stood and stared blankly at the thinning crowd. Then, collecting myself with an effort, I went my way.

Six

I STAYED WITH ABHAYA AND ROHINI BABU FOR A COUPLE OF DAYS in their new lodgings before starting out to look for my own. I helped them to settle down as I had promised but the situation repelled me and I was eager to escape. I told myself, over and over again, that all may not be as it appears on the surface, and that intricate relationships of this type are often misunderstood. Did not my own past experience bear this out? Nevertheless, as I stepped out on to the streets of Rangoon one fine morning, I felt curiously free and light-hearted.

At the time that I'm writing about, Bengalis, newly arrived in Rangoon, were not hunted down as they are today to be cross-examined and humiliated by policemen in plain clothes and uniform. I remember that I wandered around all morning, then, bumping into a man who looked like a Bengali, I asked him the way to Nanda Mistri's house. The man stopped and scrutinized my face long and earnestly.

'Which Nanda?' he said at last. 'Are you looking for Nanda Pagodi of Ribit?'

'I'm not sure. He told me he was the famous Nanda Mistri of Rangoon.'

'Mistri!' the man made a face. 'Everyone calls himself a mistri these days. Do you know how many anonymous letters Bara Saheb got when Marcott Saheb said to me, "Haripada, you are the only worker who deserves to be called mistri"? A hundred. A hundred anonymous letters! But could they damage my reputation in the least? *Aré*, if you know how to hold a saw, if you can cut first and join afterwards—who can come in your way? But the trouble is—'

I realized that I had touched the man in a vulnerable spot and that he would continue to expatiate on the glories of being a true mistri for several hours if I didn't stop him.

'Then you don't know him—' I interrupted.

'Of course I know him. I've been in Rangoon these forty years. I know everybody. But there are three Nandas in Rangoon. Which one do you want?' Then peering into my face, he said, 'You are a newcomer aren't you? From Bengal? Oh! I know which Nanda. You want Tagar's man—don't you?'

'That's the one,' I said, relieved.

'Well! Come along with me, then. How can I help you if you don't give me the details?' he grumbled, then went on, 'He's lucky to be making a living—that Nanda. But to call himself a mistri—'

He then asked me my caste and, on learning that I was a Brahmin, stopped and touched my feet. 'Has Nanda promised you a job?' he asked curiously. 'Well! he may be able to find you one. But he'll expect two months' salary as commission. Can you manage that?'

I assured him that I was not seeking out Nanda in order to ask him for a job. 'He promised to find me a lodging,' I said. 'We came on the ship together.'

Haripada Mistri looked startled. 'Nanda promised to find you a place to stay? Where? You are a gentleman. Why don't you stay in the mess?'

'I don't know where it is.'

The man looked crestfallen. He didn't know either, he admitted, but he would make enquiries and let me have the information by evening. 'You won't find Nanda in his room at this hour. He'll be at the workshop. And Tagar will be sleeping with her door bolted. And,' he stopped and threw me a searching look, 'if you knock on her door and wake her up, all hell will break loose.'

I knew that quite well and was not prepared to risk it.

'Why don't you go to Da Thakur's place for the day?' the man urged. 'Have a bath, a meal and a good rest. You can meet Nanda in the evening.'

We reached the hotel around ten-thirty. About fifteen men of the working class were assembled in the dining-room to eat the first meal of their day. The hotel was located at one end of the city. On three sides of an enormous stretch of land, workshops and sheds stood in neat orderly lines. On the fourth, one in a row of wooden hutments, was Da Thakur's hotel. This area, known as the mistri *palli* (locality) of Rangoon, as I came to know later, was a curious place. A vast number of people—Chinese, Burmese, Madrasis, Oriyas, Mussalmans from Chattogram and Bengalis from Calcutta and its environs—lived squashed together in it and followed a variety of occupations. They appeared to be a homogeneous lot despite their squabbles and rivalries. It was by living among them that I first learned that what we call *samskar* is not founded upon rock and can easily be shed.

Two English words 'instinct' and 'prejudice' together make up the full meaning of the word *samskar*. One is not the other—that of course is obvious. That the strongest of our *samskars*—the caste bias—is not instinctive and can easily be overcome, was revealed to me that very first day at Da Thakur's hotel. I was amazed at the discovery. I realized that many of us, who wear the shackles of caste imposed upon us through centuries of mandatory compartmentalization, happily, even proudly, in the conviction that we are upholding and handing down to posterity worthwhile systems of thought and action, discard them with the greatest ease the moment we enter an area where they have no relevance. The belief that to go to England is to lose caste, because stepping on English soil and partaking of beef are inseparable, has been bred into us so thoroughly that we accept it without question. Not even the strictest vegetarian is exempted, for, as the guardians of Hinduism rigidly maintain, to eat or not to eat is one and the same. Yet ninety per cent of the passengers to Rangoon, Brahmins for the most part, (Brahmins being notoriously greedy in this age and time) have no qualms about eating hearty meals from the ship's kitchen before they set foot on Burmese soil. Do they ever question what is being served by the Mussalman and Goan cooks? Or if what they eat is kept at a careful distance from what is forbidden? If any of them had the courage to peep into the cold room of the ship, as I have done, they would have seen that everything from milk and bananas to pork and beef are piled indiscriminately, one on top of another. But let us not quarrel with our blessings. Let us be thankful rather, that the necessity for a codicil to include the passage to Burma among the areas of ostracism has not occurred to our caste killers as yet.

Da Thakur received me with great deference and, leading me to a little tumbledown shed, said, 'You may stay here as long as you like and have your meals in the hotel. You need not pay till you get yourself a job.'

'How do you know I won't disappear without paying? You are seeing me for the first time.'

Da Thakur touched his forehead and wagged his head solemnly. 'What will be will be. You cannot take my fate away with you. Can you?'

'No. I have no need of it,' I said.

That his implicit faith in his destiny was justified was amply proved when, four or five months later, he disappeared from Rangoon, taking away with him several hundred rupees, rings, watches and other valuables that his clients had entrusted to his safe keeping, leaving the latter to knock their heads on the empty floor of the hotel. But that was much later. For the present his words fell soothingly on my ears and his proposition, in view of my straitened circumstances, was like a boon from heaven.

At dusk, a young Bengali serving maid came into my room and, setting a square of matting and a glass of water on the floor, got ready to serve me my evening meal.

'Why do you serve me here?' I asked. 'Why not with the others in the dining-room?'

'They are mechanics, Babu,' she answered. 'How can you eat in their company?'

'Who knows what work I'll get? I may have to work as a mechanic myself. From tomorrow I'll eat in the dining-room.'

'You are a Brahmin. It is not proper for you to eat with them.'

'Why not?'

'They are Bengalis and Hindus—it is true. But there is a Dom among them.'

A Dom! In Bengal Doms are treated as untouchables. If you happen to touch one of them you are forced to bathe before entering the house. Even in the most flexible households a change of clothes and a dash of gangajal on the head is insisted upon.

'What about the others?' I asked.

'They are from better castes. There are Kayasthas, Sadgopes, Kamars, Goalas, and Kaibartas among them.'

'Don't they object to a Dom eating with them?'

The girl smiled. 'We are in Burma, Babu—seven seas away from our native land. Who cares to guard his caste here as carefully as in Bengal? Once they go back they'll take a dip in the Ganga and eat cow-dung as penance. Then all will be as it was.'

I did not doubt her words at the time. But, subsequently, I realized how wrong she was. Many years later, back in Bengal, I had the good fortune of seeing many Indians returning from Burma. Some of them did take a casual dip in the Ganga but not one—and I maintain, not one—took the trouble of eating cow-dung or performing any other kind of expiatory rite. It was obvious that their brief exposure to a foreign country and culture was sufficient to successfully wipe away the generations of conditioning with which they had gone. I noticed that there were two hookahs in the hotel—one for Brahmins, the other for non-Brahmins. The second one passed from the hand of a Karmakar to that of a Goala, from a Dom to a Sadgope with the utmost ease.

A couple of days after I arrived at the hotel I asked a Karmakar, 'Don't you lose caste by smoking the same hookah with a Dom?'

'Of course we do.'

'Then—'

'He didn't tell us he was a Dom when he first came. He said he was a Kaibarta—'

'But when you realized that he was a Dom—didn't you say anything?'

'What could we say? It was very wrong of him to have deceived us, but if we told him we knew the truth he would have died of shame. So we went on pretending we knew nothing.'

'Is such a situation possible in your native village?'

'Oh! no.' The man trembled at the thought. 'But you know what? Leaving Brahmins aside—they are *varna srestha* and there is no comparison—the other castes are not so different from one another. Who can tell the difference between a Nabasakh and a Dom or a Goala and a Sadgope? And, after all, we are all God's creatures. We've all left our homes and families and come out to this heathen land to earn our living. And if one goes by behaviour—Hari Mandal may be a Dom but he is honest and sober.

He doesn't touch ganja or liquor. And look at the Kayastha Lakshman! If we hadn't saved him he would have been serving a sentence. What good would his high caste have done him then? He would have had to eat at the hands of sweepers.'

The man went his way leaving me wondering at the psyche of the expatriate Hindu. How could a land like ours, in which even the educated upper class devoted itself almost exclusively to seeking out and exposing the weaknesses of others, produce men like the Karmakar and his fellows—men who were liberal enough to forgive an errant colleague for robbing them of their caste, and sensitive enough to empathize with his shame and sorrow? The secret lay, no doubt, in their movement away from the stagnant cesspools of their native villages and their efforts to build a future in a land where caste is unknown. 'Mental mobility is the natural sequel of physical mobility,' I thought, 'and together they could be the making of our people.'

I did, however, find a distinct absence of the former in one area. The distrust of the lower classes for the educated upper class is as firmly embedded in the consciousness of the Rangoon mechanic as it is in that of his social equal in India. I have lived among these people for many years and have marvelled at this inconsistency. As long as they thought me an uneducated worker like themselves, they treated me like a friend and involved themselves in my welfare. But the moment they realized that I was educated and knew English, they withdrew silently but surely. They still came to me for advice but they didn't love me or trust me because the conviction that I, as a member of the educated upper class, despised them, had remained unshaken. It was this obsessive fear in them that frustrated me in many of my endeavours for their upliftment and welfare.

Yet, many women whose antecedents were cloaked in mystery were allowed to live with their families in the mistri *palli* and become part of the mainstream. Their children, when questioned about their caste, declared they were Bengalis. By this they meant that they were Hindu—not Muslims or Christians. When these children married, usually others like themselves, Brahmin pandits from Chattogram performed the ceremony. There were widows too among the women, who did not live the life of harsh abstinence that is the norm in Bengal. They did not marry (perhaps the pandits shrank from sponsoring such unholy unions, even in Burma) but they lived openly with their protectors and bore their children. The latter grew up with no stigma attached to them and when they married, pandits performed the ceremony without a demur. Only under the most severe stress did a woman change her protector, for such a change was looked down upon as unworthy and shameful in the mis tri *palli*. Treating her relationship as irrevocable, she performed all the customary rites for the welfare of her family with no less devotion than the purest of wedded wives in Bengal.

Seven

$\mathcal{A}$S LUCK WOULD HAVE IT ABHAYA AND ROHINI BABU, WITH
WHOM I had shared all the ups and downs of the sea trip and the
quarantine, were left behind at one end of the city while I took up
my quarters in the other. Thus, it was a good fortnight before I saw
them again. During that period I had occupied myself in a zealous,
though fruitless, search for employment. All day I ran around in
circles coming back late at night, bones aching with exhaustion.
When I had almost reached the conclusion that jobs are no less
elusive in Burma than they are in Bengal, I suddenly thought of
Rohini. He was worse off than I was for, knowing rural Bengal as I
did, I realized that he did not have the option I had—of going back.
They had little money between them, most of which had already
been spent. The only course left to him was taking up a job and,
as I had seen from my own experience, that was easier said than
done. Simple and childlike as well as burdened with the care of a
woman, he had even less of a chance than I had of securing one. I
felt worried and decided to go and see them the very next day. It
was evening by the time I stepped into the compound of the tiny
house that they had rented. Rohini Dada was seated on a stool in
the front veranda, his face dark and ominous.

'Srikanta Babu!' he said without much enthusiasm. 'How are
you?'

'I am well,' I replied. 'And you?'

'Well enough. Why don't you go in? She's in her room.'

'I'll do that but why don't you come too?'

'I would prefer to sit here for a while. I work hard enough all day to kill myself. I need a rest.'

Though there were no signs of an imminent death on his countenance I felt perplexed and faintly disturbed. I had never seen him like this before. On the boat and in the quarantine camp he had seemed passive and gentle. I wondered where he had hidden this gravity and self-importance all those days. As for working hard enough to kill himself—what did that mean? Was he, like me, dragging his feet all over the streets of Rangoon looking for work?

As I stood hesitating on the steps, Abhaya's face appeared from behind the door. She smiled and beckoned me to follow her.

'Come, Rohini Dada,' I said, a little uncomfortably. 'Let's sit inside and have a chat.'

'A chat!' Rohini exclaimed bitterly. 'Do you know what I wish for most urgently at this moment? Death!'

I had to confess I hadn't known when Abhaya's face appeared again. This time I followed her inside. It was a tiny house with two rooms and a kitchen. The front room, the larger of the two, was Rohini Dada's. As I stepped inside, the first thing I saw was a *thala* (plate) piled with *luchi* (puffed pancakes), fried vegetables and halwa, set before asan and a brass tumbler of water. Even the most determined optimism could not prompt me into imagining that Abhaya had made these arrangements in anticipation of my arrival.

I realized that some sort of quarrel was in progress.

'How long you have been in coming, Srikanta Babu!' Abhaya said plaintively. 'Had you forgotten our existence?'

I sat on the bed and pointed to the *thala*. 'What does that mean?' I asked.

Abhaya smiled and shook her head. 'It is nothing,' she said. 'Tell me, how have you been?'

I was silent for a few moments. 'I really can't say,' I said, at last, 'Rohini Dada just said—'

Before I could complete my sentence, Rohini Babu walked in, his torn slippers clattering on the wooden floor. Without glancing at anyone he walked straight to the tumbler of water and put it to his lips. Then, setting it down with a bang, he went out muttering, 'Does anyone care if I'm hungry or thirsty? I am all alone in this alien land, Srikanta Babu. I have no one of my own to feed me and look after me.'

I glanced at Abhaya. Her cheeks were flushed with embarrassment and her eyes glittered. But her voice, when she spoke was calm and detached. 'If you were truly hungry you would have picked up the *thala* and not the tumbler.'

Rohini Babu pretended not to hear. He went out but came back in half a minute. Then, addressing himself to me, he said, 'I work so hard at the office all day that, by evening my head starts swimming with fatigue and hunger. This is why I couldn't converse with you when you came in. You must forgive me, Srikanta Babu.'

'Certainly,' I answered.

'Can you arrange for me to stay at your lodgings, Srikanta Babu?'

I couldn't help laughing at his expression. 'I can,' I said, 'but they don't serve *luchi* and halwa.'

'I can do without all that,' Rohini answered. 'When one is hungry a glass of water and *gur* (jaggery) is food for the gods. There is no one here to give me even that.'

I looked questioningly at Abhaya. She shook her head and said softly, 'I had a headache and fell asleep in the afternoon. So my cooking got delayed and I was a few minutes late in serving his meal.'

I was so shocked that I exclaimed aloud, 'Is that an offence?'

'That is a serious offence, Srikanta Babu,' Abhaya said, deliberately. 'Not to you, perhaps, but certainly to him who feeds and clothes a woman. Why should he not extract his comfort to the last degree if he is paying for them?'

Rohini reared up like a wounded snake. 'Have I ever said that I feed and clothe you?'

'You don't need to say it. You make it obvious in so many ways.'

'I! I make it obvious! Oh my God! Did you tell me you had a headache?'

'Suppose I had? Would you have believed me?'

Rohini Babu turned to me and said, 'This is the way she talks to me all the time. And it was for her that I left my village and family. What am I today? A tramp, a wanderer with no home and no country. I—'

'You need not concern yourself about me anymore,' Abhaya said angrily. 'Go back home whenever you wish. Why should you suffer these agonies for my sake? Who am I to you? I would much rather fend for myself than hear your taunts day in and day out.'

Rohini Dada could bear it no longer. His voice broke and tears rushed to his eyes as he screamed incoherently, 'Listen to her, Srikanta Babu. Just listen to her. All this insulting talk—for a bit of cooking! I forbid you ... if you dare enter the kitchen—I'll eat in a hotel. I swear I will,' and, pressing the edge of his dhoti to his trembling mouth, he rushed out of the room.

Abhaya's face grew pale. She bowed her head in an effort, I'm convinced, to hide her tears.

Suddenly, the truth was crystal clear. Whatever they were quarrelling about had nothing to do with Abhaya's headache or the meal getting delayed. The cause of Rohini Babu's grievance and Abhaya's indignation lay deeper, far deeper, than that. I guessed that it was connected with Abhaya's determination to seek out her husband.

I stood up. Breaking the silence I began, 'I have a long way to go—'

'When will you come again?' Abhaya lifted a tense white face.

'I live very far away and—'

'Then wait a minute.' Abhaya rose and went into the inner room. Returning in a few minutes she pressed a piece of paper into my hand and said, 'I came to Burma with a definite purpose, as you know, and you promised to help me. Go through the note and do the best you can.' Saying this she knelt on the floor and touched my feet with her forehead. Before I could recover from my surprise she rose and said in a matter-of-fact tone, 'Can you give me your address?' I gave it to her, then gripping the note in my palm, I walked out of the room.

The veranda was deserted. Rohini Dada was nowhere to be seen. My curiosity was so great that I couldn't wait till I reached the hotel. Entering a dilapidated tea-shop I ordered a cup of tea and opened the note before a flickering oil lamp. It was written in pencil in a bold masculine hand. Giving her husband's name and address Abhaya had written: *I know that you have guessed the truth about us. I also know that I trust you and depend on you. That is why I asked for your address.*

I read these lines again and again but could make nothing of them. That she was intelligent enough to appreciate my intelligence had been obvious from the start. That she depended on me had been obvious, too. She had given me her husband's name and address on the boat. Why did she put it down again? And what was the cryptic message all about? Did she want me to look for her husband or didn't she? And why had she asked for my address? From Rohini's conversation I gathered that he had found himself a job—a job lucrative enough to enable them to eat *luchi* and halwa. Their financial problems were obviously at an end. Did she, then, foresee some new trouble and had sought my help in anticipation? All this and much more went round and round my head all the way home. One thing, alone, was clear. I was *not* to seek out Abhaya's husband, however great my curiosity, till I was expressly commanded to do so.

The days went by but my luck did not change. The beaming countenance of the deterministic Da Thakur did, however, gradually assume the hues of deep gloom. My meals first degenerated in quality, then got depleted in quantity. But Fortune eluded me, determinedly, deliberately. I grew frustrated—even frightened. Then, one day, I realized why Fate had favoured Rohini Babu and not me.

One morning, as I was passing through the market-place, I saw Rohini Babu buying grocery and vegetables. His shoes were broken and dusty and his clothes, grubby and worn with many years of service, hung from his emaciated frame. But one glance was enough to tell me that he was buying the best produce of the market and that too in generous quantities. I watched him from a distance as he went from stall to stall examining each item carefully, deliberating, then making his choice. The tenderness and devotion, the impulse to cherish and nurture that lay behind his effort to take home only the best, was as clear as the white-hot light that streamed from the Burmese sky. As he walked out of the market, staggering under the load of provisions, his thin, perspiring face glowed with an inner light. I knew, then, as I had never known before, why he had managed to make a living in this alien land while I hadn't. He had succeeded because he had *had* to succeed. I had only myself to look after and my efforts were attuned to that alone. He had another—far more valued and beloved than himself.

Tears welled up in my eyes as I watched Rohini Babu's frail form melt away. Wiping them on my sleeve I directed my steps homeward, marvelling all the while at the strength and endurance that flows from a true devotion. But the conditioning of centuries was not to be subdued. It rose like a cloud of moths fluttering urgently within me. 'No! No!' a voice breathed in harsh whispers. 'This love is illicit, impure. No good can come of it.'

As soon as I reached the hotel a large envelope was handed to me. Opening it I found that I had been offered a post in a reputed timber firm of Rangoon. Relief swept over me but it was mixed with a little apprehension. I had never worked before so I had no idea of what it meant, in practical terms. I was doubtful, too, of being able to retain the job for any length of time.

But my fears proved to be totally unfounded. My boss, though an Englishman, spoke fluent Bengali and was very affable. Within a fortnight he said to me, 'Srikanta Babu, from tomorrow you will work at another table and your salary will be raised by a hundred and fifty per cent.'

I thanked him profusely, in relief and happiness at the turn of events. As I shifted my files from my rickety table to a solid one of Burma teak covered with green baize, I thought of Da Thakur and his faith in Providence. I had laughed at him, not dreaming that I, myself, would prove a glowing example of his philosophy and that too in a few days.

In my new found state of prosperity I hired a carriage one evening and went to Abhaya to give her the good news. It was the same hour of evening and Rohini Babu, just back from work, was sitting down to a lavish meal. I was invited to join him, and I accepted with alacrity for the food looked and smelt delicious.

As soon as he had eaten Rohini Babu got ready to go out again. Abhaya watched him in sullen silence as he put on his shirt, then burst out angrily, 'Why do you insist on doing these tuitions? We don't need any more money. We have enough to live on.'

Rohini turned to her with a smile, 'I can't afford to keep a cook for you and you say that we have enough to live on.' And, stuffing a paan into his mouth, he went out.

Abhaya suppressed a sigh and, turning to me, said in a sombre voice, 'I'm afraid for him, Srikanta Babu. He isn't strong and all this hard work is telling on his health. But he doesn't listen to a word I say. He really believes that cooking for two is killing me.'

I smiled but did not comment.

After a while Abhaya went to her room and came back with a letter which she handed to me. Opening it I found that it was from the Burma Rail Company. The manager regretted to inform Abhaya that her husband's services had been terminated two years ago upon his committing a grave offence and that the company had no knowledge of his present occupation or address. We sat in silence for a long while.

Then Abhaya asked, 'What do you advise me to do?'

'Who am *I* to advise you?'

'Don't say that,' Abhaya burst out passionately. 'You cannot shrug off your responsibilities so easily. You are the only one here to whom I can turn. Ever since I received the letter I've waited for you to come.'

'You have some cheek,' I thought to myself, 'to land yourself in this mess and then involve me in it!' Aloud I said, 'Have you considered going back?'

'No. I can, if you want me to. But where do I go and to whom? I have no one of my own.'

'What about Rohini Babu? What are his plans?'

'He refuses to leave Burma—for another ten years at least.'

Another stretch of silence. I broke it with a question. 'Will he undertake to look after you for all time to come?'

'How do I know?' She reflected for a few moments and added, 'Even he—how can he be sure? But I would like you to get one thing clear. He is not responsible for what I did. Coming to Burma was *my* decision—only mine.'

At this point the carriage driver called out, 'How much longer must I wait, Babu?'

I stood up, relieved to be able to escape. 'I'll come again, very soon,' I said as I stepped into the carriage. I had hardly gone ten yards when I realized that I had left my walking-stick behind in Rohini Babu's room. I stopped the carriage and retraced my steps.

As I crossed the veranda, I found Abhaya lying in a heap on the floor—her body shaking with sobs. I stood quietly for a few moments—a mute witness to the agony that tore her apart—then walked out of the house.

Eight

T HOUGH I HAD HAD EVERY INTENTION OF REDEEMING MY
PROMISE to Rajlakshmi, to write to her as soon as I reached Burma,
I had not done it so far. Letter writing was a task I dreaded as a
rule. Besides, I had nothing interesting to tell her. But Abhaya's
pain lay so heavy on my heart, tonight, that I longed to ease the
burden by sharing it with someone. And who else was there for
me but Pyari? Consequently, the moment I reached home, I took
out pen and paper and wrote a long letter to her. I was sensible
of being disloyal to Abhaya as I conveyed the intimate details of
her life to another woman. But my curiosity to hear Rajlakshmi's
opinion of her was so great that it swamped all my finer feelings.
I reasoned that since Rajlakshmi had passed through a similar
ordeal herself when she had to choose between Banku and me,
she and not I was the right person to advise Abhaya.

A few days later a file was placed on my table with instructions
from the manager to handle the case. On going through the
papers I found that it was a case of theft. A Bengali clerk from
the Prome branch of our company had been caught stealing
timber and had been suspended. When I read the name I was
astounded, for it was Abhaya's husband's. While I sat wondering
what to do a Burmese clerk informed me that a gentleman was
waiting outside with a request for an interview. I had expected
this, knowing well enough that Abhaya's husband would not be
content with merely representing his case but would come from
Prome to Rangoon to follow it up.

I watched him closely as he shuffled in and sat in a chair opposite me. He was a big hulk of a fellow dressed in a suit and hat so grimy and worn that they threatened to fall to pieces any moment. Dark, heavy jowls were rendered darker by the masses of greasy black hair that grew over them. Thick lips—the lower one an inch and a half deep—were black with years of tobacco chewing. Even as he sat facing me, paan juice trickled from the corners of his mouth and ran down his chin in slimy streams.

I had been reared in a tradition that exhorted a woman to revere her husband as her God. But, try as I would, I couldn't bear to think of Abhaya in connection with this animal. Abhaya, whatever she may have done, was sensitive and refined and this creature looked and behaved like a buffalo that had strayed in from some tropical swamp of innermost Burma.

I asked him if he admitted his guilt. In answer he spluttered and gesticulated so wildly that the spray from his mouth threatened to drench my shirt. I pushed my chair back and repeated my question. His defence, as far as I was able to make out, was that he was as innocent as the babe unborn; that the real thief was his British officer; that this officer wanted his own man on the job and had, for that reason, devised an elaborate plot to remove him from office. Needless to say, I didn't believe a word.

'You are, to take you on your own valuation,' I said at last, 'a very competent and honest official. Since that is so, why does the loss of this clerkship mean so much to you? A man like you can have the best of jobs. There are not many like you in Burma.'

The man looked visibly taken aback. He hesitated for a few minutes, then said incoherently, 'You are right, but you know how it is! I'm a family man—many kids—you understand?'

'Are you married to a Burmese woman?'

'Why? How do you know? Has that British bastard written that in his report? Do you believe him?' He stood up, agitated.

I signalled to him to sit down and observed calmly, 'There's no need to get excited. What's wrong with marrying a Burmese woman?'

'Exactly! What's wrong with marrying a Burmese woman? I'm not afraid. What I do, I do boldly. I'm a man and I need a woman. And it isn't as if I have anyone back home in the village. And, after all, this is where I live and work. And this is where I shall go on living. You get me, don't you?'

I nodded my head as if to say I did but went on to ask, 'You have no one of your own in India?'

'Not a soul. If I had, would I have spent the best years of my life in this heathen land? No one at all—you understand? I was born into a wealthy and reputed family—a line of zamindars. My ancestral home still stands. It would dazzle your eyes to look at it—even today. But Fate was against me. My family got wiped out. I was young and sentimental—I couldn't bear to live alone. So I gave up my property rights and came away to Burma.'

'Do you know Abhaya?' I asked suddenly.

The man was shocked into silence. His face paled beneath the filth encrusted on it. He asked, haltingly, 'How do you know her?'

'It could be that she has come to Burma to look for you and has appealed to the company for maintenance—'

'Oh! So that's how it is,' he sounded relieved. 'I admit that she was my wife—once.'

'Now—'

'Now she has forfeited her rights. I have left her.'

'What was her offence?'

The man pulled a long face and whined mournfully, 'There are some matters—you understand? It is best to keep them within the family. But you are more to me than the closest of relations so I don't mind telling you. She's an immoral woman. Immoral and depraved. In fact that's the reason for my leaving my country and living the life of an exile all these years.'

I felt so revolted I couldn't look him in the face. I realized that Abhaya's husband was not only a liar and a thief—he was the scum of the earth; a thoroughbred scoundrel with no conscience and no heart.

'You did not announce this when you came away. You even wrote to her and sent her money for several months—'

The villain opened a vast cavern of a mouth and grinned. 'Well! You know how it is. Upper class people like us are fated to suffer in silence. I couldn't proclaim my wife's infidelity to the world like a low-caste peasant. Anyway, let's not relive unpleasant memories. It makes me sick to even utter her name. About this case. I cannot tell you how relieved I am you are in charge, Srikanta

Babu. But there is one thing that I shall insist upon. That white rascal of an Englishman must not be let off lightly. He must be taught such a lesson that he won't dare trifle with me again. Can't you get the swine transferred to the head office?'

'No,' I answered shortly.

The accused laughed and pushed the file towards me. 'That's a joke,' he said. 'Everyone knows that you have the manager under your thumb. I made all the necessary enquiries before I came. Anyhow, how you deal with him is your business. I'd like to catch the nine o'clock train back to Prome. Can you arrange to let me have the manager's order reinstating me before that?'

I was silent for a while. It is difficult to counteract flattery even when one is convinced that it springs from base and selfish motives. But I steeled myself and said coldly, 'The manager's order is not going to help you. You had better start looking for another job.'

The man's jaw sagged. 'What do you mean?'

'I mean that I'm going to recommend your dismissal from the company.'

He stood up, then sat down again folding his hands with exaggerated humility. 'Save me, Babu,' he said in a nasal whine. 'I have many children. They'll die of starvation.'

'I'm not responsible for them. Besides, I don't know you. I cannot accept your word against your superior officer's.'

His rheumy eyes stared into mine as it dawned on him at last that I meant exactly what I said. Then he burst into a fit of sobbing so loud and piteous that the office clerks, the darwan and the peon started up from their seats and crowded at the door.

I was startled and acutely embarrassed but I managed to say coldly, 'Please pull yourself together. Abhaya has come to Burma for your sake. Go to her. I don't ask you to take back an immoral wife, but if she forgives you after hearing the truth—the whole truth—get a letter from her. I'll try to help you retain your job. If not, do not embarrass me by coming to me again.'

I knew the psychology of men of his type. The male chauvinist and bully is invariably lily-livered and feeble at heart. A tremor passed over his vast bulk as he wiped his eyes and asked, 'Where does she live?'

'Come back tomorrow at the same time and I will give you her address.'

He rose and with an obsequious salaam left the room.

Abhaya sat pale and silent as I narrated the events of the day. I waited for some response, but when nothing was forthcoming I asked, 'Can you forgive him?'

She nodded.

'If he offers to take you back—are you ready to go?'

Another nod.

'You have seen what Burmese women are like. Do you have the courage to make your home with one of them?'

Abhaya raised a streaming face. Her lower lip trembled so violently that she couldn't speak for a while. Then she wiped her eyes and, clearing her throat with an effort, said, 'What else can I do?'

I suddenly found myself at a loss. I did not know if I should rejoice at her decision or shed tears over it. All the way back home I wrestled with myself trying to examine my feelings. But no matter how hard I tried I could come to no conclusion. My heart grew heavy and cold and a bitter hatred—of whom or what I could not say—pulsed and pounded in my brain. When the man came again, the next day, I did not even glance at him. He may have guessed how I felt, for he picked up the slip of paper that bore Abhaya's address without a word and, salaaming humbly, left the room.

But when he reappeared the next day all his familiar garrulity was back. Laying Abhaya's letter on the table he said, 'I can't thank you enough, Srikanta Babu. I'll never forget your kindness. As long as I live I shall remain your devoted slave.'

'Go back to your job,' I said with an indifference I was far from feeling. 'The manager has forgiven you.'

He smiled, displaying rows of large red teeth. 'I don't worry about the manager. All I ask for is your forgiveness. I have erred grievously—I admit it,' and he burst into a passionate speech so long and involved that I prefer not to strain my reader's patience by repeating it word for word. The long and short of it was that his account of his wife's infidelity was totally false; that a wife as chaste and pure as his was not to be found anywhere in the world; that he had always loved Abhaya above everyone else—even himself—and would do his duty by her. Only, this fresh complication in his life—he had never desired marriage with a local woman but had been forced into it by circumstances—had to be sorted out first. But that would not take long. He was taking Abhaya to Prome tonight and would have the Burmese slut out of the house, bag and baggage, by the day after tomorrow. As for the children—ugly, vicious brats—what use would they ever be to him? Would they feed him and clothe him in his old age or perform the proper rites over his body? No, he didn't give a damn for any of them and would drive them out of the house without a qualm.

'Are you taking Abhaya away tonight?' I asked.

'Certainly. Certainly. It was different when she was out of sight. Now that I have found her I refuse to stay away from her even for a moment. What a jewel of a wife she is! She came all the way to Burma for my sake. Have you ever seen a devotion to match that, Srikanta Babu?'

'Do you intend to keep the two woman together?'

'Oh! no. I shall take Abhaya to the postmaster's house. She'll be quite comfortable there. The postmaster's wife is a kind woman and will look after her. But only for two days. Then I'll instal the goddess of my home and hearth where she belongs—here,' and he touched his chest with an extravagant gesture.

After his departure I picked up Abhaya's letter and read the two lines she had penned, over and over again. I don't know how many hours I passed in this occupation but it seemed only a minute before the clock struck the half hour after four o'clock, and the peon stood respectfully at the door waiting to lock up.

Nine

$\mathcal{I}$ RECEIVED A LETTER FROM ABHAYA'S HUSBAND BEFORE THE MONTH was out. The first half of the letter was packed with fulsome praise of me and innumerable expressions of gratitude. The second contained a flood of invective against Abhaya.

The gist of the matter was this. Abhaya's husband had rented a big house, far beyond his means, with the intention of keeping his Burmese wife and children in one part of it and Abhaya in the other. But Abhaya, far from being overwhelmed with gratitude, had refused to leave the postmaster's protection. He had begged and pleaded but to no avail. Her disobedience and disregard of her husband's wishes had cut him to the heart. He was convinced that irreverence of this kind was being bred by the values of the world in which we lived. Oh! To have been born in the age of truth—the great *satya yuga* in which Sita and Savitri had lived—in which women walked smiling into the funeral pyres of their husbands and were engulfed by the flames even in the act of clasping their dead lords' feet to their bosoms! An age in which women carried husbands rotting with syphilis to the houses of favoured prostitutes—their faces radiant with happiness. Ah! Where had that world vanished? Where were the Aryan women of old? Where was that blind unquestioning obedience to a husband's wishes; the stubborn identification that made a woman glory in her position as shadow to her lord and master's substance? Ah! India. To what depths art thou fallen! All this and much more he wrote, filling four-and-a-half pages. He ended with the regret that Abhaya had trampled on his heart in more ways than one. Not only had she refused to move into her husband's house—she had been receiving letters and even money from one Rohini Sinha.

Although the epistle afforded me more amusement that I had had in years I couldn't help feeling a measure of annoyance at Rohini Babu's interference. After all Abhaya had come all the way to join her husband. Their relationship had yet to establish itself. In her state of doubt and bewilderment, when she needed all the help and support her friends could give her, why was he confusing and discouraging her?

And Abhaya too—what was she thinking of? Why did she go away with her husband if she had had no intention of living with him? If she expected him to abandon his existing family she was not being very fair. He had married the woman after all and fathered her children. Did she imagine that Burmese women had no feelings? Were they not justified in claiming maintenance? And, anyway, if that was her condition she should have clarified it right from the start.

That afternoon, just as I was about to leave, the peon brought me another letter—this time from Abhaya. It was a strange communication for it contained no reference to herself or her new life. But every line of it breathed her concern and fear for Rohini Babu's welfare. Reminding me of his ill health she requested me, over and over again, to look after him for there was not a soul in the world more desolate and unhappy. That this passionate plea was wrung from a heart sick with yearning was not difficult to guess. In the last line of her letter she briefly informed me that she was still living in the postmaster's house.

As I sat with the letter in my hand I was aware of a strange sensation. I felt as though I were, once again, in the presence of a chastity as dazzling and awesome as that of Annada Didi's. The wonder that had always accompanied the thought of Annada Didi's magnificent conquest of sorrow, degradation, injustice and isolation was upon me in an instant. 'There is something phenomenal about a woman's chastity,' I thought. 'It elevates her far above the reach of a man on the one hand and renders her weak and vulnerable on the other.' I was aware, of course, that I was confusing issues. Men learned in the Shastras would tell me that a woman's fidelity is the sole prerogative of a wedded husband. I had neither the capacity nor the heart to argue.

I had not visited Rohini Babu after Abhaya's departure, chiefly out of a desire to avoid seeing his misery. But after reading the two letters I decided to go to him that very evening and scold him heartily for cherishing a secret adulterous passion for another man's wife. As I knocked on the door it fell open revealing a room shadowy with twilight. The lamp had not been lit but a faint smoke haze hung in the air. The doors and windows were wide open and the shutters rattled in the breeze.

I walked a few steps and peeped into the kitchen. A column of smoke curled upwards from the hearth at one end, and at the other, a basket of vegetables by his side, sat Rohini Babu—his hand arrested in the act of slicing a brinjal. I could see at a glance that it was not the sound of my footsteps that had made him freeze like that for he did not even turn his head. I waited a few moments—then tiptoed back into the room. As I stood uncertainly in the smoky dusk I felt the presence of an overwhelming sorrow within those walls—a sorrow that brimmed over the bounds of conventions, ethics and morals. It rose from the room like a cloud of fog and, growing thicker and more impenetrable every minute, enveloped me where I stood. I had to escape. Groping my way out of the room I sank down on the stool in the veranda.

After a while I heard someone moving about inside the room. A voice called from within, 'Who is there?'

'I'm Srikanta.'

'Srikanta Babu?' Rohini Dada came forward eagerly, a lighted taper in his hand. Clutching my arm he led me back into the room.

We sat in silence for a while, then I said, 'Don't go on staying here, Rohini Dada. Let me take you to my hotel.'

'Why?' Large, innocent eyes shone out of a lined face.

'You are not happy here.'

'I'm happy enough,' he answered with a faint smile.

I had no answer. I had come with the intention of jerking him out of his abject self-surrender, of exhorting him to fight his weakness and conquer it like a man. But, in the presence of his all-consuming love, my anger and scorn melted away.

'I've given up the tuition,' he continued. 'It was too much for me. But the work in my office is terribly strenuous. I get quite tired by the evening. Otherwise—I'm all right.'

I listened quietly, remembering the day he had said just the opposite, when he had turned a deaf ear to Abhaya's pleas and dashed off to his tuition. He had been warmed, then, by the thought of keeping Abhaya in greater comfort. A machine needs fuel, I thought sadly. It cannot run on water. I repeated my offer of taking him to Da Thakur's hotel but he refused. I realized that he couldn't bear the thought of breaking up the household he and Abhaya had built together. Not that he cherished any hope of things ever being as they had been. He stayed on only for the sake of the memories that breathed all around him for they, alone, could sustain him and keep him whole—painful though they were. To leave these protecting walls would be, for him, equal to embracing annihilation.

As I stepped into my room late that night I noticed a man sleeping on the floor against one wall. I asked the maid who he was and she answered that he was a gentleman, meaning that he was not a mechanic or a coolie. I understood, now, why Da Thakur had installed him in my room.

We got acquainted after dinner. He had come, he said, from Chittagong in search of his younger brother who had left home four years ago. Only a few weeks back the family had heard that he was in Rangoon and was living with a Burmese woman. 'You've heard about the women of Kamrup,' he asked, 'the ones who change men into sheep? Burmese women are no less dangerous from what I hear. You must help me rescue my brother from the woman's clutches.'

I promised to do what I could and, with that noble intention, I made my way the next morning to the younger brother's house. On reaching it I discovered that it was his Burmese wife's ancestral home and that she was an orphan with a young sister. The young man was out on his morning promenade and the two girls and their maids were making cheroots—these being the source of their livelihood. The older sister received me with great deference. She thought, no doubt, that being a Bengali, I was a relative of her husband.

Burmese women are exceedingly industrious while the men are invariably lazy and shiftless. Since women are the principal breadwinners (and domestic servants of course) it is important for them to obtain a measure of education. Men, on the other hand can be as illiterate as they please as there is no pressure on them to provide for their families. The sight of a man living on his wife's income and frittering away his time in idle pursuits is a general one. Society does not condemn him. Neither does his wife. On the contrary, that is by and large the norm for men in Burma.

The young master of the house arrived within a few minutes. He was dressed in impeccable English attire. Rings gleamed on his fingers and a heavy watch and chain hung from his waistcoat. His Burmese wife left her work and, rising from her seat, relieved him of his hat and stick. Her sister fetched cigars and matches while the maids hurried inside to prepare tea and paan.

'Lucky fellow!' I thought. 'They treat him like a king.' I knew the man's name, but have forgotten it since. It may have been Charu or something like that.

He asked me who I was and when I told him I was a friend of his brother he shook his head in disbelief. 'You look as though you are from Calcutta, and my brother has never left Chittagong in his life. How do you know him?'

I told him that his brother had come to Rangoon with the intention of taking him back and that he was, even now, eagerly waiting to cast his anguished eyes on his long lost brother.

The next morning a tearful reconciliation took place in Da Thakur's hotel followed by a lengthy confabulation conducted chiefly in whispers. Thereafter, the younger brother appeared at the hotel morning, noon and night. Some conspiracy was obviously afoot. Three or four days later I got the first inkling of what it was. We had been invited, the day before, to drink a cup of tea in the Burmese woman's drawing-room and it was then that I first got a chance to talk to her. I found her a gentle, exceedingly humble creature, wholeheartedly devoted to the Bengali youth she loved and lived with. So when I was informed by my room-mate that they proposed to leave for Chittagong on the first boat available, my heart missed a beat.

'Your brother will return to Burma, will he not?' I asked, rather frightened.

'Heavens! No. The idea!'

'Have you told the girl?'

'If we do the whole clan will descend on us like a swarm of

locusts.' Then, winking broadly, he added, 'French leave, *moshai,*[*]
French leave.'

'It will make the girl very unhappy.' I said, acutely depressed.

The man laughed till tears came to his eyes. Then, controlling
himself with an effort, he said, 'Unhappy! Burmese women are
filthy, casteless whores. She'll catch another man before the boat
leaves the harbour. The sluts eat *neppi* (a pickle of decomposed
fish called *guanpi*) and stink to high heaven. They are not like our
women, *moshai*. Unhappy indeed!'

'Stop it!' I cried suddenly. 'You forget that she has fed and
clothed your brother and kept him like a king for the last four
years. Isn't there such a thing as common gratitude?'

The man's face flushed. He said in strident tones, 'You
surprise me, *moshai*! Young men must sow their wild oats.
Which son of a bastard doesn't? My brother's case is a little
more complicated than normal. I admit it. But must he be made
to sacrifice his future for a trifling error committed in the heat
of youth? Does he not have a country and a family? Is it not
important that he returns to them, marries, begets children and
becomes a respectable member of society? People get away
with far more serious offences. Some men I know have even
eaten fowl when they were young and headstrong. With age
and wisdom they have admitted their folly. We, as older men,
should forgive and forget. Therein lies our greatness. Think over
what I have said without passion or bias and then tell me if I'm
right or wrong.'

I was so taken aback at his assumption that eating fowl was
a more serious offence than exploiting an innocent girl's love and
then abandoning her, that I was rendered speechless. It being
time for me to leave for work I went away without another word.

When I returned that evening the gentleman beamed at me.
'I've been thinking over what you said. You were right. We ought
to prepare the girl or she might create a scene and stop him from
going. I don't trust these flat-nosed bitches. They are shameless
and depraved with no sense of right or wrong. More like animals
than human beings!'

I approved of his decision but something told me that this was

---

[*] A term of courtesy used for men.

part of a bigger conspiracy. I came to know only on the afternoon of their departure—as we were waiting for the ship to leave—how senselessly cruel and shamelessly selfish it was. It being a Sunday and having nothing better to do, I walked across to the harbour to see the brothers off.

Among the people who were assembled at the jetty with a similar end in view stood the Burmese girl holding her little sister by the hand. Her eyes were red with weeping and every line of her white face bore the marks of an inconsolable grief. Her young man was busy transporting his trunks, bedding, bicycle and innumerable other possessions on board with the help of coolies. When everything had been safely stowed away he came up to the weeping girl and, under the pretence of bidding farewell, acted out a scene that made my cheeks burn with indignation.

I've often wondered why he had to do that, why he had to damage his immortal soul the way he did. True, she was not his wedded wife. But she was a woman, a member of that fraternity of mothers, sisters and daughters on which a man is so dependent. In the four years that they had lived together she had given him an unswerving loyalty and devotion. Why did he have to ridicule her and make her the laughing-stock of the common people who stood around, even as he left her?

Clasping her neck with one arm and holding a handkerchief to his eyes, the man muttered something in mournful tones while the girl, her face buried in her veil, sobbed uncontrollably. I was standing a little distance away so I couldn't hear what he was saying at first. But, noticing some of the crowd grinning widely and others trying hard to suppress their laughter, I pushed my way towards them and heard him say in crude Bengali, 'You think I'm coming back with tobacco from Rangpur? You'll be waiting for me? Oh! My jewel! You can go on waiting for me till doomsday for I'm finished with you for ever. My only regret is that I got only five hundred out of you. Not a thousand as I had hoped. If I had only had the time I could have made you sell your house and give me the money! That would have been something worth bragging about back home. Five hundred is a paltry sum. Oh! What a cruel world it is!'

The man was obviously enjoying his own humour, and the entertainment it afforded to the Bengalis around him spurred him on to greater heights. But the girl understood nothing. She only heard her beloved's sobbing voice and, weeping louder, put up her hand to wipe his tears away. The sailors now called out to him to board for they were in the process of removing the gang planks.

The man moved towards the ship, then, coming back, took the girl's hand in his. Pointing to the large unflawed ruby she wore on her finger he sobbed, 'Ah! Let me have this—the last token of our love. I can sell it for three hundred rupees at the very least. Why do you deprive me of it, my jewel?'

The girl quickly took off the ring and slipped it on his finger. Then, crumbling suddenly, she sank to her knees on the ground. The man carried on his act as he crossed over the planks leaving his audience rocking with merriment. But the poor girl saw nothing, heard nothing—so thoroughly immersed was she in her own grief.

As the ship moved away comments like 'What a boy!' 'Really a fine young man!' and 'God! How he made me laugh!' were heard from the crowd. No one deigned to cast a glance at the abandoned woman.

As I went up to them, the little girl, who had been pulling her sister by the hand, threw me a grateful glance and said, 'Get up, sister. Look who is here!'

The girl lifted her head and, seeing the expression on my face, burst into another fit of weeping. I had no words with which to console her, but I couldn't leave her and go away either. I escorted her to her carriage and, at her request, drove home with her.

'Oh, why did I send him to Rangpur?' she said over and over again all the way home. 'A month! A whole month! How shall I live without him? How shall I bear the loneliness? And he—he'll be sick and miserable without me in a foreign land. I shouldn't have let him go. We have managed so far with tobacco from the Rangoon bazaars. Oh! Why couldn't I remain content? Why was I tempted to look for greater profit? My heart is bursting with unhappiness, Babuji. I'll go to him on the next boat.'

I sat silent, staring out of the window in an attempt to hide my tears.

'Babuji,' the girl went on, 'our men don't love us the way you do. They are not as kind or considerate.' Then, pausing to recover her breath, she went on, 'When we first started living together my kinsfolk warned me not to put my faith in an alien. But I didn't heed them and I've never regretted my decision. Now all the Burmese girls envy my happiness.'

The carriage was now approaching the crossroads from where the hotel could be reached after a short walk. I wanted to get off and make my way there but the girl wouldn't let me. Barring the door with both arms she said, 'No, Babuji. First come home with me and have a cup of tea.' I couldn't refuse. The carriage rolled on and the unhappy girl, weary with weeping, fell silent. Suddenly she sat up and asked anxiously, 'How far is Rangpur, Babuji? Have you ever been there? What sort of a place is it? Is it possible to get a doctor if someone is ill?'

'Yes,' I said shortly.

She heaved a sigh, 'Fei* will guard him and keep him well! I have nothing to fear. His brother is with him. He is a good, kind man and will protect his younger brother with his life. Indians are so noble! So full of duty! Why do I worry?'

I stared out of the window trying to assess the extent of my own involvement in the monstrous crime that had just been committed. I had to plead guilty on two counts. I had been aware of the plot but had not warned the girl. Worse, I had not made a whisper of a protest when the grisly scene of betrayal was being enacted. The thought made my face burn with shame. I couldn't bear to look into those innocent, trusting eyes.

Dusk was falling when I left her house. I was exhausted, physically and emotionally, but the prospect of going back to the clamour and bustle of Da Thakur's hotel daunted me. I wandered about in the streets of Rangoon, innumerable thoughts going round and round in my head like rats caught in a trap. But, however hard I tried, I could not subdue the gut feeling that a relationship of this kind was doomed from the start.

The Burmese have rather flexible rules regarding matrimony. There is such a thing as a social and religious ceremony. But the other kind—marriage by virtue of eating out of a common bowl and sleeping under the same roof for three nights in succession— is equally acceptable to that society. Thus the Burmese girl's

---

* A Burmese goddess.

conviction that hers was a true marriage was neither foolish nor unfounded. From the young man's point of view, however, it was as ephemeral as a summer breeze for there was no sanction for it in Hinduism. There was no way he could reconcile the presence of a Burmese wife with his rightful place in Hindu society. Only two options were open to him. One was a lifelong exile. The other—a total and complete break with his partner.

As I walked on aimlessly, speculating on the worth of a religion that inflicts such cruel suffering, my eyes fell on a wayside tea-shop. I recognized it as the one that stood opposite Rohini Babu's house—the one in which I had opened Abhaya's note. I had a cup of tea, then walking across, knocked on Rohini Babu's door. It opened and within its frame stood Abhaya.

'You!' I cried, amazed.

Abhaya blushed to the roots of her hair and, turning suddenly, ran to her own room and banged the door shut. Even in the faint starlight there was no mistaking the shame and guilt that were stamped on her face.

As I stood, irresolute, my ears were suddenly assailed by the sounds of two kinds of weeping. I had heard them that very afternoon—the bitter, heartbroken sobs of the Burmese girl and the cruel, mocking one of her companion.

I had started walking away but I stopped myself. 'No,' I said to myself, 'I cannot leave Abhaya—not this way. I have no right to humiliate her. So many dos and don'ts are ingrained in us from childhood. What are they truly worth? Who has the right to sit on judgement over another human being? Not I, certainly. Not you. Not even God.'

Ten

THERE WAS A CLICK AND ABHAYA OPENED HER DOOR AND STOOD before me.

She said, 'Forgive me for running away, Srikanta Babu. It was out of a false sense of disgrace, a momentary surrender to the conditioning of centuries. Do not make the mistake of thinking that it reflected my true feelings.'

I was amazed at her for having the courage of her convictions.

'Rohini Babu will be back in a few minutes,' she went on. 'Then you can put us both in the dock and deliver your verdict.' This was the first time that I heard her refer to Rohini as 'Babu'.

'When did you come?' I asked inconsequentially.

'The day before yesterday. You must be curious to know why.' And, lifting her arm, she pointed to where the lash of a whip had cut deep into the flesh. 'There are many like this,' she said dispassionately.

The blood boiled in my veins. If the scoundrel had stood before me I would have torn him limb from limb.

'Please don't imagine that this is the cause of my return. This is only a token of our relationship as master and slave—a small reward, you may say, for my years of wifely devotion.' After a brief silence she continued, 'A woman who pursues her husband without his leave, makes claims on him and disturbs his peace is a traitor and a rebel. No man will tolerate such audacity. Hence my husband dealt with me as a man deals with a wife in such cases.

He used every kind of ploy to get me to his house and, once there, demanded from me my reasons for coming to Burma with Rohini Babu. I told him that I had been orphaned some time ago and that I had had no one else to turn to and that I had written several letters which he had left unanswered. He unhooked a whip from the wall and said, "This is my answer,"' and Abhaya touched the mark on her arm.

The bloated, evil face of the disgusting beast came before my eyes and my stomach churned with nausea. But the conditioning of centuries—that which had prompted Abhaya to run and hide herself—was upon me. I could not bring myself to utter the words: 'You were right in leaving him.' I sat in silence for a while, then said with an effort, 'I don't blame you for coming away but—'

'That is just what I want you to explain—that "but" which stands in the way of all rational thinking. May my husband live happily with his Burmese wife. I grudge him nothing. Only one question, Srikanta Babu! Do Vedic mantras have the power to command a wife's loyalty, even after her husband has stripped her of all her rights and driven her away by brute force into the streets? Do you have an answer?'

I was silent. Abhaya looked steadily at me for a few minutes and said, 'Rights and duties are inextricably linked, Srikanta Babu. There can be no question of one without the other. My husband took the marriage vows, as I did, but they have played no part in shaping his needs and desires. They are no more to him than a piece of rhetoric, uttered in an idle moment, to be blown away at will. Yet these same vows bind me to him with iron fetters simply because I'm a woman. You said you did not blame me for coming away and added a "but". What did that mean, Srikanta Babu? Were you trying to tell me that it is my duty to atone for my husband's sins by voluntarily embracing a death-in-life? Why? Because once, long ago when I was still a child, I had involuntarily pronounced some words of which I knew not the meaning? Are those words, uttered in ignorance, all that is true and meaningful in my life? And the terrible injustice and affliction that has been heaped on my head—are they of no consequence? I am deprived of my rights as a wife and a mother. I am denied my legitimate place in society. Love, laughter and joy are not for me. Why, Srikanta Babu? Why? Simply because I had the misfortune of being chained in wedlock to a selfish, brutal, loathesome creature? And am I to be denied my womanhood because such an animal would have none of me? In no society other than the Hindu is the woman so crushed and crippled. Do you understand what I am saying, Srikanta Babu?'

I was speechless.

'Why don't you answer me?' Abhaya went on inexorably.

'Is there really any need? You did not seek my advice before you took your decision.'

'There was no time for that.'

I stared moodily at the darkening world outside. I felt sunk in gloom. After a long silence I said, 'My heart is very heavy, Abhaya. Do you know why I came here tonight? Because only this afternoon I was a mute witness to a terrible crime against a defenceless woman.' And I described the scene in the harbour. 'What future do you visualize for this young woman?' I asked.

Abhaya shuddered and shook her head.

'And now I'll tell you about two other women whose sufferings have been no less than yours.' I recounted Annada Didi's history from beginning to end. As I did so, I noticed Abhaya's body stiffen and her eyes grow large and sombre. When I came to the end she touched the ground with her forehead and, sitting up, wiped her eyes with the end of her sari.

'What happened after that?' she asked.

'After that I lost track of her. Now let me tell you about Pyari Baiji. When she was a young girl called Rajlakshmi she loved—someone. Do you know how? The way Rohini Babu loves you. Then, many years later, they met. She wasn't Rajlakshmi any more. She had become Pyari Baiji. But her lover discovered, on that very first day, that Rajlakshmi had not died. She lived and was immortalized in Pyari Baiji.'

'And then?' Abhaya asked curiously.

I told her the rest of the story ending with the sentence, 'And the day came when Pyari sent away the man she loved above all else in the world—above her own life.'

'What happened then? Do you know?'

'I do. Nothing happened.'

Abhaya sighed and said, 'Are you trying to tell me that I'm not the only one? That women have suffered these misfortunes through the ages and that their submission to suffering is their greatest achievement?'

'I'm not trying to tell you anything. I only ask you to accept the fact that women are not men. Their actions cannot be weighed on the same scales. And even if one were to do so it would not be worthwhile.'

'Can you tell me why not?'

'No, I cannot. Besides, my mind is in such a turmoil tonight that it is unfit to unravel issues of such complexity. I can only tell you of my own feelings. Many women have come into my life but only a few hold exalted positions in my heart. Do you know how? Through their capacity for suffering. My Annada Didi carried the burden of her sorrow in mute silence. Even when her burden became too grievous to be borne she did not abandon it. My heart would burst with pain if I even imagined her doing what you have done.'

After a brief silence I continued, 'And Rajlakshmi! What a grievous affliction was upon her when she sacrificed her dearest love! I have seen it with my own eyes. I don't mind telling you that it is her capacity for suffering that has won her the highest place in my heart.'

'Are you the man she—?' Abhaya began in a startled voice.

'If she didn't know what she meant to me,' I continued calmly, ignoring Abhaya's interruption, 'she would never have sent me away. She would have clung to me for fear of losing me.'

'Maybe she knows you are hers. Hence she has no fears.'

'It isn't only that. There is something beyond having and losing and I believe that Rajlakshmi has found the key to it. Which is why she doesn't need me anymore. I have suffered too—in many ways. And it is through my suffering that I've stumbled upon an important truth. Sorrow is not the negative emotion we think it is. Sorrow signifies neither absence nor loss. If unaccompanied by fear, it can be sensed and even enjoyed as fully as happiness.'

'I think I understand. You mean that sorrow can become a prop—a purpose for living. It did for Rajlakshmi and Annada Didi. But my case is different. I don't even have that to fall back upon. All I've received from my husband is rejection and humiliation. Do you ask me to live out my life with these as my only support?'

It was a difficult question. I did not even try to answer it.

Abhaya went on, 'My life has nothing in common with theirs. Millions of men and women inhabit this earth. All are not cast in the same mould. People live by different laws and find their fulfilment in different ways. We vary in our instincts, our ideas and our mental abilities. Society must find a way for the successful development of each of its members and not force all to tread a common path. Is not my experience a glaring example? I was compelled to come to my husband for all other means of living were denied me. But was my coming here of any use? Nothing of him belongs to me anymore. Yet living under his protection as his whore was the only option society left open for me. That was to be my final fulfilment, and bearing the burden of that sterility the ultimate goal of my life as a woman. Rohini Babu loves me. You are aware of it and you have seen his suffering. Do you ask me to maim his life and destroy his soul only to buy for myself the label of a virtuous woman?'

Abhaya wiped her eyes with the back of her hand and continued, 'Must I deny his love and ruin his happiness only to establish the validity of a ceremony performed so long ago that it has become a lie to both man and wife? Does God, who created love and put it in our hearts, demand such a denial? You may think what you like of me. You may call my children by any name you please. But I would like you to get one thing clear. If we live and if children are born to us they will not need to hang their heads in shame for having come out of my womb. They may inherit nothing from us but their mother will take care to give them a secure foundation on which to plant their feet and hold their heads high. Do you know what that is, Srikanta Babu? It is the conviction that they are the fruits of a meaningful relationship.'

There was a long silence. Her words hung in the air and breathed around us where we sat. I looked out at the sky and felt it shudder. I was overwhelmed by the strangest of sensations. I felt as if this great inanimate universe had a life and soul of its own that went on unseen, impervious to the thoughts and feelings of men.

Abhaya broke the silence with a question, 'What about you, Srikanta Babu? Will you withdraw your friendship and stop visiting us?'

I hesitated, trying to find the right words. 'God may forgive you for he can see into your hearts,' I said, at last. 'Man cannot—unfortunately. Another thing! You forget that the collective identity can only be preserved by adhering to certain norms and principles. It is difficult, even impossible, for society to frame different rules for different people.'

'There is a faith that is large enough and generous enough to accommodate sinners like us. Do you ask us to embrace it?'

I had no answer.

'You talk of a collective identity,' she resumed. 'Yet you cannot protect your own people when they are in trouble. Is that something to be proud of, Srikanta Babu?'

I sighed. Once again I had no answer.

'Never mind,' Abhaya went on. 'If you don't make room for us we won't complain. After all Hinduism is only one of many faiths. I take comfort in the thought that there is a place for us in another great religion of the world.'

'Protection is not everything—at least not in every case,' I said, a little hurt at her jibes at Hinduism.

'Isn't it? There is proof of it everywhere if we only had eyes to see. You do agree, don't you, that an institution based on false values cannot flourish for long. How then do you account for the spread of Islam in the twelve centuries of its history? Do you mean to tell me that the Mussalman community owes its growth and importance to the fact that it lends its support to the vicious and the depraved? And that you Hindus are falling into a decline because of your faithfulness to a lofty rule of moral law? In the few months that I've been here I've noticed that the Burmese, like the Indians, are turning more and more to Islam. Every village in Burma has a Mussalman community and a mosque . . . . You were just telling me of the incident at the harbour . . . didn't the young man betray the woman's love only because Hindu society is not large enough to accept the Burmese wife of one of its sons? Would it have been necessary for the older brother to devise such a shameless scheme of desertion if he had been a Mussalman? Instead of breaking up the happy pair he would have drawn them under the shadow of the one true God and, blessing them, would have departed in peace. Which course of action do you recommend as the more ethical, Srikanta Babu?'

I looked at her with reverence in my eyes. 'Tell me, Abhaya,' I said, 'from where did a simple village girl like you learn to speak as you do. I can say, quite truthfully, that knowledge and breadth of vision like yours is rare even among men. No child of yours need ever be ashamed to call you "mother".'

Her wan face lit up. 'Tell me, Srikanta Babu,' she urged. 'Will Hindu society be the purer for rejecting me? Will it not suffer a loss?' Suddenly she smiled a radiant smile and continued. 'But I shall not run away, Srikanta Babu. I shall live among you and be part of you however much you dishonour and defame me. If I can rear even one of my children to become a man among men I shall have had my revenge. For I will have proved that man is exalted by his actions alone—not by the accident of his birth.'

Eleven

AMONG THE PEOPLE WHO ASSEMBLED PERIODICALLY IN DA Thakur's hotel for religious singing and discourse was a man called Manohar Chakraborty. He was a wealthy man and was reported to have combined within himself the qualities of devoutness and worldly wisdom to a fine degree. He took quite kindly to me for some reason.

One morning he drew me aside and treated me to a little lecture. 'You are a young man, Srikanta Babu. Your life is before you. If you wish to make something of it I can give you a few tips. Fortune has favoured you. Not everyone who comes to Burma fares as well as you have done. You earn well but from what I hear—and I always take care to ascertain my facts—you squander away every paisa you earn. It breaks my heart to think of it. I too was careless and improvident at your age. Then someone took me in hand and gave me the advice I'm about to give you. He was an ordinary man. He earned only fifty rupees a month. But when he died he left behind him a house with an orchard and a pond, acres of paddy fields and two thousand rupees in cash. I myself . . . .' He stopped suddenly and changed the flow of his monologue. 'You too can be a rich man in a couple of years if you take my advice. You may even be able to save enough money to go back to Calcutta and get yourself a wife.'

From where he had got the impression that I was sighing my soul away for a wife, I could not say. But, since he had assured me that he never uttered a word without full and absolute knowledge, I had to accept the statement and even nod encouragingly.

'Look, Srikanta Babu,' he continued. 'Making money is not as easy as it seems. It can only be accomplished by careful planning and ceaseless toil. I won't advise you not to throw your money away in charities and such like. I know you are not such a fool as to do that. What I'm asking you to do is to follow a few simple rules that will enable you to keep the money that you have earned with your hard work. If anyone is in distress of any kind, shun him like a leper for, before you know where you are, he'll touch you for a couple of rupees. If you give him the money you lose it and your peace of mind as well, for two rupees is a tidy sum, after all, and you can't let it go without a struggle. You'll try to get it back and bitterness and frustration will inevitably follow. Is it not much better to steer clear of such complications?'

'Certainly, certainly,' I agreed.

'You are an intelligent man,' he continued, warming to his theme. 'An educated man. That is why you appreciate my advice. The mechanics and coolies here are such fools—they'll even borrow money to lend it. No wonder they never have a paisa in their pockets. What can you expect from low caste fellows like that lot. Dolts! Idiots!'

Recovering from his indignation with an effort he went on. 'Never lend money without a collateral. If someone comes crying to you that he is in trouble, just turn around and tell him it's not your fault. And he if touches you for a loan ask him for a mortgage on his house, his lands or his wife's jewellery—as the case may be. That is always good policy. Never go near any kind of quarrel. Even if you see a man being beaten to death—don't interfere. Why invite trouble? You may get a few blows for your pains. You may even have to testify before a court of law if there is a police inquiry. It is much better to slip away and lie low for a while. You can offer your condolences and a few words of advice to the bereaved party once the trouble is over. What do you say? Is my reasoning incorrect?'

'Oh! no. This is excellent advice.'

'Of course it is excellent advice. Now for the last bit. Keep at a safe distance from the sick and afflicted for they are always in need of help—financial and otherwise. To be frank I never go near such people. It is imprudent to lend a sick man money for who can prophesy the future? He may not live to repay the loan. As for nursing the sick—dear God! if I were to catch the infection and fall ill in this alien land! No, I must not even think such dreadful thoughts. Sheetala Ma have mercy on me! What am I but the dust of your feet?' and he bit his tongue and tweaked his ears in excessive humility. Observing my silence he hesitated a little before adding, 'Europeans never visit the sick. If they are very concerned, they send a card. Isn't that far more sensible? White men never get involved in one another's problems. That is the secret of their success.'

The office hour being at hand I was compelled to take a break from the moral instruction my mentor doled out so unstintingly. In any case, I didn't feel young and unformed enough to be moulded by the wise man's guidance to any great extent. A man like him is not a rarity in rural Bengal. Neither is his advice. Thus I was not unfamiliar with the type. What I was unprepared for was the speed and thoroughness with which Providence dispelled his delusions of practical wisdom and exposed him for what he really was—a spineless, contemptible, self-centred old fool. But that was a fortnight later.

I had not been to see Abhaya since the day I had surprised her in Rohini Babu's house. I had thought of her a good deal and had tried to reconcile her point of view with my own pre-conditioned one with all the arguments I could muster. I respected the independence of her thinking, her veracity and candour and her deep, passionate love for Rohini. All these attracted me immensely and I longed to renew our friendship, but the bigotry of generations of Hindu chauvinists was in my blood and it would not let me rest. I couldn't, despite my best efforts, conquer the nagging feeling that Annada Didi would not have acted as Abhaya had done. Even if the choice were between a lifetime of humiliation as a servant in some strange household and one of queenly dignity in that of a man who was not her husband she would have chosen the former without the slightest hesitation. I asked myself, over and over again, if Annada Didi's perception of physical purity and her concept of duty—derived, I had no doubt, from her unconditional

---

* The presiding female deity of smallpox, chicken pox and measles.

surrender to God's will—could be truly reduced to nothing by Abhaya's intelligent reasoning. I remembered something the latter had said—the finer nuances of which had eluded me at the time.

'Srikanta Babu,' she had said, 'the human race has been attracted to suffering from time immemorial for there is, inbuilt in the nature of man, an irresistible urge for self-chastisement. Man obsessively views himself as good or bad in proportion to the sorrow that has been his portion. This is perhaps owing to the knowledge that through the centuries of his history, man has acquired nothing without tremendous sacrifice. That knowledge has been subverted today into the erroneous conviction that the opposite is equally true. That sacrifice and sorrow bring acquisition and ascent in their wake. When a man voluntarily suppresses his natural instincts and embraces a life of deprivation, he does it in the belief that a great deal more than what he is giving up is being stored for him in some other place. His fellowmen share his conviction. When a sanyasi immerses himself in ice-cold water on a bitter winter night or stands on his head in the scorching summer sun he invariably attracts a crowd. Why? Because people are overwhelmed not only by the sight of the privations the man is undergoing but by their own visions of the luxury and comfort that awaits him in the next world. Woven into the fabric of their awe and admiration is a strand of envy and another of self-pity. Convinced that this man, alone, is doing with his body what God meant him to do whereas they are wasting theirs on earthly functions—they go back home saddened and frustrated. Srikanta Babu, the belief that self-deprivation brings happiness in its wake is the biggest lie that man has concocted for himself. It is neither true of this life nor of the next.'

'But a widow's brahmacharya—' I began.

Abhaya stopped me with a gesture. 'Speak of it as the conduct regulated for widows. It has nothing whatsoever to do with Brahma. This is another of the lies perpetrated through the ages—that abstinence and sacrifice lead widows straight to Brahma. What is good for widows should be good for everyone. Why isn't it so?'

'Oh! All right,' I laughed. 'Let's not call it brahmacharya. What's in a name?'

'You are quite wrong, Srikanta Babu,' she answered, fixing her dark, compelling gaze on mine. 'Everything is in a name. What in the world is more powerful than the word? Give the biggest lie the label of truth and it will become sacrosanct. Men, women and children will adapt their thoughts, feelings and perceptions to it and tread the groove of falsehood for centuries to come. A widow's renunciation of the pleasures of the world gets her nowhere, Srikanta Babu. All it gives her is a halo she can well do without. There is no trick so low down in the world as the one that has been played on poor, foolish, trusting, unresisting women by their male protectors. To push them on to a path of self-obliteration—what can be more cruel? What a waste of human quality, Srikanta Babu! What utter, colossal waste!'

I had no arguments with which to counter her analysis. I recalled that Doctor Babu had called her a 'forward' woman on the strength of his slight acquaintance. Neither of us had dreamed of the dimensions the word 'forward' could attain in connection with Abhaya. The girl had a way of baring her innermost thoughts and emotions before the glaring light of public opinion without the slightest hesitation. Another thing I noticed about Abhaya was that there was no gap between her words and her actions. She waged a ceaseless battle against her enemies, within and without, and strove to live by the light of her own convictions. It was this quality that often made me tongue-tied in her presence. Later, back in my own room, I found all the forceful arguments I could have used against hers. The thought of Abhaya invariably created a duality within me. The more I told myself that Abhaya was right in leaving her husband, that there was nothing else that she could have done—the more my heart and soul turned against her. I would reason with myself. I would exhort myself to respect her thoughts and actions. But, somehow, I never managed to—quite. A nagging feeling of doubt and frustration invariably dogged me, preventing me as forcefully from renewing our friendship as from forgetting her existence.

While things were in this state, plague burst over the city of Rangoon. All the efforts of the authorities to prevent its insidious progress across the Bay had come to naught. Normal life was paralysed under the pressure of a two-way exodus. Some people abandoned the centre of the town for the suburbs while others, from the latter, rushed to the former. To see a rat, alive or dead, was to run—such a state of panic had ensued.

It was a Saturday morning. I remember that well. I was walking through a congested area of central Rangoon at a quick pace when I caught sight of Manohar Chakraborty waving frantically from the upper window of a decrepit house. I waved back but did not slow my steps for I was in a hurry to get to the main road.

'Do come up, Srikanta Babu,' he called in a piteous voice. 'I'm in great trouble.'

I retraced my steps unwillingly, grumbling to myself that it was just my luck to be caught by the old bore. Outwardly, however, I smiled a false smile and said, 'You haven't been to the hotel for some days now, Chakraborty *moshai*. Do you live here?'

'No, I moved in a fortnight ago. I was suffering from dysentery—which is why I haven't been to see you—and then the plague broke out in the neighbourhood. Naturally, I left as quickly as I could.'

'Naturally,' I echoed.

'It's all very well, *moshai*,' he went on fretfully.'You understand and I understand. But my combined hand is threatening to leave. Why don't you call the rascal and give him a good scolding?'

Here I think I owe it to my readers to explain the term *combined hand*, for, living in India as they do, they have no idea of what that is. Combined hands are men who combine cooking and serving food with every other kind of menial chore. They are generally found among Brahmins from northern India who, though rabidly caste-conscious in their native village, display a remarkable flexibility in Burma. For an extra rupee or two the purest of pure Dwivedi and Chaturvedi cooks will undertake to clean dirty utensils, wipe floors, prepare hookahs and polish the shoes of their low-caste masters, for if there is one thing they cannot resist, it is the lure of filthy lucre. For them money is the most potent of purifying agents. Unlike our foolish fellows from Bengal and Orissa whose Brahminhood resists practical assaults, with the fiercest determination the Brahmin from the north simply puts a price tag on every dent in his. Anyhow, who was I to reprimand Manohar Chakraborty's servant? And why should he take it from me? This combined hand was evidently new—a concession, no doubt, to the difficulties wrought by the prolonged dysentery—for, as far as my own knowledge went, Manohar Chakraborty had been his own hand, combined or otherwise, for as many years as he had been in Burma.

'You are an eminent man, Srikanta Babu,' he continued, 'and a respected one. We have all heard of the power and prestige you enjoy in the highest circles. One line from you to the governor will ensure that the swine is punished with imprisonment upto fourteen years.'

I stared at him in astonishment. The idea that I, who didn't even know the governor's name, was capable of getting a man imprisoned for life on the strength of a single line written to His Excellency, was so novel that I staggered under its impact. In my dazed condition, with my erstwhile mentor's repeated humble requests ringing in my ears, I proceeded to the kitchen where the hapless combined hand was stationed. Crouching in the shadow of the black vault which made up the kitchen quarters, the combined hand had heard every word his master had uttered. He now came forward, pale and trembling, and folding his hands before me, begged me in a nasal whine to allow him to leave. He had no objection, he said, to working for the master if he moved to another house but this one, he was convinced, had a *deo* (a spirit) in it. Strange shadows flitted about day and night. The house was so dark and ill-ventilated that the presence of shadows did not surprise me. What did was the nasty stink that proceeded from the interior of the kitchen.

'What is that smell?' I asked

'Something rotting. Must be a rat,' said the combined hand.

'Rat?' I asked startled. 'Is there a dead rat in there?'

The combined hand shrugged his shoulders and informed me that he threw six or seven dead rats out into the alley every morning. I lit a kersosene lamp and the two of us made a thorough though futile search. I shivered involuntarily. Try as I would, I could not bring myself to advise the man not to desert his sick master. Back in the bedroom, Manohar Chakraborty treated me to an account of the virtues of the new house. Such a big house, located right in the centre of the city, was never to be had at the rent he was paying. Then again, the landlord was such a thorough gentleman, and the neighbours so decent and non-interfering. The room adjoining his had been rented out to a group of Christian boys from Madras who were as quiet as they were amiable and respectful. He even informed me that he would throw out the rascally Brahmin as soon as he felt a little better. Then, suddenly, he asked a strange question. 'Do you believe in dreams, Srikanta Babu?'

'No,' I replied without the slightest hesitation.

'I don't either. Yet—and this is very strange, *moshai*—I dreamt last night that I fell down the stairs and was hurt in the groin. When I woke up I found a swelling on it. I even feel feverish this morning. Touch me and see.'

I could feel my face grow pale with horror. I sat speechless for the next few minutes. Then, recovering myself, I checked his fever and inspected the lump in his groin. 'Have you sent for a doctor?' I asked. 'I advise you to do so immediately.'

'Everything is so expensive in this country, Srikanta Babu. A doctor will charge four or five rupees as his fee. Another two will be wasted on medicines—'

'Never mind that,' I cut him short. 'Send for one immediately.'

'Whom shall I send? Tiwari is a fool. Besides, if he goes, who'll do the cooking?'

'I'll go,' I said and went out.

After examining the patient, the doctor drew me aside with the question, 'Are you related to him?' On my answering in the negative he asked, 'Does he have any relatives in Burma?'

'Not that I know of,' I said.

The doctor's face grew sombre. 'Well,' he said at last. 'I'll write out a prescription. And you had better send for some ice to put on his head. But the best thing would be to remove him to the plague hospital. It is not right for you to expose yourself to the risk of infection. And another thing—don't bother about the fee.'

After the doctor had left I went back to Manohar Babu and, very hesitatingly, broached the subject of shifting him to a hospital ward. But at the word 'hospital' he burst into tears. 'Don't send me to a hospital please, Srikanta Babu. I've heard that the doctors there kill off the patients. I'll never come back.'

Disengaging his clinging hands I went to look for Tiwari with the intention of sending him out to buy ice and medicines. But the combined hand had vanished. There was not a trace, in the house, of him or his possessions. I calculated that he had overheard the doctor's remarks and though he had understood little else, the word *plague* had been sufficient inspiration for him to bolt. I had no choice but to lock the door and go out myself. I returned within an hour with medicines, an ice bag and ice, and the long vigil began. The morning dragged on hot and weary. The patient was in high delirium. Continually threshing his arms and legs, he tried to throw off the ice bag from his head. Then around two o'clock in the afternoon, he slipped into a coma.

There were some lucid intervals, however. Towards evening he opened his eyes and, gazing into mine with full consciousness, he said, 'I'm dying, Srikanta Babu.'

I made no answer. He fumbled painfully for the key that was secured by a string to his waist and handing it to me with a trembling hand said, 'I have three hundred guineas saved up. Send them to my wife. You'll find the address and the money in my trunk.'

I sat through the long dreary afternoon and evening watching the sick man die. From time to time I heard snatches of conversation and light footfalls from the adjoining room. Around dusk there was a sudden burst of activity. Sounds of furniture being shifted were interspersed with low whispers. Then all was still. I got up to investigate and found a lock on the door. Thinking that the inmates had gone out for a stroll and would soon be back, I took up my place, once more, at Manohar Babu's side. An acute depression took hold of me. The hours passed and no one returned. Around midnight I got so restless that I went up to the door once again. The lock was still there and all was silent, but through a chink in the wooden wall a beam of light shone into the passage. Fitting my eye to it, I peeped into the room.

The blood froze in my veins as the full impact of what I saw hit my consciousness. Two young men lay sleeping side by side, their heads resting on a single pillow. A row of candles, burning low in their sockets, stood on the headboard. I had heard of the Roman Catholic ritual of keeping a light burning at the head of a corpse and I knew, to a certainty, that these sleepers would never awake. Another two hours and Manohar Babu sank into the same restful sleep. As I sat guarding the body, I marvelled at the fate that had singled me out to take charge of the worldly possessions and mortal remains of one who had advised me, most emphatically, to keep away from the sick and the afflicted.

The next morning and afternoon were taken up in collecting the death certificate, handing the body to the authorities and arranging for the guineas to be sent to the family of the deceased. Bidding goodbye to Manohar Babu's corpse as it lay in the police wagon on its way, it is hoped, to heaven, I returned to my den in Da Thakur's hotel. I was weary to the bone. Not a drop of water had passed through my lips in thirty-three hours, and my eyes burned with the night's long vigil.

As I sank down on the bed I became aware, for the first time, of a dull throbbing at the back of my ear. Probing gently with a finger I felt, or thought I felt, a lump. I wondered if this were preordained; if Manohar Chakraborty, in his infinite worldly wisdom, had ensured that I follow him to heaven to render a true account of what I had done with the guineas. All night I tossed and turned in my bed and, by constantly prodding the inflamed area, rendered it even more painful. I woke up the next morning with one thought in my head. I had to find some place to dump myself before I passed out altogether. I had many friends and acquaintances in Rangoon but they were all, without exception, righteous and devout. They didn't deserve the terrible fate of having a plague patient thrust on them. If I did so I would incur the wrath of God as surely as I still lived and breathed. Far better to seek out a sinner. I knew of one—an immoral, depraved woman who lived in sin at the other end of Rangoon. I had despised her and scorned her for a long while now. Who, better than she, deserved the punishment of nursing me through the dreaded illness? She might even catch the contagion and die and, in doing so, justly atone for her sins. Reasoning thus I sent for a carriage to take me to Abhaya's house.

Twelve

THAT MORNING WHEN I STOOD FACE TO FACE WITH ABHAYA, DEATH warrant in hand, my fear of dying was swamped by a terrifying humility. Abhaya's face turned deathly pale but the words that issued from her lips were these: 'You were right to come to me for who, in this alien land, cares more for you than I do?'

Tears rushed to my eyes. 'I am going, Abhaya,' I said. 'I have to suffer the agony of the passage. No one can take that away from me. I came to you in my helplessness but, seeing you, I am ashamed of bringing my troubles to your door. The carriage is waiting. I will not lose consciousness for another hour at least. I can reach the plague hospital before that. Only you—you must be firm and tell me to go.'

In answer, Abhaya took my hand and led me to the bed. Then, wiping her eyes, she laid a hand on my fevered brow and said, 'I am grateful I have a door to which you could bring your troubles. My home is truly a home now that you are in it.'

What I suffered from was obviously not the plague for I was up and about in a fortnight. But Abhaya would not let me go back to the hotel. While still in her house I received a letter from Pyari—her first after I came to Burma. I had written to her several times but never received a reply.

Touching lightly on the subject she wrote:

If I die, someone or the other will inform you of the fact but while I live my news can be of no interest to you. That is why I do not write. The reverse is not true. I pine for news of you. Write me a line whenever you can so that I have the satisfaction of knowing how you fare in that God-forsaken land.

Then she came to the real purpose of the letter.

I'm writing to you in the hope of securing your permission for Banku's marriage. I wish to arrange it within this month. You have always maintained that a man should not marry before he is capable of supporting a family and I have agreed with you. Nevertheless, I am being forced to take this decision. Do come home as soon as you are able and judge the situation for yourself.

Towards the end of her letter there was a reference to Abhaya. I had been so shaken and bewildered after my argument with Abhaya on the day she had arrogantly asserted her right to spurn her brute of a husband and live openly with the man she loved, that I had poured out my feelings in a four-page letter to Rajlakshmi. Referring to that communication Rajlakshmi wrote:

I don't know if you've spoken of me to Abhaya. If you have I beg you to give her my humblest and sincerest regards. I don't know if she is younger or older than me in years. I don't need to know either. Her indomitable spirit and vigour of thought and action have ensured her a far higher place than ordinary mortals like us can ever dream of reaching. Srikantada, whenever I think of Abhaya I am reminded of something my gurudev said to me on the day of my indoctrination. I had everything arranged and ready in my house in Kashi. Gurudev entered the puja room and seated himself on the carpet. I watched him as he sat, still and silent as a figure of stone, then, suddenly afraid, I threw myself at his feet and wept, 'Gurudev, don't give me the mantra. I don't deserve it.'

He put a hand on my head and asked, 'Why, child, what ails you?'

'I am a sinner.'

'If so, you are all the more in need of the word of God.'

'I lied to you,' I sobbed. 'I dared not reveal my true

identity. If you knew what I am you would never have crossed my threshold.'

'I crossed your threshold with full knowledge and I shall give you the mantra all the same. I may not approve of Pyari but what prevents me from loving my daughter Rajlakshmi?'

I sat speechless for a few minutes. Then I said fearfully, 'My mother's guru refused to give me the mantra. He said he would be doomed to eternal punishment if he did. Was he not right?'

Gurudev smiled. 'He must have been. But I have no fear of eternal punishment so I can give it to you.'

'Why do *you* have no fear?'

'Why is one member of a household stricken with a disease while another is untouched?'

'No one is untouched. The strong can resist the disease. The weak succumb.'

Gurudev stroked my head and said, 'Always remember that, child. What kills the weak and petty makes the strong stronger and finer.'

'But good and bad are equally so for everyone, surely, irrespective of strength or weakness? Is it not unjust to have different laws for different people?'

'No. That is how God created the world. What is good for one is not necessarily good for another. A drug that kills a child of five may have no effect whatsoever on a man of thirty. You may not agree with me—at least not today—but bear this in mind. There are some among us in whose breast the fire of God burns bright and clear. There are others who have not the faintest spark—only a heap of cold, dead ashes. Can they both be subject to a common law? No, child, no.'

Srikantada, I have not seen Abhaya but from what you write about her, I can sense the fire Gurudev spoke of, flaming fiercely in her soul. Don't be hasty in your judgement of her. Don't weigh her actions on the same pair of scales as you do those of ordinary women like me.

I handed the letter to Abhaya. She read it once, twice and yet a third time. Then, suddenly overcome, she crumpled the piece of paper in her hand and, throwing it on the bed, ran out of the room.

I realized that the respect and admiration that breathed from every line of Rajlakshmi's letter was too great for Abhaya's hurt, humiliated womanhood to bear. She had to hide her face, torn with pain and happiness, from my insensitive male eyes. She reappeared half an hour later. I could see that she had washed her face clean of the tell-tale tears.

'Srikanta Dada,' she began.

'Good heavens! Since when have I become your *dada*?'

'From this minute.'

'Oh! No,' I groaned. 'What will become of me if all my girlfriends make me their brother?'

Abhaya laughed. 'So that was your little plan, was it? You are a terrible man. Is this the return you make to poor Rohini Babu for sheltering you and looking after you in your illness?' Then, sobering down, she added, 'What a pity I didn't think of sending a telegram to Rajlakshmi when you were sick! If I had she would have been here by now and I would have had the good fortune of seeing her.'

'Yes,' I agreed.

Abhaya looked thoughtful. 'From the tone of her letter I get the feeling that she needs you desperately. Why don't you take a month's leave and go home, Srikanta Dada?'

I didn't admit it to Abhaya but I too had got the feeling that Rajlakshmi needed me. Next morning, I applied for a month's leave and made all the arrangements for the journey back to India. Just before I stepped into the carriage that was to take me to the harbour Abhaya touched my feet and said, 'I want you to make me a promise.'

'Yes. What is it?'

'Certain situations arise at times, which men are powerless to deal with. If, and when, that happens you must write to me and ask me for my advice.'

I nodded my assent and got into the carriage.

'Another thing,' Abhaya called after me. 'Look after yourself. Be very careful, particularly on the ship.'

I looked back smiling, to see Abhaya's eyes swimming in tears.

Thirteen

THE FIRST PERSON I SAW WHEN THE SHIP TOUCHED THE SHORE WAS Banku. He ran up the steps and, touching my feet with great reverence, said, 'Ma is waiting in the carriage. Why don't you join her? I'll collect your stuff and bring it in.'

I stepped on the jetty to encounter a grinning Ratan. He fell at my feet in an excess of devotion then, leading me to the carriage, opened the door and bid me step in.

'Come,' Rajlakshmi said and, turning to Ratan with a distracted frown, added, 'We are leaving, Ratan. It is two o'clock and Babu is tired and hungry. You hire another carriage and come home with Banku and the luggage. Tell the coachman to start moving.' As we moved on, Rajlakshmi bent down to touch my feet. Then, raising her head, she asked, 'Was the journey uncomfortable?'

'No.'

'You were very ill—'

'I *was* ill but not very. What about you? You look far from well yourself. When did you arrive?'

'The day before yesterday. I left Patna as soon as I got Abhaya's wire intimating your arrival. I would have come a few days later in any case. We have a lot of work waiting for us in Calcutta.'

'It can go on waiting. Tell me, is anything wrong?'

A little smile flickered on Rajlakshmi's face at the sight of which the full realization of what I had been deprived of all these months overwhelmed me. A sweeping, blinding desire swamped all my other feelings but I had to crush it, perforce, with all the will power I was capable of. There was only one witness to my agony of the moment, and that was God. A sigh, wrenched from the depths of my being, made Rajlakshmi look up in surprise and ask, 'Do I look different? Am I thinner than I used to be?'

She was a little thinner and paler, it was true, but that was not all. There was a look, on her face, of excessive fatigue and strain, as if she had just returned from a nightmarish journey across the world, so weary and exhausting that she could barely support herself. On my remaining silent she repeated her question adding, 'Tell me. How am I different?'

'I won't tell you.'

Rajlakshmi gave her head a little shake and begged like a child, 'You *must* tell me. People say I've become old and ugly. Is that true?'

'It is,' I answered solemnly.

Rajlakshmi laughed. 'You are the rudest man I've ever met. Anyway, what does it matter if I've lost my looks? Is our relationship dependent on my youth and beauty that I should die of worry?'

'You needn't die of worry. For one thing, no one has told you that you have lost your looks. For another—even if someone has, you don't believe it. You know very well that—'

'You of course know everything about everybody,' Rajlakshmi said angrily. 'But tell me truthfully—am I exactly as I was when you first saw me at the hunting party?'

'No. You are far more beautiful.'

Rajlakshmi turned her face to the window to hide her delight from my admiring gaze. She sat silent, for a while, apparently absorbed in the sights and sounds of the Calcutta streets. Then, turning to me with a worried gaze, she asked, 'What was it that made you ill? Did you find the climate unsuitable?'

'It is different,' I answered, 'but since I'll have to live in Burma I may as well get used to its air and water.'

Even while making this statement I anticipated a violent protest from Rajlakshmi—an unconditional turning down of my proposal of going back to an environment that, I had admitted, did not suit my constitution. But nothing like that happened. She answered softly, 'That is true. Besides, there are many Bengalis in Rangoon. If they have got used to the climate, you will too—in time.'

The cool indifference with which she made this statement cut me to the quick. All through my convalescence in Abhaya's house I had fantasized about the moment of reunion with Rajlakshmi. I had wrought the scene with care adding colour and depth as I went along. I had imagined the storm in her breast as I told her how I had nursed a plague patient and then succumbed to the dreaded disease. I had seen the tears pouring down her cheeks. But now a terrible shame and humiliation engulfed me. What a blessing it was, I thought, that one cannot look into another's heart! I decided that nothing would induce me to tell Rajlakshmi of my near encounter with death.

As we entered the house she had rented in Bowbazaar, Rajlakshmi pointed to the staircase saying, 'Go straight up to your room on the second floor and rest for a while. I'm coming in a moment.' And with that she moved briskly towards the kitchen. It was not difficult to identify my room for it was a replica of the one I had had in Patna. All my books were there. My hookah, with its long pipe, stood in its usual place by the bed and my velvet slippers sat decorously, side by side, on the footstool. My clothes, my writing materials and all my personal possessions, down to the last detail, had been remembered and brought over with meticulous care. As I looked around I noticed something new. A magnificent sunset in oils that I had always admired in Pyari's bedroom now hung on one wall of mine. I walked over to the armchair at the window and, leaning back, shut my eyes. Tears pricked my eyelids as I felt the waters that had been ebbing away gather themselves, and flow once again from an old strong source.

Exhausted by the journey, I dozed off after lunch. When I awoke I found the afternoon sun streaming on my feet through an open window and Pyari leaning over me wiping the sweat from my face, neck and chest. She said, 'This room faces the west and is very hot. I must move you from here. The one next to mine on the first floor would be cooler I think. See how you're perspiring! The sheet and pillowcase are drenched.' Then, seating herself very close to me on the bed, she started fanning me vigorously with a palm leaf fan.

Ratan entered the room. 'Shall I bring Babu's tea up here?' he asked.

'Yes,' answered his mistress, 'and tell Banku I want to see him.'

I shut my eyes. After a few minutes the sound of slippers could be heard flapping on the marble steps and Pyari's voice called out, 'Is that Banku? Come up here.'

I heard Banku step cautiously into the room. Pyari continued fanning me as she said, 'Take up a piece of paper and a pencil and make a list of the things we need. Then take the darwan with you and buy them.'

This was something new. Except in my illnesses, Pyari had never sat on my bed and ministered to me the way she did now. Even more surprising was the unashamed candour with which she admitted our intimacy before Banku and the servants. The wondrous beauty and boldness of her action filled my heart with emotions I could not describe. I remembered the day she had asked me to leave her house because of what Banku might think or feel.

After Ratan had brought up the tea and Banku departed with the list, Pyari put a question I hadn't expected, 'You say Rohini Babu and Abhaya love each other but whose love is the stronger? Can you tell?'

'Abhaya's—obviously!' I laughed. 'After all, she's the one who has been haunting you for the past six months.'

'What makes you think that?'

'I *know* it. Contradict me if you can.'

'You may be right but *I* believe Rohini Babu's love to be stronger. He has had to pass a more difficult test than Abhaya.'

I was surprised at her reasoning. 'I don't agree,' I said. 'I think Abhaya's struggle has been more painful and bitter than Rohini Babu's. He is a man, after all, and our society is far more supportive of the male than of the female. Don't forget that.'

'I forget nothing,' she said. 'But let me get this clear. You are saying, are you not, that our society is more lenient with men than with women where extra-marital involvements are in question? That, once the affair is over and the woman abandoned, the man is welcomed back to the fold and the passage is made smooth and easy for him? I agree, but then—only the lowest and the most contemptible of men take advantage of that kind of support. Rohini Babu does not belong to that class. Neither do you. Just think of what life is for a man like Rohini Babu. Since he cannot abandon the woman who has trusted him, he is a ready target for the taunts and jeers of his fellowmen. There is no protection for him, for he cannot confine himself within the four walls of his home the way a woman can. He has to go out into the world to earn a living and support the woman he loves. The burden of protecting his beloved and the mother of his children from the assaults of the outside world also falls on him. And as if all this is not torture enough there is, to add to it, the temptation that he has only to lay down his weary load, leave the woman to her fate and his old comfortable world will take him back with open arms. This temptation gnaws at his vitals like a canker, destroying the love for which he had once defied the world. Can you imagine the strength of the love that can withstand all these pressures?'

I saw the force of her reasoning. I remembered Rohini's gentle, self-effacing ways and the stark pain and bewilderment in his eyes after Abhaya left him for her husband.

'But you sent your humblest and sincerest regards to Abhaya and not to Rohini,' I said laughing.

'I did. And I still give her what is her due. I firmly believe that whatever base metal there may have been in her nature has long since been burned to ashes by her inner fire. If it hadn't, she would have been just as low and degraded as any other fallen woman.'

'Why low and degraded?'

'The sin of rejecting a husband is a grievous one—'

'If you had seen Abhaya's husband you wouldn't have said that.'

'Men have been wayward and dissolute through the ages, *and* oppressive to their women. That cannot condone a woman's running away from her husband. Women must submit to their sufferings. The world cannot go on otherwise.'

Her words confused and irritated me for, in them, I saw the reasoning of a passive female who glories in her subordinate status. 'Then what is this fire you were talking about?' I asked, a trifle impatiently.

Rajlakshmi smiled. 'I have just received a letter from Abhaya, giving me an account of your illness. She had been through hell and had just begun to live, when you stormed into her life bringing the plague with you. Your presence threatened to destroy the delicate web of happiness that she had woven for herself. But did she shrink from you? On the contrary, she gathered you to her bosom as spontaneously and fearlessly as a mother would her child. Her strength and discipline, her belief in duty before self, emerge from what I call the fire in her soul. Why is fire referred to as all consuming? Because it makes no distinction between sorrow and happiness and draws both to itself with equal triumph. Something else that she wrote in her letter impressed me. She is determined, she wrote, to make Rohini Babu a success in all his capacities—as a man, a husband and a father—for it is only through one's own fulfilment that one can ensure that of others. Frustration breeds its own likeness and multiplies rapidly. It's very true, isn't it?'

She sighed. We had nothing to say to one another for a long while. Then, running her fingers through my hair, she asked timidly, 'Is Abhaya a very learned woman?'

'Yes,' I answered. 'She seems well educated.'

'That is the secret of her strength. But she has concealed something from me—her yearning to be a mother.'

'Does she have such yearnings? I know nothing of them.'

'What woman doesn't? No one proclaims it before the world.'

'Do you?'

She blushed and hung her head to hide her flaming cheeks. The red-gold beams of the setting sun were streaming in through the window. They shimmered over her lustrous black hair and flashed from the facets of the diamonds in her ears. 'Why should I?' she said, at last, sitting up proudly. 'Do I not have children already? My daughters are married. My son is about to be married. I shall soon have grandchildren. What more do I want?'

I didn't have the heart to contradict her.

After dinner that night, Rajlakshmi said, 'Banku's wedding is a fortnight away. We can go to Kashi and get back well in time. Let's go. I want my gurudev to meet you.'

'Am I worth the trouble?'

'That's the beholder's problem. You don't have to worry.'

'But what is the point of it? What good will our meeting do him, or me for that matter?'

'It is of no consequence to either of you. But it means a great deal to me. Come for my sake.'

I had to agree. Owing to a dearth of auspicious days in the coming months there was a glut of weddings in the city. As we drove to the station on the day of our departure we got caught in a wedding procession. We managed to extricate ourselves with difficulty and as soon as we did so, Rajlakshmi said, 'If you had your way, only the rich would be allowed to marry. How would the world go on?'

'You needn't worry about the world,' I answered, the notes of the bagpipes still shrieking in my ears, 'for there are few in it to take my advice.'

'I'm glad of that. Why should every happiness and comfort be reserved for the affluent? Are the poor not human? Don't they have desires and aspirations—the same as the rich?'

'They may have desires and aspirations, as you put it, but there's no need to give in to them.'

'Why not?'

I was silent for a while. Then I said, 'I hold this view only with regard to the genteel poor. And I think you know my reasons.'

'Your view is lopsided,' Rajlakshmi said stubbornly.

But I, too, could be stubborn. 'You, of all people, know very well it is not. The day Banku's father married you and your sister for the paltry sum of seventy-two rupees is not so far off that you have forgotten it. The only redeeming feature of the case was that he was interested in the money alone. If it hadn't been for that, you would have had the added bonus of a string of children. What would you have done then?'

Rajlakshmi's eyes flashed rebelliously. 'God would have looked after them as he does all his creatures. You are an atheist. That is why you ask such a question.'

'This is a practical approach indeed! To believe that God exists only to bail one out of one's troubles—'

'Even if God turned away from me I wouldn't have despaired. I would have begged from door to door to feed my children. It would have been a far better fate than living the life of a singing girl.'

I gave up the argument. I realized that we were treading dangerous ground: a frequently assaulted, exceedingly vulnerable area of Rajlakshmi's heart!

The day being a Saturday and the time early afternoon, crowds of office employees were seen heading towards the station to catch the two o'clock or two-thirty trains to their respective villages. As our carriage moved jauntily through the jostling masses I noticed that all the men were carrying something or the other in their hands. One had a couple of large lobsters dangling from a string; another, a bit of mutton tied in a kerchief. Grapes and pomegranates peeped out of bursting bags—delectable luxuries to be enjoyed once in a while. Writ large on the faces of the men was the fact that they were going back to their loved ones for a brief but ecstatic reunion.

Rajlakshmi tugged at my sleeve and whispered urgently, 'Why are all these gentlemen rushing to the station? Where are they going? What's today?'

'Today's Saturday. They are going home for the weekend.'

'Yes. That must be it. Look, they all have sweets or fruits in their hands—for the children.'

'Yes,' I murmured.

'How excited the children will be!' Rajlakshmi's imagination had taken wing. 'How they'll jump and dance around their fathers and call out to their mothers,' and Rajlakshmi's cheeks glowed at the thought.

'That they will,' I agreed.

My companion's bright eyes devoured the pedestrians from the window of the carriage for a while longer, then, with a sigh, she turned to me and asked, 'How much do they earn?'

'Twenty or twenty-five rupees,' I said, carelessly. 'Most of them are clerks.'

'But they have wives, mothers and children to support.'

'One two widowed sisters,' I added to her list. 'Guests. Expenses on weddings or funerals. The mess bill in Calcutta. Doctors and medicines. In short, everything is paid for out of those twenty rupees.'

Rajlakshmi's eyes grew enormous and the colour drained from her cheeks. 'You can't be sure of that,' she said. 'They may own property in the village. I'm certain they do.'

I hesitated a little before disenchanting her. I knew what I was about to tell her would hurt her terribly. 'I've lived among them and I know that nine out of ten have nothing beyond their income. And if they lose their jobs they starve with their children or beg.'

Rajlakshmi covered her ears with her hands and wailed, 'Don't tell me anymore. I won't listen to another word.' Her face was flushed and tears trembled in her eyes.

I turned away and resumed my contemplation of the moving scene. There was a long silence. I knew that Rajlakshmi was fighting a mute battle with herself and I let her fight it alone. Then there was a tug at my sleeve. Curiosity had won.

'Tell me about the children,' she whispered. But don't exaggerate their misery—I beg of you.'

The nature of her request and the humility with which she made it, amused me but I kept a solemn face and said gravely, 'The question of exaggerating does not arise for the simple reason that even the bare truth would pain you beyond endurance. I wouldn't have revealed it, had you not stated a while ago that you wouldn't mind begging from door to door to feed your children. The concept that God looks after those he sends into the world is a fine one indeed and not to be convinced by it is to be an atheist! Anyhow, I'll tell you what I know, and leave it to your own logic and reason to work out the extent of God's commitment to those he sends into the world, and that of the unfortunate parents who give them birth.'

I glanced at her anxious face and continued, 'A new-born child is the mother's responsibility. She keeps it alive by suckling it at her breast. My faith in God's abilities is boundless and my conviction of his mercy—supreme. Yet, I confess I have not, to his day, seen Him offering to take on this responsibility.'

'What nonsense you talk,' Rajlakshmi said, half-laughing, half-angry.

'Wait,' I held up a hand. 'Do you know how quickly a woman's milk dries up in families like theirs?' I pointed a careless finger at the crowd. 'Do you know why? If you wish to know, go have a look at what a young mother gets to eat in a middle-class home.' Rajlakshmi's eyes raked mine as a I went on, 'You know how expensive milk is? And how difficult to procure—particularly in a village.'

'I do. Unless you have a cow of your own there's no way you can get hold of milk. I've seen it myself.'

'Then what does a baby eat once the mother's milk is gone?

Water from a slimy, green pond and some barley powder from a tin. And even if a few drops are left for him he cannot enjoy them for long. Within three or four months his successor sibling takes possession of the maternal womb and works actively towards his deprivation. You understand me?'

Rajlakshmi blushed crimson and said sharply, 'Yes, yes. Go on.'

'What happens next is that the malnutritioned child falls prey to two dreaded diseases—dysentery and malaria which attack him by turns. When this happens it becomes the father's duty to provide quantities of raw quinine and barley powder, which the mother mixes in pure, unadulterated pond water and pours down the hapless infant's throat up to the time—needless to say—that her own labour pains overtake her. Then, upon her falls the task of crying bitterly for the old one with the new one in her lap.'

'Crying! Why crying?' Rajlakshmi asked, white to the lips.

'That's a mother's foolishness. Far from being grateful at God's taking charge of those he sends out into the world, a mother will weep and beat her breast over a dead child—even in a middle-class home.'

'God! My God!'

I had been talking all this while with my face to the window. I turned sharply at this low cry and fixed my eyes on my companion's. The expression in them hit me like a physical blow. I felt ashamed and angry with myself. Why had I told her all this? What had I gained by destroying her illusions? She could have gone through life without this knowledge like others of her kind.

Rajlakshmi wiped her eyes and cried passionately, 'What are you made of? You talk of people's misfortunes in that mocking way because you have never known any!'

I did not contradict her, knowing it to be useless. I said softly and humbly, 'I have not known their happiness either. Look at the faces of those men.'

In an instant Rajlakshmi's face become a study in light and shadow. That's exactly what I say!' she cried joyously. 'They are hurrying home to their children. How happy they must feel! So what if they are poor? If they have little money, they don't have expensive tastes either. Anyway, I don't believe they earn as little as twenty rupees. They must be paid a hundred or a hundred and fifty at the least.'

'You may be right. I may have got my figures wrong.'

Rajlakshmi sat up in her excitement. My admittance made her greedy. A hundred and fifty rupees was not enough for her petty clerk. 'Do you think they are solely dependent on their incomes? I'm sure most of them earn a good deal more.'

'How?' I sneered. 'Do they consort with princes who shower money and jewels on them?'

A cloud passed over Rajlakshmi's face. She averted her eyes and said, 'The more I see of you the more disillusioned I get. You know I'm bound to you from childhood. And you test your power over me by wounding me whenever you can.'

I took both her hands in mine and tried to tell her what lay in my heart. But the moment passed. The carriage reached its destination and in the bustle of the arrival my words were left unsaid.

The two-thirty local was about to depart as we stepped on to the platform. As we walked along it, an elderly man, carrying a bag full of vegetables in one hand and a clay bird on a stand on the other, came rushing up from the other end and collided violently with Rajlakshmi. The bird flew from his hand and was shattered to splinters on the platform. With a piercing wail the man sank to his knees and began picking up the pieces even as Banku and Pandeji descended on him, angrily cursing him for being a blind, old fool. I managed to ward them off and turning to the old gentleman, said urgently, 'Your train is leaving. You'd better board it at once.' Torn between the moving train and the broken bird he scrambled to his feet and, apologizing humbly to Rajlakshmi, ran in the direction of a third-class compartment. But too late! The train picked up speed and snaked away. The man returned and resumed his task of picking up the pieces.

'What will you do with those bits of clay?' I asked, smiling.

'My little daughter, she's been sick these many months, has been begging me for a clay bird. I paid two whole annas for it— the shopman wouldn't take a paisa less—but look at my luck! The poor girl will cry her eyes out. I'll show her the pieces and tell her that the first thing I'll buy, on getting my salary, will be her clay bird.'

Saying this the man walked away, clutching the pieces to his breast. Banku and Pandeji had already strolled away to the other end of the platform. I turned to Rajlakshmi, who had stood silent all this while. Tears streamed down her cheeks like monsoon showers.

'What is the matter? Are you badly hurt?' I asked, alarmed.

Rajlakshmi wiped her eyes and said hoarsely, 'Yes. I *am* badly hurt—in a place that you have not the eyes to see or the heart to feel.'

Fourteen

*B*ANKU, IN HIS ENTHUSIASM, HAD RESERVED A FULL COMPARTMENT for our journey to Kashi. In the middle of scolding him for this unnecessary extravagance (the situation was awkward for her, as I well understood) Rajlakshmi's eyes fell on the elderly gentleman sitting on a bench, patiently waiting for the next train. She nudged me and whispered, 'Where is he going? Why don't we take him with us? He can save the ticket money.'

'He must have bought his ticket already.'

'But he can travel in greater comfort!'

I was in a perverse mood. 'People like him are used to discomfort,' I said.

'I don't care. I want to take him with us,' she said stubbornly.

'Why do you want an outsider? Am I not enough for you?'

Nevertheless, I went up to the man with Rajlakshmi's offer, and needless to say, he accepted.

In the train, Rajlakshmi struck up a lively conversation with her travelling companion. Within a few minutes, he had poured out the whole story of his life into her willing ears. By the time the train reached Bardhaman station where he was to alight, Rajlakshmi had gleaned a mass of information on life in the villages of north-west Bengal. Just before the station came into view she opened her trunk and, taking out a sari of brilliant green silk, held it out to him with the words, 'Give this to Sarala as a compensation for her broken bird.'

The old man shrank from her gift. 'No, no. This is too expensive,' he cried out in alarm. 'Please don't put yourself out. I'll buy her another bird.'

'It isn't too expensive and even if it is I'm her *mashi* (maternal aunt) and I want to give it to her. Tell her from me that she must get well soon and then wear it—to please me.'

Tears stood in the old man's eyes. 'You are very kind,' he said. 'But I'm a poor labouring man. My daughter will never find an occasion to wear a sari like that.'

He looked at me for support, but I urged him to take it, 'If Sarala's *mashi* wants to give her a present, it is your duty to accept it on her behalf. I only wish I had a *mashi* like hers.'

The man's eyes shone with gratitude as he took the sari from Rajlakshmi. But I was not interested in his feelings. A question, one that I had asked myself many times in the last one year, came to me again. What was Rajlakshmi heading for? Where would it all end? Giving away a sari worth ten or twelve rupees, in charity, was nothing much to her. But the direction in which all her sympathies were flowing was too clear to be mistaken. A torrent of mother love, gushing from her breast, raced joyously over rocks and boulders, green meadows and dark forests towards a destination unknown. I was afraid for her. I understood Rajlakshmi. I knew that the passion and yearning of her youth, enshrined in the person of Pyari, was dying a slow death—so that the very name brought her pain and humiliation. Gone were the enchanted days, the intoxicated nights of the singing girl, Pyari Bai. She was dying and in her death pangs was being born a woman consumed with mother love—a thirst so deep that not all the waters of the world could quench it. Banku was not enough for Rajlakshmi anymore. Her love encompassed and suffused all the children of the world.

For a long time after the train had left Bardhaman station Rajlakshmi sat silent with her face turned towards the window. 'For whom these showers of salt water? Sarala or her father?' I asked, at last.

'Eavesdroppers—' she began furiously.

'Eavesdroppers have no option but to hear. What else could I do when I was not allowed to speak? Who are you weeping for?'

'That is none of your business.'

'It *is* my business. If your tears are for Sarala's father I will feel extremely threatened.'

I thought the joke would make her laugh and restore her good humour. Instead she turned away completely and fixed her eyes on the passing scene. I made another attempt. 'We should have bought something to eat from Bardhaman station.' On her remaining silent I persisted, 'You weep buckets for the misery of others but have no thought for the members of your own household. From where did you pick up these foreign ways?'

This time she turned around and, fixing her eyes on my face, said, 'I am well aware of the needs of my own household. When the time comes to serve you I shall not be found wanting.'

At the next station, Rajlakshmi sent for Ratan to prepare my hookah and, opening a hamper she had brought from home, filled a huge *thala* with a variety of sweets and savouries. One glance confirmed that all my favourite foods were there. I ate with relish, then lay back comfortably sucking at my pipe. I heard Rajlakshmi say, 'Take the rest of the food to your compartment, Ratan, and if you can't eat it all, give it away.'

'Aren't you going to eat?' I asked, surprised.

'I'm not hungry. Go, Ratan—what are you waiting for?'

I noticed that Ratan's face was red and embarrassed. He turned to me and said, 'I'm very sorry, Babu. I handed the hamper by mistake to a Mussalman coolie. I—'

'Will you go?' Rajlakshmi thundered.

After Ratan had left and the train had started moving, Rajlakshmi came up to where I lay, and running her fingers through my hair, said, 'Don't misunderstand me. I have nothing against Mussalmans. I don't really believe their touch to be polluting. I wouldn't have served you the same food, if I did.'

'Why did you refuse to eat it, then?'

'It is different for women.'

'What do you mean?'

'Men are free to do what they like, eat as they will and go wherever they wish. For them it is enough to be happy. Can men suffer the tribulations that women do as a matter of course? Look at yourself. You were getting peevish because you were hungry.'

'There is nothing great in enduring affliction for its own sake. Neither for you nor for us.'

'For women, suffering is a part of living. We are a race of slaves.'

'Who told you that? Your gurudev?'

Rajlakshmi brought her face close to mine and whispered, 'Everything I've learned in my life, I've learned from you. You are my first and greatest guru.'

'Then you've learned the opposite of what I've tried to teach you. I have always believed that women are equal to men.'

Rajlakshmi's eyes shone, 'I know that. If only all men were like you, the world would be such a wonderful place. No woman would mind being a slave.'

'Do you feel no sense of humiliation when you think of yourself as a slave?'

'No,' Rajlakshmi answered gravely.

'Really!' I said, exasperated. 'The women of our country have been so conditioned by their subordinate status that they have become insensitive to humiliation. As a result they sink lower and lower everyday.'

Rajlakshmi sat up. Her eyes flashed. 'That is not true. Women don't sink of their own volition. It is men who have kept them low and, in the process, have sunk even lower themselves!'

The passion in her voice startled me. I was confused at first. Her words were enigmatic but slowly took on meaning.

'You were laughing at the old gentleman,' she continued. 'Do you know how much I have learned from my conversation with him?'

On my confessing that I did not, Rajlakshmi said, 'You must *want* to know first! A man as self-centred as you—one who runs away from the real world for fear of endangering his own privacy and comfort—can know nothing of others: Yet it is people like you who think they know everything. You hold forth endlessly about how women are being oppressed. Why don't you forget about women for a change and worry about yourselves? Why don't you raise your- selves to a higher level first?'

'I don't know where this argument is leading us, Rajlakshmi. Let's stop for a while. I'm extremely sleepy.'

Rajlakshmi was silent for a few minutes. Suddenly she murmured—quite out of context, 'Greed! Insatiable greed has become the curse of our society. High or low—no one is exempt from it. And that is at the root of all our social evils today. I understand that clearly.'

'That is quite true. But what made you come to this conclusion?'

'Experience. Who has been a greater victim of greed than I? Who ever heard of a mother selling her daughter in the olden days? People were natural then. They followed their fundamental instincts and did not run after money. Today I have all the wealth in the world! But what has it brought me? Even the beggar in the street is happier than I.'

I took her hands in mine and asked gently, 'Are you truly that unhappy?'

She sighed and said, 'Only my Maker can answer your question.'

'Tell me, Rajlakshmi. What do you want from life? What will enable you to pass the rest of your days in contentment?'

'I've thought about that a great deal,' she said promptly. 'I want to be stripped of all my wealth. If I am left destitute—only then ....'

I read between the lines easily enough.

'Since when have you been thinking of such a thing?' I asked softly.

'Ever since I heard of Abhaya.'

'Abhaya has barely started her life with Rohini Babu. She may face a lot of unhappiness in the future.'

'But she'll never be as unhappy as I am. I'm convinced of it.'

I thought for a while, then I said, 'I can sacrifice everything I have for your sake, Lakshmi. But I can't compromise my honour.'

'Have I asked you to do so? And if you can't compromise your honour—which is the only thing worth compromising— why talk of sacrifice?'

'A man who loses his honour is as good as dead. Barring that—I can give up everything for your sake.'

Rajlakshmi drew her hand away from mine. 'Please do not take the trouble. I'd like to ask you one question though. Is honour the sole prerogative of the male? Haven't you heard of women who have thrown away their honour as easily as they would a filthy rag for the sake of the men they love?' I was about to say something when she stopped me with a gesture. 'Enough has been said on the subject. No more! You are not what I believed you to be. Let us put an end to this conversation.' And she rose and moved away to her own seat.

We stepped off the train the next morning and took up our residence in Pyari's enormous mansion in Kashi. I noticed that, barring a couple of rooms on the top floor, the entire building was crammed with widows of varying ages.

'They are my tenants,' Rajlakshmi informed me, laughing.

'What is so amusing? Don't they pay their rents?'

'On the contrary. I pay to keep them.'

'What do you mean?'

'I pay so that they may live to pay me in the future. Don't you understand simple logic? Besides, many among them are my kinswomen.'

'Really?' I asked puzzled.

Rajlakshmi gave me a wry smile. 'The fact that I met my death here in Kashi is common knowledge. It is only fair that those who helped my mother arrange my funeral should be rewarded. Besides, they are so free with their services that they need to be restrained. I have undertaken to do so.'

I stood as if turned into stone. It wasn't as if I was hearing anything new. Yet the laughing remark shook me as never before.

'We've come to Kashi quite uselessly as it turns out,' Rajlakshmi informed me that night. 'Gurudev is away on a pilgrimage.'

'That doesn't disturb me in the least. You'll go back to Calcutta, I suppose.'

'Yes.'

'Is it necessary for me to accompany you? If not I'd like to move on to Prayag.'

'I'll come too. I haven't bathed in the Ganga at Prayag for many years.'

I was in a quandary. I had planned to stay with an uncle. Besides I had many friends and relatives in Prayag. Pyari read my thoughts like a book. 'You are afraid of someone seeing us together, are you not?'

'The trouble is,' I said, acutely embarrassed, 'that even if a relationship is innocent people are liable to misunderstand. One has no option but to be wary of public disapproval.'

Pyari gave a forced little laugh. 'Quite true,' she said. 'Last year around this time, I spent twenty days and nights with you in my arms. How fortunate that no one saw us then! Don't you have any friends in Ara?'

'Why do you taunt me with what is over and done with?' I exclaimed, stung. 'I have never denied that I'm an inferior being—far lower than you in courage and character.'

'Taunt you?' Rajlakshmi flew into a passion. 'Are you suggesting that I rushed to your side to provide myself with the means to taunt you? There's a limit to human endurance. Don't cross it.'

'You saved me from sure death. But I was not worth the trouble. I am petty, worthless. There can be no comparison between you and me.'

'If I saved your life,' Rajlakshmi said arrogantly, 'I did it in my own interest. Not in yours. But I have never thought of you as petty and worthless. It would be easier for me if I could.' And Rajlakshmi walked away without waiting for an answer.

Next morning, as Rajlakshmi handed me my tea, I asked, smiling, 'Are we on talking terms?'

'Why not? Do you wish to say something?'

'Let's leave for Prayag tomorrow morning.'

'Go—by all means.'

'You come too.'

'You are very gracious!'

'Don't you wish to come?'

'Not at present. If I do, someday, I'll let you know.' And she went about her own business.

At noon, as I sat down to my midday meal, I said to Rajlakshmi, 'Do you really believe you can turn away from me? Why this effort in futility?'

'When you are before me I can't. No one can,' Rajlakshmi answered. Then after a pause, she continued, 'I've been thinking. We must put an end to this struggle. It *is* a struggle for both of us. I admit that the mistake was mine. I've been stupid and shameless. Heaven knows what my son thinks of me! And the servants! I've made a spectacle of myself in my old age. Really and truly! You go on to Allahabad as you planned. But look me up before you leave for Burma—if you can.'

And saying this she went out of the room. My appetite vanished in an instant. I knew, from her face, that this was no lovers' quarrel. She was a woman with her mind made up.

When the maid brought my afternoon tea I was surprised, for Rajlakshmi had always made it a point to serve me my meals herself. On asking for her I was told that she had left the house earlier in the afternoon and had not returned yet. I had no idea where she had gone or for what purpose. Yet an acute depression assailed me. Her laughing words about meeting her death in Kashi echoed and re-echoed in my ears. I decided to go for a walk. I wandered aimlessly about the streets for hours. When I reached home at ten o'clock I was informed that Pyari had still not returned. Panic seized me. I was about to call Ratan and question him when I heard the sound of approaching hooves. An enormous phaeton drawn by a pair of superb white horses rolled in and stopped by the porch. There was a murmur of male voices within as Pyari alighted. Suddenly, the moon sprang out of the clouds and rained its beams on her. Her bosom, swathed in glowing tissues, heaved like a sea of beaten gold. Jewels flashed regally from her ears, throat and arms and twinkled in the masses of her hair. Her eyes held mine as she stood moon-washed and still—an enigmatic smile on her lips.

Fifteen

WHEN RAJLAKSHMI ENTERED MY ROOM A LITTLE LATER I JUMPED UP from my chair and declaimed theatrically, 'Cruel, cruel, Rohini! Have you forgotten Gobinda Lal? Oh! for a pistol or even a sword….'

'What will you do with a pistol? Kill me?' Rajlakshmi asked in a frightened voice.

'No, Pyari dear. Why would I deprive my fellowmen of such a very excellent thing as you? Who would block a gold-mine with a piece of rock? On the contrary, my blessings are eternally with you, oh queen of dancing girls! May you live long and take the three worlds in your stride. May the strains of the divine lyre well out of your voice and your feet twinkle like the stars of the firmament, so that even Urvashi and Tilottama are put to shame.'

'What is the meaning of all this?'

'Don't look too deep for meanings. Be satisfied with facts. I'm leaving tonight by the one o'clock train, first to Prayag then to that ultimate pilgrimage of the Bengali clerk—Burma. I'll see you before I leave if I can.'

'Won't you ask me where I went?'

'Certainly not.'

'You mean you'll make an issue of this and leave me forever?'

'I am a weak and miserable sinner. I dare not make a permanent commitment. For the present I'll be grateful to get out of the maze in which I am caught.'

'You are really leaving tonight? Do you have the right to punish me for something I have not done?'

'By no means. But I claim the right to go away if I like.'

'You won't let me tell you where I went?' Rajlakshmi asked after a pause.

'I see no reason to do so. You did not take my permission before you went. Besides, I don't have the time or the inclination to listen to your story.'

'Neither do *I* have the time or the inclination to tell it,' Rajlakshmi lashed out like an angry snake. 'I'm nobody's bondwoman that I must take permission before I leave my own house. You may go wherever you like.' And she walked away imperiously, leaving a trail of scent and colour in her wake.

An hour later, when the carriage I had ordered stopped at the door, Pyari re-entered my room and said, 'Do you really think you can walk out on me like this? Why do you humiliate me before the servants?'

'Your servants are your concern. Not mine.'

'What about Banku? How can I explain your absence at the wedding?'

'Tell him the truth. Tell him I've moved on to Prayag.'

'Is my crime so great that I can't be forgiven? If you show me no mercy, who will?'

'Pyari,' I said smiling, 'You are using a bondwoman's language. It isn't fitting.'

A burning flush spread over Pyari's countenance. She stood irresolute, biting her lip. As I put out a hand to pick up my bag she made a quick movement. 'Don't leave me. Not in this way,' she pleaded. 'Punish me if I have erred but don't humiliate me before my entire household.'

I dropped my bag and sank into a chair. 'The time has come,' I said solemnly, 'for a final reckoning. I forgive you for what you did tonight. But one thing is certain. Our relationship must end. I have thought it over carefully and I have arrived at this decision.'

'Why?' Pyari asked in a small voice.

'Can you stand the truth?'

'I can.'

Hurting a loved one is hard—even harder than being hurt. But, my mind was made up. I said, 'Lakshmi, you are beautiful, wealthy and sought after. You have power over many men. This power is like a heady wine that you will never be able to resist fully. You love me and respect me—I know that. You can sacrifice a great deal for me. But the glamour of your old life will always colour your vision. You can never be totally free from it.'

'You mean I'm liable to stray even when I'm with you?'

I was silent. So was she.

'What then?' she asked at last.

'Then everything we've built together will fall apart. Save me from that fate. It is too miserable, too low. Set me free, I beg of you.'

Pyari sat, her face downcast, for a long long while. When she lifted it at last it was bathed in tears. She asked softly, 'Are you afraid I'll involve you in my degradation? Is that what you mean when you talk of a miserable fate?'

'No. You are incapable of degrading yourself. Still less me. But people don't know that. For them you are not the little Rajlakshmi of Manasa pandit's pathshala, but the notorious Pyari Baiji of Patna. Don't you see that?'

'God can see me for what I really am.'

'True. But since God is invisible, we must accept the vision of his created beings as reflecting his own. We cannot defy the society in which we live.'

Pyari lifted her head and said with a strange smile, 'You are afraid of social disapproval. I can see that. Well, go if you must. I won't stop you. But to put public opinion above me—the greatest friend you have ever had or will have—can never be right. I don't accept it and never will.'

Pyari left the room. I glanced up at the clock. There was just enough time to catch the one o'clock train if I hurried. I crept stealthily out of the house and took my place in the carriage. The driver whipped his horses in a mad rush to the station. But it was useless. The train to Allahabad was already on its way out by the time I arrived, puffing and panting, on the platform. As I stood wondering what to do next, a wave of nostalgia for my native village came upon me. I boarded a Calcutta bound train and, instead of travelling west, set my face towards the east.

I reached my destination at dusk of the following day to find my ancestral home swarming with relatives—some so distant that I had never seen them in my life. I noticed that a number of faces turned pale in alarm even as they exclaimed at the merciful Providence that had brought me once again in their midst. The elderly among them exhorted me to give up my wandering ways, to marry and settle down in my native village.

'That is exactly what I plan to do,' I assured them. 'But I need a rest first. Could I be accommodated in my mother's room?'

But the lady who occupied it with her large family (I discovered later that she was my father's second cousin) looked so woebegone at the prospect that I was forced to amend my proposal. 'I'll sleep in the outer room then,' I said and regretted my generosity immediately afterwards. For, on opening the door, I found it was being used as a godown for building materials. There was nothing for me but to wedge my cot between a pile of stone-dust nearly touching the ceiling and some twenty or twenty-five sacks of lime.

I lay down but could not sleep. My head ached and my limbs felt as if they had turned into stone. Ever since the illness out of which Abhaya had nursed me back to health, I had suffered from periodic bouts of fever. So I wasn't particularly worried or surprised.

'It is heat fever,' Ranga Didi diagnosed. 'It will pass.'

After a week, when the fever did not pass but went on rising steadily, I had my first moments of panic. Doctor Govinda was sent for. He lifted my eyelids, felt my chest, tapped my abdomen with zest and made me swallow quantities of bitter medicines, but to no avail. The fever defied all medical logic and rose higher and higher.

Thakurdada* was frightened. One day, he came to my bedside and said, 'I'd better write a letter to your Pishima. What do you say?' I shook my head violently and begged him not to do so.

Five days passed. On the sixth day I discovered that my wallet was missing. I turned my bag upside down and rummaged frenziedly among its contents, but the small black object was conspicuous by its absence. The doctor who stood by, waiting to be paid, said with a note of alarm in his voice, 'What is the matter? Have you lost anything?'

'No—nothing.'

But when I could not pay him, he understood. 'You should

---

* This is Srikanta's great-uncle, though the word means 'grandfather'.

have been more careful, son,' he said. 'But don't worry. I won't stop your treatment because you've lost your money. You can pay me later—after you've recovered.'

'Please keep this to yourself,' I begged.

There was no question of borrowing money for I had nothing to pledge. I was aware of the fact that not even a four-anna coin was lent without a collateral in the villages of Bengal. I decided to write to Abhaya but before I could do so the news of my loss spread within the household. The loving faces around me turned sullen and gloomy and the tender concern of yesterday gave way to indifference, even hostility. Burma was a long way off. I couldn't afford the luxury of not stooping to Rajlakshmi any longer. I wrote two letters describing my plight and entreating her to send me some money. Addressing one to Patna and the other to Calcutta I lay waiting for the post feeling sick and miserable and utterly degraded.

I had no doubt at all that Rajlakshmi would send me the money, but when two days went by and nothing arrived I felt as though the ground had been cut from under my feet. I lay with my face to the wall trying hard to subdue the painful throbs of my heart.

Suddenly, I heard the sound of carriage wheels. They grew louder and then stopped by my door. I raised my head and saw Ratan on the box. I sat up in excitement. And then my eyes beheld something that was beyond my wildest imaginings. Rajlakshmi was stepping out of the carriage. She had come, in broad daylight, to the very village in which her mother had announced her death only a few years ago.

Rajlakshmi entered my room and, touching my forehead and chest, said with a composure I was far from feeling, 'The fever has broken. Do you feel well enough to travel? We could leave by the seven o'clock train.'

'Are you taking me away?' I asked, my eyes fixed on her face. Then, before she could answer, I said, 'Were you not afraid of coming here? Do you really think no one will recognize you?'

'Why would I think that? I'm sure everyone will recognize me.'

'Then …?'

'One must follow one's destiny. Why did you choose to fall ill here of all places?'

'I didn't ask you to come. You could have just sent the money.'

'You know I couldn't do that—not after hearing you were ill. I was distracted with worry.'

'Well! Your worry is over. And mine has begun. How can I explain your presence here—to all these people?'

Rajlakshmi touched her forehead. 'We only carry out God's will,' she said.

'God's will!' I exclaimed, sitting up angrily. 'What about shame? Don't you have any? How did you dare to show your face here?'

'From today I depend on you to cover my shame.'

What could I say after that? What could I do? I lay back exhausted. After a while I asked, 'Where are you taking me?'

'First to Calcutta, then to Patna.'

'Why to Patna?'

'Because the deeds of gift have been drawn up there.'

'What deeds? What are you gifting and to whom?'

'I'm giving the two houses in Patna to Banku and the one in Kashi to Gurudev. As for my jewels and company holdings—I have divided them up as fairly as I could. But the deeds will be registered only after you approve of them.'

'What have you kept for yourself?' I sat up, alarmed. 'Suppose Banku doesn't look after you?'

'I don't want him to look after me, I'm not giving up my possessions to become his ward.'

'But why are you doing such a thing? Whom will you turn to in your old age?'

'The one I'll turn to, will not forsake me. Do not excite yourself. Go to sleep.'

I turned my face to the window. The sun had almost set. Earth and sky swam in a haze of misty gold and out of the blue and violet shadows of dusk the star of the evening rose—pure as a rain-washed pearl. Never had the world seemed more beautiful. Tears rolled down my cheeks and peace flooded my being. How long I lay in this state I cannot tell. The sound of approaching footsteps made me look up. Thakurdada and Doctor Babu walked in.

Thakurdada has always been a man of great sagacity. Glancing briefly in Rajlakshmi's direction he asked, 'Who is the girl, Srikanta? I think I've seen her before.'

'So have I,' his companion chimed in. 'Her face is familiar.'

I let my eyes rest on Rajlakshmi's face. It was suffused with a deathly pallor. Suddenly, a voice murmured within me, 'Be kind to her, Srikanta. She has forsaken everything for your sake.' To hell with the truth, I thought. I put out my hand and taking hers, said gently, 'You have come to your husband, Rajlakshmi. You have nothing to be ashamed of. Go make your *pronams** to Thakurdada and Doctor Babu.'

I saw the elderly gentlemen exchange glances as Rajlakshmi rose and pulled her veil over her face. Then, kneeling before them, she touched her brow to the ground at their feet.

---

*   to make obeisance

Forbidden Fruit

One

ONCE AGAIN I DRAW BACK THE CURTAIN ON THE SCENE AS I LEFT IT so many years ago. I had thought of ending this narrative. I had thought that I would keep the look on Rajlakshmi's face when my great-uncle hastily drew his feet away mumbling vaguely, 'Good, good. Live long and be happy,' to myself alone—not share it with others. But now I'm glad to unburden myself, glad to open up that chamber of my heart within which lie secret mysteries that cry out to be unravelled. For years I kept the door locked allowing doubts and suspicions to batter at it. Today, the lock has rusted away and all stands open to view.

Rajlakshmi looked at Thakurdada's retreating back and said with a pained smile, 'He was afraid I would touch him.' Then, turning to me, she said sadly, 'Why did you have to tell him that? It didn't do us any good. It only—'

I agreed with her. The lie didn't do either of us any good. I should have known that to any law-abiding Hindu, marrying a widow was no better than marrying a prostitute. I had pushed Rajlakshmi into a deeper humiliation and in doing so, had humiliated myself.

Rajlakshmi sat immobile as a statue. Then she rose suddenly with a jerk and said urgently, 'We'd better leave at once or we'll miss the train.' And calling out to Ratan, she ordered him to prepare for our departure. Within ten minutes my bag was packed and stowed away, my bedding rolled up, and I found myself sitting in a corner of the carriage. Not a word passed between us.

I had entered my ancestral village only a few days ago. No one had welcomed me then and no one bade me a tearful farewell now. But it was the same twilight hour. Conch shells blew from little homesteads. Snatches of kirtan and a clashing of cymbals came from the mandir adjoining the mansion of the Basu Mullicks. Everything was the same—yet how different!

I had never attached any particular significance to the crumbling walls that my ancestors had raised in this remotest of remote Bengal villages. I had never thought of losing my place within them as a loss. Yet, that day, when the prospect of going back to it had become as distant as the northern star, this sodden, malaria-ridden, unhealthy village of Bengal drew me with a thousand arms.

As we clattered along the winding path I thought of my grandmother being borne along it—a child bride in a yellow palki. I thought of the bridal bullock-cart that had carried my mother from her father's village through the shadows of the very trees that spread its branches over our heads. And it was along this path that they had journeyed on the shoulders of their sons to be immersed in the Ganga to the chant of Vedic mantras. This path had not been so perilous then, so dark and depressingly choked with weeds and *bainchi* bushes. The air had been clean, the sun bright. Food there had been in plenty—food, life, warmth and kindness. Tears flooded my eyes.

I gathered the dust from the carriage wheel and touched it to my head. 'I am your unworthy son. I have never loved you, never valued you. But, today, when I leave you, perhaps never to return, the image of your suffering motherhood trembles in my eyes. These are the first tears I shed for you but they are wrung out of my heart. I will never forget you.' I looked up and saw Rajlakshmi sitting in her corner, eyes shut, head resting on the window. She seemed deep in thought. 'Think hard, Rajlakshmi,' I said to myself. 'It is up to you to see us safely across the river over which we are floating. Avoid the whirlpools and find the shore as best as you can.'

I had studied my own mind often enough. I knew its qualities and its limitations. It couldn't take too much of anything—not even health, happiness and well-being. Too much love disturbed me, it made me feel hemmed in. I felt suffocated and yearned for escape. Yet, I had voluntarily enslaved myself to Pyari. What pain there was in my surrender only my Maker knew.

I glanced out of the window at the sky now black with night and then at the dim form of Pyari. I folded my hands humbly—before whom I did not know. 'I've tried to resist the tide of her love,' I thought. 'I've tried to escape it but all my separate paths, like an intricate maze, only led me back to her. Of what use is this struggle? Far better to surrender to one whose success in lifting herself out from a cesspool of vice and degradation will ensure my survival.' Immersed in these thoughts, it took me some time to notice that Rajlakshmi hadn't said a word since her command to Ratan to get ready for departure. Even after we reached the station she stood by a pillar, mute and expressionless, while Ratan, instead of rushing to the ticket office, proceeded to spread my bedding in a corner of the waiting-room. I understood, from his action, that we were not to catch the train to Calcutta for which we had hurried but the morning train. But what our destination was—Kashi or Patna—I did not know. Nor did anyone care to enlighten me.

Ratan came up to Rajlakshmi and said, 'Ma, the coolies tell me that there is a shop a little further on where the food is clean and well-cooked.' Rajlakshmi undid a little knot at the end of her sari and taking out a few coins handed them to Ratan with the words: 'Go and buy some. But be very careful about the milk. Make sure it isn't stale.'

Ratan hesitated a little, then said jerkily, 'Some fruit for you—anything?'

'Nothing.'

We were all familiar with Rajlakshmi's stubborn ways—Ratan most of all. Still he stood his ground, shifted his feet and mumbled, 'But you haven't eaten anything for the past two days—'

'Are you deaf, Ratan? Didn't you hear what I said?'

Ratan was forced to withdraw. He knew, as well as I did, that Rajlakshmi, despite her denial, had a streak of orthodoxy in her that would never permit her to eat anything on a train journey. Going without food was nothing to Rajlakshmi. She kept many fasts—most of them utterly without meaning. Another thing I had noticed about her was that she rarely ate except the barest minimum of the coarsest of food. Every kind of delicacy was to be found in her kitchen, but none of it ever passed through her lips. If I teased her about this rigorous disciplining of her body she would laugh and exclaim, 'I discipline my body! That's a joke. Why, I eat everything!'

'Do you? Then let me put you to the test.'

'Now? Goodness, no! I'd die if I had to eat anything now.' And she would go about her business, serene in her resolution to save herself from death.

The habit of self-deprivation had become so much a part of her that it often went unnoticed. But I couldn't help wondering, from time to time, when it had first started and why. It was obviously before I came into her life for the second time. I've often thought how difficult it must have been for her, in the beginning, to deny herself the luxuries she had grown accustomed to—luxuries bought with her money and enjoyed freely by the people around her. Was not this ability to stand firm in the face of temptation to be lauded? And had she not passed the final test only a few hours ago in her solemn resolve to surrender all her possessions for the sake of her love?

The waiting-room was empty except for the two of us. Ratan had disappeared. I went up to Rajlakshmi where she sat motionless beneath a flickering lamp. I placed a hand on her head and said gently, 'Why are you sitting here in this dust and litter? Come and sit with me on my bed.' I pulled her up by the hand giving her no opportunity to refuse, but once together we had nothing to say to one another. I took her hand in mine and stroked it tenderly. I saw her tears fall, one by one. Then, as I put up my hand to wipe them away, she threw herself at my feet, sobbing uncontrollably.

I allowed her to weep for a while, then I said, 'I have something to say to you, Lakshmi.'

'What is it,' she whispered hoarsely.

I hesitated. It was hard to say what I wanted to. But I did not allow myself to weaken. 'I'm yours from this moment onwards— to do what you like with. Whatever happens to me—good or bad—is your responsibility.'

Rajlakshmi smiled through her tears. 'What use are you to me? You can't play the tabla or the sarangi. And—'

'And? Can I serve paan and tobacco? Most emphatically not.'

'But the other two?'

'I can try my hand at them.'

'Can you really?' She sat up in her enthusiasm.

'Well! I hope I can.'

Rajlakshmi looked at me with a strange expression in her eyes. Then she said, very softly, 'Somehow I always believed that—even when you went around with a gun in your hand. Then I would remind myself that one who delighted in shooting innocent animals couldn't possibly have a feeling for music, could never know its divine agony! My conviction of your insensibility helped me to overcome the pain you've inflicted on me so often.'

It was my turn to fall silent. I could have countered her accusations with well-chosen arguments but a strange lassitude overtook me. Something, deep down, told me that she was right—that she had instinctively sensed what I had only rationalized. She had put it clumsily but her words brought home a supreme truth. I understood for the first time, that the pain of awakening that had come to her slumbering consciousness was linked with her growing love for music. Hence her self-denial, her sacrifice. Hence the pristine purity of her soul!

I could have told her that man's nature was made up of contradictions. If it wasn't so, how could I, who couldn't bear the death of an ant in childhood, who often starved so that stray dogs may eat, shoot down wild animals and birds with an unflinching eye? And Rajlakshmi herself? How could I reconcile her—whose heart and mind stood as clearly revealed before me, tonight, as that moon in the sky—with the opulent, infamous Pyari Baiji of Patna? But I couldn't bring myself to utter the words. Not only because I wished to spare her pain but because the truth of today could easily be the falsehood of tomorrow. Where a man is being driven, by what Gods and demons—he does not know. How else can one explain the transformation of a man of many appetites into a yogi? What changes the cruel, grasping landlord into a selfless philanthropist? Where, in what dark closet of the human soul, lie those unconscious yearnings that, suddenly awakening into life, assume mastery? No one can tell. I scrutinized my companion's face in the feeble light and thought, 'She sees my capacity for inflicting pain to the exclusion of everything else. That I endure it—day in and day out—is unknown to her. In fact, she forgives me my inability to suffer out of the greatness of her love!'

'Yet you willingly sacrificed everything for one you consider so cruel?' I smiled up at her.

'Not everything,' she answered. 'I haven't sacrificed you.'

Two

$\mathcal{I}$ WAS SUFFERING FROM MALARIAL FEVER—COMMON IN THE villages of Bengal. That it held me well in its grip was evident even before the train entered Patna. I was carried, half-fainting, out of the station and for a month after that I lay confined to bed with the doctor and Rajlakshmi in attendance. When the fever subsided the doctor advised a change of scene. Preparations to leave Patna commenced. These, I noticed, were somewhat more elaborate than usual.

One day, I called Ratan to my side and asked, 'Where are we going, Ratan?'

He threw a surreptitious glance at the door before answering in a lowered voice that it was to an obscure village in Birbhum called Gangamati which Rajlakshmi had never set eyes on. He himself had visited it briefly in the company of the *mukhtiar* (an attorney), Kishen Lal, when the land had first been bought. I could see from his face that he disapproved heartily of the plan but did not dare say so for fear of incurring his mistress' wrath.

'Where in Birbhum is this village?' I asked with a sinking heart.

'About twenty miles in the interior from Sainthia station. One has to get there in a bullock-cart. The land is bare and pebbly—red in places and burned black in others. Nothing grows there. There's hardly any water. And the people are so rough and coarse. Why we must leave our beautiful city to live among the lower castes in a strange village—I really don't understand.'

But I understood. I sighed and said, 'The doctor has advised a complete change for me, Ratan. I'll never recover if we go on living here.'

'But Gangamati is not the only other place in the world. People are falling ill all the time. They don't all go there.'

'There are diseases and diseases, Ratan,' I said. 'Perhaps Gangamati is the only cure for mine.'

'There's nothing there,' Ratan persisted, 'but this piece of land, and a caretaker to look after it. Ma has sent him two thousand rupees with instructions to get an earthen house built. Can we live in such a house, Babu?'

'Don't go there if you don't want to, Ratan,' I said softly. 'No one can force you to.'

But my words failed to pacify Ratan. He pushed out his lower lip and said, 'Ma can. I don't know what power she has over us but even if she were to order her servants to go to hell we wouldn't dare disobey.' And Ratan left the room, his face like a thunder-cloud.

It suddenly dawned on me that his words—though uttered in anger—were absolutely true. I was not the only one who was in Rajlakshmi's power. She held her entire household in the hollow of her hand. 'By virtue of what?' I asked myself. Had I been a superstitious man I would have put it down to some tantra or mantra. I thought of the many ways I had tried to escape her. I had left her after a violent quarrel believing, quite honestly, that I'd seen the last of her. I had become a sanyasi. I had even left my country, voluntarily embracing exile so as never to see her again. And all I had done was go round and round in a circle that led me back, unfailingly, to her. I hated myself for my weakness. Yet I succumbed to it over and over again.

Even as these thoughts passed through my head, I saw Rajlakshmi hurrying past my room with a bowlful of something in her hands.

I called out to her, 'Rajlakshmi! Do you practice witchcraft?'

The shapely brows came together. 'Do I practice what?'

'Witchcraft. Everyone says so.'

'Yes, I do.' She flashed her eyes at me and was about to leave the room when she suddenly stopped and said, 'Isn't this the same shirt you were wearing yesterday?'

I squinted down at it. 'Yes. I believe it is. It looks quite white, though.'

'That doesn't make it clean. When will you learn that everything is not as it appears on the surface?'

Rajlakshmi put down her bowl and, fetching a fresh shirt, handed it to me. As I stripped off the old one I noticed that the inside was sweat-stained and grimy. I don't know why the fact depressed me but it did.

Rajlakshmi's insistence on cleanliness and purity in all things had always seemed an obsession—meaningless and oppressive to others. Today, suddenly, I felt differently. It was not that the old irritation vanished without a trace. It did not. But her insinuation that I judged only by the surface of things set me on another track of thought. I thought of the two lives that had run, in apparent contradiction, for so many years. I thought of the child, Rajlakshmi, and of how she had nurtured her love in silence and in secret and how, when the time came to reveal it, the tempestuous beauty, Pyari, had dived deep down below the slime and rank weeds of her day to day living to come up in triumph—the radiant, myriad-petalled lotus in her hand. But was that Pyari? No! No! No! My whole being protested. That was Rajlakshmi—Rajlakshmi alone.

I didn't know the whole of Pyari's history—or Rajlakshmi's for that matter. All I knew was that they had nothing in common, that they flowed out in opposite directions from a secret old source. Thus, when the blossom of love was unfolding its tender petals in the calm waters of one, the raging torrent of the other could not touch it. Not a petal was bruised. Not a spot marred its dazzling whiteness.

The shadows of evening grew longer and dusk was upon me. 'Pyari is dead,' I thought. 'But was Pyari only a beautiful body sullied by time and tide? Shall I judge her by that alone? And Rajlakshmi? She who had burned herself to ashes in the fire of sorrow and degradation and emerged pure gold—shall I turn my face away from her? Shall I judge man by the animal in him that snarls and bites and knows not its Maker or shall I seek out the hidden angel that suffers and surrenders in silence?'

It was not so long ago that I had given myself up—weak, exhausted and vanquished—to Rajlakshmi. The humiliation of defeat was still upon me. But, now, a strange peace descended on my soul. A voice whispered in my ear, 'Let Pyari, whom you do not know, lie buried in oblivion. Rajlakshmi was yours and is yours. Put out your arms and draw her to your heart. That it all that lies in your power. Leave the rest to Him who sees and knows and cares.'

Preparations to leave Patna went on. One afternoon, I saw Pyari engaged in the task of packing enormous quantities of brass and silver utensils in a big trunk.

'Why are you packing so much?' I called out to her. 'Are you leaving the house for good?' Even as I said the words I remembered that she had given the house away to Banku. 'What if you don't like the place after a while?' I asked.

'You needn't worry about that,' she answered with a faint smile. 'You may come away the moment you like. I won't stop you.'

I was hurt by her tone and did not care to carry on the conversation. It was not for the first time that Rajlakshmi had deliberately twisted my meaning and insinuated that my commitment to her was of an ephemeral kind. This conviction had become so firmly embedded in her consciousness that nothing I could say or do could shake it. The most innocuous of remarks from me could release a torrent of suspicion and mistrust. I wondered when this would end and how.

Another week went by before we set off for our destination. I was irritable and depressed on the journey though not as much as Ratan who sat, glum and rebellious, in his corner of the compartment. My heart sank every time I thought of what lay at the end of the journey. It was not that I was apprehensive of the possible absence of comforts and conveniences in Gangamati. Its unfamiliarity daunted me. The thought of the strange new life ahead lay like a heavy burden on my heart. I glanced at Rajlakshmi, gazing quietly out of the window, and suddenly thought that I had never loved her in my life, yet, like a fool, I'd put myself in her power and left no loophole for escape. I had believed, only a day ago, that my only chance of breaking out of the labyrinth of Rajlakshmi's love lay in my surrender. 'I am yours, Rajlakshmi, to do what you like with,' I had said. How easy it had been to say the words. But now my heart burned with painful feelings. Who had known that the reality would be like this?

WE REACHED SAINTHIA STATION LATE IN THE AFTERNOON TO BE met by two men with a letter from Kashi Ram, the caretaker. Apologizing for not being there to welcome us (he was busy preparing for our arrival in Gangamati) he informed Rajlakshmi that he had made all the arrangements for a safe and comfortable journey to the village. Four bullock-carts, two open and two covered, were waiting outside the station. The first two would carry the luggage. Of the covered carts, the one that had a thick carpet of straw and palm leaf matting over it was for the mistress. The other was for the servants. He concluded the letter with the advice that we should set off immediately after a meal, preferably before dusk. Assuring Rajlakshmi that the journey was perfectly safe (there were no thieves or bad characters about) he advised her to have a good night's rest in the cart.

Rajlakshmi's lip curled a little as she read the epistle. Then, turning to the man who had brought it, she asked, 'Is there a pond nearby where I can have a dip?'

'Yes, mistress. There it is behind those trees.'

Rajlakshmi walked away in the direction indicated, with Ratan accompanying her. I wanted to warn her about bathing in a strange pond which might be infested with malaria for all we knew. But I didn't, knowing it to be useless. Besides, she might, just possibly, eat something after a bath. Without it not a drop of water would pass through her lips.

Returning in a few minutes, Rajlakshmi got busy serving my evening meal. Spreading an asan under a tree she got a fresh green banana leaf upon which she arranged, in orderly piles, the food she had brought from home.

I had barely begun eating when I heard a deep voice behind me call, 'Narayan! Narayan!'

I looked back, startled, to see a tall handsome young sanyasi striding purposefully towards us. He was not more than twenty years old. His complexion was like beaten gold. His eyes, nose lips and brow seemed carved out of marble but his saffron robes were torn in places and tied in knots. I stared at this paragon of male beauty in wonder. Rajlakshmi rose and, pulling her veil a little lower over the damp knot of her hair, knelt and touched her forehead to the ground at his feet.

'The servants will give you water to wash,' she said. 'I'll serve your meal in a few minutes.'

'You are welcome to do so,' the sanyasi said calmly, 'but I come to you for something else.'

'I know. You want the money to go back home.' And Rajlakshmi turned her face away to hide a smile.

'You are quite wrong,' the sanyasi said solemnly. 'I heard you were on your way to Gangamati. So am I. I want you to carry a box for me on your luggage cart.'

'That is quite easy. But you—?'

'I can walk. It is only twenty miles away.'

Rajlakshmi said nothing. She got busy preparing another banana leaf for her guest. We ate in silence for a few minutes and then Rajlakshmi said, 'What is your name, Sadhuji?'

'Bajrananda Swami.'

'Goodness! What a mouthful! And your real name?'

'I have left that behind me. It is of no consequence to me now—or to anyone else.'

'Very true,' Rajlakshmi said meekly though she looked as though she would burst out laughing any minute. However, she controlled herself and asked another question, 'How long is it since you ran away from home?'

I looked up. Such vulgar curiosity was not worthy of Rajlakshmi, I thought. My eyes fell on her face. There was an expression on it that I hadn't seen in a long time. I had forgotten what Pyari had looked like. Now suddenly she was there before me—the old Pyari with the dimpled cheeks and gleaming eyes. Even her voice had changed: it was low and husky.

A morsel of food must have gone down the wrong way, for the sadhu burst into a fit of coughing. 'The question is discourteous and irrelevant,' he said severely, between coughs.

Rajlakshmi was not put out in the least. She nodded and said demurely, 'Very true. I ask it only because I had a bad experience—once.' Then, turning to me she said, 'Why don't you tell Sadhuji about your camels and mules? *Durga*! *Durga*! Someone is remembering you, Sadhuji. Have some water.'

I had not spoken a word in all this while. Nor had the sanyasi addressed himself to me. Now he asked me gravely, 'Were you a sanyasi too—once?

My mouth was full of *luchi*. I lifted four fingers of my right hand and spluttered, 'Not once. Not once. Four! Four!'

The sanyasi's reserve broke down and he burst into a peal of merry laughter. After a while he asked, still laughing, 'What made you change your mind?'

I pointed a finger at Rajlakshmi.

'What lies you tell!' Rajlakshmi exclaimed in mock anger. 'Well, once perhaps! No, not even that. It was your illness, not me, that made you change your mind. Anyway, what about the other three?'

'The mosquitoes are to blame. My skin wasn't thick enough to withstand their assaults er—'

'You may call me Bajrananda,' the sanyasi said smiling. 'And your name—'

Rajlakshmi spoke before I could, 'You may call him Dada and me Bowdidi* if you wish. We are both older than you.'

The sanyasi blushed. I too was taken aback. Rajlakshmi was being too familiar, I thought. But, looking on her face, I changed my mind. Pyari's eyes looked out of it—those old, clear, trusting, loving, happy eyes. This was the same Pyari who had fought and argued and wept because I had taken up the old man's challenge of visiting the burning-ghat at midnight; the same Pyari who had

---

*   Elder brother's wife.

insisted I part company with the prince. Her heart had gone out to the nameless boy who had left his loved ones forever. All the pain of parting that had been his mother's was now hers.

'I don't mind calling you Dada,' the sanyasi said to me. 'But—' He glanced at Rajlakshmi and lowered his eyes.

Rajlakshmi was not embarrassed in the least. 'But what?' she asked him archly. 'What does a sanyasi call his brother's wife? Not Mashima, surely, or Pishima?'

The boy smiled shyly. 'I'm with you for another five or six hours. I'll call you Bowdidi—if the need arises.'

Rajlakshmi took a handful of barfis and pedas from the pot of sweets at her side and placed them on his leaf. 'And I'll call you Sadhu Thakurpo.* Shall I?'

'As you wish,' he answered indifferently.

But, despite his cryptic comments and stern expression, he displayed a voracious appetite. The speed with which the luscious milk sweets Rajlakshmi kept piling on his leaf disappeared, alarmed me not a little. A deep sigh escaped me at which Rajlakshmi looked up sharply and said, 'You have had a long journey and you must be tired. Go and rest in the cart.'

The sadhu looked up from his leaf and said, 'The pot is nearly empty. It *is* something to sigh about.'

'There's plenty left,' Rajlakshmi said, glaring at me.

Precisely at this moment, Ratan came up to where we sat and announced in all innocence, 'Ma! I bought the *chire* as you said. But what will you eat it with? Not a drop of milk or curd is to be found in the bazaar.'

The sadhu turned a red embarrassed face to Rajlakshmi and said, 'I have been very selfish. I—'

He attempted to rise but Rajlakshmi put out a hand and pulled him down crying wildly, 'No. Don't get up. If you do, I'll throw the rest of the food in the dust. I swear I will.'

The passion in her voice must have surprised him for he stared at her and said helplessly, 'But what about the rest of you?'

'There's plenty of food for the servants. As for me, I'll be happy with a handful of *chire* and a gulp of water. But if you go away

---

* Husband's younger brother.

hungry I won't have even that. Ask him if you don't believe me.' And she waved a hand in my direction.

'That is quite true,' I said. 'Don't waste your time arguing with the woman. Carry on the good work and complete it before sundown if you can. After that—even the *chire* and water will lose their purity.'

The sanyasi stared at her and asked in a wondering voice, 'But why?'

Rajlakshmi blushed and, pulling her veil a little lower, resumed her task of serving the one who had given up worldly pleasures in favour of a life of abstinence.

The night of the thirteenth moon was barely upon us when the line of bullock-carts started moving slowly towards Gangamati. I was in front, comfortably ensconced in the cart meant for Rajlakshmi. She herself was in the middle, with the servants and luggage behind her. The sadhu, his tall form clearly visible in the moonlight, strode on ahead.

'Brother!' I called. 'It is a long way to walk. Sit with me in my cart for a while.'

'I will when I get tired. Just now I prefer to walk.'

'Then walk by my side as my bodyguard,' Rajlakshmi's voice was heard in the dark. 'We can talk as we go along. I can judge by your accent that you do not belong here. You are probably from our part of the world. What are you doing here and where are you going?'

'To Gopalpur,' was the brief answer.

'How far is it from Gangamati?'

'They are neighbouring villages, or so I've heard. To tell you the truth I know nothing of them. I've never been there in my life.'

'How will you find the village, then, so late at night? Or the house you're expected in?

'To find the village will not be difficult. I've been told that it lies two miles south of a dried up tank that falls right on the track. As for being expected anywhere—there is no such thing. Once there I'll look for a tree under which I can sit and wait for the dawn to break.'

'You'll spend this bitter, winter night under a tree? With only that thin blanket to cover you?' Rajlakshmi cried out in an anguished voice. 'No, Thakurpo, I can't let you do that.'

There was a long silence. Then the sadhu's voice was heard

saying, 'But I have no home, Didi. The shade of a tree is my only shelter.'

It was Rajlakshmi's turn to fall silent. After a while her voice fell, soft and gentle, on my ear. 'Not when your sister is with you. Come home with me tonight. Go wherever you wish after daybreak. I won't stop you.' Calling Ratan, she told him that no luggage was to be moved without her express command.

'Then give up walking in the cold wind, bhai,' I broke the silence that followed. 'Come into the shelter of the cart.'

'I will, presently. Let me talk to Didi for a while.'

It was obvious, now, that he had given up the struggle and surrendered heart and soul to Rajlakshmi.

The hours went by. Snatches of conversation came to my ears between the noise of the night—the creaking of wheels, the baying of jackals and the sleepy voices of the servants. I dozed off once in a while waking up with a jerk. I heard Rajlakshmi ask after one such rude awakening, 'What do you have in your box, Ananda?'

'A few books and medicines.'

'Why medicines? Are you a doctor?'

'I'm a sanyasi. Have you not heard of the cholera epidemic in these parts?'

'No. I know nothing of it. But you—can you cure cholera?'

'No man can cure anything. He can only serve his fellowmen as best as he can. The rest lies in the hands of God.'

'Was that why you became a sanyasi? To serve your fellow-men?'

'One of the reasons. We have another mission—to free our country from the foreign yoke.'

'Is it necessary to renounce the world for that?'

'I haven't renounced the world. I'm too small a man to make such a claim. I've only exchanged some responsibilities for others.' Then, pausing for a few moments, he added, 'You are pained at the thought of all I've lost just as if you were my true sister. But if you had seen those for whom I've left my home and family, if you had seen their agony, their helplessness, their sheer numbers—you would never ask me to abandon them.'

I could guess from her silence that the sanyasi's words had touched a vulnerable spot in Rajlakshmi's heart. I myself was not unaware of my country's condition. I had witnessed her suffering and suffered for her. But this young boy had done more. He had pledged himself to a lifetime of service. The sleep vanished from my eyes and hot tears pricked my eyelids. I don't know what Rajlakshmi's new brother made of her silence. But I knew what lay in her heart.

The impassioned young voice came echoing through the dark. The sanyasi described the plight of rural India where ninety per cent of our countrymen live. He spoke of the poverty and degradation, the polluted air and germ-ridden water. He lashed out at the primitive faith of our people: their superstitions, their obscurantism. He condemned the white foreigners who had ravaged our land and were steadily bleeding her white. My eyes burned with shame and sorrow as I listened. Never had my country's humiliation lain heavier on my heart.

The cart's wheels creaked and the bullocks' feet were a steady patter on the stony path. The land stretched away on all sides—arid and waste. The smell of dust was in the air even as the night dews were falling. It was cold, bitterly cold, and the moon, pale with frost, hung high in the heavens.

Suddenly, the voice changed. It became gentle, everyday. 'I met you only a short while ago, but I think I know you, Didi. I wish I could show you the millions of our brothers and sisters I spoke of. You would have understood them and suffered with them.'

Rajlakshmi was silent for a long, long while. Then, clearing her throat, she said huskily, 'How can that be? I'm a woman, Thakurpo.'

'All the more because you are a woman, Didi.'

Four

I WOKE UP, CRAMPED AND COLD, TO THE SOUNDS OF ARRIVAL AND the twittering of birds in the pearly dawn. As I sat up, I was alarmed to find myself surrounded by what seemed to be a sea of faces. Crowds of naked children and half-naked adults swarmed about the carts as they stood at the entrance of our new dwelling house. I had heard Ratan complain that only the lowest of the lower castes lived in Gangamati. Looking on the faces about me I was forced to admit the truth of his statement.

As the children squirmed and pushed, in an attempt to catch a glimpse of the mistress, Ratan descended on them angrily. 'Get away—shoo, scram! How dare you get so close, you vermin? What are you staring at? Are we here for your entertainment? Look, Babu! Look at their cheek. Pushing their way in as though they belong here. Filthy untouchables!'

Sadhuji, meanwhile, was busy unloading his trunk from the luggage cart. Opening it he took out a bell metal pitcher and, approaching the nearest child, pressed it into his hand and said, 'Run and fetch some water from the nearest pond, boy. I'm going to make some tea.' Then, turning to a ragged-looking man who stood idly by, he asked, 'Dada, does anyone nearby happen to own a cow. I could do with a bit of fresh milk.'

All this while, Rajlakshmi had sat motionless in her cart watching the scene with anxious eyes. But when Sadhuji turned to her, saying heartily, 'Fresh cow's milk, Didi! What fine tea it will make,' she could contain herself no longer.

'Ratan,' she called, her voice sharp. 'Take the pitcher to the nearest pond and fill it. Be sure to scour it well first.'

As was to be expected, Ratan's temper was not improved by this command. To be rudely woken out of a sweet slumber by an unruly mob was bad enough. To be expected to venture forth in the biting cold to look for a pond from which to fill a pitcher that belonged to an unknown sadhu, was not to be borne. His face gradually assumed the character and dimensions of a hornet's nest that had been violently disturbed. He made a rush towards the hapless urchin who stood gaping, pitcher in hand, and roared, 'Why did you touch the pitcher you vicious imp? Come with me and scour it out or I'll—'

The sadhu and I burst out laughing. Rajlakshmi said with a pained smile, 'You've managed to turn the village upside down, Ananda. Do sanyasis have to have their tea at crack of dawn?'

At this moment, Rajlakshmi's caretaker, Kashi Ram Kushari, came hurrying in with three or four men behind him. One carried a basket of fresh vegetables and greens, another had several pots of milk and curd with him and yet another dangled an enormous *rui* by a string. I watched him closely as Rajlakshmi stepped down and made her obeisance. He was a lean, elderly man of about fifty years of age with a fair clean-shaven face. There was a simplicity about him that I liked. We greeted each other with instant approval. Sadhuji, disdaining these conventional niceties, had, in the meantime, relieved the men of their burdens and was now examining the contents with a lively interest.

Announcing that the vegetables were freshly picked and the milk thick and creamy he proceeded to deliver a short sermon on the weight, size and anticipated flavour of the *rui*.

'Don't be alarmed, Kushari *moshai*,' Rajlakshmi said with a glance at the former's anxious eyes. 'The sanyasi is my brother. This is not my first attempt to transform an ascetic into a householder.'

Ananda retaliated with a laugh, 'Do your best, Didi. I assure you, you won't succeed. Not this time.'

Entering the house we found it to be large and well appointed. The time given him being too little to build a new house, Kushari *moshai* had, with discreet additions and alterations, converted the old court-house into a comfortable dwelling place. There was a large sitting-room, two fair sized bedrooms, a kitchen and a storeroom—all with packed mud floors and freshly thatched straw roofs. In addition, there was an enormous yard neatly fenced in with high mud walls. A sweet-water well stood in a corner of the yard and rows of basil, oleander and jasmine bushes adorned it.

We were delighted with the house—the sanyasi most of all. He went from room to room, examined the flowering trees and shrubs, tasted the well water, and declared that everything was perfect. Rajlakshmi busied herself in the kitchen and refrained from expressing an opinion. But, from the look in her eyes, it was easy to see that she was not disappointed. Only Ratan's face remained as glum as ever. He sat motionless, his back against a bamboo post, making no effort to help Rajlakshmi or explore his new surroundings.

The sanyasi gulped down two cups of hot tea with the remains of the previous day's sweetmeats and said, 'Let's go for a walk. We can have a look at the village and bathe in the canal on our way back. Why don't you come too, Didi? There are no genteel folk around so you needn't feel embarrassed. I must say that I envy you your property. It is a fair one.'

'Sanyasis are greedy and envious by nature,' Rajlakshmi said, dimpling at her guest. Then, calling out to the Brahmin cook she had brought with her, she said, '*Maharaj*!* I'm going to the canal for a bath. Don't touch the fish till I get back. I wish to cook it myself.'

At this, Ratan, who hadn't uttered a word all this while, declared in a solemn voice, 'The canal is crawling with leeches, each a-yard-and-a-half long.'

Rajlakshmi's face turned pale. She looked about her with an air of helplessness. 'That's what I heard this morning,' Ratan said in a voice that seemed to clinch the matter.

But the sadhu turned on him with an oath, 'You rascally son of a barber! So this is your game—is it? Don't let him frighten you with his lies, Didi. I'll get into the water first and if I'm not bled to death by the leeches you can join me.'

But the joke was lost on his Didi who stood where she was and

---

* A term of respect used for Brahmin cooks from UP and Bihar.

said, 'It is better not to be too rash. We know nothing of this place. Get up, Ratan, and draw some water out of the well. I'll have my bath here. And you too,' she turned to me, 'you are not well enough, yet, to go bathing in strange canals.'

'What about me?' Sadhuji asked laughing. 'Am I of no consequence that you send me to meet my death among the leeches?'

At these words, uttered so lightly, Rajlakshmi's eyes filled with tears. She smiled at him tenderly and said, 'You are beyond human control, bhai. One who hasn't obeyed his parents is not likely to obey a stranger.'

The sanyasi stopped short in the act of moving towards the door and said abruptly. 'Don't call yourself a stranger. I left home and family to make the rest of the world my own.' He walked rapidly away with me following close behind.

We wandered about the village for several hours. It was small and densely populated with men, women and children from the lowest strata of the caste order. Except one family of Kumahars and another of Baruis the entire community was drawn from the Jal Achal order of Doms and Bauris. The latter worked as wage labourers and the former wove baskets and mats and sold them to the few upper caste families who lived in the village of Porhamati on the other side of the canal. They were so poor that their houses were not more than shacks and their living little better than that of street dogs who are born only to be kicked and starved to a miserable death.

I wondered at their resilience. 'This is how they have lived for centuries,' I thought, 'expecting nothing from life, making no demands and dreaming no dreams. We have taken away their humanity. We treat them like polluted beings. And so encased are we in the armour of our superior caste that their agony and humiliation makes not the slightest dent.'

Lost in my thoughts, I became aware of the sadhu's intent gaze only after a while. Fixing his eyes upon my face he said, 'Dada, this is a true picture of our people but don't torture yourself with thoughts of their misery. They aren't miserable in the least.'

'What do you mean? What kind of talk is this?' I exclaimed, angered by his careless dismissal of the anguish of his fellowmen.

'If you had travelled as widely as I have, you would have understood. What is it that tells a man he suffers? The mind—is it not? But do these people have minds left to them? Have we not squeezed the life, the mind, the spirit out of them and reduced them to animals? They genuinely believe that to ask for more is to err against God!' He laughed heartily and continued, 'What fine rogues our ancestors were! What a dirty trick they played on millions of their countrymen. And for so many years!' And he laughed again—peal after peal of gay laughter.

His words made me uncomfortable. I couldn't join in in his mirth.

Presently, he sobered down and said, 'There's been a terrible drought this year and the winter paddy has failed. Famine will stalk the village sooner or later. God has seen fit to send you among your subjects in this dark hour of their lives. Don't abandon them. Don't go back to the city till the worst is over. You can't do much—I know that. But you can see their suffering with your own eyes and suffer with them. It will wipe out the sin of living off your fellowmen—to a certain degree'

I sighed. The sanyasi obviously saw me as a powerful zamindar who made a luxurious living by exploiting his miserable subjects. How far it was from the truth! But I didn't react. It was past noon by the time we had bathed in the canal and returned to the house. The midday meal was ready and Rajlakshmi served it to us. She had done the cooking herself and therefore, as was to be expected, the sadhu got the best part including the head of the fish and the creamy top of the curd. He ate with a relish that only an ascetic was capable of. No householder of my acquaintance could have matched his enormous appetite and tremendous zest for food. In between mouthfuls, he carried on a conversation with Rajlakshmi.

'I'm delighted with your zamindari, Didi, and feel sorry to leave it.'

'Have I asked you to?'

'You mustn't be too kind to sadhus and fakirs. They start taking advantage of you at the first opportunity. But the village is truly charming. Not a house has a full thatch on it. They look just like the ashrams of the rishis. Only the people who live in them are, without exception, all untouchables.'

'That's what Ratan tells me. There's not one family whose water is acceptable. I don't think we can stay here for long.'

The sadhu's lips twitched a little. I noticed it but it didn't have the power to hurt. For I knew, better than all others present, the terrible power of age-old prejudices and irrational beliefs. The very fact that this kindest, most loving of women, could betray such a shameless assumption of superiority was proof of that power. 'Lakshmi,' I said to myself, 'the work a man does may be low—even degrading. He himself, by virtue of his birth, is the highest of created beings. If that were not so, Pyari could never have transformed herself back to Rajlakshmi.'

I ate in silence till, the meal over, Rajlakshmi handed us our paan and left. An hour or so later she reappeared with the astonishing news that the sadhu was about to depart. We hastened outside to find Ananda dressed and ready and his heavy trunk already lodged on the head of a man from the village. Although Rajlakshmi had promised to let him go as soon as he wished she cried out in alarm, 'Are you really going, Ananda?'

'Yes, Didi. If I don't hurry I won't reach before sunset.'

'Where are you going? Who will look after you?'

'Let me get there first.'

'When will you come back?'

'I can't say. I may come back some day when my work is concluded.'

'No! No.' Rajlakshmi shook her head violently. 'I can't let you go like that. You must come back in a few days.'

'I've told you why I'm going—'

Rajlakshmi burst into tears and ran inside. The sadhu turned a red, embarrassed face to me and said, 'I'm really sorry but I can't stay.'

I nodded. I understood his predicament. His mission was as important to him as Rajlakshmi's heartfelt appeal and he had to suffer the pain of choosing. He glanced towards the door, sighed, and smiled ruefully, 'Ours is a strange country, Dada,' he remarked. 'Here mothers and sisters are strewn in the streets. There's no escaping them.'

He walked away leaving me wondering at Rajlakshmi's foolishness. How could she expect to hold a man who had left his own mother and sisters in response to the call of a million others? How did she ever hope to entice him with her puny bribes of fish heads and creamy curd?

Five

RECLINING AGAINST A CUSHION, I WATCHED THE DAYLIGHT FADE
from the high walls of the courtyard. Stray thoughts continued to
flit in and out of my head as they had done ever since the moment
of Ananda's departure. I marvelled at the Providence that had
rendered one we hadn't known above a few hours so much a
part and parcel of our lives. Rajlakshmi had not left her room
ever since she had rushed in weeping and slammed the door. As
for me, an overwhelming lassitude—the consequence, no doubt,
of my prolonged illness—took hold of my body and soul. I felt
myself in the presence of a power, mysterious and terrifying,
even as the wintry dusk crept in, chilling my blood and clutching
at my heart with numb fingers.

The door opened with a click and Rajlakshmi walked in. Her
face was composed but her eyes were red and swollen. She sat by
me and, smiling apologetically, murmured, 'I fell asleep—'

'That isn't surprising,' I answered. 'You must be tired to death
after all the strain of packing and travel. If I were in your place I
would have slept for a hundred years.'

'You didn't sleep at all?'

'No. But I will now.'

'No, you won't. Not at this hour. Tell me, did Ananda say
anything before he left?'

'Such as?'

'Such as where he is going or—' she smiled painfully,
abandoning her sentence in mid-stream.

'You know very well where he is going. As for the "or" part of it—he has said nothing. I have no hopes of his return.' I paused a little and asked curiously, 'Did you know Ananda before we met him in Sainthia? Is he someone you recognized the way you recognized me in the prince's tent?'

'No.'

'Have you ever seen him before.'

'I often get confused about people,' Rajlakshmi answered smiling. 'I think I've seen them before when I really haven't. It was like that with Ananda.' She thought for a few minutes and added, 'I've promised myself that if he ever comes back I'll make him go back to his parents.'

'What do you hope to gain by that?'

'A boy like him cannot be allowed to waste himself the way he's doing. You became a sanyasi once. Did you find anything of true worth in the calling?'

'I was a fraud. My impressions would not be worth repeating. Ananda is different.'

'Is it necessary to leave the world in order to realize God? Is spiritual enrichment out of bounds in the lives of ordinary men and women?'

'Since I've never been interested in either, I cannot answer your question.'

'It seems strange to me that a boy of Ananda's years, one who had everything to live for, could detach himself so easily from the world. *You* couldn't.'

'No. For one thing I didn't have a world to renounce or not renounce. For another, I was not attracted in the least to that Omnipotent, Omnipresent, Omniscient Being who rules the Universe. I've lived all my life without Him and will continue to do so. As for Ananda, I don't really believe that he is on a spiritual quest. None of the sadhus I've known—and there have been quite a few—believe that God is to be found among the starving millions. And not one of them has ever dreamed of substituting prayer and ritual with a box of medicines. And you've seen with your own eyes how much Ananda loves good food—'

'Are you implying that he left the world on a whim? Is everyone like you?'

'Oh! No. Ananda, unlike me, has a definite mission. He has pledged himself to his country. His path may not be a short cut to heaven but it will encompass it. His leaving his home and family, therefore, doesn't amount to leaving the world. He has merely renounced a smaller family for a larger one.'

Rajlakshmi looked thoughtful. I wasn't sure she had comprehended. Then she asked again, 'Are you sure he said nothing—nothing at all before he left?'

'Nothing of any consequence.'

I didn't know why I hid the truth from her, why I didn't repeat the sadhu's words, 'Ours is a strange country. Here mothers and sisters are strewn in the streets. There's no escaping them.' I marvelled at the boy's sensitive understanding of our miserable land, and many half-buried memories came up to the surface clamouring for light. I thought of the innumerable sins of omission and commission whose accumulated weight, through the centuries, had buried our motherland in the slough of degradation in which we now live. And, though only a boy, Ananda had perceived the truth about her.

Rajlakshmi sat up with a jerk and said, 'If that is true, if he has left home on a mission to serve his fellowmen, he will have to return. He has no idea of the terrible frustration that falls to the lot of one who strives unselfishly for another's good. I've been through it, so I know. A day will come when his cup of agony will brim over as mine has done.'

'You may be right,' I answered. 'But I have a feeling that he has had a taste of it and knows what to expect.'

'No. Never!' Rajlakshmi shook her head violently. 'No one could suffer the same humiliation over and over again.'

Banku had told me of Rajlakshmi's efforts at community welfare in her husband's village and of the humiliations she had suffered in consequence. I realized, of course, that her position *vis-à-vis* the villagers was quite different from Ananda's. But knowing how deep her hurt was, I refrained from telling her that. I sat silent, wondering why it was in the nature of man not to accept his own good simply and without question. I decided to ask Ananda for his opinion if he ever came back.

*

One morning, a few days later, I woke to the melancholy strains of a flute floating in through my window. 'There's a wedding in the village,' I said to myself.

As I rose from my bed I saw three or four men step into the yard followed by Ratan who called out in a hearty voice, 'Ma! These good men are here from the village to pay you tribute. Come, don't be afraid. Come forward and speak to the mistress.'

The elderly man, to whom the latter part of his speech was addressed, now stepped forward. He was wearing a dhoti of ceremonial yellow and had a string of wooden beads around his neck. In his hand was a sal leaf with a silver rupee and a betel nut on it which he laid humbly at Rajlakshmi's feet with the words, 'My daughter is to be wedded tonight, mistress.'

Rajlakshmi picked up the gift and asked in a bright voice, 'Is this what is given when one's daughter gets married?'

'People give what they can,' Ratan the know-all said philosophically. 'These men are Doms. They hardly have anything for themselves. How much can they spare for their zamindar? Even the one rupee—'

At the word 'Dom' Rajlakshmi put down the leaf and exclaimed, 'Then why are you giving it to me? Take it back and use it for the wedding expenses.'

The rejection of the proffered tribute disconcerted Ratan even more than it did the bride's father. He declared vehemently that Rajlakshmi would have to accept it; that she would be violating an age-old custom if she didn't, that the rites of a marriage could not be solemnized if she refused the tribute, and much more in the same strain. I also understood why Ratan was so loud in his protestations. It was obvious that he had constituted himself the guide and guardian of the Doms and that they knew and he knew that if the tribute were to come through the proper channels, that is through Kushari *moshai*, one rupee would not suffice. Hence Ratan's alarm at Rajlakshmi's refusal.

I walked quietly up to the group and picked up the rupee saying, 'I accept it. Now you may go back and attend to your duties.'

Ratan beamed at me and Rajlakshmi relaxed visibly. Madhu Dom twisted his hands obsequiously and said, 'The rites will be solemnized soon after dusk. If you would have the kindness to step into my humble dwelling I—'

We assured him we would. Rajlakshmi said, 'Open the big trunk, Ratan, and bring one of my new saris for the bride. Are there no sweets to be bought at the village? Then buy some sugar puffs and give them to her.' Then turning to the Dom she asked, 'How old is your daughter, Madhu? And where is the groom from? Are lots of people invited to the wedding? How many of you are there in the village?'

Taken aback by so many questions, all together, from no less a personage than the zamindar's lady, Madhu folded his hands humbly and stuttered out that his daughter was nine years old, that the groom was in his prime—not more than thirty or forty; that they lived in a village ten miles north of Gangamati where a flourishing community of Doms lived, that they were not practising Doms but farmers with enough money to live on. It was obvious, therefore, that his daughter would be happy. It was not the girl's future that was worrying him but the anticipated events of the night. His arrangements were all complete. The *chire* had been bought and the curds and molasses. He had even procured a large sack of sugar puffs to feast the bridegroom's party. Still he was not sure that all would go smoothly. He was relying on us to help him out if anything untoward happened.

'All will go well.' Rajlakshmi smiled sweetly at him. 'Your efforts will not go waste. The groom's party will be pleased with your arrangements.' Madhu touched his forehead to the floor of the yard in great reverence and departed. His face, however, was no less worried and anxious than when he had first come.

In spite of our promise we had no intention of actually attending Madhu's daughter's wedding. But that evening, as I lay idly on my bed listening to Rajlakshmi's account of her expenditure of the day, the clamour of the wedding festivities took on a harsher, more alarming note. Rajlakshmi raised a laughing face and said, 'What is that? Are quarrel and assault included in the rites of a Dom wedding?'

'Why not? After all, Doms have emulated their superior castes for centuries. Have you forgotten what happened at your own wedding?'

Rajlakshmi's face reddened. She sighed and said, 'The way we treat our women in this wretched country! From the highest to the lowest it is the same story. I found out from the men who came this morning that Madhu has sold his daughter to the groom's father for twenty-four rupees. She's their property now. They will take her away tomorrow morning and she may never see her parents again. How she will weep for her mother! What does a nine-year-old know of marriage?'

I had seen so many marriages of this kind that they no longer had the power to move me. Receiving no answer she went on, 'A Hindu marriage, whether a Brahmin's or a Dom's, is part of our dharma. If it were not for that—'

Words trembled on my lips. I wanted to ask her why she complained if she truly believed all Hindu marriages to be sacrosanct. What was the worth of the dharma that brought rebellion and anger in the minds of its upholders instead of peace and serenity? But, before I could utter a word, Rajlakshmi said in a tone of finality, 'The ancient rishis who wrote the Shastras could look into the past, the present and the future. The laws they made were for the good of mankind for all time to come. Who are we to question their dictates? How much do we know—ignorant mortals that we are?'

Her speech effectively silenced the retort I was about to make. It was not for the first time that Rajlakshmi had expressed such sentiments. As at the other times, I was silent. I knew that a bitter quarrel would ensue if I even hinted that no code of laws could ensure the welfare of humanity for all time to come. I have mentioned elsewhere in this narrative, that Rajlakshmi had a gift of reading my thoughts as if my face were a mirror in which they were reflected. The soft lamplight in which we sat may have dimmed her vision but did not obscure it.

'You doubt my words,' she continued after a pause. 'You do not believe that anyone can predict the needs of the future. But I say that our rishis could and did. If it were not so, the mantras that still govern our lives would have been lost in oblivion ages ago. You do agree, don't you, that our Hindu mantras are living and dynamic? How else could they have withstood the onslaughts of time and history? Why is it that the most mismatched of Hindu marriages evolve, with time, into the firmest of unions. I don't deny the presence of unholiness and immorality among us. But isn't that true of every race? Besides, where else in the world will you find female chastity of the high order that exists in our country?'

'Nowhere,' I answered dully, knowing that I was up against a blind faith I could not fight with reason. Had this been an objective discussion I could have named several countries in the world in which female chastity is held in equally high esteem. I could have reminded her of Abhaya and asked why the mantras that had been pronounced at her marriage had not had life enough to bind her husband to her. Why did this 'firmest of unions' hold good only for the woman and not for the man? But, knowing argument to be useless, I was silent.

I had a dim notion of the direction in which her thoughts had been drifting of late. She had suffered, as few had, from the laws she upheld so steadfastly. She had known the pain and guilt of bringing down one she loved above life itself, to her own level of self-indicted degradation. A desperate battle was raging within her, between a slowly awakening fundamentalism and the overwhelming needs of her heart. These two, like turbulent rivers, washed over her, turn by turn, shaking her to the core of her being. Would they ever come together to form a cool and tranquil sheet of water over which her tortured soul could float, calm and pure and free? She herself saw no such prospect. But I did. I had a sense, a very faint one, that the passionate yearning that had driven her all these years, intoxicating her body and firing her mind, had dimmed in these few months of possession. Some subtle, scarcely perceptible, manner of speech and look told me that she was now taking stock of her losses and gains. I wondered what would become of me if her scales weighed down in favour of the former. My life, as far as I could see, had taken on the quality of a discarded fishing net—torn and flimsy and heavy with dust. Where, among all these holes, would I find a space to tie a knot and begin again? There was only one ray of hope. I had been a wanderer for many years. I could take up that life again. If all else came to naught there was always the road.

The strange thing was that even as we were arguing about the power of the marriage mantra, a drama was being enacted around it in the house of the Doms. We knew nothing of it, till a crowd of men, carrying sticks and lanterns, burst into the yard calling, 'Huzoor! Babu *moshai*!' I started up and ran to the veranda. Rajlakshmi came and stood by me but we could make nothing of their clamour. Ratan shouted to them to talk one at a time but, delirious with excitement, they all shrieked together in high voices. It took me a long time to understand what they were saying but when I did I was both shocked and amused.

What had happened was this. The priest attending the groom's party had alleged that his counterpart from the bride's party was pronouncing the mantras incorrectly and that the marriage that was being performed was not a true marriage. Not content with making this allegation he had actually clapped his hand over the other's mouth and had swept away his flowers and gangajal, scattering them in the dust. I had heard of many grisly crimes being committed by the priesthood but to burst in from an alien village, insult a fellow-priest and prevent him from uttering the 'living' mantra must surely be the worst of them all.

Rajlakshmi was struck dumb by this strange communication but Ratan, more conscious than ever of his caste superiority in this village of Doms and Bauris, thundered, 'Priest! You dare talk of priests! Since when has a marriage between Doms become equal to one between Brahmins or Kayasthas or Nabasakhs that a real priest will solemnize the rites?' And he glanced from my face to Rajlakshmi's, his own bursting with pride. Here it is appropriate to remind the reader that Ratan was a barber by caste.

Madhu Dom was not present (he had been at the point of giving his daughter away when the fight started) but his brother-in-law spoke up. He admitted the truth of Ratan's statement that Doms are too low to be united in matrimony by a proper Brahmin priest but added that their own Rakhal pandit, though a Dom, was as good a priest as any Brahmin. He wore the sacred thread, knew all the mantras and followed the sacred laws as strictly as any Brahmin. He led a life of such purity that not a drop of water touched by a fellow Dom ever passed through his lips. In the face of this evidence of Rakhal pandit's greatness even Ratan's arguments about true priests and false priests lost their force.

By this time the wedding clamour had risen to alarming proportions. I prepared to go, and Rajlakshmi, unable to contain her curiosity, agreed to accompany me. As we stepped into Madhu Dom's yard we saw the two rival factions in full battle. About thirty men of the groom's party were screaming abuses and gesticulating wildly at an equal number from the other side while the powerful, hefty Shibu pandit held the pale, emaciated Rakhal pandit firmly in his grip. He let go as soon as he saw us and stood glumly in a corner. Lowering myself on the mat that was respectfully placed for us I asked Shibu to explain his behaviour.

'Huzoor!' he replied. 'This rascal here is ignorant of the first letter of the mantra. And he calls himself a pandit. He was reducing the rites to a mockery.'

'Rites to a mockery!' Rakhal echoed, sticking out his tongue and grimacing fiercely at his opponent. 'I have been conducting all the marriages and funerals in these five villages for the last thirty years. Who are you to come in from nowhere and teach me my mantras?'

I had come to mediate and I did so. After a prolonged argument it was decided that Rakhal would be given another chance but that if he made another mistake Shibu would take his place. Rakhal marched up triumphantly to his seat and thrusting some flowers into Madhu Dom's hand, he began his recital of the Vedic mantras in a manner that I have not forgotten to this day. Hearing him I could not help wondering if the mantras that had come down to us had retained the forms given them by the rishis of old. I was also quite sceptical about their immortality. Even if I were to admit Rajlakshmi's assertion that they had been animate when first created, I had not a shadow of doubt that, like all created beings, they had died a natural death in due course of time.

Rakhal pandit said to the groom, 'Repeat after me: *Madhu Domaya kanyaya namaha.*' (Madhu Dom's daughter, salutations!)

The groom obliged.

Rakhal now turned to the bride. 'Repeat after me: *Bhagwati Domaya putraya namaha.*' (Bhagwati Dom's son, salutations!)

The little girl looked frightened and burst into tears. Her father was on the point of helping her out when Shibu jumped up and announced in a thundering voice, 'All wrong! The mantra is all wrong! The marriage has misfired.'

I felt a tug at my sleeve. It was Rajlakshmi. She had stuffed the edge of her sari into her mouth to prevent herself from laughing out aloud. Her face was red and her eyes bright with suppressed laughter. The rest of the company now begged Shibu to take over, to give Rakhal a quarter of the dues and keep the rest. Rakhal was about to plead his case but the crowd would not let him. However, at this moment of supreme triumph, Shibu decided to be magnanimous. 'There's no use blaming Rakhal,' he said kindly. 'The truth is that, barring myself, no one in these parts knows the right mantras. I'm not greedy for money. I'll recite the mantras from here and Rakhal can repeat it after me.'

With that the great pandit, renowned for his knowledge of the Scriptures, started his recital in a booming voice. Rakhal, recognizing defeat when he saw it, argued no more.

Shibu said, 'Repeat after me: *Madhu Domaya kanyaya bhujya patrang namaha.*' (Madhu Dom's daughter, leaves and food offerings! Salutations!)

'*Madhu Domaya kanyaya bhujya patrang namaha,*' echoed the groom.

Shibu said, 'Madhu, repeat after me: *Bhagwati Domaya putraya sampradanang namaha.*' (Bhagwati Dom's son, I give thee away! Salutations!)

And so it went on. The company looked respectfully on. At last the marriage was being conducted as a proper marriage should! Shibu thrust a couple of flowers into the groom's hand and said, 'Bipin, repeat after me: *Jata din jibanang tata din bhat kapadh pradanang swaha.*' (As long as I live I'll give away rice and clothes into the sacrificial fire.)

Bipin stammered and stuttered and made a mess of this most wonderful of mantras. But Shibu was satisfied. He pronounced the final, the climactic mantra with considerable aplomb.

'Bride and groom repeat together: *Jugal milanang namaha.*' (Union of two, salutations!)

'*Hari! Hari!*' the crowd chanted. Conch shells blew and the bride and groom were taken into the house. People whispered to one another, 'Did you hear the mantras? Rakhal pandit has been cheating us all these years.'

The nuptials over, I rose solemnly and departed with Rajlakshmi. As soon as we reached home Rajlakshmi threw herself on the bed and, doubling over with laughter, mimicked what she had just heard. 'What a great pandit! What knowledge of the scriptures! Rakhal has been cheating us all these years.'

I, too, burst out laughing. Then controlling myself I said, 'Rakhal must be a great pandit too since his mantras have been forging those "firmest of unions" you spoke of, for the last thirty years. Don't forget that the girl's mother and grandmother were married by Rakhal.'

Rajlakshmi stopped laughing. She sat up and glanced sharply at my face, then, turning her own away, she fell into a reverie.

Six

*W*HEN I WOKE UP THE NEXT MORNING RAJLAKSHMI INFORMED ME that we had been invited to have our midday meal in Kushari *moshai's* house.

'Am I to go alone?'

'No. I'm coming too.'

Her answer surprised me. The act of eating, in Hindu society, is hemmed in by innumerable rules and restrictions. Rajlakshmi was aware of them and had respected them all these years. I didn't know much about Kushari *moshai* but it was obvious that he was a practising Brahmin. It was also obvious that he knew Rajlakshmi's history. Yet he had invited her to a meal in his house. And, most surprising of all, she had accepted his invitation.

The bullock-cart arrived. I came out to see Rajlakshmi standing near it. I stared at her and asked, 'Aren't you coming?'

'I was waiting for you,' she said and climbed in. Ratan, who was to accompany us, stared too. Rajlakshmi wore little jewellery at home, as a rule. But this morning, it seemed to me, she had deliberately denuded herself. Only a thin gold chain hung around her neck and a pair of plain gold bracelets clasped her wrists. Even the bangles she had worn till yesterday, or so it seemed to me, had been removed. Her sari was of simple cotton—one she kept for everyday use.

I took my place next to her and remarked. 'You are giving up all your luxuries, one by one, Lakshmi. I'm the only one left.'

'It may be that everything worthwhile is contained in the one that is left. That is why all that is redundant is drifting away from me.' Rajlakshmi glanced behind her to make sure that Ratan was not within earshot and continued, 'You know that you mean more to me than anything else in the world. Help me to find the power to renounce even you in favour of Him.' I was so startled that I couldn't think of an answer and Rajlakshmi did not press me for one. She picked up a pillow and curled up with it close to my feet.

Porhamati was only a ten-minute walk if one went over the bamboo bridge that spanned the canal. By bullock-cart it was a good two hours distance from our village. Not a word did we exchange during that time. But she put out her hand, took mine, and held it close to her neck. For the rest of the journey she lay motionless, pretending to be asleep.

It was well past noon when the bullock-cart finally stopped at Kushari *moshai's* door. Quite a crowd had gathered to see us. The master and mistress of the house came forward and took us in with great ceremony. I realized that the norms of the city were not applicable in this remote village of Bengal and that it was perfectly in order for inquisitive neighbours to mill around the guests of the house.

Rajlakshmi and I were led right inside to a veranda, over-looking the yard, where two asans were laid ready, side by side. Our host and hostess, still busy with the preparations, left us in the care of their widowed daughter who stood behind us waving a palm leaf fan above our heads. Despite Rajlakshmi's presence, several men crowded around me making inane remarks and plying me with questions about the nature of my illness, the length of my stay in Gangamati, and the difficulties of running a zamindari in an absentee state. I answered briefly and looked around me with some curiosity.

There was no doubt that I had entered a household of plenty. The house itself was built of earth but it was large and sprawling, with many rooms. Two immense paddy bins built of straw stood in the yard with a couple of husking pedals between them. A spreading shaddock tree bearing globes of glistening fruit stood in one corner. Beneath it were several grates for boiling paddy, now cold and clean and raked of their ashes. Two plump calves, tethered to the tree, slept in the shade. Their mothers were not to be seen but I hadn't a doubt that they were somewhere close at hand, ready to provide the household with vast quantities of rich creamy milk. Against one wall of the veranda on which we sat, stood several enormous jars balanced on coils of straw. They shone clean and bright in the afternoon sun. It was easy to see that they were not abandoned or empty. I was sure that they were filled to the brim with lentils, spices and treacle. Rows of hooks on another wall had bundles of jute and flax hanging from them.

Kushari *moshai* came hurrying in and, apologizing for the delay in attending to us, announced that the meal had been served. I rose instantly, glad of the respite from the curiosity of his neighbours. However, I discovered to my dism y that a single place had been laid and that I was to eat alone. My host explained, with shy pride, that he was a vegetarian and that he had continued the observance of eating in seclusion and silence that he had been initiated into during his thread ceremony. I accepted his explanation without comment but when I heard that Rajlakshmi was fasting that day and would not partake of cooked food, I was both surprised and amused. Was there really any need for such a pretence, I thought. Rajlakshmi, who always read my thoughts even before they were properly formulated, said instantly, 'Don't let that spoil your appetite. Enjoy your meal. Everyone here knew of my fast.'

'Only I didn't,' I said. 'But why did you take the trouble of coming then?'

Kushari *moshai's* wife answered for her. It was the first time she spoke that morning. She said, 'It was at my insistence, Baba. I knew the mistress would not eat here but I couldn't resist the temptation of receiving our patroness in my humble dwelling. Isn't that true, Ma?' And she smiled at Rajlakshmi.

I looked at her with some curiosity. I had not expected to find such dignity and grace in the speech of a simple, unlettered village woman. But there was another surprise awaiting me. I had not dreamed that there was another woman in the same village whose acquaintance would turn out to be the memory of a lifetime.

'We are hardly what you call us,' I said. 'And if we are, we give so little that you wouldn't miss it if it were withheld.'

She shrank a little at these words and her benign, motherly face paled and grew solemn. After a brief silence she said, 'It is true that we enjoy God's bounty as few people do. But I feel, sometimes, that it would have been kinder to us if He had given us less. What use are all these riches to me when I have no one of my own to enjoy them with except a widowed daughter? My loved ones have been taken away from me—' Her voice broke and her lip trembled. She must have lost a grown son, I said to myself, and was silent, respecting her grief. Rajlakshmi took her hand and held it without a word. But her next sentence jerked us out of our speculations. 'They are your subjects just as we are. Make them come back to us I beg of you.' And she lifted the edge of her sari and touched it to her eyes.

Rajlakshmi and I exchanged glances. I realized that she was as much in the dark as I was. But the situation was so strange that neither of us knew how to react. After a while our hostess collected herself and slowly, haltingly, told us the whole story. How much of it was true, I cannot say. But there was no doubt that it was a strange one. The facts, as she related them were as follows.

Her husband's parents had died many years ago leaving their infant son, the present Jadunath Nyaya Ratna, in her care. Although only fourteen years old at the time, she had taken the motherless child to her bosom and cared for him as her own. They were poor and life was a bitter struggle. All the ancestral property that her husband had inherited was a one-roomed earthen house, two bighas of land and a few families of disciples. What we saw now was his own acquired property. The younger brother had contributed nothing to it. Nor had anyone expected him to.

'I see,' I said. 'He's demanding more than his fair share.'

'Oh no!' The kindly matron shook her head. 'He demands nothing. He doesn't have to. It is all his. He would have had it all if his wife Sunanda hadn't stopped him. It is she who has taken him away from me and poisoned my whole existence.' Her voice broke. She cleared her throat and continued. 'God is witness that I've never failed in my duty to the boy. So are my neighbours. But he, himself, has forgotten the past altogether.' She wiped her eyes and took up the narrative once again. 'After Thakurpo's thread ceremony my husband sent him to Mihirpur to study Sanskrit in the *tol* (a school where Sanskrit is taught) of the famous Shibu Tarkalankar. I loved him so much that I couldn't bear the separation. I wept and wept till my husband took me to Mihirpur. Even that he has forgotten! Anyway, the years passed one by one and I got used to his absence. Then, when his studies were nearing completion and his brother had started looking around for a suitable bride, he came home. He had a wife with him. He had married Sunanda, the daughter of Shibu Tarkalankar, without informing us, leave alone asking for permission.'

'Did he have a reason for doing that?'

'Of course he had. Her family did not match ours in lineage or status. Besides, they are from a lower order of Brahmins. My husband was so disappointed that he didn't speak to them for a whole month. But I wasn't. I loved Sunanda from the moment I saw her sweet face. Then, when I heard that her mother was dead and her father had become a sanyasi, my heart went out to her. What that girl meant to me I cannot describe. And this is how she has repaid me!' And the good woman burst into tears.

'Where are they now?' Rajlakshmi asked gently.

Our hostess was so overcome that all she could do was shake her head helplessly. We understood that they were in that very village. But the mystery was still to be cleared. After a few minutes of struggling with her emotions she continued. 'Our property, as you see it, belonged originally to a weaver of the village. He died some years ago and my husband acquired it. One morning, some months ago, his widow came to the house holding a little boy by the hand. She was in a state of great agitation and accused my husband of robbing her minor son of his inheritance. It may be that what she said was a lie but Sunanda believed every word. She was preparing to go for her bath when the commotion started. She stood where she was for a long time, even after the woman had left. I called out to her, "Chhoto Bou,* make haste and start the cooking. It is getting late," but she didn't move an inch. I looked at her face and was frightened. She was as pale as death but her eyes burned like living coals.

"Didi," she said, "You must return the weaver's property. Will you deprive a fatherless boy of his rightful inheritance?"

"What nonsense you talk," I said angrily. "Kanai Basak was neck-deep in debt. His property was auctioned off and your brother-in-law bought it. Does one give away what is rightfully one's own?"

---

*   Youngest daughter-in-law of the house.

"From where did he get the money to buy such a large property?"

"That I don't know," I snapped. "Go ask him!" and thinking that the matter had ended I proceeded to the prayer room.'

'If the property was auctioned off,' Rajlakshmi said in a wondering voice, 'why should Chhoto Bou insist on returning it?'

'That's just it,' said our hostess, but a shade of embarrassment came over her manner. She added feebly, 'The property wasn't auctioned in the usual way. My husband was the Basak family's kul (clan) guru. Kanai Basak left everything in trust to my husband before he died. Who knew, then, that he was so deeply in debt?'

At these words a strange feeling came over me. I felt the presence of something vile and treacherous all around. Suddenly the rich food lay heavy in my stomach. I looked at Rajlakshmi. Her face was pale and her eyes held a curious expression. But Kushari *moshai's* wife seemed not to notice. She went on with her narrative.

'A couple of hours later I returned to find Sunanda sitting at the same spot. She hadn't had a bath or moved to the kitchen. My husband was about to return from the court-house. Thakurpo had left early to inspect the granaries and he had taken Binu with him. They too would be arriving any minute. And the cooking hadn't even begun. "Have you decided not to enter the kitchen, Chhoto Bou?" I asked exasperated. "What is the matter with you? Do you trust that wicked woman more than us?"

"Didi," Sunanda said lifting her chin and looking straight into my eyes, "I will neither cook nor eat in this house if you do not return what is not yours. I cannot snatch the food from the mouth of a defenceless child and feed it to my husband and son." And she walked into her room and shut the door.

'I knew Sunanda well. I knew that honesty was basic to her nature. I also knew that her father had educated her in the Shastras as thoroughly as the best of his pupils. But I was still to find out how far she could go. She did not leave the room even after I started cooking the midday meal and her husband and son returned. But the moment my husband sat down to his simple meal she came and stood outside the door. "Sunanda," I begged with folded hands, "say what you must after he has eaten." But she turned a deaf ear to my pleas.

'She spoke in a voice as brittle as glass. "I wish to know the true circumstances of the transfer. From where did you get the money to buy the weaver's property? I have heard you say, often enough, that my father-in-law left nothing when he died."

'This was the first time that my husband had heard Sunanda speak. He asked in a surprised voice, "What do you mean by such talk, Bou Ma?"

"You know what I mean well enough. The weaver's widow was here this morning. There is no point in repeating what she said. If you do not return what is not yours—we have nothing more to do with you. Not a grain of rice from this house of sin will pass through the lips of my husband and child. Not while I have breath in my body."

'I couldn't believe my ears. "Either I'm dreaming," I thought, "or Sunanda is possessed by a demon." My husband was too shocked to speak for a while.

'Then he answered her, his eyes blazing, "The property is mine—not your husband's or son's. If you do not wish to stay here you are welcome to leave." He left the meal uneaten and went out of the house.

'I ran, weeping, to Thakurpo. "I have tended you like my own child," I said. "Is this the reward I get?"

'His eyes were full of tears. "Bou Than," he said, "You are the only mother I've ever known and Dada the only father. But my conscience is more important to me than anything else in the world. Sunanda was right in what she said and I support her. Her father's only gift to her on our marriage was the blessing: *Seek the truth with honesty and purpose and a way will be shown to you.* I have known her from childhood onwards. She does not compromise with her conscience."

'The day was *Bhadra Sankranti*.* The sky was overcast and rain fell in torrents. Sunanda took her son by the hand and walked out of the house in the pouring rain. I ran after her screaming, "Where are you going?" But she didn't answer. There's a crumbling old house at the end of the village that had once belonged to a disciple of my father-in-law. It had been abandoned many years ago and

---

* The last day of the fifth month of the Bengali calendar, falls in mid September.

was crawling with toads, snakes and jackals. If was to this house that she was taking her husband and son.

"What will you eat?" I asked in despair.

"My father-in-law left two bighas of land. One bigha is legally mine."

"Accursed wretch!" I wailed. "That won't feed you for a day. Starve to death if you will. But why do you punish my Binu?"

"What about the son of Kanai Basak? Don't you ever think of him, Didi?" And, with that, she walked away.

'The house became like a house of death. I didn't have the heart to light the lamps or cook the evening meal. My husband spent the whole night leaning against that post and staring up at the sky. Tears rushed into my eyes everytime I thought of Binu. I had reared him so tenderly. What was he eating now? Where was he sleeping? As soon as dawn broke, I sent the cowherd over with a cow and a calf but Sunanda returned them with the message that she was going to change Binu's diet and train him to eat the coarse food of the poor.'

The elderly voice trembled and the pain of parting with those she loved so dearly was stamped on every line of her motherly face. A deep sigh escaped Rajlakshmi. Our hostess cleared her throat, wiped her eyes and nose and continued. 'The whole village was talking. My husband became pale and thin with worry and humiliation. He had brought up Thakurpo as his own son and the child was dearer to him than life. "They can't go on like this forever," he would say at first. "They'll have to come back." But I knew Sunanda. She would break but not bend. After some days he sent them a message asking them to return. He promised to see that the weaver's family was provided for. But Sunanda's condition was not to be shaken. Either all was returned or they lived apart.'

I had stopped eating for a long while. I dipped my hand in a glass of water and asked, 'What do they live on?'

The poor woman covered her ears and answered with a trembling lip, 'Don't ask me that, Baba. It is too distressing to bear thinking or talking about.'

A clatter of wooden clogs in the distance announced that Kushari *moshai's* meal was concluded. But he did not come near us. We sat in silence for a while—till it was time to depart.

As we took our places in the cart, Kushari *moshai's* wife gripped Rajlakshmi's hand and whispered urgently, 'They are your subjects, Ma. The land from which they get their living is in Gangamati. And the house in which they live is at the edge of the canal. You can see it from your house.' Rajlakshmi nodded.

The cart started moving. Neither of us spoke. Rajlakshmi seemed deep in thought. I interrupted her reverie with the words, 'Trying to help a person who is self-sufficient is a futile exercise, Lakshmi.'

Rajlakshmi smiled at me and said, 'I know that very well. I've learnt it from you.'

Seven

ANALYSING THE PAST, AS I OFTEN DO THESE DAYS, I DISCOVER
THE presence of several women whose personalities are marked
indelibly in my memory. One of them is Kushari *moshai's* rebellious
sister-in-law. I have not forgotten Sunanda to this day. Neither
have I overcome my gratitude to Rajlakshmi whose sensitive
concern and generosity made this acquaintance possible.

Jadu Nyaya Ratna's dilapidated dwelling stood right across
the bleak, barren field that stretched westward to the edge of the
canal. It was only a minute's walk over the bridge to the cluster
of mud rooms that huddled together in the shade of an ancient
tamarind tree. I had often seen it from my window but had
never known that it was inhabited by a fiery female who defied
social norms with impunity. Looking on it, the morning after
my visit to Porhamati, I thought how true the maxim was that
nothing could be judged from the surface. Who would ever have
thought that classics like *Kumar, Raghu, Shakuntala* and *Meghdoot*
were contained within those crumbling walls? Or that serious
discourses on the nature of *morality* and *law* took place between
a young preceptor and his pupils? Or that a young woman's
personal vision of *right* and *truth* dominated the entire household,
compelling its members to embrace a life of want and struggle?

As I looked at the shapeless mass with an inexplicable pain
and yearning in my heart, I became aware of voices in the yard.
One, loud and enquiring, was Rajlakshmi's. The other, low and

indistinct, was Ratan's. But the moment she saw me, Rajlakshmi put the responsibility for the disturbance squarely on Ratan. 'Really, Ratan!' she said. 'You must learn to lower your voice. You woke Babu up with your shouting.'

Ratan and I were both used to being blamed for what we hadn't done. So neither of us bothered to contradict her. On the ground, at Rajlakshmi's feet, was a large basket filled with rice, lentils, spices, oil, salt, sugar and a variety of vegetables. I gathered that Rajlakshmi was trying to persuade Ratan to carry the basket over to somebody's house and that he was mumbling excuses about its size and weight.

'Why don't you get someone from the village to carry the basket? Ratan can go with him wherever you're sending it,' I said, realizing that it was the indignity of carrying a load that was upsetting Ratan.

'Go then,' Rajlakshmi commanded. 'Fetch someone from the village since you are too grand for such lowly work.'

'Where is all this going so early in the morning?'

'If foodstuff is to be sent to anyone—it must be done first thing in the morning.'

'But where are you sending it? And why?'

'I am sending it to the house of a Brahmin. As to why—the answer is simple. So that the family may eat.'

'And who, may I ask, is the Brahmin?'

About to mention a name, Rajlakshmi thought the better of it and smiled. 'One shouldn't brag about one's good deeds or name names. Go wash your face. Your tea is ready.'

Around ten o'clock that morning, as I sat in the outer room lazily leafing through an old journal for want of anything better to do, an unfamiliar voice fell on my ears. 'Namaskar, Babu *moshai*.'

'Namaskar. Please take a seat.'

I took stock of the stranger who stood before me. That he was a Brahmin was obvious. That he was exceedingly poor was even more so. He wore no shirt and his feet were bare. A fold of his frayed dhoti was taken around his shoulders and a couple of knots were clearly visible where the material had given way. He lowered himself on to a bamboo stool and said, 'I am one of the humblest of your subjects. I should have come to pay my respects much earlier. Do forgive me for the lapse.'

Any reference to me as a landlord or zamindar embarrassed

and annoyed me and this was no exception. I answered coldly, 'You needn't apologize for the "lapse" as you call it. I am not in the habit of demanding courtesies. What is your business with me?'

My guest looked bewildered at these words. 'I have come at the wrong time,' he said, rising. 'I am disturbing you, perhaps. I'll come some other day.'

'But what have you come for? What do you require from me?' I cried not caring to hide the impatience I was feeling. He was silent for a while. Then he spoke with a simple dignity. 'I am a small man and my requirements are few. The mistress sent for me. I have not come out of any need of my own.'

The answer was sharp but not rude, considering my question. It would not have disturbed me anywhere else. But, steeped in adulation as I was in Gangamati, I had lost the capacity for taking a rebuff. Such is the power of authority, albeit surrogate, over human beings! I was suddenly, violently angry. A harsh rejoinder rose to my lips. But, before I could make it, Rajlakshmi walked into the room.

She touched her forehead to the ground in reverence to the unknown Brahmin and said humbly, 'Please don't leave. I have something important to discuss with you.'

'Ma!' the stranger said, equally humbly. 'You have sent enough food to tide us over the next fifteen days. But, considering that this is a lean time of the year for religious rites and observances, my Brahmini wondered—'

Rajlakshmi cut him short with a laugh. 'I'm sure your Brahmini is well versed in the dates of religious observances. But if she wishes to learn the correct timings for interacting with one's neighbours let her come to me.'

I was afraid that the arrogant Brahmin would take exception to such talk and make an insulting remark but Rajlakshmi did not give him the chance. She threw him the sweetest of her smiles and said, 'I've heard that your Brahmini has quite a temper. She might object to my visiting her without an invitation. If I were not afraid of her I would have gone to your house myself.' At this reference to his beloved's temper (I had realized, by now, that the young man was Jadunath Kushari) his own anger melted. He burst out laughing with a happy sound that filled the room.

'You are quite wrong, Ma!' he said at last. 'She is not bad-tempered at all. She is a simple, straightforward girl. We are too poor to offer you the hospitality due to you, should you come to us. It is more fitting that she comes here to pay her respects. I'll bring her here myself.'

'How many pupils do you have in your care, Nyaya Ratna *moshai*?'

'Five. It is not easy to find scholars in these parts.'

'Do you have to provide them with food and clothing?

'Not all of them. One stays with my brother and another with his parents in Gangamati. Three have made their home with us.'

Rajlakshmi digested this information in silence. Then she said in a voice as tender and melancholy as the smile that flitted across her face, 'It must be hard for you—in the circumstances.' The genuine concern in her voice shattered what was left of the Brahmin's reserve.

He admitted his poverty and cares quite openly, adding, 'Only my wife and I know how hard it is. But what can I do to make things better? Being a scholar and preceptor is the Brahmin's caste vocation. He owes it to society. I must return to others what I've received from my acharyas.' He paused a little, then added, 'There was a time when maintaining the Brahmin was the responsibility of the lord of the land. Now things are different. The zamindar has lost his power and with it his sense of responsibility. All he does now is squeeze the life blood out of his subjects and wallow in the lap of luxury.'

'There may be one or two,' Rajlakshmi said, 'who genuinely wish to take up their responsibilities. I hope you won't stop them.'

'I quite forgot whom I was addressing.' Kushari's thin face reddened with embarrassment. 'But why should I stop you? It is your duty to take care of your subjects.'

'You have a duty too—to deprived women like me. I use Sanskrit mantras for worship but I neither know the meanings nor the correct pronunciations.'

'I'm ready to teach you whatever you wish to learn.' He glanced at the sky and, seeing that it was nearing noon, he took his leave.

'You must have your bath and meal a little earlier than usual,' Rajlakshmi said to me as soon as our guest left the room.

'Why?'

'We're going over to Sunanda's house this afternoon.'

'Why me?' I asked, surprised. 'Why don't you take Ratan with you?'

'No. I've decided not to go anywhere without you.'

'As you wish—'

I closed the argument.

Eight

RAJLAKSHMI STEPPED ACROSS THE THRESHOLD OF JADUNATH Kushari's dwelling house leaving me standing outside by the broken wall.

In a minute or two a good-looking boy of about seventeen appeared. 'The acharya is not at home,' he said. 'But Ma asked me to take you into the house.'

Leading the way through an arch, which may have had a door once but didn't anymore, he took me across a crumbling yard with an ancient husking pedal in a corner, to a high earthen veranda where Rajlakshmi was sitting. A slim, dark woman of about twenty was engaged in puffing rice at an earthen stove in a corner.

She rose and, spreading a strip of blanket on the ground, pointed to it with a hand as divested of ornament as the house itself. Smiling shyly she said, 'Please sit.' Then, turning to the boy, she said, 'There is some fire left in the stove, Ajoy. Prepare a hookah for the master. I'm sorry I can't offer you a paan, Didi,' she glanced in Rajlakshmi's direction. 'There's no such thing in the house.'

'No paan in the house?' the boy asked in astonishment.

Sunanda laughed gaily and said in a voice like a bell, 'You know very well we never have any paan. Why do you pretend?'

Acutely embarrassed, the boy mumbled, 'I'm not pretending. I only—'

Rajlakshmi smiled at him and reprimanded Sunanda in a

gentle voice, 'He's a man, Sunanda. How is he to know what you have in the house?'

'You don't know him, Didi!' Sunanda doubled over with laughter. 'My Ajoy is the real mistress of the house. He knows what we have better than I do. In fact he manages us all. Only he won't admit that there is any poverty or hardship in the way we live.'

'Why shouldn't I admit it,' Ajoy cried, his face as red as the embers in the stove. 'There's nothing to be ashamed of in being poor. I only—' and leaving the sentence unfinished, he dashed out of the yard in search, perhaps, of a hookah.

Rajlakshmi took Sunanda's hand and said, 'Sit by me for a while and let me talk to you.'

I glanced at Sunanda and thought, 'Poverty means nothing at all if you learn to ignore it. This girl—an ordinary village girl with nothing special about her—has managed to keep poverty at bay by simply refusing to acknowledge it. Before the glaring light of her personality all want, all hardship is reduced to a shadow. It cannot touch her or those about her. Yet, only a few months ago, her life was different. She had wealth, power over people, friends. But she cast it all away as easily as she would a torn garment in rigid protest over an act of treachery. Yet, there is no rigidity in her person nor any mark of struggle.'

'I thought Sunanda to be a grown woman. But she's no more than a child,' Rajlakshmi said, addressing me.

But, before I could answer, Sunanda pointed to Ajoy who approached, hookah in hand, and said in a bright voice, 'You call me a child? A woman with hulking sons like that one? You make me laugh, Didi.'

Ajoy handed me the hookah and asked her, 'Shall I put it away then?'

Sunanda nodded. Muttering something under his breath Ajoy walked up to where the yellowing pages of some ancient manuscript lay fluttering on a wooden plank. It was clear that the disturbance in his study session had not met with his approval.

'What manuscript is that?' Rajlakshmi asked curiously.

'The *Yoga Vashishtha*.'

'Were you reading it out to your Guru Ma?'

'Oh no. She was taking a lesson.'

Sunanda blushed and snatched the words out of his mouth,

'A lesson indeed! As if I have learning enough for that. The boys come to me when their guru isn't home. But I don't have answers to half their questions, Didi.'

There was a long silence. Then Rajlakshmi sighed and said gravely, 'If my house were a little closer I would have become your pupil, Sunanda. I have had so little education that I can't even pronounce my prayers correctly.'

I had heard this particular lament often enough. So I made no comment. What surprised me was that Sunanda didn't either. She smiled and was silent. I wondered what lay behind her smile. Was it disdain at Rajlakshmi's concern for the correct pronunciation of words whose meanings eluded her? Or was her smile one of modest self-abnegation? If it was the former, if Sunanda had relegated Rajlakshmi to the category of women who habitually express similar sentiments only to forget them a minute later, she had made a terrible mistake. A time would come when she would be compelled to revise her opinion. Rajlakshmi, who had an instinctive understanding of people's reactions, expressed or otherwise, clammed up immediately. She didn't mention the subject again but commenced talking, in a low voice, of ordinary everyday matters. I was left alone to pull at my hookah and pursue my own thoughts.

There's a general belief, and I share it, that the male of the species has subordinated the female and forced her to occupy a position of extreme degradation. Exactly how he managed to do so was a question I had considered from many angles over many years but my speculations had never yielded any satisfactory results. That afternoon, sitting in Sunanda's broken veranda, I got my answer. Had I never met her I would have remained in the dark to this day.

I had seen and heard of many forms of women's emancipation both in my own country and abroad. I have already mentioned the sight that met my eyes on my first day in Rangoon—of three women belabouring a hefty male with sticks of sugar-cane. I remember Abhaya muttering dejectedly, 'If only our women were like them.' I have heard an uncle of mine rail against a Marwari woman who had boxed his ears and nose in a railway compartment for daring to report her to the authorities and I remember how my aunt had sighed wistfully and regretted that such a system was not to be found among us. While sympathizing with the women of our land I still failed to see how 'such a system' would have given them the enhanced status they sought. Looking at Sunanda I realized where the trouble lay. Sunanda's father had given her little of material things but he had educated her as he would have educated a son. He had exposed her to the doctrines and philosophies of learned men and had encouraged her to think and act for herself. It was here, in this freedom of thought and action, that the source of her power over self and environment lay. It was from this power that she had derived the courage to walk out of her husband's ancestral home, to entertain a man in his absence and become a mother to young men of her own age. Her husband didn't dream of criticizing her actions or of imposing restrictions. Neither did anyone else. Her father had given her a good deal of learning but what she was to do with it was her own concern.

The shadows of evening were falling, yet Nyaya Ratna *moshai* did not return. I rose unwillingly, for the desire to meet him again was strong.

Rajlakshmi said, 'I'll come again if you don't mind,' and I added, 'I have no one to talk to. I, too, would like to visit you sometimes if I may.' Sunanda smiled and bent her head.

On the way home, Rajlakshmi said enthusiastically, 'She's a fine girl. Husband and wife are perfectly matched. I didn't bring up the subject of their breaking away from the family because I'm not sure I understand Kushari *moshai* well as yet. But there's no denying that the wives are excellent women.'

'True,' I admitted. 'Why don't you try to reconcile them? Your power over human beings has been tested often enough.'

'Don't judge by your own case. Anyone could have done what I did.' Rajlakshmi smiled and tossed her head.

The afternoon had been shadowy, cool and calm. But now an angry black cloud swam over the sun causing the western sky to glow like a flame. In that unearthly light, the expanse of the dun-coloured earth over which we walked, became a sheet of gold. A twisted tamarind and a clump of bamboos in the distance seemed smudged in lamp black against a sky of deepening rose and violet. The beauty of the scene flushed my being, entering my very soul.

I glanced at Rajlakshmi. The smile was still on her lips. Never had she appeared more beautiful to my eyes. Was it only the colour of the sky that had thrown this web of enchantment on a familiar landscape—external and internal? Or was the colour and light derived from the person of the woman I had just left? Rajlakshmi may have felt as I did for she heaved a sigh of deep contentment. This day has been a memorable one. I feel I've found a true friend and companion.'

But the moment we stepped into the house we were flung into the glare of harsh reality and the peace and serenity that had been ours was rudely shattered. The yard was full of people. Ratan, evidently in the act of delivering a fiery oration, stopped short on seeing us and said in a triumphant voice, 'Ma! I've told you over and again that this would happen, haven't I?'

Rajlakshmi looked bewildered. 'What has happened? What have you told me over and over again? I don't understand—'

'Nabin has been arrested. He has murdered Malati.'

The blood drained from Rajlakshmi's face. One of the men spoke up quickly, 'No, mistress. He has beaten her badly but she isn't dead.'

'How do you know?' Ratan bore down aggressively on the hapless optimist. 'Has anyone seen her? Who knows if she's alive or dead since she's not to be found? Don't forget that you'll all be under suspicion if—'

'Go stand in that corner, Ratan, and don't speak till you're spoken to.' Rajlakshmi threw him a burning glance and, turning to Malati's father who stood trembling like a leaf, she said in a commanding voice, 'I want to hear the truth. Don't try to hide anything or you'll be in trouble.'

The old man (his name was Bishwanath) said that, following the previous evening's incident, his daughter Malati had left her husband's house and come to her father's. This afternoon, as she was filling her *ghara* (pitcher) at the pond, Nabin had rushed out from behind the bushes where he had been hiding and, falling upon her, had beaten her mercilessly. With blood streaming down her face from a deep cut in the head, and weeping bitterly, she had first come here and not finding us at home had gone to Kushari *moshai's* house. Not finding him there either she had gone to the thana and filed a case. She had arrived with a constable just as Nabin was sitting down to his midday meal. The constable had kicked away the rice Nabin had been about to eat and, binding him with iron fetters, had taken him away.

Rajlakshmi's face turned a fiery red as she heard the story. She disliked Malati heartily and had no love for Nabin but the full force of her anger was directed against me, 'I've told you a hundred times not to meddle in the filthy affairs of these low-caste people, but would you listen? Now manage the situation as best as you can. I have nothing to do with it.' And sweeping into her room, she slammed the door with the parting shot, 'Nabin ought to be hanged. And if that slut is dead—it's a good riddance.'

A death-like silence fell on the people in the yard. 'She is right,' I thought. 'Had I not mediated and brought them together, this would never have happened.' But I forget that my readers have not been introduced to Nabin and Malati and are unaware of the events of the previous evening. I'll go over the facts briefly.

Ever since I had come to Gangamati I had been hearing of the exploits of Malati, the young wife of Nabin Dom. She was like a smouldering coal that threatened to kindle the heart of any man who came near her. All the women of Dom Para were terrified of her power. Pretty, vivacious and sharp-tongued, she stood out from them all in appearance and personality. She wore fine saris with broad, black borders, drenched her long hair in lemon oil and marked her lovely eyebrows with a green beetle's glittering wing. She was not unduly bashful and the sight of her uncovered face atop an arched neck was often to be seen in the lanes of Gangamati. It was said that she had refused to cohabit with her husband till he went away to the city and, working for a year, returned to the village with a tin trunk, a pair of silver bracelets, some expensive saris, coloured ribbons and a bottle of rose water. With these riches he had been able to buy, not only her presence in his household but her heart as well. However, all this is hearsay. Unfortunately, beautiful relationships do not last. No sooner had Malati surrendered heart, soul, and body to their rightful owner than Nabin began suspecting her of an illicit relationship. Violent fights broke out and beatings became quite frequent. A cut in the head was nothing new. Perhaps that was why Nabin had sat down to his meal without any qualms or fears. He hadn't dreamed that Malati would set the police on him and have him arrested.

The previous evening, when Malati's shrieks rent the sky more piercingly than usual, Rajlakshmi had said disgustedly, 'This is not to be borne. Why don't you give her some money and tell her to leave the village?'

'Nabin is equally to blame,' I answered. 'He doesn't do a stroke of work. All he does is drink toddy and beat up his wife.'

Needless to say, these were habits he had picked up in the city.

'There's nothing to choose between them,' was Rajlakshmi's verdict. 'He would have worked if she hadn't occupied all his time.'

It was true that the situation was becoming intolerable. I thought of sending for them and giving them a talking to but before I could do so, they arrived at my door—followed by a crowd of eager spectators.

'Babu,' Nabin said in a solemn voice. 'This woman is a whore. I can't keep her in my house.'

'Make him break my conch bangles and take off my iron hoop,' Malati, the shrew, screamed from behind her veil.

'You must return the silver bracelets first,' was her husband's condition.

Malati pulled them off her wrists and threw them in the yard. Nabin picked them up and said, 'You can't keep the trunk either.'

'I don't want to keep it.' Malati fumbled for the key that was tied to one end of her sari and flung it at his feet. Now Nabin marched up to her and broke her conch bangles with the air of a conquering hero. Then, pulling off the iron hoop from her wrist, he flung it over the wall. 'Go,' he roared at her. 'I've made you a widow.'

I was too shocked to react. An old man in the crowd explained that without this ritual, Malati could not marry again. Her brother-in-law's younger brother had been wooing her for the last six months. He was a rich man and had offered Bishu Dom a bride price of twenty rupees. No wonder Bishu was tempted. The suitor had also promised Malati silver anklets, silver bangles and a gold nose stud and had even deposited these articles with her father. I felt sickened and unhappy for I realized that this conspiracy had been going on for some time now.

'I'm tremendously relieved,' Nabin puffed out his chest and said importantly. 'Now I can go to the city and work in peace. There's such a good time to be had in the city! As for a wife—I can marry twenty like you. Hari Mandal of Rangamati has been begging me for years. His daughter is a hundred times prettier than you.' Saying this, he tucked the bracelets and the key into his waist and departed. But the look on his face belied his brave words. It was clear that the prospect of working in the city and marrying Hari Mandal's peerless daughter did not enthuse him in the least.

Ratan came to me and said, 'Babu! Ma says you must rid the house of all these people at once.' At these words, Bishwanath and his daughter rose and left the house. The others followed. I entered my bedroom with a heavy heart. I tried to tell myself that what had happened was for the best. It was much better to end an incompatible relationship than to live a cat and dog life together, particularly when remarriage was permissible for both.

But what I heard the next day left me utterly confounded. It seemed that Nabin's proclamation of his wife's widowhood meant nothing at all. He had retained his right to beat and abuse her. I stood at my window looking out into the twilight and wondering where the girl could be. I was not sorry for Nabin. 'Serves the scoundrel right,' I said to myself. 'The poor girl can breathe freely at last.'

Rajlakshmi entered the room with a lamp in her hand. She stood looking at me for a few seconds, then turned to leave the room. But, before she could cross the threshold, there was a sound as that of a heavy body falling. The lamp wobbled and fell from her hand but it didn't go out. She picked it up and held it close to the bundle that clung to her feet. The broad black border of Malati's sari was not to be mistaken.

'Why did you touch me, you wicked girl?' Rajlakshmi wailed. 'Now I'll have to bathe in this twilight hour and catch my death. *Ma go*!* What is this on my feet?' I took the lamp from Rajlakshmi's hand and held it aloft. The blood, streaming freely from the wound in Malati's head, was flowing all over Rajlakshmi's feet.

'Save him, Ma! Save him,' Malati knocked her head harder on Rajlakshmi's feet.

'Why? What do you want now?' Rajlakshmi asked in a tone of anguish.

'The constable says he will be jailed for five years,' Malati shrieked between sobs.

'So what?' I thundered. 'He deserves it.'

'What is it to you if Nabin is alive or dead? You are not his wife anymore,' Rajlakshmi said bitterly.

---

*   Oh! My mother!

'Don't say that, Ma! Please don't say that. Save us this time—
only this time. We will leave the village and never trouble you
again. The constable kicked his rice away. He has had nothing to
eat all day. I'll die if you don't save him,' and Malati wept as if her
heart was breaking.

Rajlakshmi's eyes glistened. She put out a hand and touched
the dark head. 'Be quiet,' she said huskily. I'll see what I can do.'

The rest of us saw too. A couple of hundred rupee notes
disappeared from Rajlakshmi's coffer that night and neither
Nabin Mandal nor Malati was seen in Gangamati from the next
morning onwards.

Nine

MALATI AND NABIN WERE SOON FORGOTTEN BY ALL CONCERNED. The only exception was Ratan. It was obvious that he disapproved of Rajlakshmi's action though, wisely, he kept his feelings to himself. As for Rajlakshmi herself, her passion for improving her Sanskrit pronunciation became more and more intense as the days went by. A visit to Sunanda's house became part of her daily routine. I have no idea of how much information was imparted within those mouldy walls. All I could see were the consequences which were unexpected, even alarming. I was, habitually, a late riser and my bath and morning meal were seldom concluded before noon. Rajlakshmi had always grumbled about it and scolded me heartily but never in a manner that forced me to mend my ways. But now, in these days of her spiritual awakening, I was made to feel acutely ashamed of any delay, however minimal. 'If you don't care to look to your own health, you might consider the convenience of the servants,' she would say with a sullen face. 'When are they to have their own meals and rest if you insist on delaying yours?'

The words were the same—yet not quite the same. The tone of loving tolerance had been replaced by one of simple irritation—so obvious that even the servants saw the difference. So I would, out of consideration for the servants, have my morning meal before I was hungry. How much they valued this sacrifice I cannot say. But ten or fifteen minutes later, Rajlakshmi would be seen crossing the field that led to the bridge on the canal. Sometimes, Ratan went with her but more often than not she went alone. I spent the day in my lonely room, idle and vacant, while she spent hers in a state of tense excitement. And thus, we gradually drifted apart.

I knew that I didn't enter her thoughts even momentarily, that my unhappiness and frustration made not a dent in her consciousness, yet I could not stop myself from gazing at that lithe figure stepping over the sun-baked earth, till it was lost from sight. I would rub my eyes and strain them to see if there was even a speck of her in the distance, then, sighing, I would turn from the window and seek refuge in my bed. Sometimes I would sink into a heavy, dreamless sleep induced by the terrible weariness of an aimless existence; sometimes I would lie awake for hours staring at the babla bushes out of which the cooing of doves fell softly and plaintively on my ear. On hot afternoons, when the warm winds set up a sighing and rustling amongst the bamboo leaves, I had the strangest feeling that these sounds came from within me and not without. At such moments, the premonition that this phase of my life was soon to end was upon me. If Ratan tiptoed in, as he often did, to see if I needed anything, I would feign sleep out of fear that he would see the pain and bewilderment in my eyes.

That afternoon, after Rajlakshmi's form had merged into the haze of sky and sun, I was suddenly reminded of Burma. I sat down to write a letter to Abhaya. I thought of writing one to my British officer in Rangoon but what I would write and why... I could not think. As I sat, pen in hand, a woman, her veil pulled low over her face, walked rapidly past my window. There was something familiar about her form and the way she walked. I thought it was Malati but by the time I got to the window all I could catch a glimpse of was a red-bordered sari, before it turned the corner of the wall and disappeared from view.

A month had passed since Malati, the shrewish daughter of Bishu Dom, had knocked her head on Rajlakshmi's feet and begged her to secure her husband's freedom. Everyone in Gangamati had forgotten about her—Rajlakshmi most of all—but I hadn't. I often thought of her and wondered where she was and what she was doing. Genuinely believing that she had taken the right step in leaving Gangamati and its base temptations, I visualized her living happily with her wedded husband in some distant village.

I went back to my letter but had barely started writing when Ratan appeared at my elbow—a hookah in his hand.

'Leave it, Ratan. I'm busy,' I said

'Babu,' Ratan said by way of introduction as he always did, 'Ratan Paramanik can see the future as clearly as in a mirror. The only thing he can't predict is the hour of his death.'

I looked up and smiled. 'But since I can't predict anything at all you'd better tell me what you've come to say.'

'Didn't I tell Ma not to get taken in by these wily Doms? Didn't I beg her not to give Malati the two hundred rupees?'

As a matter of fact, Ratan had done nothing of the kind. No one, not even I, had the courage to contradict Rajlakshmi these days. But there was no point in arguing about it.

'What is the matter, Ratan?' I asked.

Ratan told me. How it had all happened he could not say (he was still in the process of collecting information) but Nabin Mandal was rotting in jail serving a five-year sentence and Malati had married her brother-in-law's wealthy brother and had returned to Gangamati this morning. Had I not seen Malati only a little while ago I would not have believed him but, having done so, there was no reason to doubt his words. An acute depression weighed me down at the thought of the treachery and deception the human race was capable of and bitterness welled up in my heart.

Rajlakshmi heard the story that night as she served me my meal. 'What are you saying, Ratan?' she asked in a wondering voice. The wench played a likely trick on us all. Two hundred rupees she got out of me and made me bathe at midnight! What is the matter with you? You have eaten nothing.'

I remained silent as I generally did on occasions like this. Rajlakshmi had always kept a vigilant eye on what I ate and how much I ate. She would weep, scold, sulk, and coax by turns to make me eat a little more, just a little more. But that was long ago! Of late her senses had become dulled to everything other than her hours with Sunanda. Her remark that I had eaten nothing, after so many months of neglect, brought tears to my eyes. I rose hastily, before she could see them, and, entering my room, lay down on the bed.

My days passed, one by one, in an endless round of drab and meaningless routine. I was well looked after, but beyond that my life held nothing. I rose the next morning, had a bath and a meal and sat by my window looking out at the expanse of bleak stony ground—the long, hot afternoon stretching out before me like a nightmare. I watched Rajlakshmi's form moving rapidly away from the house and then, when it had disappeared from view, I took up the letters I had been writing the day before. I completed them with the intention of catching the three o'clock post but, as I re-read the letter I had written to Abhaya, something caught at my heart and stalled my hand. I had written—

> I haven't had news of you for a long time. Not that I have tried to acquire any. I have only imagined, from time to time, your life with Rohini Babu. Your happiness or possible unhappiness has not been my concern. I leave that in the hands of God as I did the day we parted from one another. I have not known you for long but our relationship cannot be measured by time. It began at a point of intense suffering for you and Rohini Babu and ended at a similar point—for myself. Stranded in an alien land, sick to the point of death, friendless and helpless, I turned to you and you took me under your wing without a moment's hesitation. Someone else had done the same for me on a similar occasion in my life. Today, sitting hundreds of miles away from you, I see the difference. The love, courage and sincerity that were yours were not different from hers in degree or quality. But in yours there was a selflessness, a general aloofness that saw nothing beyond my recovery and ultimate welfare. Too much love suffocates and swamps me! Perhaps that is why I long to see you again. Till I do, so much of what I think and feel will remain a mystery—even to me.

By the time I completed the two letters it was past three o'clock and the post had gone. I was not disappointed. On the contrary I breathed a sigh of relief at the thought that I had another day in which to re-read my letter to Abhaya. As I was putting away my writing materials, Ratan came in with the message that Kushari *moshai's* wife was waiting outside to speak to me and, within minutes, the lady was in the room.

'Rajlakshmi is not at home,' I said awkwardly. 'She won't be back before evening.'

'I know that. I hear she seldom returns before dusk.' And unrolling a mat, she seated herself calmly on the floor.

I had heard that her newly acquired wealth had made her so haughty that she seldom condescended to visit anyone. She had come to this house only twice before—once to pay her respects to the zamindar's lady and the second time in response to an invitation. Why she chose to come that afternoon and seat herself even though the mistress was absent, baffled me.

'I hear that she and Sunanda are very close these days,' she began, touching a sore spot in my heart with a careless finger.

'That is true,' I admitted. 'She visits her quite often.'

'Often? Every day—or so I hear. But does Sunanda return her visits? Oh no! Sunanda is too high and mighty for that.' And she searched my face for tell-tale marks.

Till that moment I had concerned myself solely with Rajlakshmi's visits to Sunanda. Her words gave me a bit of a jolt, but what was there for me to say? However, the purpose of her visit was revealed by this outburst. She hoped to excite my indignation and enlist me on her side. I had the strongest impulse to tell her that she was making a grievous mistake if she thought I had any power or influence over Rajlakshmi. I was helpless and worthless and could do nothing for her.

But these things can't be said and to pay for my silence I was forced to hear a passionate account of her sufferings of the last ten years. The weary monologue went on and on. I must have missed quite a bit for my thoughts trailed away after a while. Then, on a new note creeping into her voice, I sat up and asked, 'Why? What has happened?'

'Thakurpo was seen at the *haat* (a village market) last evening. He was selling brinjals.'

'Selling brinjals?' I asked astonished. 'Why would he do that? And where would he get them in the first place?'

'They have a vegetable patch behind the house. It is all that wicked girl's doing. How can we live on in the same village if they insist on humiliating us like this?'

'Why should you feel humiliated? You don't live together anymore. They needed money. They had something to sell and they sold it. That's all there is to it.'

'If that is your verdict I have nothing more to say.' She looked at me with dazed and saddened eyes. 'I'll take my leave.' Her voice shook.

I said gently, 'Isn't it better to ask your mistress to intervene? She might be able to help you.'

She shook her head. 'No one can help me now. Nor shall I ask for anyone's help. I admit defeat. If Sunanda could make her husband sell vegetables—she can do anything.' She paused a while and continued. 'There was a time when she loved and respected us as if we were her own parents. But ever since she saw the weaver's widow she has turned hard and cold as stone. I used to send her things for the house pretending they were from other people. My husband believed that she knew where they really came from. But I knew Sunanda. The moment she discovered the truth she sent everything back. She'll watch her only son die of starvation but she won't touch anything of ours. She is cruel and heartless. If only I could be like her!'

She rose to leave but she suddenly turned around at the door. Her eyes were streaming and her hands were folded in humble supplication. 'I hear Ma has a lot of influence over her. Can nothing be done? My heart is breaking, Babu. I can't bear it anymore.'

I had nothing to say. She waited for a while then, wiping her face with the end of her sari, she walked quietly away.

Ten

WITH RAJLAKSHMI'S HECTIC PREPARATIONS FOR THE LIFE hereafter, many of the shackles that she had lovingly fitted on me crumbled and fell away. It brought a measure of relief, for I was no longer constrained to consider my 'poor health' or the 'convenience of the servants' and sit down to a meal almost as soon as I left my bed. Now I was free to eat when I liked and as little as I liked—that is, as little as I could without offending the cook. The ordeal over, I would sit by my window looking out on the glaring plain of dust and sun and wonder about our relationship.

That Rajlakshmi still loved me, I knew without a doubt. I was closer to her than any other human being in the world. But what of the world beyond? I had no document in my possession that would enable me to claim kinship with her in our next birth and, orthodox Hindu as she was, the fact had not escaped her. She realized now, as never before, that this world was not an end in itself; that there was another—a more glorious one—to strive for and attain and that her love for me would not prove to be an asset in that endeavour.

While she reasoned thus and acted upon her reasoning, my days passed in ever-widening circles of monotonous inactivity. The weary mornings trailed off into wearier afternoons and the sun set every evening on a soul throbbing with anguish. Ratan looked after my comforts as best as he could. Sometimes he brought a hookah, sometimes tea. I thought I saw pity in his eyes.

'Let me shut the window, Babu. There's a burning wind outside.'

'No. Leave it, Ratan.' I liked the feel of the wind on my face. It brought with it memories of many of my loved ones—now lost to me. I thought it possible that the same wind had passed over the form of my childhood friend, Indranath, before streaming in through my window. It bore the breath, perhaps, of Annada Didi if she still lived. As for Abhaya—Burma was just around the corner. I often had the illusion that in the smell of hot dust and withered leaves was mixed the faintest scent of Abhaya's hair. The wind had carried it across the sea out of pity for my sufferings.

Abhaya! I imagined her sitting by the window, even as I was, stitching a tiny vest or pillowcase, her eyes resting from time to time on the face of her sleeping infant. That wondrous being, innocent and pure as a new-blown flower, breathed out a fragrance of honey dew. Yet it had to be hidden from the public eye out of the fear that it might be mocked or reviled for being born of shame. What a travesty of morality this was! What a shattering comment on the human race!

The hot wind dried my tears as fast as they came. Thoughts of Abhaya crowded into my mind, possessed me, and would not let me rest. I asked myself, over and over again, why Abhaya had not abandoned me even at a time when the plague was raging like a hundred-headed demon in the city of Rangoon, when brothers fled from a sick brother's side and children left parents to their fate in a desperate endeavour to save their own lives? Why did she risk the tearing apart of the fragile web of happiness that she had wrought for herself with so much pain and so many tears?

Suddenly, I had the answer. Suddenly, I saw the truth about Abhaya. I saw that she had a steel-like quality about her that feared nothing—not want, not sickness, not even death. But it wasn't only fear that she had conquered. She had conquered desire. The needs of her body, the cries of her heart were as nothing to her. She could brush them away with as careless a hand as she could a cobweb from a mouldy wall. This revelation left me with the strangest feeling. I felt small, insignificant, low. I thought of how our lives had changed. She had changed hers, voluntarily, with strength and purpose while I was trapped in my own passivity and incapacity for action.

Exhausted by the weary indolence of the long, hot afternoons, I generally went out walking in the evenings along the dusty tracks over which the bullock-cart had brought me to Gangamati. On one such walk, as I stood aside to allow a horseman enveloped in a cloud of dust to pass, a voice fell on my ears. 'You are Srikanta Babu, aren't you? Don't you recognize me?'

'That is my name, but I'm afraid I don't recognize you.'

The man jumped off his horse and came forward. He wore a threadbare suit of English tweed and a sola topi. 'I am Satish Bharadwaj. We were in school together.'

'Frog!' I exclaimed (that was the name we had had for him at school). 'Where are you off to, all suited and booted?'

'I'm a sub-overseer for Railway Constructions,' he said with a hint of pride in his voice. 'We are building a new railway line from Sainthia. I have to wear English clothes or the coolies won't obey me. Why don't you join me for a cup of tea? My camp is only a mile away.'

'Some other time,' I demurred.

Frog asked me where I stayed, what I did, how many children I had and many other questions. Needless to say my answers were brief and evasive. But Frog was a simple soul who took everything as it came. Instead of trying to bore holes in the wall of my reserve he proceeded to tell me all about himself. The life he lived was comfortable enough. The place was healthy and vegetables were cheap. Fish and milk were difficult to procure but he had tremendous powers of management. The evenings were lonely (there was practically no company) but were made endurable with the aid of a little liquor. The work was hard but the pay was good. He could put in a word for me with the bara saheb if I was interested in a similar job. Walking his sickly horse, he came with me part of the way and after extracting a promise that I would visit him soon, he rode away.

I reached home rather late that night. As I sat down to my evening meal, Rajlakshmi came in. Dropping down on the floor by my side she said with a radiant smile, 'Promise me you'll give your consent.'

'I promise.'

'Without hearing what I've come to say?'

'If you feel like telling me, do so—sometime.'

Rajlakshmi's smile faded and her face grew tense. Suddenly, her eyes fell on my *thala*. She asked angrily, 'Why are you eating rice? Do you want to fall ill again?' Then, raising her voice, she called out to the cook, '*Maharaj*! I've told you a thousand times that Babu is to be served *luchi* in the evening. I'm going to cut a month's salary for disobedience.'

The loss of a month's salary was a threat that Rajlakshmi often held over the heads of her servants. But it was never carried out and they knew it. This evening however, the *maharaj* chose to take offence. 'Ma,' he said irritably, 'I've told you several times that there is no ghee in the house but you don't seem to remember anything these days. How can I make *luchi* without ghee?'

Rajlakshmi's face paled. 'Since when—?' she began.

'For the past six days.'

'Six days! You've been giving Babu rice for six days? Ratan, you could have got the ghee, couldn't you?'

Ratan wasn't very happy with his mistress' behaviour of the past month or so. Her constant absence from the house and her neglect of me had not met with his approval.

'How could I? Have I ever done anything except on your express command?' he said—all servantly obedience. 'I thought you didn't send for the ghee on purpose—it being so expensive.'

Rajlakshmi swallowed the barb, then rising, she slowly left the room.

That night I was very restless. It was very hot and sleep wouldn't come. As I tossed and turned on my bed, the door opened and Rajlakshmi came in.

'Are you asleep?' she asked softly.

'No.'

'I've wanted you all my life from early childhood,' she whispered. 'I've done everything I could to possess you. With even half that effort, God would have been mine. But you didn't give yourself to me.'

'Perhaps human beings are more elusive than God.'

'Human beings!' she echoed. 'Love is a kind of bondage. I admit it. And you find it irksome.'

I was silent. This particular argument was old and oft repeated. It had started with the genesis of the human race and was still going on. I was surprised, however, that Rajlakshmi did not press me for an answer to the question that was so important to both of us. She said instead, 'Nyaya Ratna *moshai* was telling me of a religious rite that is very difficult to perform. It goes on for three days. Sunanda is very keen on taking it up and so am I. If you have no objection we can do it together.'

'Are my objections of any value?'

'Of course they are.'

'Then I forbid you to take up anything of the kind.'

'But why? You are teasing me—'

'I'm not. I genuinely dislike these elaborate rituals.'

A cloud came over Rajlakshmi's face. She hesitated a bit, then said, 'But all my arrangements are made. Half the things are bought. What shall I tell Nyaya Ratna *moshai*? And Sunanda will be so disappointed! I know you are teasing me. Please, please give your consent.'

'You've never concerned yourself with my likes and dislikes, Lakshmi, and I've never claimed any right to guide your actions. Why is my consent so important all of a sudden?'

'It is and you must give it without any reservations, or the entire ritual will be useless,' she said in a small voice.

'You win,' I turned over to my side. 'I give my consent for whatever it is worth. You'll be leaving early tomorrow morning. Go, get some sleep.'

Rajlakshmi did not leave the room. She sat at the foot of my bed and trailed her fingers over my feet. All through my convalescence, after she picked me up from Ara station, she had put me to sleep thus. I had never asked for such devotion, not knowing what to do with it. I had fought her with all my strength but she had forced her way into my life with the passion and turbulence of a mountain stream, shattering all resistance. Now the stream was changing direction with the same ruthlessness with which it had come and my faint cries of distress were lost in the sound of rushing waters.

Rajlakshmi left the room after a long time. She thought I was asleep but had she taken a closer look she would have seen the tears dropping slowly from my fevered, burning eyes. An overwhelming sense of loss was upon me at that moment. I stifled it as best as I could but the tears went on falling.

Eleven

$\mathcal{I}$ AWOKE THE NEXT MORNING TO FIND RAJLAKSHMI GONE. THE COOK informed me that she had bathed at crack of dawn and had set out for Jadunath Kushari's house taking Ratan with her. She had left word for me that she would be away for three days. I had no idea which religious rites were being performed in the crumbling house across the canal or how far they would carry Rajlakshmi on the road to heaven. I was not curious to know either.

Ratan came home every evening and said with a hint of censure in his voice, 'You haven't visited Ma even once, Babu!'

'Is it necessary to do so?'

'Well, yes. Not really.' Ratan would dither at a straight question like that. 'But you know how people are. They may think you disapprove. It is awkward for Ma.'

'Has she ever said so?'

'No. She hasn't exactly said so. But we all know how she feels. When people question her about your absence she tries to cover up by telling them that you're still recovering from your illness.'

'I'm not a religious man, Ratan. Pujas and yagnas make me uncomfortable. Is it not better for me to stay away in the circumstances?'

Ratan would agree with a nod of his head.

One day, Ratan came with the news that Kushari *moshai* and his wife had moved into Nyaya Ratna's house in order to look after the mistress' comfort. He then proceeded to describe how the elderly matron had clasped Binu to her bosom and wept as if her heart would break; how Sunanda had washed her sister-in-law's feet and wiped away her tears and then fed her with her own hands, how Kushari *moshai* had cried like a child and everybody had wept in sympathy.

'I have a feeling the two families will come together now,' Ratan prophesied. 'And the credit for it goes to Ma.'

Knowing Sunanda, as I did, I did not share Ratan's optimism. But a great deal of my gloom was blown away. I realized that Rajlakshmi had planned this moment and worked for it all these months. My heart sang with happiness! I welcomed the thought that by today's sunset the third day would be over. Tomorrow Rajlakshmi would be home!

But she did not come. Around noon Ratan arrived with the message that his mistress had left for Bakreshwar—a place of pilgrimage near Gangamati—and would not come home for another week. Another week! I had looked forward to seeing her and I was disappointed but strangely, neither hurt nor angry. I understood that all her rituals, prayers and pilgrimages were part of a passionate endeavour to wipe out the past. Pyari was dead but her memory lay like a weary load on Rajlakshmi's heart, afflicting and tormenting her beyond endurance. Hence this frantic beating of wings against the bars of her present existence, this desperate struggle to escape into the world beyond. And the terrible irony of it was that I, whom she loved, was the principal bar. It was my presence that disrupted her flight, dashing her back to the floor of her cage, over and over again. 'Shall I, whom nothing and no one could bind, stand in the way of Rajlakshmi's happiness and ultimate welfare?' I asked myself. 'No,' I resolved. 'I'll set her free, not like the last time out of anger and jealousy, but out of love and pity for her suffering.'

I remembered the afternoon when I was leaving Patna. Rajlakshmi had stood motionless, on an upper veranda, watching me step into the carriage. Her lips had not spoken but the desperate cry of her heart, tortured with the pain of parting, had filled my ears all the way home. Not heeding it I went away to distant Burma. But I couldn't escape that passionate appeal—formless and soundless though it was. It had floated over land masses and oceans as effortlessly as a ghost and, reaching me, had pierced me where it hurt most. The scene of our second parting was being set, even now. She would watch me go away, mute and still as an image of stone. But would her heart cry out to me as it had done the time before? I thought not.

I woke up the next morning with a curious feeling of displacement. I felt an alien, an intruder in the house and in the village. Even the fields and the canal seemed remote and unreal. An overwhelming desire to get up and walk away across the fields and over the bridge to where the sky was huge and soft with morning light took hold of me but, overcome with lassitude, I lay awake listening to the noises of the household. Kushari *moshai* arrived with our rations of milk, vegetables and fish and departed shortly afterwards. The cook hummed a little tune as he chopped vegetables and washed rice. And then Ratan came to wake me up. He said that his mistress had made him promise that I would be looked after exactly as I was in her presence. I was to be served my morning meal by eleven o'clock and my evening meal by eight. The servants were to get a month's extra salary if her instructions were carried out to the letter.

I rose and had a bath and meal, not wishing my apathy to stand in the way of Ratan's gain. Then, exhausted with the effort, I sank into a heavy slumber. When I awoke it was past four o'clock. I had a cup of tea and prepared to go out for a walk. I had barely stepped out of the door when a stranger came up to me with a letter in his hand. It was from Satish Bhardwaj. He was very ill and wanted my presence at his side as soon as possible

'What is he suffering from?' I asked the messenger.

'Cholera.'

'Let's go,' I said instantly, glad to escape the pressures of my immediate environment for the time being.

Dusk was falling by the time I reached the construction site which was six miles away from Gangamati. I had formed all sorts of ideas about the status and comfort enjoyed by that exalted being, sub-overseer, S. C. Bhardwaj. What I saw did not make me lament my own fate. A plump Bauri woman was cooking something over a wood fire in a corner of a shed. She rose as I entered and led me to a tattered tent on the floor of which, on some equally tattered and soiled sheets, lay the sick man.

Frog was, by now, in a state of coma. There was a Punjabi

doctor with him who rose to leave the moment he heard I was the patient's childhood friend. His trolley was ready, he said, and he couldn't delay leaving any longer. As it was he would not reach headquarters before midnight. I must hasten to add that he wasn't callous or heartless for, before he left, he gave me some medicines together with innumerable instructions on their use. He even told me to keep an eye on the rest of the camp for, cholera being extremely contagious, the coolies might get affected at any moment. Then, warning me not to drink any water from the quarry, he departed.

I stood, dazed, watching him mount the bony back of his dispirited nag and ride away. I realized that I'd just landed myself in a mess. And it wasn't for the first time either. Rajlakshmi had come into my life in a similar situation and so had Abhaya. Sighing in self-pity I turned to the Bauri woman, Kalidasi, who, as I guessed rightly, was Frog's mistress. 'Is there no better bedding to be found in the camp, Kali?' I asked.

Frog's beloved shrugged and pushed out her lower lip.

'Could you get me some straw?'

'Straw?' she giggled. Rows of white teeth flashed in a shiny black face. 'Do we keep cows here?' Then, leaning over her protector, she asked, a practical note creeping into her voice, 'Will he live—do you think?'

'This is true love,' I thought. Aloud I said, 'These sheets are filthy. Doesn't Babu have a dhoti I can spread under him?'

She shook her head. Then, rummaging in a bundle, she brought out a pair of torn trousers. 'Pantaloon?' she asked brightly. But I shook my head. Pantaloons, though European articles of clothing and highly valued by natives, cannot, unfortunately, be used in lieu of sheets. Suddenly I remembered seeing a piece of canvas lying outside the tent. I dragged it in and, spreading it against one wall, lifted Frog's inert body onto it with Kali's help. Then, seating myself on a packing case, I prepared to keep a vigil. Kali finished her meal and, curling up in a corner, proceeded to snore so violently that the flimsy walls of canvas shook to the ground.

Around midnight, Frog's limbs started stiffening with cramp. I shook Kalidasi awake. 'Get up and light a fire. We must warm Babu's feet and hands or he will die.'

'Where's the wood?' Kali asked briefly before turning over to a more comfortable position. Within a few minutes she was snoring as energetically as ever. I walked over to the shed that was Kali's kitchen and found that she hadn't lied. There was nothing fit to burn except the shed itself and, unwilling to consign my friend's living body to the flames, I decided not to take the risk. I set fire, instead, to the packing case on which I had been sitting. Taking off my shirt I rolled it into a ball and, warming it at the fire, began fomenting the patient's limbs.

Around three o'clock a couple of men, carrying a lantern, called loudly at the door of the tent, 'Doctor Babu! Doctor Babu!' I came out to be informed that my presence was urgently required as two in the coolie camp had been taken violently ill. Taking the doctor's medicines with me, I followed my guides across a barren tract of land to where a line of trucks stood silhouetted against a steel grey sky. My surprise knew no bounds when I was told that my patients lay in the trucks for, as I learned later, the trucks served as conveyers of stones and earth during the day and coolie quarters at night. I climbed the bamboo ladder that led to the floor of the first truck and flashed the lantern in the face of the sick man. I saw that he was very old and on the verge of death.

'Where is the other one?' I asked.

'There!' A crowd of frightened faces pointed to a truck at the far end of the line. This time it was a young woman in her twenties. There were two children sleeping by her. I was informed by the other occupants of the truck that she had been abandoned by her husband a year ago. He had fallen prey to the recruiters and gone off to work in a tea garden of Assam in the company of a younger woman. Sadly, apart from vivid descriptions of her brute of a husband, I got nothing out of the sick woman's neighbours. Not one of them came forward to help me treat her or take care of the children.

By morning, another, a young boy, was smitten. And Frog's condition grew steadily worse. I sent a message to the Punjabi doctor at Sainthia but the messenger returned with the depressing news that the doctor was on a visit and could not come. Two days and three nights I spent on the trucks. Not a wink of sleep did I get during that period nor anything to eat, for I had no money. What was worse, not a drop of water passed through my lips, for, drinking the quarry water had been forbidden and there was no other source. Added to all this was a sense of agonizing defeat. Despite all my efforts I couldn't save one life—not even Frog's.

I buried Frog's body (there was no money for a cremation) on the third day and returned to the trucks. I could do nothing much but I couldn't abandon them either. There was a young boy who kept crying for water but no one agreed to walk down to the village well and fetch it. The coolies continued to drink the quarry water despite my repeated appeals. They would risk death but would not undertake any work that did not yield hard cash. Besides, who had the time? Those who were still fit went back to their digging for the prospect of a weekly wage was dearer to them than the lives of their fellows. The railway line was a government project and could hardly be abandoned because cholera had broken out in the coolie camp. I noticed a kind of callousness among the workers that I've never seen in a village. With all its feuds and tensions, a village has a composite inner life that binds its member with invisible threads. In a labour camp, where people, uprooted from their natural habitat, are massed together with only one common interest—that of making a living—no links, either of love or hate, are formed. The civilized élite knows this and since its financial expansion depends on its capacity to dehumanize a man and get an animal's work out of him, it has resorted to this trick from time immemorial.

Every evening the workers returned drunk on toddy. Every night there was singing and dancing and unabashed love-making in the open trucks. Life and death went hand in hand. Even as the ground was being dug for corpses, the wails of newborn infants rent the sky. Sickened by the tumultuous, teeming life around me I sat, a little apart, watching over a sick mother and child. The boy opened his eyes and, passing a stiff tongue over cracked lips, murmured, 'Water.'

'There's no water, son.'

He nodded weakly and shut his eyes. My eyes burned and bitterness welled up in my heart. It wasn't only the indifference to another's pain that tortured me. It was the meek acceptance of one's own. This wasn't self-control. This was a state of insensate inertia—subhuman, bestial.

Above my head, the stars and constellations hung like golden lamps out of a blue-black sky of incredible beauty. At my feet lay the dying. Suddenly a red-hot rage swept over me, stiffening my spine and misting my eyes with flecks of blood. 'Die,' I muttered between clenched teeth. 'Spawn of vermin, die! But curse your oppressors! Curse them with your dying breath—you who bear the burden of the civilized world on your backs! Drag it down, down to the bottommost layer of human history though your bones and sinews be ground in the process.'

Twelve

THE BOY DIED THE NEXT MORNING AND TWO OTHERS WERE afflicted. I handed out medicines and sent another message to Sainthia. Then, crossing the field, I stepped on to the path where, just ahead of me, two elderly gentlemen dawdled along holding umbrellas over their heads.

'Is there a village nearby?' I asked.

'There!' one of the men pointed a finger.

'Can I buy something to eat?'

'Why not? Rice, dal, ghee, vegetables—whatever you wish.'

The other turned to me and fired a volley of questions with the aim of ascertaining my caste, parentage and business in the locality. I tried to satisfy his curiosity as best as I could but the moment I mentioned the name of Satish Bharadwaj, the two old men spluttered in rage, 'Cheat! Drunkard! Scoundrel!' Expletive after expletive was hurled at the unfortunate Frog.

'All railway employees are like that—thieves and rascals!'

'I'm afraid he has gone to a place where your abuses can't reach him,' I said, pointing to the mound under which the dead man lay.

This shocked them into silence. At last one of them said in a voice that shook, 'He was a Brahmin.'

'I know, but there was no money to buy wood.'

'You could have come to us,' the other said, his face red and swollen. 'To bury a Brahmin—'

'Are you a relative?' the first asked curiously.

I heard later that he was the headmaster of the village school. I told them who I was and how I came to be there and how I hadn't eaten anything for three days. The old men clicked their tongues in sympathy. 'Come home with me,' the headmaster said. 'You need a bath and a good meal. It is extremely dangerous to starve when surrounded by cholera patients.'

I was dying of hunger and thirst and needed no second invitation. Agreeing instantly, I began to follow them to the village.

'I don't blame Satish Bharadwaj,' the headmaster said as we walked along. 'Everyone who works for the British is corrupt. Such is the contagion they spread among us.' And, with this introduction, he proceeded to elaborate on the politics of British rule. 'Look around you, young man,' he said ponderously. 'We have no tanks, no wells, no ponds—no proper sources of water. People die like dogs in the summer heat. Our villages are infested with malaria. Cholera claims the lives of a third of the villagers every year. But does the government do anything about it? No. Instead, it spends lakhs of rupees on another railway line. There was no railroad in my childhood. How cheap things were then! How plentiful! Whatever grew in the village—mangoes, jackfruit, rose-apples—everyone got a share. Now, thanks to the railway line, even the greens that grow in one's backyard are sold in the city for a few coins. It is shameful the way men, women, even children are caught by the lure of money.'

I had my own reservations about the railway. I had not a doubt that this immense network with its insidious links was responsible for the disappearance of food from Indian villages. Rice, lentils, vegetables—the staple food of the people and that which sustained life—were being bartered for worthless luxuries imported from abroad. And how many of us enjoyed them? There had always been a gap between the rich and the poor in India, but now it was no longer a gap. It had assumed the dimensions of a vast abyss. Yet I argued for the sake of argument, 'Is there anything wrong in converting excess food into money?'

'Yes, there is,' came the ready answer. 'That is a Western concept not born out of the soil of India. There is no such thing as excess where food is in question. Is it enough only to fill our own stomachs? Do we have no duty towards our fellowmen? Do we have to emulate our conquerors and snatch the food out of the mouths of the weak and afflicted?'

'I agree with you up to a point. But I don't go the whole way. Charity ennobles the giver but degrades the taker. Why shouldn't every man work for his own living? Besides the British pay for what they buy. We needn't sell if we don't wish to.'

The old gentleman got terribly excited. He jumped up and down on his little feet, 'You talk like an Englishman. Put a hand on your heart and ask yourself which is better—to barter the produce of the country and fatten your bank balance or to feed your starving brothers? In the pre-rail days there were some idlers and wastrels in every village of Bengal. They had to be looked after and someone or the other did so, grumble and curse though he may. Yet they were an integral part of the community. They were the chief entertainers at weddings and celebrations and chief pall bearers at funerals. They ran errands and sat up nights in sickness and death. Today, thanks to the rail and the pressures of civilized living, that breed is extinct. But are we better off without them? Have they not taken away with them much of the joy of living?'

I must confess that his words startled me. In appearance he was an elderly semi-literate rustic of the kind commonly found in Bengal's villages. But what he was saying went beyond him somehow. I said, hesitating a little, 'I'd like to ask you a question if I may. Are these ideas your own? That is, are they born of your own experience?'

'They are Swamiji's,' he answered without a trace of embarrassment. 'Swamiji never lies.'

'Who is Swamiji.'

'Swami Bajrananda. Young as he is, he is a great scholar and—'

'Bajrananda!' I cried. 'Do you know him?'

'Know him?' the headmaster, whose name was Jadav Chakravarty as I later found out, said with a curious mixture of pride and humility. 'He resides in my house as Krishna did in the house of Vidhur. He came among us a couple of months ago. He started the school in which I teach. And he doctors the sick—'

This was the same Ananda who had walked in our company from Sainthia station to Gangamati. How Rajlakshmi had wept when he went away! How she had pleaded with him to come back to her! But, true sanyasi that he was, there was no room in Ananda's heart for a woman's tears. He was living within a few miles of Gangamati but had never thought of visiting her. 'When my time comes to leave her, as it will very soon, can I find the same detachment?' I asked myself. 'No, never,' came the reply. 'You are too weak, too abject in your love.'

The village we were bound for was called Mahmudpur but I was assured by my companions that the name was deceptive. 'There are no Mussalmans in the village. And no untouchables either,' Jadav Chakravarty said, with an arrogant lift of his head. Then, turning to his friend, he sought confirmation, 'Are there, Naren?'

'Not one! Not one!' the man called Naren cried enthusiastically. 'Only Brahmins, Kayasthas and Nabasakhs! We wouldn't dream of living in a village which had Mussalmans and Doms.'

What he said was probably true. But what was so wonderful about living in a village exclusively inhabited by upper class Hindus I could not see. Particularly as they were self-confessed disciples of Swami Bajrananda!

The first person I saw on entering Jadav Chakravarty's house was Ananda. His eyes lit up and he came forward eagerly. 'Dada! What are you doing here?' My host and his friend stared and a new respect crept into their eyes. It was obvious that they thought I was no ordinary mortal. Why else would that divine being, Swami Bajrananda, greet me the way he had?

'You look ill,' Ananda said, scanning my face.

'He hasn't eaten for three days,' Jadav Chakravarty answered for me. 'He was in the coolie camp nursing the sick.' And he gave a heart-rendering description of the suffering he hadn't seen. Ananda didn't look particularly disturbed.

Continuing in his own line of thought, he said under his breath, 'Three days of starvation couldn't wreck you on this scale. It has a longer history. What was it? Malaria?'

'Something of the kind,' I smiled.

'How did you manage to get involved with the coolies?'

'Fate!' I touched my forehead.

'I have my doubts. You have quarrelled with Didi and left home in a huff. She must be worried sick by now.'

I smiled. 'I left home—but not in a huff.'

Ananda nodded. He thought he understood the situation perfectly.

After a bath and meal I felt considerably refreshed. I would have liked to rest but Ananda led me to the door. A bullock-cart stood outside. 'Your royal equipage is ready to convey you back to my sister. Do step in,' he said, smiling.

'I can't go home just yet. I must go back to the camp.'

'Don't nurse your anger, Dada,' Ananda said, his voice gentle and pleading. 'You have suffered enough, have you not? You are neither a doctor nor a sanyasi. I'll do what I can for the coolies. Trust me and go home. Tell Didi her Ananda is well and happy.'

I thanked my host and stepped into the cart. Ananda walked along with it for a while. 'You have lived the major part of your life in the west, Dada,' he said. 'Your body is attuned to its climate. Go back where you belong. The air and water of Bengal are making you sick and languid. Tell Didi I said so.'

I sighed. Ananda had no idea of the enormity of the task he was assigning to me!

'You have not asked me to visit you even once,' he said, breaking the long silence.

'You are a busy man. Your good works are innumerable. How can I ask you to waste your time in idle visiting?'

The truth was that I didn't want Ananda anywhere near Gangamati. I feared his keen intelligence. He would perceive the degradation into which my life had fallen at a moment's glance. There was a time when I wasn't afraid of facing the naked truth. I could cut my losses with a smile. Even a year ago I could have told Ananda, 'Don't grieve at my fallen estate. I have riches stored up which lie beyond your powers of perception.' But today, I lacked that power. A wave of self-pity swept over me. I saw myself as a worthless parasite—weak, vulnerable! A sick, broken man with only a host of broken dreams to keep me company.

'I'll come on the strength of the old invitation, then,' Ananda said, smiling.

'When?' I asked, dully.

'Don't be alarmed. I promise not to come before you two are reconciled.'

I lacked the energy to repeat that there was no quarrel and therefore the question of a reconciliation did not arise. Ananda turned and walked away. The cart moved on, creaking and groaning over ruts and furrows, over bleak, stony ground.

Ananda's words rang in my ears. But where was the question of quarrels and reconciliations? Why would I quarrel with Rajlakshmi? What was her offence? Disputes over water rights make sense only when the stream is full and flowing. When the source itself is dry, what is to be gained by dashing one's head against the bank?

These thoughts ran round and round my head like rats in a trap and I lost my sense of time. Suddenly I sat up with a jerk. The bullocks had tumbled into a ditch. Pushing aside the sacking that hung in front of the cart I poked my head out. The afternoon light had mellowed and the sun was about to set.

'Why don't you keep to the road, boy?' I asked the driver, a good-looking hulk of about fifteen.

'The bullocks climbed down. It was not my fault.' The boy's answer came sharp and clear in the Rarh* dialect.

'You're supposed to control the bullocks.'

'I'm not used to them. They are new.'

'It will soon be dark. How far is it to Gangamati?'

'How do I know? Have I ever been there?'

'Then why did you offer to bring me?'

'I did nothing of the sort. Mama** said, "Take Babu to Gangamati. Keep going south till the road forks. Then turn east."'

'I hope we aren't travelling north instead of south and west instead of east.'

'We may be. Who knows?'

The boy's cryptic, arrogant answers angered me. 'You are a fool and a scoundrel,' I shouted. 'Why did you come if you don't know north from south? Who is your father?'

'He's dead.'

'And your mother—?'

'She's dead too.'

'Good for them. Looks like we will both join them shortly. Come on, get going.'

The bullocks ambled along for a hundred yards or so.

---

* The ancient name for the part of Bengal lying on the western bank of the Ganga.
** Maternal uncle.

Suddenly the boy broke down. 'I can't go any further. I'm tired.' And he burst into loud sobs.

'What will you do?'

'I'll go back home.'

'What about me?'

'You must fend for yourself, Babu. The fare is one rupee, four annas. Mama will beat me if you give less.'

I looked around me with apprehension. Dusk was falling. Soon it would be dark. The best course would be to go back with the blubbering boy. But, at the thought, a tremor passed through my frame. I couldn't face Ananda again. I scanned the landscape. Wasn't that dark mass a grove of mango and jackfruit? Then human habitation couldn't be far off. I would find shelter for the night. If I didn't, I could walk on and on—away from Rajlakshmi, away from my familiar world. I had done it before. I could do it again.

I climbed down and paid the boy. I saw that his actions were suited to his words. His tears dried as if by magic. He changed direction within seconds and, even as I stood there, became a speck on the horizon.

Thirteen

As I WALKED THROUGH THE TREES IN SEARCH OF A NIGHT'S
shelter, a curious feeling came over me. A sense of encroaching
on someone's private preserve oppressed me. I tried to tell myself
that this was not the first time, that I had accepted people's
hospitality often enough before. But the feeling persisted. I
thought, at first, that it was prompted by the fact that my roving
had hitherto been outside Bengal. This was Rarh. I knew nothing
of it. But, by the same logic, I had known nothing of Burma when
I first set foot on it. Yet, I had felt no shame, sensed no humiliation
in throwing myself on Da Thakur's charity.

The truth, as I saw it now, was that I myself had changed.
I had been free then. I could float, effortlessly as a bird, from
experience to experience. Now, bound to Rajlakshmi as I was, the
desire to lose myself was a travesty, an imitation of the old. Yet,
not knowing what else to do, I kept on walking.

Suddenly, I caught a glimmer of white through the dark
branches on my left. Changing direction I walked on till I came to
an old derelict building with a high iron gate. But the hinges had
rusted away and many of the spikes were gone. Inside, two rooms
opened out on to a veranda. I entered one. Four iron cots stood
in the corners. They had mattresses on them but the covers were
ripped and torn and the stuffing bulged out in places. Some plates
and glasses of thick enamel, encrusted with dirt and grime, lay
scattered about. The air was mouldy and smelt of bat droppings.

As I looked around, a man, pale and gaunt as a ghost, materialized from one of the corners. I guessed that the place was a hospital and this shadowy creature its sole inmate.

'Can you spare me a few annas, Babu?' he said in a nasal whine.

'Why?' I asked, surprised.

'I'll buy something to eat. I'm starving.'

'You are a patient. You shouldn't be eating food from the bazaar.'

He was silent.

'Don't they feed you here?'

'I get a bowl of sago in the mornings. By the evening I get so hungry that I stand at the gate and beg from the passers-by. If I get a little money, I buy *muri* (puffed rice) or *chire*. If I don't, I starve.'

'Doesn't the hospital have a doctor?'

'Yes. He comes once a day—in the mornings, usually. There was another man. He did everything—from mixing medicines to cleaning lanterns. But he left last month. He said he hadn't been paid for over a year. He hasn't been replaced.'

'Do you know whom the hospital belongs to?'

In answer the man led me to the veranda where, fixed on the wall, was a vast marble plaque. On it, inscribed in gold leaf, was the name of the hospital and the date of its inception together with a panegyric in honour of the English magistrate who had performed the ceremony. There was also a kind of family tree of the founder—one Rai Bahadur, who had immortalized the memory of his dead mother by this tremendous service to the nation. Unfortunately, as I gathered, after meeting the expenses of the building and the plaque, he had had no money left to run the hospital. His interest, too, had waned and finally disappeared.

In return for a few annas, the man gave me the heartening news that within a hundred yards of the hospital lived a family of Chakravarty Brahmins who were renowned for their hospitality. They would be happy to give me a night's lodging. In fact, he would take me there himself on his way to the grocer's.

A few minutes walk brought me to my destination. I had thought, from the man's description, that the people whose hospitality I sought were well-to-do, generous folk. What I saw depressed me considerably. The house was in the worst state of disrepair imaginable. And, for all my companion's tributes to their gracious hospitality, the inmates turned a deaf ear to his calls.

'Thakur *moshai!*' he cried, over and over again, banging on the door with all his might. But a death-like silence pervaded the little house.

I tried to stop him but his tenacity was really admirable. I understood, now, how he had managed to keep alive in that mausoleum of a hospital. After hours, or so it seemed, when the frail door was on the point of bursting at the seams, a fretful voice answered from within, 'Not today. I can't give you anything today. Please go.'

My friend was not put off in the least. 'Come out and see who's here,' he cried. I was horribly embarrassed. He spoke of me as though I was the family's gurudev and my sole purpose in coming was to bless the household.

'Who is it, Bhim?' The voice changed. It became gentle and had a glow in it. There was a click and within seconds a lean, faded man in a ragged dhoti stood in the doorway. 'Who is it?' he asked again, peering up at me.

'He's a gentleman, a Brahmin!' Bhim answered enthusiastically. 'He lost his way and came to the hospital."Don't worry, Babu," I said, "I'll take you to Thakur *moshai*. He'll look after you."'

I must admit that Bhim had not exaggerated. My host received me with great warmth. Spreading a mat on the floor, he invited me to sit down. Then he proceeded to prepare a hookah mumbling apologetically, 'My servants are all ill with fever.'

As I digested this piece of information, a woman's voice boomed from the inner room, 'Who is it? Who is being entertained at this time of night?'

My heart missed a beat at the sound. I guessed that this was the voice of the mistress. The master of the house trembled visibly as he answered, 'He's a Brahmin, *ginni*,* a great man from the city. He lost his way and needs a place to stay. He's our guest for the night—only the night. He will leave as soon as dawn breaks.'

'Everyone loses his way. And manages to find it to this house,' the voice came loud and clear. 'What are you going to feed him

---

* Mistress of the house.

with? Ash from the hearth? You know very well that we have no food—'

The blood froze in my veins. The hand that held the hookah shook. I attempted to rise but my limbs were paralysed. Chakravarty *moshai* said quickly, to hide his embarrassment, 'Come, come, *ginni*. What nonsense you talk! No food in my house! Come to the kitchen. I'll arrange everything.'

'What will you arrange? There's a handful of rice in the jar. I'm going to cook it and give it to the children. You are mistaken if you think I'll deprive my own babies to feed that hulk.'

After this a marital war ensued in which all norms of civilized behaviour collapsed and disintegrated. I tried to rise but Chakravarty *moshai* grabbed me by the shoulder and pushed me down. 'You are my guest. And a guest is akin to Narayan. If you leave—I'll hang myself.'

'An ideal solution,' the voice came prompt and sharp. 'If I'm rid of you I'll gladly beg from door to door to feed my children.'

I couldn't bear it anymore. I stood up and said in a resolute voice, 'That may be the best course for you, Chakravarty *moshai*. But kindly do it at your leisure. For the present, either let me go or get me a length of rope so that I may hang myself and be relieved of your hospitality.'

There was a stunned silence. Then my host addressed his opponent, 'Did you hear that?'

'Hunh,' said the voice from within.

Suddenly an arm appeared through the door and set a brass pitcher, with a bang, on the floor. 'Take this to the grocer's and bring back rice, dal, salt and oil. See that the devil Srimanta doesn't cheat you.'

'No! No!' My host was happy again. 'I'm not a child.' Then peering into the hookah he said, 'The fire is out. Change the bowl, *ginni*. I'll have a few puffs before I go. I won't be long.' He pulled at his hookah with tremendous enjoyment and departed. Thus, husband and wife were reconciled.

After an hour or so I was invited into the kitchen. My appetite had vanished and I felt sick and exhausted. I had spent many nights of my life under strange roofs but nowhere had I witnessed the kind of scenes that I had in that house. Yet, I couldn't get out of the situation either. I followed my host with a heavy heart but that night was, obviously, one of surprises. On entering the kitchen I found that, instead of a cooked meal, rice, dal, ghee, salt and vegetables lay in mounds on pieces of banana leaf. A fire roared in the hearth and a brass pot stood before it.

'Put everything in the pot and set it on the fire,' my host directed, fairly dribbling at the mouth. 'The dal is excellent—*khari musuri**—*and so is the ghee. It will make a fine kedgeree.'

I didn't understand the situation in the least, but, afraid of sparking off another controversy, I did as I was told. My ignorance of the art did not escape the eyes of my hostess.

She came out of the shadows and addressed me directly, 'You know nothing of cooking,' she said in the voice that still had the power to make me tremble.

'No,' I admitted humbly.

'My husband wanted me to cook the meal. He said, being a stranger, you would never come to know. But I refused. My conscience would not allow me to rob you of your caste. We are Agradani** Brahmins. Our touch is polluting for high caste Brahmins like you.'

I didn't dare tell her that I had eaten at the hands of people far lower in the caste ladder than she. I cooked the meal according to her instructions and forced myself to swallow it. But the 'fine kedgeree' tasted like sawdust and felt like a pile of nuggets in the pit of my stomach. I wished, desperately, for the night to be over. I would walk out of the depressing house the moment I saw a glimmer in the east.

I steeled myself and went on eating but the moment I washed my mouth everything came up and I vomited, violently, all over the floor. I wanted to clean up the mess but, overcome with exhaustion I couldn't move a muscle. A dark mist swirled before my eyes. I said, gasping, 'Let me lie down for a few minutes. Then I'll get up and clean the floor.'

'Hush, child!' said a voice, surprisingly soft and maternal, and a pair of gentle hands took hold of me. 'Come and lie down on my

---

*   Husked but whole lentils.
** A Brahmin who performs funeral rites for a living and is, in consequence, socially degraded.

bed. I'll clean it up in a minute.' She led me to her room and I shut my eyes, surrendering to the inevitable.

When I awoke, it was morning and the sun was high over the horizon. My head ached unbearably and my body burned with fever.

'Are you awake, Baba?' the voice of last night spoke from the foot of the bed. I opened my eyes painfully. I saw a woman in her forties, dark and pock-marked with commonplace features. But not a trace of the harshness that had emanated from her person last night was evident this morning. Most prominent in her physiognomy were the marks of a lifetime of struggle and suffering.

'I didn't see you properly last night,' she said. 'You are very young indeed. Had my eldest son lived, he would have been your age.' She placed a cool hand on my forehead and murmured, 'The fever is quite high.'

I felt acutely guilty at the thought of the burden I had become on this poverty-stricken family. 'The hospital is not too far off. I can walk to it—with a little help,' I said, my throbbing eyes shut against the glare.

I couldn't see her face but the voice that answered was suffused with pain. 'I said some unforgivable things last night. Don't take them to heart, son. Hardship and constant anxiety have worn away all my patience. Don't go to the hospital—that hell of hells. Stay here with me. The sick are not bound by any rules—so the Shastras say. I'll cook you sago and barley water and nurse you till you are well.'

I stayed in her house for four days and during that period I had first hand experience of the oppressions inherent in the Brahminical hierarchy. As if the grinding poverty was not bad enough, life was made hell for these Agradanis by other Brahmins of a higher order. I heard from my hostess that Chakravarty *moshai* had once been a prosperous landowner but, owing to his excessive generosity and lack of a sense of self-preservation, he had lost all he had. Loss of prestige had followed and they were living in a state of excommunication from the Hindu order. And their chief persecutors were those very Brahmins who were in their debt.

On the second day of my stay I proposed shifting myself to

the outer room but my hostess shook her head. 'It is going to rain and the roof leaks. You'll catch your death.'

'Why didn't you get the roof repaired before the rains came?' I asked.

She pointed to a pile of straw standing just outside my window. 'No Hindus will work for us—such is the rule of the village. We hire Mussalman peasants from the neighbouring village to thatch our roof every year. This year no one came.' Then, bursting into tears, she continued, 'There's no end to our troubles, Baba. When my eight-year-old daughter died of cholera, not a soul came forward to console us or help to take the body to the burning-ghat. My husband carried her in his arms and my younger son went with him. But he wasn't allowed to cremate the body. He had to dig a hole and bury the child—his own child—' She broke down, sobbing uncontrollably.

My fevered brain pulsed and pounded and pain tore at my eyeballs as I heard this terrible tale of suffering and humiliation. Centuries ago a Brahmin ancestor of theirs had committed the heinous crime of accepting alms in return for performing the pre-cremation rites of a dead man. That single act had branded him and his descendents as Agradanis and relegated them to the lowest rung of the Brahmin caste ladder for all time to come. Yet the acceptance of alms is mandatory. Without it the rites are incomplete, according to the Shastras. This paradox is embedded in the system to this day and given unquestioning respect, leaving Agradani Brahmins vulnerable to all kinds of social and moral pressures. The moral perversity that is reflected in the treatment meted out to Agradanis is peculiar to Hinduism and is not to be found in any other religion of the world.

Controlling herself with an effort, the woman said, 'Sometimes I wish we would move to a Mussalman village. We might be better off.'

'But you'll lose caste—' I began.

'My husband's uncle went away to Dumka and became a Christian. His troubles are over,' she said by way of an answer.

I was silent. The thought of Hindus defecting to other religions was painful. But what were the alternatives? I had believed that only the lowest of the low, the untouchables, suffered persecution on this scale. I realized, now, that it was inherent in the system and not a single caste was protected against it.

I found out years later that some enlightened Hindus do admit to this defect in our religion. Yet they are prepared to live with it and perpetuate it. Not even one of the men I conversed with even tried to offer any viable alternatives or proposals of constructive change. It has left me speculating on the future of Hinduism. I'm convinced that a religion that saps the moral fibre of its followers to the extent that Hinduism does cannot last for long.

On the fourth day I got ready to depart. 'Bid me farewell, Ma,' I said, 'I'm going.'

My hostess came to the door. 'We are poor, wretched folk,' she said, her face flushed, eyes swimming. 'All we've given you is a share of our suffering.'

I was silent. Formal speeches of thanks never come easily to me. I remembered Ananda's words, 'This is a strange country, Dada. Here, mothers and sisters are strewn on the streets. There's no escaping them.'

Chakravarty *moshai* had procured a bullock-cart with great difficulty. As I took my place in it his wife called upon the gods to protect me from harm and made me promise to come again if I was ever in these parts. I never saw her again. Later, much later, I learned that Rajlakshmi had paid the mortgage on much of their land and helped to bring the family back to a position of comparative stability.

Fourteen

$\mathcal{I}$T WAS TEN O'CLOCK BY THE TIME I REACHED THE HOUSE IN Gangamati. As I stepped down from the cart, I noticed that the doorway was hung with a garland of mango leaves. Banana fronds were placed on either side and consecrated pots stood next to them. The outer room was full of men, many of whom came crowding in at the door on hearing the sound of the cart. One of them came rushing out with a happy laugh. He was no other than my old friend, Swami Bajrananda. While he plied me with questions, informing me mischievously that search parties had been sent in all directions to look for me, Rajlakshmi came and stood quietly by the door.

'Where were you all these days?' she asked. 'We were all sick with worry. Ananda, I told you he would come today, didn't I? I felt it in my bones.'

'You did?' I asked, smiling. 'Is that why you've placed these auspicious symbols at the door? To welcome me home?'

'No, no, Babu,' Ratan intervened enthusiastically. 'Ma is feeding Brahmins today to mark her return from the holy pilgrimage of Bakreshwar—'

'Ratan,' Rajlakshmi fixed him with a stern glare. 'Stop jabbering and go and attend to your work.' Her cheeks were flushed and her eyes bright.

Ananda threw a brief glance in her direction and said, 'Didi found it impossible to endure the worry of your disappearance.

She organized the Brahmin bhojan to take her mind off—for a short while at least. You know how it is. The idle mind is a breeding ground for all kinds of tensions and fears. But you still haven't told us where you were all these days. The cart driver's boy told us he had dropped you off on the road to Gangamati.'

I recounted the history of the last four days. He heard it carefully and said, 'Don't repeat the disappearing trick, Dada. You have no idea of what Didi has suffered.'

I knew it well enough so I did not contradict him. In a little while Ratan brought me a hookah and a cup of tea. Ananda rose to leave. He said, 'If I sit here a moment longer I'll earn the curses of a good woman. Why take the risk?' He left the room and Rajlakshmi came in.

'It is very late,' she said. 'I suggest you don't bathe at this hour. Have a wash and change your clothes.'

'I'm very hot and sticky. I must have a bath.'

'Then let me help you. You are still so weak—you can't manage by yourself.' She burst out laughing and added, 'Don't try to punish me. You'll only end up punishing yourself. Take my advice. Don't bathe. The fever will return if you do.'

This was typical of Rajlakshmi. I have not known her equal for foisting her wishes on others. This was a small thing she asked of me, but she dominated, equally easily, in other, more important areas of my life. Yet she was never offensive, never jarring. And it wasn't only in her relation with me that she wielded this power. It was apparent everywhere. As she rose to fetch me my meal I said, 'Let the good work be concluded first. I'll eat after your Brahmins have been fed.'

'Oh no, you won't,' she answered instantly. 'That may go on till late in the evening. If I keep you starving till then I'll end up in hell instead of heaven,' and she left the room, laughing.

Sitting down to eat I noticed that I was served with the very light food that is usually given to convalescents. I realized that Rajlakshmi had prepared it especially for me with her own hands. She sat by my side encouraging me to eat as she had always done. But the old habit of command had gone. She begged humbly where she had protested passionately—even a few days ago. 'She's a changed woman,' I thought and a wave of melancholy swept over me.

Late that night Rajlakshmi tiptoed into the room and, dimming the lantern, moved towards her bed. 'Your Brahmins were fed long ago,' I spoke from out of the dark. 'What were you doing all this time?'

Rajlakshmi gave a little start. 'I thought you were asleep. That's why I walked in as quietly as I could.'

'I kept awake on purpose. I wanted to talk to you.'

Rajlakshmi lifted the mosquito net and sat on my bed. Then, running her fingers through my hair in the old manner, she asked tenderly, 'Why didn't you send for me, then?'

'Would you have come if I had?'

'Do I have the power to disregard your call?'

I knew she didn't but, weak as I was, I lacked the power to admit it.

'Why are you silent?' she asked after a while.

'I'm thinking.'

'What of?' She lowered her head till the soft cheek rested on my forehead. 'You were angry with me. That's why you left home, didn't you?'

'How did you know?'

'Wouldn't you know if you were in my place?'

'Perhaps I would.'

'There's no "perhaps" about it. These feelings are instinctive.'

'I know.'

'If you do, why do you say things that hurt me?'

'I don't. I haven't for a long time now. Only you haven't noticed it, have you?'

The old Rajlakshmi would have reacted violently to this statement. She would have sulked and probed and asked a hundred questions. Now, silence fell between us. After a while she sat up and said, 'I'm told you had a fever. Why didn't you send for me?'

'There was no one to send. Besides, I didn't know where you were.'

Then I recounted my experience of the last few days. Tears of gratitude and humility coursed down my cheeks as I described the poor woman who had nursed me as tenderly as she would her own child even while bowed down by toil and care. Rajlakshmi wiped them away and said softly, 'Why don't you send her some money?'

'If I had the money I would.'

Any suggestion that her money was not mine had always offended Rajlakshmi. She would reject it outright and the argument would end, invariably, in a quarrel. But, as before, today she was silent. When she spoke her voice was changed. 'A letter has arrived for you—from Burma. It was in an official envelope so, thinking that it might contain some urgent message, I asked Ananda to open it.'

'What does it say?'

'The manager of the company informs you that your request for re-appointment has been granted. Your old post is open for you any time you choose to claim it. Shall I fetch the letter?'

'There's no hurry. I can read it tomorrow morning.'

Another silence fell between us, pregnant with meaning. I felt torn apart. I didn't know what to do, what to think. I wanted to speak but didn't know how. Suddenly a teardrop fell on my forehead. I said softly, 'I have been offered my old job again. That is not bad news, Rajlakshmi. Why do you cry?'

Rajlakshmi wiped her eyes and said, 'Why didn't you tell me you were planning to go back? Did you think I would stop you?'

'No. I'm convinced you wouldn't have stopped me. You may even have encouraged me. I didn't tell you because I didn't think you would care to waste your time on trifling matters like these.'

The hands in my hair stiffened and became cold and rigid and her voice, when she spoke, sounded far away, insubstantial. 'I deserve your reproaches. I realize, now, that in dragging you here to Gangamati I have sinned grievously against you. This aimless, idle existence into which I've pushed you is akin to death—for a man. I can never forgive myself for destroying you as I have done.'

'When did this realization dawn on you?'

'I went on a pilgrimage but I didn't find God. Wherever I looked I saw *your* face—broken, vulnerable. You have suffered enough at my hands. It is time I released you. Go back to Burma. Live your own life with meaning and purpose.'

At these words the anger melted away from my heart and I became whole and pure again. 'You, too, have suffered, Lakshmi. Gangamati is no place for you. You belong—' I stopped myself in time. What I was about to say would offend and humiliate her.

But, though my unspoken words hit her where it hurt most,

she forgave me this time. 'On the contrary,' she said gently. 'I'm not fit for Gangamati. Others may believe that I've paid for my love by surrendering the pleasures of the city. But *you* should know better. You should know that I've lost nothing that I valued: I've only shed the terrible weight that people hung round my neck and forced me to carry from childhood onwards. And you—whom I've desired above all else from the beginning of memory itself! In possessing you, did I not acquire ten thousand times what I surrendered? You should know that.'

I tried to speak but words would not come. My breast heaved with indignation for Rajlakshmi. 'Fool, fool and thrice fool!' I chastised myself. 'You have misjudged her! You don't deserve her love.'

'I thought I would keep this knowledge from you in your own interest,' she continued. 'But I couldn't help myself. What hurts me most is your belief that I've neglected you in the hope of a place in heaven.' A shower of tears fell on my face. I took one of her hands in mine and pressed it without a word. She wiped her eyes with the other and stood up. 'I had better go and see if the servants have eaten. Try to sleep.' And, gently pulling her hand away from mine, she left the room.

I lay awake for hours after that. Innumerable thoughts chased one another in an unending circle. But the one that dominated, recurring over and over again in an unchanging pattern, was that she had truly cut me loose at last and, in doing so, had set herself free.

I awoke the next morning to find Rajlakshmi's bed empty. She had either not come in at all last night or had left before dawn. I rose and went into the outer room where the ascetic, Swami Bajrananda, looked eagerly on as Rajlakshmi fried some delectable delicacies on a stove in the corner. Against one wall sat Ratan pouring tea out of an enormous kettle. Bajrananda greeted me heartily, 'Come, Dada, let's fall to while everything is piping hot.' Then, peering into my face, he added, 'You don't look too good. Let me feel your pulse.'

'No, Ananda,' Rajlakshmi protested. 'Don't treat him like a patient. You'll be recommending a diet of sago any minute.'

'I've been living on sago for the last four days. I refuse to eat it now—even on doctor's orders,' I said, stretching out my hand.

Rajlakshmi put some *singaras* (samosas) and kachauris on a plate and handed it to me. Then, pushing the vessel that contained the rest towards Ananda, she said, 'Come, bhai. Eat.'

'So many?' he asked, amazed.

'Why not? Why are you a sanyasi if you can't eat more than ordinary men? You could just as well have been a householder.'

Ananda's eyes softened. 'If it weren't for sisters like you I would have torn off my saffron robes and thrown them into the river long ago. But I have a request, Didi. You have been fasting for the last three days. Why don't you share our breakfast?'

'Goodness, Ananda! Some of my Brahmins are yet to be fed. Not all could come yesterday.'

'Then there is nothing for me but to go in search of them. Give me their names and addresses. Let me drag the rascals to your feet by the hair of their heads.' He suited the action to the words by pulling the pot of snacks towards himself and falling upon it with a vengeance. Rajlakshmi smiled a crooked little smile and said, 'What a fine sanyasi you are, Ananda! How deep is your respect for gods and Brahmins!'

The morning was bright and clear and my spirits rose with Ananda's banter. Rajlakshmi looked relaxed and happy. I persuaded myself that her mood of last night had been induced by her prolonged mental strain and her self-inflicted mortifications of the flesh. All my fears and worries drained away and a sense of well-being flooded my body and soul.

All day the Brahmins came, singly and in twos and threes, ate and departed. In the evening, her work over, Rajlakshmi came into the outer room where Ananda and I sat having our tea.

'Welcome, Didi,' Ananda called.

'What makes the sanyasi so happy this evening?' Rajlakshmi dropped down by his side.

'Your wonderful snacks and sweets! We sanyasis never resist the temptations of the flesh. Householders have a different code. Just look at yourself. While we ascetics are enjoying one good meal after another you are killing yourself with your innumerable fasts.'

'Killing myself? On the contrary! This wretched body flourishes day by day.'

'That is the wonder of it!' Ananda looked at her with admiring eyes. 'Every day I see you, you are more beautiful. And your beauty is not of this world. It is unearthly, ethereal!'

Rajlakshmi blushed and lowered her face. Ananda turned to me and said, 'It is obvious you do not see with my eyes. If you did you would never have attempted to go back to Burma. I wonder which deity, in his malignance, planted this blind man in your path, Didi.'

Rajlakshmi laughed and answered, 'It was all my own fault, Ananda. I blame no one—him, least of all. He was the head boy of the village pathshala and I, a junior pupil. He had a whip which he laid about my shoulders whenever I forgot my lessons. That didn't aid my memory in the least but it created—other feelings. Child as I was, I roamed the woods picking *bainchi* berries and stringing them into garlands to appease him. I wish I had strung the thorns in between.'

'What a blood-thirsty woman you are, Didi!'

'I would still do it—if he had someone to pluck them out for him,' and laughing, she left the room.

Ananda turned to me after she left. 'Are you still planning to go to Burma? Didi will never go with you.'

'I know that.'

'But why must you go? You don't need the money. Why tie yourself to a desk from morning till evening?'

'It is a good habit I believe.'

'You haven't got over your annoyance with Didi. That's what it is.'

'Can't you think of any other reason?'

'Frankly, I can't.'

I felt like asking him why he involved himself in something that didn't concern him. But, fearing unpleasantness, I desisted.

When Rajlakshmi came in again, Ananda said to her, 'Dada says that enslaving oneself is a good habit. My question is that why go to distant Burma, why not do so right here? We could work together for our country.'

'But he is not a doctor, Ananda,' Rajlakshmi pointed out.

'There are other ways of serving the country. We must build schools, dig wells and teach the villagers to value themselves as human beings. The poor are deprived in so many ways.'

Rajlakshmi glanced at me out of the corner of her eye and shook her head gently. She was afraid, perhaps, that I would agree.

'Why do you shake your head, Didi?'

'No, Ananda,' she smiled. 'I know our country is in a shocking state. But I don't see what a single man can do about it. If you take him with you you'll spend all your time and energy looking after him. You'll have nothing left with which to serve the country.'

Ananda laughed at her fears. 'Rest assured, Didi. I won't steal him away from you. But you were wrong when you said that a single man can do nothing. It is not the number of people who rise at the call of the motherland but the strength with which they rise that matters. The power of the will is a tremendous power. Do not underestimate it.' He was silent for a while. Then he continued, 'It is true that I can achieve very little by myself. But one thing I can, and do. I share the misery of the poor and degraded to the best of my ability.'

'I know that. I have known it from the very beginning.'

'I needn't have done it. My father is a wealthy man. I could have had a life of ease and comfort. But I turned my back on it. The fact that I have overcome the desire for good living is virtue enough for me. My conscience is at rest.'

At this point, Ratan came in and announced that the evening meal was ready. Rajlakshmi ordered him to start serving and turned to me. 'I am very, very tired. I'll retire as soon as you have eaten.' Weariness was stamped upon her face but it was the first time that she had admitted it. We stood up and followed Ratan without a word. Suddenly the bright, beautiful day was over and a wraith-like gloom descended on the house. My old depression returned.

Ananda left the next morning. Rajlakshmi accompanied him to the door. I remembered the last time she had bidden him farewell. How bitterly she had wept! How inconsolable she had been for so many days! Now her calm, clear gaze rested on his face as she asked, 'When do I see you again, Ananda?'

'I'll come as soon as I can. I promise.'

'But we're leaving Gangamati. Will you come to me, wherever I may be?'

'If you command me, can I disobey?'

'Then give me your address. I'll write to you as soon as we reach—'

Ananda fished in his pocket for a pencil and paper, and writing his address, handed it to Rajlakshmi. Then bidding us farewell he walked slowly away.

Fifteen

WHEN SWAMI BAJRANANDA LEFT WITH HIS TIN TRUNK AND CANVAS bag, he took away with him all the joy of living that had remained with us. Not content with that he had, it seemed to me, packed the vacuum created by his absence with the deepest and most active gloom. Our lives had been like a stretch of sea water that had retained a measure of clarity by dashing against the coral reef that was Ananda. With its removal, the water stagnated and became foul and evil-smelling. A week went by. Rajlakshmi went out every day—where, I did not know. Nor did I want to ask. In the evenings she spent hours discussing business with Kushari *moshai*. I yearned for Ananda as I had never yearned for anyone before. I knew Rajlakshmi did the same. At times the irony of the situation was too much to be borne. We, who had loved one another and had sought to create a little world of our own away from the public eye, were reduced to seeking a stranger's presence in our midst.

One day, Ratan came in beaming from ear to ear. He looked around him surreptitiously, even though Rajlakshmi was away from home, and whispered, 'Have you heard the news, Babu? We are leaving Gangamati in a day or two. Pray to Goddess Durga that Ma doesn't change her mind.'

'Where are we going, Ratan?'

Ratan threw another furtive glance at the door. 'That I don't know, yet. It has to be Kashi or Patna. Ma has a house in each of these cities. Where else could it be?'

I was silent. Mistaking my lack of enthusiasm at his great news for lack of faith in his communication, he continued, 'It's true, Babu. It's absolutely true. We *are* leaving. Ma has finalized the arrangements with Kushari *moshai*. All we need to do now is pack up and leave. It's wonderful news, isn't it?' And, bursting with the anticipated pleasures of the city, Ratan left the room.

It was obvious that Ratan looked upon me as a mere member of the retinue that went with Rajlakshmi wherever she chose to go. He knew that my likes and dislikes held no ground before hers and that, like the rest of the company, I was completely dominated by the will of the mistress. Ratan, in his innocence, was unaware that he had filled my cup of agony and humiliation to the brim with his words. 'How weak I am,' I thought and marvelled at her strength. I saw now, more clearly than ever before, that I was merely a pawn in the game Rajlakshmi was playing—that of testing her own strength. She had employed all the force of her magnetic beauty and overwhelming desire to bring me to her feet. And I had been powerless to resist. But now I was redundant. Fool that I was, I had allowed myself to be dragged through the dust and believed I was flying on golden wings. I had valued myself against the riches she had discarded for my sake not knowing that, for her, they had no value.

Ratan's words were confirmed the next morning. After her morning bath and prayers, Rajlakshmi came up to me and asked softly, 'If we leave tomorrow morning, around this time, we can catch the train going west, can't we?'

'Yes.'

'I've concluded the arrangements here. Kushari *moshai* will continue to look after the property as he has been doing.'

'Very good.'

Rajlakshmi hesitated a little and said, 'I've written to Banku. I've asked him to reserve a compartment and wait for me at Sainthia. I'm not sure—'

'You needn't worry. Banku will never disobey you.'

'He'll try not to. But—would you like to come with us?'

I didn't know where she was going or why. But I could not ask. I answered hesitantly, 'I'll come—if you want me to.'

Rajlakshmi couldn't reply for a few seconds. Then she spoke, changing the subject all of a sudden, 'Where is your tea? Hasn't Ratan brought you your tea?'

'Not yet. He must be busy.'

Such an aberration, in the early days of our relationship, would have been enough to spark off a domestic disturbance lasting for days. But now Rajlakshmi did not even call Ratan and demand an explanation. She hung her head, as if in shame, and quietly left the room.

On the day of our departure, Rajlakshmi's subjects came to pay their respects. I missed Malati in the throng but I knew that she had left Gangamati and was now happily settled with her new husband in his ancestral village. The Kushari brothers arrived with their families at crack of dawn to bid us goodbye. Rajlakshmi had managed to bring them together—how, I did not know. But it was evident from their faces that the quarrel over the weaver's property was at an end and amity and concord had been restored.

Sunanda brought her son over to me and said, 'Asking you not to forget me is unnecessary. So I won't do that. I seek your blessings for my son.'

'Even that is unnecessary, *bon*,' I replied. 'A child of yours is blessed in his birth. He needs no other blessing.'

Overhearing the conversation, Rajlakshmi said, 'Pray that he grows up to acquire a heart and soul like yours.'

'Like mine?' I laughed. 'You must be joking.'

'A mother doesn't joke when the good of her own child is in question,' Rajlakshmi's eyes filled with tears. 'I love the boy as if he were my own and that is my prayer for him.'

We left Gangamati amidst tearful farewells. Even Ratan wiped his eyes unashamedly every now and then. The inhabitants of Gangamati clamoured about their mistress begging her not to forget them, to return as soon as she could. Only I stood apart, like a spectator watching the last scene of a play—poignant and bittersweet. Soon it would be time to ring the curtain down. The lights would go out, one by one. The viewers would rise and shuffle out of the theatre to take up the separate burdens of their everyday lives. But I was not one of them. I stood alone, apart, like a star wrenched out of its socket. I drifted aimlessly in space, apathetic and lustreless. Trapped in a maze of clouds, I had lost my sense of direction.

We reached Sainthia before dusk. Banku had obeyed Rajlakshmi's instructions and was waiting at the station. As soon as the carts rolled in, he got busy stowing away the luggage and directing the servants to their third-class seats. Then, taking his place with his stepmother in their reserved compartment, he proceeded to converse with her in a low voice. He ignored my presence but not very overtly. I knew why. He was now a full grown man, wealthy and powerful in his own right, and he had no use for such as me.

As I walked up and down the platform (my train to Calcutta was not due before midnight) my eyes fell on Rajlakshmi beckoning me through the window of her compartment. She grasped me by the hand the moment I reached her and said, 'Won't you come and see me once—before you leave for Burma?'

'Certainly—if you desire it.'

'I don't desire it,' she answered with a sigh. 'At least not in the way I did. But I would like to see you once before you leave. Will you come?'

'I will.'

'Write to me as soon as you reach Calcutta.'

I nodded. The final whistle sounded and the green light came on. Rajlakshmi released my hand and I stepped off even as the train moved with a jerk and glided away from the dim light of the station towards an enveloping darkness.

On reaching Calcutta, I wrote my promised letter to Rajlakshmi. Then I started preparations for my departure from the country. A fortnight went by. I had promised Rajlakshmi that I would visit her but my heart quaked at the prospect. I hadn't a clue to her present state of mind. She might take it into her head to stop me from going to Burma. It was true that in the letter that she had written from Kashi, she had not reminded me of my promise. But, weak as I was, I persuaded myself that that was normal in the circumstances. Even I, I reasoned, would not humble myself to that extent. The truth was that Rajlakshmi had become so much a part of my life that I couldn't live without her. Suddenly I longed to see her again, so passionately that I was lost to all sense of propriety. Glancing up at the clock I saw that, if I made haste, I could catch the train to Kashi. I didn't even pack a change of clothes. I told myself that she, to whom I was going, knew my requirements better than I did. I rushed out of the house and, buying a ticket, boarded the train to Kashi. All night I tossed and turned on my narrow berth. Then morning came. A fierce sun rose and blazed white hot in the sky. Everywhere, the light was pitiless and glaring. But a mist lay over my eyes and coiled its damp and streaky strands around my heart. And so I arrived at my destination.

The first person I saw, on entering the house, was an elderly Brahmin smoking a hookah.

'Yes?' he asked, fixing his tranquil gaze upon my face. 'Are you looking for someone?'

'Is Ratan—?' I murmured—my heart sinking.

'Ratan has gone to the market. He'll be back in a few minutes.' His eyes took in my dishevelled hair and clothes grimy with smoke and sweat. 'Please sit down.'

'Is Banku Babu at home?'

'Yes, yes, of course.' The old man called a servant and instructed him to fetch Banku. Banku was extremely surprised to see me. 'We thought you were in Burma,' he said, not specifying who 'we' were. 'Are your things in the carriage?'

'I have no luggage with me.'

'No luggage? Are you returning tonight, then?'

'Yes. That's what I had planned.'

Banku rose and went about his work. A servant came in with water, towels and fresh clothes but no one else came near me. After a long while, a message came from within that my meal had been served. I followed the servant to a flagged veranda where two *thalas* were laid side by side. As I took my place beside Banku someone entered from a side door and everything—Banku, the shining *thala* with its surrounding bowls, and the black and white marble of the floor—swam before my eyes. Only for a moment, however. Then, recovering myself with a desperate effort, I commenced eating.

Rajlakshmi came forward and sat by me. She was wrapped in widow white from head to toe and not a speck of gold remained on her person. Not only had she stripped herself ruthlessly of all adornment—she had even cut off the long black river of her hair. The shorn locks tumbled about her face—now harsh and worn with prolonged austerities. I had parted from her only a month ago. She had aged ten years in the interim.

My eyes burned and the rice stuck like glue in my throat. I wanted to get away from her—far, so far away that I need never see her again. I couldn't bear to look at her face or even hear her voice. I swallowed mouthful after mouthful in a fierce determination that she should not get a chance to comment on my lack of appetite.

'Banku tells me that you are leaving tonight,' she said, after a while.

'Yes.'

'So soon? But your ship leaves on Sunday.'

I glanced up at her face and she shrank before the look in my eyes.

'There are still three days to go,' she murmured.

'Yes, but I have a few things to tie up before I leave.'

She hesitated a little, then said, 'My gurudev is here.'

I gathered that the old gentleman I had met on my arrival was Rajlakshmi's gurudev—the one she had talked about and wanted me to meet. Since my train was to leave at midnight, I had ample time in which to make his acquaintance. I found him a good, kind man, fiercely protective of his personal religion but also open to that of others. He knew the truth about us for Rajlakshmi had hidden nothing from him but, far from looking down on me, he sought my company and conversed with me for a long time. He spoke words of comfort and sympathy and gave plenty of advice. I have forgotten much of what he said but I remember that he expressed his faith in Rajlakshmi and said that he had anticipated the change that had come over her. 'I have had many disciples but not one like her,' was his comment. 'Her unwavering faith and devotion to duty are incomparable.'

The hour of my departure drew near. The carriage that was to take me to the station stood at the door. I took leave of Gurudev and stepped in. Rajlakshmi's face appeared at the window. Her lips trembled but no words came. I thanked my Maker that my face was hidden from her view. Inside the carriage, everything was dark.

The stinging tears poured down my face in blessed release as the horses bore me away from Rajlakshmi. 'We cast ourselves adrift together,' I murmured to myself. 'I, hapless that I am, will never sight the shore but your goal is before you, fixed and immutable like the northern star. May it be ever so. May peace and happiness be yours.' I repeated this prayer over and over again as the rushing wheels and galloping hooves took me further and further away from her. Suddenly I felt as I had that last day in Gangamati—a spectator watching the last scene of a play. It was a glorious conclusion to a sordid tale of human weakness and error. But even while the triumph and glory that were Rajlakshmi's awed and uplifted me, I suddenly thought of Rohini Babu. He and I were two of a kind, floundering and sinking in a slough of base desire. But for him there was Abhaya. I remembered her as she stood at her door bidding me goodbye, tears trembling in her eyes, steadfast and unwavering in her love. The breadth of her vision, the courage of her convictions and the innate purity of her soul came upon me in a flash. I would go to her and she would not forsake me.

The moment the carriage stopped, a figure leaped nimbly from the box and touched his forehead to the ground at my feet.

'Ratan!' I exclaimed.

'Yes, Babu. If you need a servant in that foreign land where you are going—send for me. I'll serve you faithfully to the end of my days.'

The light from the flare of the carriage fell on his face. 'Why? What makes you cry, Ratan?' I asked in genuine surprise.

He wiped his eyes with the back of his hand and walked away rapidly. I stared at his retreating back. Ratan offering to accompany me to Burma! Wonders will never cease.

Journey's End

One

ALL MY LIFE I HAVE REVOLVED LIKE A SATELLITE AROUND A luminary I never possessed but could not disown. I dared not go too near it but I lacked the power to wrench myself out of orbit. So it has been for me from early childhood. The years spent as a poor relation in my aunt's house saw a physical transmutation. My frail child's form expanded, filled out and became that of an adult's. But a corresponding mental progression was denied me. My mind remained as it was in its infancy—dependant, trusting, vulnerable.

I realized that Rajlakshmi was as good as dead in my life. I stood by the bank watching the dark waters swirl around the glorious image I loved, drowning it inch by inch till nothing remained. Then, when the last ripple was still, I came away—a sense of loss weighing heavily on my heart. I bore it alone for I had none of my own with whom to share it. It seemed only the other day that I first saw Pyari in Kumar Saheb's tent and gained a whole world I had done nothing to deserve. Yet I hadn't deserved to lose it either, as I had now. 'The loss has outweighed the gain,' I thought. 'It encompasses the whole world. However far I go—to Calcutta, to Burma even, all is dark and unreal. Only the journey remains. May it never cease.'

'… *Aré!* That is Srikanta! Look, look. It is Srikanta.'

I hadn't realized that the train had stopped. Shaken out of my reverie I looked up to see Thakurdada's face at the window. Close behind him stood Ranga Didi with a girl of seventeen or so by her side. All three were laden with boxes and bundles and looked harassed from running up and down the platform.

'The crowds in the other compartments—you wouldn't believe—' Thakurdada wiped the sweat pouring down his face. 'Is yours reserved? Can we come in?'

I opened the door. They tumbled in, scattering their belongings all over the floor.

'Is this a first-class coach? I hope they don't clamp a fine—' Thakurdada looked around nervously as if expecting a guard to leap on him any moment.

'Oh no. I'll go down and speak to the collector.'

On my return, I found my guests sprawled comfortably all over the padded seats—all signs of apprehension wiped off their faces.

'How thin you've become, Srikanta,' Ranga Didi commiserated as soon as the train started. 'Were you ill again after leaving us? Why didn't you write? We were so worried about you.'

Fortunately, no one expects answers to questions like these so my silence was received without comment. Instead, Thakurdada rushed into explanations with characteristic gusto. He said that they were on their way back home from a pilgrimage to Gaya and that the girl with them was Ranga Didi's sister's granddaughter. Her father was willing to give a dowry of a thousand rupees for her but a suitable bridegroom could not to be found. They were taking her along with them in the hope of acquiring one in their own village.

'Putu!' he called after this introduction. 'Open the pot of pedas. I hope you haven't left the curd behind, *ginni*! Give Srikanta and me some on the sal leaves we've brought with us. It's the best curd you've ever tasted, Srikanta. I promise you that. No, no, Putu, wash your hands before touching the pot. Remember you are serving someone special. It is time you learned these things.'

Putu obeyed Thakurdada's instructions very carefully and soon a sal leaf, with a mound of curd and a handful of pedas on it, was placed before me. Though this in itself was not unwelcome, the accompanying emotions were. Putu's docility was faintly alarming. I hoped I was not under consideration as the 'suitable bridegroom' worth a thousand rupees. As the train moved further and further away from Gaya, Thakurdada and Ranga Didi outdid each other in their praises of Putu. They needn't have exerted themselves so much, for I could see that she was pretty enough and pleasant enough. Neither of them mentioned Rajlakshmi. It seemed as though they had forgotten that part of my life altogether.

Next morning, around ten o'clock, the train arrived at my ancestral village. Thakurdada expressed so much concern at parting from me, and Ranga Didi was so loath to let me go on without a bath and meal, that I was forced to alight. Once in the house, I was treated like a distinguished guest by everyone, including Putu, and within a few days the whole village knew that I was the lucky man who was to receive her and her father's thousand rupees. Putu's parents were sent for. Thakurdada was eager for the rites to be solemnized soon—that very Baisakh,* if possible. It was to be a grand wedding with all their relatives attending.

'Wonder of wonders!' Ranga Didi pronounced triumphantly over and over again. 'Whoever would have thought that our own Srikanta?' etc. etc. This kind of talk went on and I was powerless to stop it. I ignored it at first and tried to leave but the bonds of love were tied too tightly for me to break. Then I grew really alarmed. I felt the net closing around me but I could not escape. I even started wondering about my own commitment in the affair. Had I, in some unguarded moment, given my consent?

One day, on Thakurdada's enquiring if I had a horoscope, I took my courage in my hands and asked him point-blank, 'Are you planning a marriage between Putu and me?'

Thakurdada stared at me as if I had gone mad.

'What a question, Srikanta!' he said.

'But I haven't made up my mind.'

'You haven't? Then make it up fast. The girl is well past the age of marriage and—'

'That's not my fault.'

Thakurdada found my answer illogical to a degree that was not to be borne, 'Is it my fault, then?' he shouted, losing his temper. At the sound of his voice, the girl's parents, Ranga Didi and even some of the neighbours crowded near the door. Tears and recriminations followed. The men of the village decided that I was the biggest scoundrel they had ever seen and threatened to teach

---

*   The first month of the Bengali calendar (mid April to mid May)

me a lesson. My wily Thakurdada shut up like a clam and so did everyone else. But above all considerations loomed the spectre of the girl who had passed marriageable age five years ago. Putu crept about the house in abject humiliation and her mother cursed her incessantly. 'Ill fated, wretched girl!' she lamented over and over again. 'She was born to bring me disgrace and ruin. What accursed destiny made me bear her in my womb!'

I thought the cursed destiny was Putu's—not her mother's. My heart went out to her and to all the miserable girls who had had the misfortune of being born among us.

I gave Thakurdada my Calcutta address the day before I left. 'I need someone's permission before I marry,' I said. 'If I get it, I'll come back.'

Thakurdada's face crumpled and he took my hands in his old trembling ones. 'Do your best to get it, son. The girl is as good as dead—as you can see.'

'I'm confident there'll be no objection.'

'When shall I come to you?'

'In a week or so.'

Ranga Didi and Putu's parents came with me to the door. There were tears in everyone's eyes. I felt a curious relief. I had as good as given my word. Now there was no looking back. Rajlakshmi would give her consent. I had not a doubt of that.

Two

$\mathcal{I}$ REACHED THE STATION JUST IN TIME TO SEE THE CALCUTTA TRAIN glide past. There were a couple of hours to go before the next one came. I was looking around for some diversion when a young man came up and peering into my face asked, smiling, 'You're Srikanta, aren't you?'

'Yes—'

'Don't you recognize me? I'm Gahar.' He grasped me by the hand so tightly that I winced. Then, twining an arm around my neck, he said, 'Where were you going? To Calcutta. Go another day. Come home with me.'

Gahar was a friend of my pathshala days. He was four years older than I and had always been somewhat eccentric. For one thing, he would never take 'no' for an answer. I could see that, with age, this inability had grown. I realized that I was in his clutches, for the night at least, and the thought made me quake. Oblivious of the fact that I had not responded with half his fervour, he slung my bag across his shoulder and, calling a carriage, practically pushed me in. The village in which he lived was a couple of miles away from mine along the river-bank. We had played about in the woods, as children, shooting birds with an ancient musket that had belonged to his father. I used to go to their house often in those days. His mother was always glad to see me and would give me big bowls of *muri* mixed with milk, banana and molasses. They were wealthy and had plenty of land.

'Where were you all these years, Srikanta?' Gahar asked as soon as the carriage started moving.

'Here and there.' I gave a brief résumé of my past and asked, 'What do you do, Gahar?'

'Nothing.'

'How is your mother?'

'Dead. I've lost both my parents. I'm alone in the world.'

'You didn't marry?'

'She's dead too.'

I understood why he was so eager for company. For want of anything better to say, I asked, 'Do you still have that musket, Gahar?'

Gahar laughed delightedly. 'What a memory you have, Srikanta! Yes, I have it. And a rifle I bought some years ago. If you wish to go shooting I'll come with you. But I don't kill birds anymore. I can't bear to see them die.'

'Strange! There was a time when you thought of nothing but shooting birds.'

'True. But I've given it up.'

There was another side to Gahar's personality. He was a poet. As a child he had a marvellous gift. He could reel out rhymed stanzas on any subject conceivable. I realize, now, that the rhymes were doggerel and the ideas trite but I can never forget the excitement with which I would hear him recount the exploits of Raja Tikendrajit in the battle of Manipur.

'You remember you wanted to write a *Ramayana* that would put Krittibas to shame? Have you abandoned the project?' I asked with a mixture of amusement and curiosity.

Gahar's face grew solemn in an instant. 'Such projects are not conceived to be abandoned, Srikanta. I've been working on it day and night—for years. It's my whole existence. I'll read out some extracts to you, tonight, if you don't believe me.'

His eyes shone with poetic fervour while mine grew dim with anxious fears. If he carried out his threat I may well be kept awake the whole night. 'It was an idle question, Gahar,' I said, quickly. 'I knew you would do it. I'm proud of you.'

'You'll be prouder after you've read what I've written. I shouldn't boast about it, but—'

'I don't feel well at all,' I said, desperately. 'I've been feverish since morning. I'm dying to go to bed.'

But the vanquisher of Krittibas brushed my ailments aside. 'You remember that part,' he cried enthusiastically, 'when Sita is being carried away in the flower-chariot? When she flings off her ornaments, one by one? I tell you, truly, Srikanta, whoever reads it has tears in his eyes. You will too.'

'But—'

'You remember old Nayan Chand Chakravarty? He comes over every evening. "Baba Gahar," he says "Just read that passage out to me once again. You are no Mussalman, my son. The purest of pure Brahmin blood must flow in your veins to make you write like that?"'

The name Nayan Chand, being an uncommon one, rang a bell. 'Nayan Chand Chakravarty?' I exclaimed. 'That wily old man who was your father's bitterest enemy—'

'The same. There was a long court case and Chakravarty *moshai* lost it. His property was auctioned and my father bought it up—lands, orchards and even the ancestral house. After Baba's death I returned the house and the bit of pond from which they draw their water. They are very poor, Srikanta. I couldn't bear the old man's tears.'

'I trust his tears have dried by now,' I said, beginning to understand the old man's fascination for Gahar's verse.

'He is a good man at heart,' Gahar replied. 'He did worry Baba a great deal, I know. But that was because he was up to his ears in debt. All men turn nasty when they are cornered. We have a mango grove of theirs, each sapling of which Chakravarty *moshai* planted with his own hands. The trees get laden with fruit every summer. He has so many grandchildren and I have no one—'

'True. Why don't you return it to him?'

'I ought to. The poor are so deprived, Srikanta. When all the other villagers are gorging themselves on mangoes and jackfruit, the little ones look on with hungry eyes. All my other orchards are leased out to traders but not this one. I've told Chakravarty *moshai* that his grandchildren can pick as many mangoes as they like.'

I told myself that Gahar was a poet. Naturally he was indifferent to material things. And if poverty-stricken Nayan Chakravarty was making a living out of this indifference, who was I to complain?

It was the middle of Chaitra* and spring was in the air. Gahar opened the door of the carriage and a warm, sweet wind, laden with the scent of bakul flowers, gushed in.

'The wind from the south,' Gahar murmured. 'Do you feel it, Srikanta?'

'Hmm.'

'Do you know how the poet welcomes spring? *Aaj dakshin duar khola* (the door to the south is open today). Have you heard the song, Srikanta?'

Before I could reply, the wind churned up masses of dust and dried leaves from the path and lashed out at our clothes and hair. 'Shut the door, Gahar,' I said irritably. 'Or you may have to change the words of your song. Yama may walk in through your *dakshin duar* if you're not careful.'

Gahar laughed and cried ecstatically, 'Spring! Enchanting Spring! The shaddock trees are bursting with bloom. You can smell them a kos (two miles) away. The rose-apple tree in my yard is smothered with madhavi vines. The malati vine is yet to flower but every tendril is heavy with buds. And the mango trees are weighed down with *moul* (fruit blossoms). Bees hum from out of the flowers and nightingales and cuckoos sing all day long. Even the nights, warm and sweet with moonlight, are resonant with the cuckoo's call. If you keep your window open you won't sleep a wink for the scents and sounds of the night. I'll tell you straight away, Srikanta. I'm not letting go of you in a hurry. As for your meals—Chakravarty *moshai* will arrange everything. I only have to tell him. He'll look after you as if you were his gurudev.'

I was carried away by Gahar's warmth and memories of our shared boyhood. I was seeing him after so many years but he was the same Gahar, the simple unaffected boy of nature he had always been. His delight at our reunion was genuine and heartfelt. A wave of nostalgia swept over me!

Gahar came from a line of fakirs. I have heard that his grandfather went from village to village singing Ramprasadi songs and begging for alms for a living. He had a pet blackbird whose singing prowess was famed in those days. Gahar's father had abandoned the family vocation and started a jute business that had

* The last month of the Bengali calendar (mid March to mid April).

brought him plenty of money. He acquired a lot of property and, later in life, became a prosperous moneylender. It was obvious that Gahar had not inherited his father's business capabilities. He was a throw-back of his fakir ancestors and their love of poetry and music flowed strongly in his blood. I had grave doubts about his ability to hold on to the wealth that his father had amassed for him.

As the carriage clattered over the narrow track, I was overwhelmed with memories. I dimly recalled the house and the thick jungle one had to cross in order to reach it. Suddenly Gahar gave a shout, 'Stop! Stop!' and the horses were jerked to a halt startling me considerably. Gahar leaped out of the carriage crying, 'Get out, Srikanta. Give me your bag.'

'What's the matter?'

'The horses can't go any further. Don't you see there's no path?'

It was true. In front of me, as far as the eye could see, stretched a sea of thornberry bushes and clumps of reeds so tall and thick that they blotted out whatever light was left in the sky. I followed Gahar into the dim wilderness, my clothes getting torn and skin being pricked by thorns and rough branches. By the time we reached the poet's haven, the sun had set and the soft darkness of a spring night was upon us. Around the house were dense forests of bamboos and reeds out of which, if one were to believe Gahar, cuckoos and nightingales sang all day long, driving the poet to the brink of a divine frenzy. But now they were silent. The only sounds to be heard were the rushing of the wind and the crackle of fallen leaves as they swept into the house, covering the yard and the veranda and even the floors of the rooms. Soon a bright moon would rise, silvering the forest and lending it magic and mystery, but now there was no light except from the lantern that Gahar had lit to guide me to my room. An elderly servant turned a key in a rusty old lock and said, 'You will sleep here, Babu.'

I peered into the room. The wind from the south had come in before me through a window our host had left hospitably open, and had covered the wooden cot and floor with dry leaves and creepers. I was afraid to step in for who knew what lurked in the masses of leaves? Even in the dim light I noticed a couple of holes in the earthen floor. 'Don't you ever use this room, Gahar?' I shivered involuntarily.

'I don't need to,' he answered, carelessly. 'One needs only one room to sleep in. I'll get it all cleaned up tomorrow, Srikanta.'

'But there might be snakes in these holes.'

'There were two snakes,' the servant informed me, 'but they've gone. Snakes never stay indoors in spring. The south wind draws them out.'

'Who told you that, *mian*?'

Gahar gave a roar of laughter. 'He's no *mian*.* He's Nabin. Don't you remember? He used to look after the cows. Now he's my friend, guide and counsellor. He does everything for me and knows what I have better than I do.'

I remembered Nabin but that didn't help me overcome my fears. I was convinced that he had caught the 'south wind' fever from his master and was not to be trusted. 'What you say may be true, Nabin,' I said. 'The wind may draw them out of doors. But what is to prevent them from coming in?'

Gahar realized that my fears were genuine. He said in a comforting tone, 'Even if they come in they'll crawl on the floor. You'll be on the bed. Besides, snakes are everywhere. How can one escape them? Even Raja Parikshit couldn't. Who are we? Sweep the floor, Nabin, and put bricks over the holes. What will you eat tonight, Srikanta?'

'Whatever I get.'

'We have *muri*, milk and molasses. If you could make do with that—just for tonight.'

'Excellent! Excellent! That's just what I'm used to eating in this house. But please get a large brick to cover the hole, Nabin. I don't want the creeping pair to come romancing into my room after they've had their fill of moonlight.'

Nabin peered under the bed and shook his head mournfully. 'Impossible!' he said.

'What is impossible, Nabin?'

'To cover the holes. There are far too many of them. We'll need a cartload of bricks.'

Gahar didn't seem unduly agitated by the announcement. 'Get

---

* The word *mian* is normally a term of respect used to address Muslim men. However, Gahar uses it here to imply 'Mussalman'.

it done tomorrow,' he told Nabin. 'Now fetch water for Babu to wash. And some *muri* and milk.'

'What will you have, Gahar?' I asked after a while, digging into my bowl.

'An old aunt of mine lives with me. I'll have whatever she has cooked. After we've both eaten, I'll read out the passage I promised. Shall I ask Nabin to make the bed? I can spend the night here with you, if you like.'

'No, Gahar. I'm very tired and need some rest. I'll hear what you've written tomorrow morning.'

'Will you have the time?'

'Why not?'

Gahar thought for a while and said, 'I've got an idea. You could lie down with your eyes shut while I read. I'll go away the moment you fall asleep.'

'No, Gahar,' I begged. 'Not tonight. I can't insult your *Ramayana* by falling asleep in the middle of it. Tomorrow morning, when my brain is fresh and clear, I'll hear it with full concentration.'

A shadow fell across Gahar's face. My heart was saddened as I watched him leave the room. I realized that his ambition of a lifetime would never be fulfilled. No one would publish his work. Nor would anyone read it. He had hummed snatches from his *Ramayana* in the carriage as we came and I had known, instantly, that they held no promise. He had inherited a love of poetry from his fakir ancestors but had done nothing to cultivate it. He had little education and no knowledge at all of what lay outside his native village. All he had was faith— in himself and in the world. I lay on my bed and murmured to myself, 'Twelve years of unstinted labour! Twelve years of unwavering devotion to an idea conceived in childhood! And what is it worth? Not even the cost of the paper it is written on.'

Gahar shook me awake early next morning. He wanted me to experience the full glory of a spring morning in rural Bengal. From the way he was behaving I might have come from England. Having had a taste of his insistence, I made no effort to shake him off. I washed my face and accompanied him to the yard where a partially blighted rose-apple tree stood in a corner. A madhavi vine had entwined itself in some of its branches and a few bunches of flowers bloomed half-heartedly right on top of the tree. A young malati vine, newly in bud, was seen climbing up the ancient trunk from the other side. My poet-friend wanted to give me some flowers but they were so far beyond his reach and such streams of black ants darted up and down the trunk that even he was daunted.

'I'll pull some down with a pole after the sun rises. Come along,' he said, taking my arm.

Nabin, who had been puffing away at his early morning hookah in a corner of the yard, coughed and spat noisily. 'Don't go into the jungle,' he said, shaking an authoritative hand.

'Why not?' Gahar asked testily.

'Some mad jackals are on a rampage.' He thrust his chin out in the direction of the jungle. 'A number of children and cows have been bitten.'

I stepped back a pace. 'Where are these jackals, Nabin?'

'How can I say? They lurk about in the bushes. Keep a sharp look out if you insist on going.'

'I'm not going, Gahar.'

'Not going? Dogs and jackals get into a frenzy sometimes in this season but people don't lock themselves in their houses because of that.'

Having no arguments to counter Gahar's, I was obliged to follow him into the jungle to feast my eyes on the beauties of nature. As we walked through a mango grove, innumerable insects flew down from the globes of blossom, buzzing around my ears and getting into my eyes and hair. At my feet, masses of dry leaves, sticky with the dripping juice of new-forming fruit, clung to my shoes making them slip and slither uncomfortably. At places, the narrow track was overgrown with reeds and sprawling bushes of ghentu flowers and wild fig. I remembered Nabin's warning and quickened my steps.

And thus we came to the edge of the river—the same river along whose banks we had played as children. I remembered it as broad and beautiful and swollen with monsoon rain. But now the banks stretched vast and dry on either side of a thin trickle and the bitter, pungent smell of drying lichen and rotting hyacinth was foul in my nostrils. Some silk-cotton trees on the opposite bank were splashed with scarlet blooms but even the poet was too discouraged by now to point them out to me.

'Shall we go home, Srikanta?'

'Yes.'

'I love the earth and sky of the month of Chaitra. I thought you would too.'

'I will—when I can see them with your eyes.'

'Are my eyes different? Is that why the villagers—'

'The poet's eye is always different. It imbues the commonest reality with beauty and enchantment. That doesn't mean your vision is defective. What you see is as true as what the rest of the world sees. Be satisfied with that, my friend.'

On the way back, we came across a tree whose trunk had been stripped of its bark—for medicinal purposes, presumably. Gahar started trembling at the sight and tears sprang up in his eyes. Looking at him I stumbled on a profound truth. Nayan Chand Chakravarty had not regained his property through flattery and wiles as I had thought. The reason for it lay within Gahar himself, his excessive sensitivity to suffering. Much of my anger and dislike of the old man melted away.

As soon as we reached home Gahar took out his manuscript—the size of which would have daunted men far more daring than I. 'You'll have to read the whole of it,' he said, 'and give me your opinion. Promise me you won't leave before you've reached the end.'

I didn't make any promises. Nevertheless, seven days passed before I took my leave. This period was spent in reading and discussing, sessions which were neither educative nor entertaining. But, during those seven days of close companionship, I gained something of great value. I gradually awoke to a true sense of the beauty of Gahar's character.

One morning, Gahar said, 'Do you *have* to go to Burma, Srikanta? We are both alone in the world. Why don't we spend our lives together, here, where we were born?'

'I'm not a poet like you, Gahar,' I said with a laugh. 'I don't understand the language of the trees. I would get stifled to death in this dense jungle.'

Gahar's face grew solemn. 'You are right, Srikanta. Trees have a language of their own. And I know it. You don't believe me, do you?'

'I find it difficult, I must confess.'

'Yes, it is difficult,' Gahar murmured. Suddenly he posed a question, 'Have you ever been in love, Srikanta?'

I looked up, startled. I had been up half the night writing a long letter—perhaps my last—to Rajlakshmi. I had described my meeting with Thakurdada and the circumstances in which I was caught. I had also sought her permission to marry Putu. With that letter still in my pocket I laughed and answered, 'No.'

'If you ever do, if such a day comes in your life—write me a letter.'

'Why, Gahar?'

'I'll come and stay with you for a few days. And if you ever need money, don't hesitate to ask. Baba left me a lot of money. I have no use for it—but you may.'

Tears pricked my eyelids. I said, 'I'll remember your offer, Gahar. But, if you truly love me, pray that the need never arises.'

On the day of my departure, Gahar came with me to the station my bag slung, once again, across his shoulder. I tried to take it away from him. So did Nabin. But he clung to it as if it were his dearest possession. As I stepped onto the train, he burst out crying loudly and unashamedly—like a woman.

'Come and see me, Srikanta, once at least, before you leave for Burma.'

I couldn't turn down his appeal. 'I promise,' I said.

'Write me a letter as soon as you reach Calcutta.'

'I will.'

When I reached my lodgings, late that evening, I found Ratan outside, on the steps.

'Why, Ratan? What brings you here?'

'I've been here since yesterday waiting for you, Babu. I've brought a letter.'

I understood that the letter was in reply to mine. 'It could have been sent through the post,' I said. 'Why did you have to come all the way to Calcutta?'

'The post is for ordinary people like you and me, Babu. Ma's letters have to be carried by a special messenger or they get lost. It doesn't matter if he starves and dies on the way—'

I found out, later, that Ratan's allegation was false. It was he, himself, who had begged and pleaded with Rajlakshmi to send him to me. The discomfort of the journey and the long wait outside my door had harassed him to a point of gross injustice to his mistress.

'Come in, Ratan,' I said. 'Have a bath and something to eat. The letter can wait.'

Ratan touched my feet and stood up.

'Yes, Babu,' he said.

Three

THE SOUND OF A LOUD BELCH MADE ME LOOK UP. RATAN STOOD IN the room patting his stomach lovingly.

'Had a good meal, Ratan?'

'Yes, Babu. A very good meal. Our Bihari *maharaj* can learn a thing or two from the Calcutta cooks, whatever you may say.'

I don't remember ever holding a brief for the *maharaj* either before Ratan or anyone else. But I did not point that out. I understood that this was in a manner of speaking, an expression of his supreme satisfaction at the meal he had eaten.

'The journey was rough,' he continued, suppressing a yawn. 'I need some rest.'

'Spread your bedding in a corner of the veranda and go to sleep. We can talk tomorrow morning.'

For some reason I was not anxious to see the letter. I knew what it contained and the knowledge depressed me. However, when Ratan brought it out from the pocket of his *fatua*(a cotton vest), I put out a hand and took it. It was in a long envelope heavily sealed with lac. I turned it over in my hand, hesitating.

'I'll lie down just below the window,' Ratan said. 'There's a fine breeze blowing. Thank God there are no mosquitoes here like in Kashi.'

'How are they all in Kashi, Ratan? Well, I hope.'

'Well, enough, I suppose,' Ratan pulled a long face. 'Thanks to Gurudev the outer rooms are crammed with people from dawn to dusk. And, within the house, Banku Babu and Bou Ma(his wife) hold court with their servants and maids. And Ma? Well, you know Ma. I'm a very old servant and a barber by caste. No one can fool me. That's why I offered to go with you to Burma. I knew that serving you would be the best way of serving her.'

I looked at him in surprise. I didn't understand.

'Banku Babu is a grown man now—a married man,' Ratan continued. 'What is more, he has had some education and takes himself very seriously on account of it. He is his own master and he wants everyone to know it. He has managed to acquire quite a bit of property in his own right—thanks to the deed of gift. But how long can that last?'

I still didn't understand, though an idea was slowly forming in my mind. But, by now, Ratan was on a different track. 'You've seen, with your own eyes, how often she has asked me to leave her service. I can go back to my village. I have enough to live on. But I don't. Do you know why? Because it is through her generosity that I acquired whatever I have. And if I cause her pain it will all vanish before my eyes. I have never told anyone about my past because Ma has forbidden me to talk about it. But I'll tell you, Babu. I had to leave my ancestral village, in search of a living, after my uncles cheated me out of my inheritance. It was my great good fortune that I found service with Ma. After a year, when I asked for leave to see my wife and children, Ma put a bundle of notes in my hand and said, "Don't quarrel with your uncles, Ratan. Buy back your share with this money." There were five hundred rupees—can you believe it, Babu? I thought I was dreaming. And Banku Babu! He contradicts her to her face and says cutting things and grumbles within her hearing. I tell myself that his spell of luck is coming to an end.'

I was shocked, for I hadn't anticipated anything like this. Ratan went on, his breast heaving with indignation. 'Ma has never stinted over anything. She has given Banku more than he ever dreamed of having in seven lives. That is why he has lost his head. He treats his benefactress like a liability. After one has drained out all the honey, of what use is the comb? Fool that he is, he does not know that with even one of the jewels she still has in her possession she could buy five houses of the kind she has given him.'

I hadn't known either. 'Really!' I exclaimed. 'Where does she keep them?'

'In safe custody,' Ratan smiled. 'Ma is not a fool. The only person for whom she would willingly give up everything is you. Banku does not know that, while you live, Ma needs no other protection. And while Ratan lives—no other servant. Ma's heart was torn to pieces the day you came away from Kashi. Only I could see it. Not Banku. Not even Gurudev.'

'But your mistress didn't want me to stay. You know that well enough.'

Ratan touched his ears and bit his tongue, a gesture that apologized for his presuming to contradict me. 'I'm only a humble servant, Babu. But I'll say that's a lie. I won't hear a word against Ma.' He left the room. He was fatigued with the journey and needed his sleep.

I sat up for a long time after Ratan's departure, mulling over the news he had given me. I had first seen Banku in Ara when he was a boy of sixteen. I remembered his loving tenderness for the stepmother who had taken him out of an obscure village, brought him to the city, educated him and given him an identity. Now he was twenty-one, married, and a man of means. If his complacency outweighed his gratitude who could blame him? Was it not the way of the world? If he was insensitive to Rajlakshmi's deepest feelings—so was Gurudev, if one was to believe Ratan.

I slit open the envelope and drew out the letter. Rajlakshmi had evidently taken great pains with her writing for it was much more legible than her usual hand. The reason was obvious. This was one letter she wanted me to read from beginning to end, word by word. I didn't expect anything much beyond a permission to marry Putu and a few words of sympathy and advice. Nevertheless, my hand trembled as I held it. This is what she wrote.

Kashidham

With her humblest greetings your servant presents:

I've just read your letter for the hundredth time. And I wonder which of us has gone mad—you or I. I didn't pick you off the trees as I did my *bainchi* berries. God gave you to me after a long and arduous struggle. Thus the right to abandon me does not rest with you.

In my earliest childhood I strung garlands of *bainchi* and

gave them to you as tokens of worship. My little hands bled from the thorns and the rose-coloured berries were stained with the hues of the deepest crimson. But, blind as you were, you could not read the letters that were etched in blood over your neck and breast. God could and he did. My garland reached his feet though it did not touch your soul.

Then a terrible storm burst over my head. Dark clouds spread like a stain over my moon-washed sky. I look back and wonder. Was it a dream? Was it really I who was so grievously afflicted? I do not search too deep for fear of losing my sanity. But, at moments, when memory is rudely awakened, I try to drown it by muttering a name over and over again. I cannot mention that name. No one can. But I have not a doubt that if he forgives me—God will, too. Here my courage does not fail.

What was I saying? Oh! Yes. A storm burst over my head. Shame and humiliation blotted out the light of my eyes. The garb of disgrace was flung on me. But it was only a garb, wasn't it? The real me eluded the world and lay waiting in silence, in secret. If it wasn't so, if the demon of my past had truly swallowed me up, would I have had the power to receive you when you came?

Twenty-seven summers have passed over this frame. Youth is a thing of the past and so are its desires. Don't misunderstand me. If you do, the shame would be too grievous to be borne—even though my life admits nothing but shame. Banku is no longer a child. I have a daughter-in-law. How shall I face them on the day of your wedding? With what shall I support the humiliation? And if you are sick or in trouble who will look after you? Putu? And I? Shall I receive your news from the servant and come away from your door? Will I ever live down the disgrace?

Now *you* may pose a question. You may ask if you are, then, to be condemned to a solitary existence for all time to come. But whatever be your question, it is not for me to provide the answer. That task is yours. If you can't, if your mind and brain are truly dead, I can lend you some of mine. You needn't repay the loan but don't forget to acknowledge it. You believe, don't you, that Gurudev has educated me in the value of renunciation, the Shastras have shown me the path and Sunanda has instilled in me her own devotion and piety. And you—you have been the burden on my back. How blind you men are!

I have a question I want you to put to yourself. We parted when I was but a child. When you came back to me I was a woman of twenty-three. Where, in all those years, was Sunanda? Or Gurudev?

I had thought I would wipe out my sins. I had wanted to purify myself. Not in the hope of heaven but in the hope of being reborn. Do you understand why? The stream of my life had become muddied and foul. I had sought to cleanse it. I never dreamed that it would dry up at the source. If it does, of what use are my prayers, my fasts, my penitential rites?

I have no desire to take my own life. But I can't live the life of an outcast. I can take poison from your hand but banishment—never. You know me. If the sun sets I shall not have the patience to wait for another dawn.

Rajlakshmi

I breathed a sigh of relief as I folded the epistle. Its commanding tone hurt but the words fell like a blessed rain on my heart. By withholding her consent, Rajlakshmi had saved me from marriage with Putu. But what was I to do now? How I was to elude my captors, was a problem she had completely ignored. Thakurdada would be here any day for I had promised him that the permission would be forthcoming. Preparations for the wedding would have started and the unfortunate girl, past marriageable age, would be ecstatic at the prospect. Her parents would have given over cursing and lamenting their fate and started treating her with kindness and consideration. I knew what I would tell Thakurdada but I didn't know how. The ruthless dunning and irrational insistence that I anticipated hardened my heart but the thought of Putu and her treatment at the hands of her baulked and infuriated relatives melted it and brought tears to my eyes. I lay awake in bed hour after hour. Memories of Gangamati wove in and out with thoughts of Putu and Thakurdada. Gangamati! Those brief weeks of tasting the forbidden fruit. Those honeyed days of sunshine and laughter. Those nights—deep and tender and poignant. There had been moments of pain, of separation even, but we had borne them with dignity. No taunts or recriminations ever darkened the sky of Gangamati. The villagers loved us. They awaited our return not knowing that the blossom of dawn wilts and withers by dusk and is blown away by the wind.

My eyes burned with staring into the dark but I prayed, like one possessed, that the night be endless. My supplications—to whom I did not know—grew more agonized as the night wore on. The image of Rajlakshmi, going about her work with a smile on her lips, in the little thatched house with the earthen yard, flashed over and over again before my eyes. Never again would I know the peace and contentment of those days.

As I lay awake, ruminating, I made a curious discovery. I had always thought of myself as weak and ineffectual and had been caught by Rajlakshmi, time and again, in thoughts and acts of cowardice. Tonight, I discovered where *her* weakness lay. She knew I was sickly and often ill. She couldn't endure the thought of another woman looking after me while she stood outside—an alien in my life. She could give up everything in the world but not the right to nurse me in sickness. She would gladly embrace a physical death but she could never support the psychic death that such a deprivation would bring in its wake. The threat contained in her letter was not an idle one.

I must have fallen asleep with the first glimpse of dawn for it was broad daylight when Ratan shook me awake. 'There's an old gentleman downstairs asking for you. He's just arrived in a carriage.'

Thakurdada! But would he come in a carriage?

'There's a girl of seventeen or eighteen with him.'

I rose from my bed, trembling with anger. The old man's shamelessness and insensitivity were really insupportable. To drag the poor girl all the way to Calcutta! 'Bring them upstairs to this room, Ratan,' I commanded. 'I'm going down for a wash.'

When I returned, an hour or so later, Thakurdada rose to welcome me as if he was the host and I the guest. 'Come, come, son. I trust you are in good health. Putu!'

Putu, who had been standing by the window, came forward and touched my feet. Thakurdada said, by way of explanation, Putu's *mashi* is married to a hakim in Diamond Harbour. He's a very rich man—earns five hundred rupees a month. They can't come to the wedding so I thought I'd bring the girl along to visit them before she gets married.' He paused to take a breath and continued, 'They may be rich and important but I won't let them off so easily. I'll insist they come to the wedding. The presence of a hakim will prevent all kinds of mischief. You don't know our village politics, Srikanta.'

I had a feeling that this information was significant in some way. Ratan brought tobacco in a new hookah and offered it to Thakurdada who gave him a long and level stare. 'I seem to have seen this man somewhere,' he said in a sombre voice.

'Yes, Babu,' Ratan said enthusiastically. 'I came to your house when Srikanta Babu was ill.'

Thakurdada's face grew dark and ominous as he remembered the incident. He was an extremely wily man, so he swallowed his wrath and said in a voice he fought to control, 'I thought it best to complete the formalities of betrothal as soon as possible. So I looked into the almanac before coming. Today is a good day. I can take your servant with me to the new market and buy everything we need. After all, this is Calcutta.'

I was so agitated that I couldn't frame a full sentence. I shook my head violently and said, 'No!'

'Why not? The hours of the forenoon are extremely auspicious. Do you have an almanac?'

'I don't need one. I am not getting married.'

Thakurdada rested his hookah against the wall and prepared himself for battle. He said gently but gravely, 'A girl's marriage is no joke—as you well know. You can't go back on your word. The arrangements are all complete.'

I was aware of Putu standing by the window and of Ratan listening by the door. Nevertheless, I said as firmly as I could, 'You know, as well as I do, that I made no promise. I said I would ask someone for permission.'

'You didn't get the permission?'

'No.'

Thakurdada thought for a while and said, 'Putu's father is ready to spend a thousand rupees. If we put a little pressure he will raise the sum by a hundred or two. What do you say?'

Ratan entered the room and stretched out a hand for the hookah. 'Shall I change the tobacco, Babu?'

'Yes. What is your name, boy?'

'Ratan.'

'A fine name. Where do you live?'

'In Kashi.'

'Oh! So madam is in Kashi, is she? What does she do there?'

Ratan reared up suddenly. 'Is that any of your business?'

Thakurdada lifted a hand and smiled benignly at him. 'Why do you lose your temper, son? I didn't mean any offence. I've known her from the time she was a little girl. Naturally, I'm interested in her welfare. Besides, I may have to visit her shortly. Who knows?'

Ratan took the hookah from his hand without a word and brought it back, freshly packed, in a few minutes. Thakurdada took a few deep pulls and rose abruptly. 'Wait, wait,' he cried. 'In which direction is the lavatory? I had to leave very early, so I—' and he ran out of the room after Ratan's retreating back.

Now, Putu turned from the window and said, 'Don't believe a word of what Dadu (Grandpa) says. My father is a poor man. He doesn't have a thousand rupees. He borrowed the ornaments for Didi's wedding and now her in-laws have driven her out. They are arranging another match for their son.'

'You mean it's all a bluff? Your father can't spend a thousand rupees?' I cried, shocked.

Putu shook her head. 'Baba earns only forty rupees a month and there are so many of us. My brother's name got struck off the school register because we couldn't pay the fees. He cries and cries—' Her lips trembled and her eyes grew moist.

'Is that why your father can't find a husband for you? Because he has no money?'

'Yes. Baba wanted to marry me off to our neighbour—Amulya Babu. His daughters are much older than I. Ma threatened to jump into the well so Baba was forced to call it off. But now—'

'Are you prepared to marry me, Putu?'

Putu blushed and nodded.

'But I'm old too. Nearly fifteen years older than you.'

Putu smiled and looked down at her feet. She didn't speak.

'Was any other match ever arranged for you?'

'Yes.' Putu lifted her head and a note of happiness crept into her voice. 'With Kalidas Babu's youngest son—Sasadhar. You know Kalidas Babu of your village? Sasadhar is only a little older than I and very clever. He has passed his BA.'

'Do you like Sasadhar?'

Putu giggled delightedly.

'But suppose Sasadhar doesn't like you?'

'He *does* like me. He walks up and down the path outside our house. Didima (Grandma) says it's because of me.'

'Why didn't the marriage take place then?'

A shadow fell across Putu's laughing face. 'His father wanted a thousand rupees in cash and another thousand in gold ornaments. And the expense of the wedding would come to another five hundred. Where would my father find all that money? Only a zamindar could spend so much on one daughter. Ma fell at his mother's feet and begged. But they wouldn't listen—'

'Didn't Sasadhar say anything?'

'What could he say? He's very young and he can't go against his parents.'

'True. Is he married already?'

'Not yet. I hear a marriage is to be arranged for him—very soon.'

I put a hand on her head and asked gently, 'Supposing you are the bride and they don't love you—what will you do then?'

'Why shouldn't they love me? I can cook and sew and do every kind of housework. I'll do all their work for them.'

I sighed. That is all that simple village girls like Putu know, I thought. To toil like beasts and hope for love! I smiled at her. 'Putu, you promise you'll work hard and win their love?'

'I promise.'

'Then go home and tell your mother that Srikanta Dada will send the money as soon as he can.'

'You'll give the money?' Putu lifted her large, dark eyes to my face. 'Then you'll come to the wedding?'

'I will.'

At this point, Thakurdada walked in wiping his face with the edge of his dhoti. 'Ahh!' he sighed in satisfaction. 'Where is Ratan? He can fetch me a fresh bowl of tobacco, can't he?'

Four

THAT GOOD ADVICE IS USELESS, FOR THE SIMPLE REASON THAT IT IS never taken, is a fundamental truth. Yet, like all truths, it has exceptions. One such exception occurred in my life and I'd like to tell my readers about it.

Hearing my proposal, Thakurdada beamed from ear to ear. Putu fell at my feet and knocked her head on the tiles in gratitude. But the moment they left, I was overcome with regret. I felt so frustrated—I could've banged my head against the wall. What had I done? Why had I pledged the savings of my years of exile to people I knew nothing about and cared for even less? Who was the girl? What was she to me? Till I saw her on the train, I hadn't even known she existed. And that oily scoundrel, Thakurdada! How cleverly he had caught me in his web! I wished he would never get home. I wished him dead on the spot but something told me that men of his type were indestructible. He would be here next weekend, the hakim with him, perhaps, and would get the money out of me even if the world came to an end. The more I thought about it, the more enraged I got—with myself, with Putu, with Thakurdada and the whole clan of parasites.

The thing to do was to escape—to Burma. I rushed to the booking office but, alas, all the tickets were sold. There was nothing for me but to wait for the next boat and that was not due for another week. I thought of changing my lodgings but that was easier said than done. Who would rent me rooms for only a week? Matters were further complicated by the continued presence of Ratan. He made no move, whatsoever, to go back to Kashi.

'I've written a letter to your mistress, Ratan,' I hinted delicately. 'Would you like to take it back with you tomorrow?'

'Oh no!' Ratan said, comfortably. 'Now that I'm here I'll stay for a while and see the sights. I have never been to the museum or the zoo. Who knows when I can come again?'

'But your mistress will be worried about you.'

'I've written to her saying that I need a rest. My bones are still rattling from the train journey.'

'But my letter—'

'Give it to me. I'll send it by registered post. Ma will get it in a couple of days.'

I sat in glum silence. The sly fox of a barber was too clever for me! His next sentence confirmed not only his intelligence but his superior knowledge of the world.

'I would like to ask you a question, Babu, if you don't mind the impertinence.'

'Yes. What is it, Ratan?'

'Two thousand and five hundred rupees is a great deal of money. Who are these people? What is the girl to you that you pledged such a large sum for her wedding? Besides, anyone can see that the old man is a crook. You shouldn't have fallen into his trap, Babu.'

Ratan's comment was just what I was looking for. It strengthened and comforted me. 'You are right, Ratan,' I said. 'I should have been more careful. But I haven't given him the money yet. I won't give it—that's all.'

'You think he'll let you off?' Ratan stared.

'What can he do? I haven't put down anything in writing, have I? Besides, I may not even be here when he arrives. I may have left for Burma.'

Ratan smiled ruefully and shook his head. 'You don't know the old man and his breed, Babu. Where money is in question he'll let nothing stand in his way—shame and censure least of all. He'll beg, weep, sulk, threaten, even blackmail but he'll get it out of you. And if you aren't here when he comes, he'll catch the first train to Kashi and get it out of Ma. That will be terribly humiliating for her. You'd better abandon your plan, Babu.'

Ratan's words shocked me into silence. He was right. I had

indulged the emotion of a moment and I would have to pay for it. There was no way out.

Thakurdada returned on the fourth day, bursting with pride and reflected glory. 'Your fame has spread over seven villages, Srikanta. Never has generosity like yours been seen in this degenerate age in which we live. To save a poor Brahmin from social ostracism! You don't know what you've done! You're no ordinary man, Srikanta. You were made for immortality.'

'Have you fixed the date?' I asked coldly, cutting off his flight of rhetoric.

'Yes. The rites are to be solemnized on the twenty-fifth. We have just ten days in which to arrange everything. We're having the betrothal tomorrow morning as the evening hours are inauspicious. But if you can't attend, I'll cancel everything. Here, Putu sent you this letter. I must say this for her. She's a jewel among women. You'll never find another like her.'

And, saying this, he handed me a square of yellow paper thickly covered with a close, neat hand. I opened the letter but before I could start reading it, Thakurdada sighed and exclaimed, 'Chamar! He is nothing but a chamar for all his money. Kalidas Babu wants the entire sum in his hands before the betrothal. He's getting his own goldsmith to make the ornaments. He trusts no one. Not even me!'

This was unforgivable indeed. To trust no one. Not even Thakurdada!

We set off the next morning. Before we left, Thakurdada assured himself that I was really taking the money by saying point-blank, 'I'd better count the money before we leave. We are not gods—only erring mortals. You may have made a mistake.' I handed him the packet without a word.

Ratan had left for Kashi the previous evening, bearing my letter to Rajlakshmi in his pocket. 'So be it,' I had written. And, regretting my inability to send her my address, I had begged her forgiveness.

On our reaching the house in the village, everyone heaved a sigh of relief and I was overwhelmed with the love and attention. I made Kalidas Babu's acquaintance the next morning. I found him a harsh and arrogant man with only one mission in life—to apprise the whole world of his wealth. 'I'm a self-made man, *moshai*,' he declared several times in the course of the morning. 'I don't believe in Fate and Chance and rubbish like that. I neither ask the gods for any favours nor do I blame them when things go wrong. I alone am responsible for my success. I trust only the power of my own hands.'

Those among his neighbours who had been invited to the betrothal, nodded their heads in agreement for Kalidas Babu was a rich man and the sole moneylender of the village. Who would dare to offend a man like that? Tarkalankar *moshai* even recited a *shloka* (a Sanskrit couplet) in support of Kalidas Babu's views. The lion of the gathering beamed in self-satisfaction and threw a careless glance around the room. His eyes rested on me for a brief moment before turning away in disdain. He obviously thought me to be some kind of hanger-on in the house of his future kinsman. I was burning with fury at the loss of my money and I couldn't bear the glance.

I cleared my throat and said, 'You know your hands and their power better than I do. But I cannot accept your statement that Fate plays no part in success—particularly in the acquiring of money.'

'What do you mean?' Kalidas Babu asked in an ominous voice.

'I mean that I'm a living example of the manoeuverings of Fate. I have nothing to do with either the bride or the bridegroom but it is my money that is paying for everything—from the bride's necklace to the bridegroom's ring. It is possible that the money you will spend on your son's reception will also come from my pocket. You said just now that you've never asked the gods for any favours. Yet you are taking a favour from me—an ordinary mortal and a complete stranger.'

A death-like silence pervaded the room. Thakurdada rose and tried to speak but couldn't utter a sound. Kalidas Babu's face turned a fiery red. He said in a voice of thunder, 'How was I to know you were giving the money? Why are you giving it, anyway?'

'I can't tell you why I'm giving it. You wouldn't understand even if I did. But your first question is strange—to say the least. Everyone present here knows I'm paying the dowry. Only you, who are to receive it, doesn't. So be it. But you knew, didn't you, that the bride's father earns only forty rupees a month? That he doesn't have forty paise saved up? Have you ever asked yourself where he found the two thousand and five hundred rupees with which he is buying your graduate son? Didn't your wife tell you that the girl's mother had clutched her feet and begged for mercy?

However, many men enrich themselves by selling their sons. You are no exception. Only don't brag about the power of your hands, in future. Remember that you got two thousand and five hundred rupees by a sheer stroke of luck. That was a windfall—you must admit it.'

At this speech everyone present turned blue with fear. They thought, doubtless, that Kalidas Babu would never forgive this insolence and would have us all whipped before throwing us out. But there were no such dire consequences. Kalidas Babu sat motionless for a few minutes then, raising his head, he said quietly, 'I'm not taking the money.'

'You mean you are breaking off the engagement?'

'No. I don't mean that. Kali Mukhopadhyaya does not go back on his word. What is your name, young man?'

Now Thakurdada came forward eagerly and introduced me. Kalidas Babu knitted his eyebrows and said, 'Oh! So that's who you are. I filed a case against your father once—a criminal case. However, that was long ago. Had my eldest son lived, he would have been your age. You must come to the wedding, son. I invite you to attend.'

Sasadhar, who had been sitting meekly all this while, threw me a grateful glance. I rose and touched Kalidas Babu's feet. 'I accept your invitation and will certainly come. But I must beg your forgiveness. I spoke harshly—'

'You did, but I forgive you. Sit down, Srikanta. Have some refreshment before you go.'

At the beginning of the chapter I made a reference to the uselessness of good advice. I conceded, however, that there are exceptions. Putu's wedding was one of these. In our country, where the social laws are such that the bridegroom's father can enrich himself with the greatest of ease at the expense of the bride's, what fool will refrain from doing so? We may rave and rant at the unequal laws but we can do little else. Paradoxical as it may sound, change can be brought about in society—not by the parents of the groom but by those of the bride.

Five

GAHAR WAS NOT AT HOME BUT NABIN WAS VERY PLEASED TO SEE me. On my enquiring after his master he pulled a long face. 'He hasn't come home all night. If you want to see him, go to the *akhra*[*] at Muraripur where the Vaishnavi harlots are selling their wares.'

'Vaishnavis! Where did they come from, Nabin?'

'Things are no longer the same, Babu,' Nabin sighed. 'When old Mathura Das Babaji died, a young man called Dwarika Das came in his place. He is a colourful personality and surrounds himself with women. My master has struck up a great friendship with Dwarika Das. He spends all his time in the *akhra*.'

'But your master is a Mussalman. Don't the Vaishnavis object?'

'These belong to the lowest sect of *auls*[**] and *bauls*.[+] They don't make any distinction between Hindus and Mussalman. All they want is to strengthen their numbers.'

'But when I was here last time, Gahar didn't mention the *akhra* or visit it even once.'

'That was because of Kamal Lata. He was afraid of the truth coming out. The moment you left he went back.'

In the course of my conversation with Nabin I gathered that

---

[*]   A place where Vaishnavs assemble for religious worship.
[**]   A religious mendicant.
[+]   A wandering minstrel.

Dwarika Baul was a poet and composer and that Kamal Lata was a young Vaishnavi who had recently come to the *akhra*. She was beautiful and intelligent and had a fine singing voice. Many men were attracted to her and much money had been poured at her feet.

I had heard of the *akhra* of Muraripur in my childhood. It was reputed to be very old, the founder being a disciple of Mahaprabhu* himself and many generations of Vaishnavs had lived and died within its hallowed walls.

I decided to go and investigate. 'Will you take me to the *akhra*, Nabin?' I asked.

'No, Babu,' he answered with an emphatic shake of his head. 'I have a lot of work to do this morning. If you take the road going north you'll come to the *akhra* in half an hour. There's a lake with a bakul tree growing by it. The dalliance that goes on there is equal to that of the gopis of Vrindavan. You can't miss it.'

'What do they do at the *akhra*, Nabin? Sing kirtans?'

'Day and night. Their drums and cymbals never get a rest.'

'There's no harm in that surely,' I said smiling. 'I'll go fetch Gahar.'

'Do that,' Nabin said with a smirk. 'But take care not to fall into Kamal Lata's web. Men can't resist her.'

'I'll go and try my luck,' I said and, leaving the house, strode purposefully towards Kamal Lata Vaishnavi's *akhra*.

Twilight was falling by the time I came to the bakul tree by the lake. It was an ancient tree, gnarled and black, with a circular platform around its base. But that too was old and crumbling and totally worn away in places. There was no sign of anyone and no sounds of singing or beating of drums was borne upon the wind. I stood, uncertain, for a minute or two, then discerning a faint track in the foliage at my feet, I followed it till I came to the river. Here, on a bit of raised ground, neatly swabbed with cow-dung, sat Gahar and a man who, I presumed, was Dwarika Das—the present incumbent of the *akhra*. I could see him clearly even though the light was failing. He was a young man—in his mid-thirties perhaps—tall, slim and dark. His hair was swept up into a knot on the top of his head and a dark, velvety stubble covered his cheeks and chin. His eyes were large and bright with suppressed laughter.

---

*   Sri Chaitanya Dev.

I stood by them, unnoticed, for both were absorbed in the scene before them. Across the shadowy streak that was the river, the sky had taken on the hues of sunset. And, out of the rose and gold, a thin slice of a crescent moon glimmered, pale and watery, with the evening star beside it winking like a jewel. The woods stretched away, blue-black in the weird light, as far as the eye could see. The tattered clouds tossed and turned, changing colour and form as though at the whim of any unruly child who, gigantic brush in hand, dipped and splashed paint in reckless abandon. The painter would return, any moment, and snatch his brush away and the colours would dim and fade and turn to ashes in the deepening dusk.

I glanced down at the river. The moon and the stars flickered in its depths and little flashes of light appeared on the surface like streaks of gold on a touchstone. Somewhere in the woods masses of wild jasmine were unfurling their petals. The air was full of their scent, sweet and heady. The branches above my head were astir with the flutter and hum of nesting herons. The water gleamed dully, still and soundless, in the enveloping twilight. And silhouetted against the greying expanse of sky and river, sat the two men.

'Gahar!' I called softly.

Gahar came out of his trance and stared at me with unseeing eyes. His companion nudged him with an elbow, '*Gosain*!* Isn't that your friend—Srikanta?'

Now Gahar sprang up and clasped me to his bosom in a passionate embrace. I extricated myself with some difficulty and, walking over to where Dwarika Das sat, I asked, 'How did you know me, Babaji?** You haven't seen me before.'

'Of course I have seen you,' came the reply. 'You are no stranger, *gosain*! We were together in Vrindavan, don't you remember? I recognized you by your eyes. They hold oceans of love—like Kamal Lata's eyes. I knew her the moment she stepped into the *akhra*. "Kamal Lata," I cried, "where were you all these years? Why did you go away from me?" "I've come back," she said.

---

*   A term of address used for Vaishnav men.
**   A term of address used for gurus.

"I'll never leave you now." She became mine all over again. Our love encompasses the three worlds. It flows like an unending stream, eternal and infinite. True love is religion, *gosain*; true love is God consciousness.'

'But where is Kamal Lata? I have come all the way to see her.'

'And so you shall. Though it won't be for the first time. You've seen her often enough in Vrindavan. You've forgotten her, haven't you? It was so long ago. Gahar *gosain*! Go call Kamal Lata from the *akhra*. Tell her Srikanta has come to see her.'

'You've heard of me from my friend, haven't you?' I asked as soon as Gahar left.

'Yes. When I asked Gahar *gosain* why he hadn't come to the *akhra* for a whole week, he answered, "Srikanta was here!" He told me you would come again before leaving for Burma.'

I breathed a sigh of relief. I had feared, for a moment, from his recognition of me, that he possessed superhuman powers. But now I knew that he had guessed my identity from Gahar's description. So far so good. Dwarika Das seemed a nice man, simple and uncomplicated, though slightly addled by his passion for Vaishnav philosophy. I took an immediate liking to him.

In a little while, Gahar reappeared with the Vaishnavi. Kamal Lata was about thirty, dark, slim and taut, with quick, graceful movements. She had bangles on her wrists, whether of gold or brass I could not say. The long hair flowing down her back was held by a knot at the end. She had a string of basil about her throat and another in a little pouch in her hand. She may have marked her brow and the ridge of her nose with sandal paste, as Vaishnavis do, but most of it had rubbed off. I glanced up at her and was startled. I was convinced that I had seen her before. Even her walk seemed familiar.

Kamal Lata looked straight into my eyes and said without a trace of self-consciousness, 'Do you remember me, *gosain*?'

'No, but I think I've seen you somewhere.'

'You've seen me in Vrindavan. Hasn't Bara *gosain* told you that?'

'Yes, but I've never been to Vrindavan in all my life.'

'Of course you have. It was so long ago that you've forgotten.

You drove the cows out to the meadows and picked fruit from the trees. You wove garlands of flowers and hung them around our necks. Don't you remember?' And she pursed her pretty mouth and smiled. I smiled with her, admitting her pleasantry.

'It is getting dark,' she said presently. 'We had better go in.'

'I must leave you now. I have a long way to go. I'll come tomorrow morning.'

'Who showed you the way to the *akhra*? Nabin?'

'Yes.'

'Didn't he tell you that men get caught in Kamal Lata's web and can't escape?'

'He did.'

The Vaishnavi's laugh rang out like a peal of bells. 'He has your welfare at heart,' she said. 'You should have heeded his warning.'

'Why do you say that?'

Kamal Lata didn't answer my question. She said, instead, 'Gahar *gosain* tells me you are leaving the country to take up a job in Burma. Why should you do that? After all, you have only yourself to fend for.'

'What else can I do? How else do I make a living?'

'You can live as we do. On Govindaji's prasad. No one can deprive us of that.'

'I know. I have been a *bairagi** once.'

'I knew it the moment I saw you,' the Vaishnavi cried. 'Why did you give it up? Didn't the life suit you?'

'Not for long.'

'It is better so. Come into the *akhra* and meet the others. I'm only one in a wilderness of *kamal* (lotus).'

'I believe so. But I can't come in now. It is getting dark and I have a long way to go.'

'You think we'll let you cross the jungle at this hour? The night may be long and dark, *gosain*, but dawn is sure to follow. Go home in the morning.'

'As you say.'

---

*   A Vaishnav anchorite.

'*Gour! Gour!*'[*]

'*Gour! Gour!*' I chanted after her. And we both entered the *akhra*.

Six

T HOUGH NOT A RELIGIOUS MAN MYSELF, I HAVE NEVER BEEN irreverent towards the religion of others. The academics of Hinduism are too convoluted for me to understand, but I do not doubt the veracity of those who claim that they do. Thus, the universally acclaimed swamiji (the guru) is as much the object of my devotion as the self-proclaimed sadhuji (the ascetic). I am prepared to listen to their discourses with equal attention.

Many scholars of antiquity believe that the true spirit of Hinduism is contained in the Vaishnav tradition and that, among all the provinces of India, it is in Bengal that this tradition is preserved in its purest form. I have rubbed shoulders with the sadhus and sants of Bihar without much enlightenment, as my readers may remember. But here was the real thing! I decided not to miss the opportunity of getting to the heart of our spiritual heritage. Since I had promised to attend Putu's wedding reception I could not leave for Burma just yet. Why spend the few days left to me in the boredom and isolation of my lodgings in Calcutta when I could employ them, far more profitably, in pursuit of a higher knowledge? I decided to stay on in the *akhra*.

On entering it I found that Kamal Lata's claim was not without foundation. Here, indeed, was a wilderness of *kamal*. But the blooms were ravaged and scattered as though a herd of elephants had passed over them. There were Vaishnavis of every age, appearance and colour—each employed in her own allotted task.

One was engaged in cooking milk into a delicious-smelling kheer. Another was kneading a large pat of dough. Yet another was rolling coconut and sesame balls between her palms while a fourth sliced and stoned a heap of fruit. All this was, obviously, in preparation for the *bhog* (cooked food offered to a deity) that would be offered to Sri Sri Govinda Jiu, the presiding deity of the *akhra*. A young Vaishnavi sat in one corner, stringing flowers into a garland while her companion (another young woman) smoothed and folded bits of bright satin and silk. I understood that these were to be worn by Govindaji after his ritual bath the next morning. The women were all equally absorbed in the work they did but their lips moved, soundlessly, at the same time, in silent incantation of the 108 names of Krishna. Darkness had set in and a lamp or two flickered here and there.

Kamal Lata said, 'Come. Let us make our obeisance to Govindaji. But I haven't found a name for you. What shall it be? Natun *gosain*?'

'Yes. If Gahar can become a *gosain* in your *akhra*, why can't I? I am a Brahmin, after all. But what is wrong with my name? Why not call me Srikanta with a *gosain* added on?'

'Oh no.' The Vaishnavi dimpled and smiled. 'It is not for me to utter that name. I would be guilty of misconduct.'

'Why so?'

'You are very persistent. Do you have to have answers to all your questions?'

At this, the young Vaishnavi in the corner giggled and bent her head over her garland. I followed Kamal Lata to the shrine where half a dozen images of Radha and Krishna in black marble and bronze stood in a semicircle. Here, too, I saw Vaishnavis at work busy preparing for the evening arati. After bowing my head before the images, with the correct amount of reverence, I followed Kamal Lata through several rooms and courtyards till I came upon a veranda facing east. Here, Kamal Lata spread an asan and invited me to sit.

'Rest yourself, Natun *gosain*, while I get your room ready. I won't be long.'

'Do I stay here tonight?'

'Of course. Why do you ask? You won't suffer any discomfort while in my care.'

'I know that. I'm worried about Gahar. He might take offence.'

'Leave that to me. When your friend hears that it was I who prevented you from going back, he won't be offended in the least.' And she walked away, laughing.

I sat and watched the Vaishnavis. So busy were they that not one deigned to cast a glance at me. By the time Kamal Lata returned, they had completed their work and left.

'Are you the mistress of the *akhra*?' I asked.

Kamal Lata bit her tongue in embarrassment. 'We are all servants of the Lord. No one is higher than another. We have our appointed tasks. Mine is—' And, turning her face in the direction of the shrine, she closed her eyes and folded her hands.

'Where are Bara *gosain* and Gahar *gosain*?' I asked.

'They'll be returning in a little while. They've gone for a dip in the river.'

'In the river? At this time of the night?'

'Yes.'

'Gahar too?'

'Yes. Gahar *gosain* too.'

'Why didn't you send me with them?'

'We don't send anybody anywhere. People do as they think best. A day may come when you'll follow their example—if Govindaji so desires.'

'Govindaji is unlikely to be interested in me. I am not rich ... like Gahar.'

The insinuation was not lost on the Vaishnavi. She was about to burst into a passionate protest when she controlled herself and said quickly, 'You are not poor either. One who can give away thousands of rupees in charity is not poor in the eyes of the Lord. It is possible that Govindaji may draw you to Him.'

'That's a fearful prospect. However, since I have no control over my destiny, all shall be as Govindaji wills! But tell me, from where did you get the news of my giving away thousands in charity?'

'We beg from door to door. All the local news reaches our ears. We had heard of your generosity in paying a poor girl's dowry long before we saw you.'

'As a matter of fact, I didn't pay it. But that doesn't seem to have reached your ears—yet.'

'You didn't pay it?' the Vaishnavi asked in a surprised voice. Does that mean they've broken off the engagement?'

'No,' I smiled at her agitation. 'The engagement stands. If anything is broken—it is Kalidas Babu's ego. The groom's father has realized that enriching himself at the expense of a stranger is inconsistent with his dignity as a zamindar and a man of means. And that was a stroke of luck—for me.'

'I've never heard of anything like this in all my life.'

'As Govindaji wills! Gahar *gosain's* bathing in a stagnant river just before the evening arati is not the only manifestation of His power. After all, the whole universe is Govindaji's sporting ground.'

As soon as I uttered these words I realized that, this time, I had gone too far. But Kamal Lata did not react. She turned her face, once more, in the direction of the shrine and bowed her head as if begging forgiveness on my behalf. At this moment, a Vaishnavi crossed the veranda on her way to the shrine. She bore an immense *thala* piled high with *luchis* in her hands.

'The *bhog* seems special tonight,' I observed. 'Is today a feast day?'

'Oh no! It is the same every day. We have enough and to spare by the grace of God.'

'That is a happy thought. The arrangements are on a larger scale in the evenings, I suppose.'

'No, again. The morning *bhog* too—if you stay with us for a few days, you will see everything with your own eyes. Slaves of slaves as we are, our lives are dedicated to His service. We work at His bidding from morn till night.'

'What work do you do?'

'You have seen some of us at work.'

'I've seen Vaishnavis chopping vegetables, grinding spices, boiling milk, stringing flowers and dyeing bits of material. Is that all you do?'

'Yes. That is all we do.'

'But these are domestic tasks. All women do them. What are your hours for prayer and meditation?'

'From dawn till dusk. Work is our prayer and meditation.'

'Do you mean to tell me that fetching water, kneading dough and cooking are forms of worship?'

'Work is worship, *gosain*. We are the lowest of mortals. What else do we have to serve Him with but our hands?' Tears glistened in the Vaishnavi's eyes and the lines of her face softened. I suddenly thought it the most beautiful face in the world.

'Kamal Lata,' I asked gently, 'where is your home?'

The Vaishnavi wiped her eyes with the edge of her sari and smiled. 'Under the trees,' she said.

'But it wasn't always so,' I persisted.

'No. I lived in a house of bricks and mortar—once. But that is a long story. We haven't time for it now. Come, let me show you your room.'

It was a charming room, clean and bright with lamplight. Against one wall stood a bamboo rack with a neatly folded tussore dhoti hanging from it.

The Vaishnavi pointed to it and said, 'Change into that and come to the shrine. Do not delay.' And she walked rapidly away.

A neatly made bed stood in one corner. There was a small table beside it with a few books and a *thala* of bakul flowers on it. Someone had just lit the lamp and filled the air with incense smoke. I was tired from my long walk and, having avoided the gods all my life, I decided to take a nap instead of proceeding to the shrine. I changed my dhoti and lay down on the bed. I wondered whose it was. Had Kamal Lata lent me her own room and bed for the night? In other circumstances, such a thought would have made me uncomfortable. But it didn't now. I felt I had come to my own people and a strange peace descended on me. I closed my eyes and drifted away—for how long I cannot tell. I awoke to the sound of an insistent rapping on the door accompanied by the words, 'Natun *gosain*? Aren't you coming to the shrine? They have sent me for you.'

I sat up hastily. The sounds of kirtan-singing accompanied by the tinkling of cymbals wafted in through the window. This was no loud chorus of clamouring voices. It was a woman's voice—sweet and clear. I knew, without a doubt, that the voice was Kamal Lata's. It was with her singing that Kamal Lata had woven a spell around Gahar, according to Nabin. I didn't wonder at it for the voice was melodious enough to deserve all the attention it could get. I entered the shrine and sat quietly in a corner. No one looked up for all eyes were fixed on the divine pair.

In the centre of the ring of devotees stood Kamal Lata. She swayed from side to side, clashed her cymbals and sang:

Madan Gopal jai jai Jashoda dulal ki
Jashoda Dulal jai jai Nanda Dulal ki
Nanda Dulal jai jai Giridhari lal ki
Giridhari lal jai jai Govinda Gopal ki....

(Glory be to thee, Madan Gopal
Son of Yashoda, son of Nanda
Glory be to thee Giridhari Lal
Glory be to thee Govinda Gopal.)

Tears poured down the Vaishnavi's cheeks as she repeated the few lines over and over again with slight variations. Her voice dipped and swelled, threatening to break with the intensity of her feelings. I stared at her in wonder. This was not the Kamal Lata of an hour ago—the bright, laughing woman who had teased me and taken care of me. She had become an instrument, a medium through which a torrent of love and devotion was passing. Her audience listened, mesmerized. Dwarika Das Babaji leaned against one wall, eyes shut, as if in a trance. The women who had been engaged in petty domestic tasks only a while ago and whom I had thought ordinary, even ugly, had undergone a transformation. In the dim lamplight, rendered dimmer with incense smoke, their faces took on an incredible beauty. Even I, though not generally moved by the spiritual, felt uplifted, pure. I had the strangest feeling that those graven images lived and breathed and heard Kamal Lata's song.

Afraid of being swamped by the religious fervour that flowed around me, I rose and left the shrine. I found Gahar sitting outside in the courtyard, motionless as a statue. He didn't move or open his eyes at the sound of my footsteps. I waited for a few moments but he showed not a flicker of recognition. As I crossed the courtyard I was aware of a curious sensation. I felt alienated, abandoned—as if all the inmates of the *akhra*, Gahar included, had set off on a journey to some distant land leaving me behind. I yearned to go with them but the path was strange and beset with many fears. I went back to my room, blew out the lamp and lay down on the bed. I knew myself to be superior to them all. I was a man of intelligence and learning whereas they were crude, unlearned rustics. Yet I felt as though I had failed at something they had all passed with flying colours. The thought saddened me and large tears rolled from the corners of my eyes and fell on the pillow. I don't know when I fell asleep or how long I slept. I was awakened by a voice calling, 'Natun *gosain!* O, Natun *gosain!*'

'Who is that?' I woke up with a start.

'I'm your friend of the evening—don't you remember? What a sleeper you are!'

'I saw no sense in keeping awake. I've enjoyed a good nap and I consider the time well spent.'

'I can see that. I came to ask if you were ready for the prasad.'

'I most certainly am.'

'How do you expect to get it if you go on sleeping?'

'I know I'll get it. My friend of the evening will not abandon me—be the night as long and dark as it will.'

'Only a Vaishnav can claim that privilege,' the Vaishnavi smiled. 'Why should you?'

'I too can become a Vaishnav and the slave of your slave—if you give me hope. If you could make Gahar a Vaishnav why not me?'

The smile left Kamal Lata's face. Her voice grew deep and solemn as she said, 'Don't mock our sect, *gosain*. It isn't worthy of you. And don't jump to conclusions about Gahar *gosain*. He is not a Vaishnav. His own people call him a kafir but he hasn't abandoned the religion of his ancestors. He is a good Mussalman.'

'It doesn't seem so from the way he behaves.'

'That is the wonder of it. But don't delay anymore. Come for your prasad.' She turned to go, then thought the better of it. 'Shall I bring it to your room?' she asked.

'Do that. But where is Gahar? Why don't you serve the two of us together?'

'You don't mind eating in his company?'

'I've eaten with him all my life. Besides, Gahar is a poet. Poets have no religion or caste.'

I couldn't see the Vaishnavi's face for she had moved away from the light. But I heard her suppress a sigh. 'Gahar *gosain* isn't here. I don't know when he left the *akhra*.'

'I saw him sitting in the yard a while ago. Don't you allow him to enter the shrine?'

'No.'

'You accused me of mocking your sect. But are you not making a mockery of your God, Kamal Lata? I saw Gahar's face this evening and—'

The Vaishnavi walked away, stopping me in mid-sentence and re-entered the room a few minutes later with a *thala* full of prasad in her hand. A young Vaishnavi followed her, carrying a lamp and an *asan*. Kamal Lata arranged the bowls with neat, deft fingers and said. 'This may not be your idea of a good meal, Natun *gosain*, but nothing passes through our lips except Govindaji's prasad. While in the *akhra* you'll have to be content with that.'

'Rest assured, my friend of the evening. I won't spoil this beautiful moment with complaints about the food. I'm not such an oaf. You'll find I've licked the *thala* clean when you return.'

'Good. That's the way to eat Govindaji's prasad,' said Kamal Lata.

Early next morning, I was awakened by a loud clamouring of bells. The morning arati was in full swing. In the pauses between the rhythmic clash of metal on metal I heard snatches of kirtan sung in a morning raga, mellifluous and tender:

> *Kanu gale banamala biraje*
> *Rai gale moti saje*
> *Arunita charane manjari ranjita*
> *Khanjana ganjana laje….*

(A string of wild flowers adorns the neck of Kanu
Pearls sway on Radha's breast
Blossoms blush crimson at the touch of her rosy foot
And her eyes—fluttering like the wings of a bird
    Are lowered in shame.)

The rest of the day was devoted to a worship of Govindaji that did not flag for an instant. The inmates of the *akhra* were all equally occupied in an endless round of prayer and kirtan-singing interspersed with the rituals of bathing and feeding the Lord, wiping his body and covering it with sandal-paste, then dressing it up in bright silks and garlands of flowers. It occurred to me that such unwavering attention and persistent service was possible only because the recipient was a figure of stone. Flesh and blood could not endure it and would have rebelled. Last night I had asked the Vaishnavi, 'What are your hours for prayer and meditation?' and she had answered, 'Work is our prayer and meditation.' Today, I acknowledged the truth of her statement.

Nevertheless I snatched a brief moment in which to ask her, 'You are not like the others, Kamal Lata. Tell me, honestly, do you really believe that the symbol of God that you worship, that stone image in the shrine—?'

Kamal Lata raised an imperious hand. 'Symbol?' she cried. 'He *is* God. Don't ever use that word again, Natun *gosain*.' Her vehemence startled me. I glanced at her face and saw that she had a high colour almost as though she blushed for me. I felt foolish and uncomfortable.

'I know nothing of the spiritual, Kamal Lata,' I said humbly. 'I only asked a question. Do you really think that an image of stone can be imbued with the power, the consciousness of God?'

'I don't think. I know. I've seen Him manifest himself with my own eyes. People like you, who believe power and consciousness to be vested only in the human body, are miserably deluded. That is because you cannot break out of the conditioning your education has imposed on you. Why shouldn't God be found in a stone? Is He not everywhere? Why else do we call him Omnipotent and Omnipresent?'

As an argument, this was neither clear nor conclusive. And it was certainly open to question. But she drove home her point with the authority of a divine edict. Her words were an expression of a deep-rooted conviction. Before her unswerving faith, I felt lost and vaguely defeated. I couldn't summon up the courage to argue, to prove her wrong, for I knew that, try as I would, I couldn't fight it. I realized that her whole-hearted surrender to an object, whatever it might be, was the source of her strength. And the same was true of the others. They were not children playing a game. Had they believed that, even for a moment, the whole cult would have disintegrated. It stood by virtue of their faith, their genuine belief that they served Him who was above all others. And so their numbers grew and their joys multiplied a hundredfold.

'Why don't you speak?' the Vaishnavi asked.

'I'm thinking.'

'Of whom?'

'Of you.'

'Really? I feel flattered.' She paused a moment and added, 'Yet you are leaving me and going off to Burma. Do you really need a job that badly?'

'I do, for the simple reason that one must live somehow. If I had a throng of devoted disciples and the wealth of a *math* (a monastery) to enjoy, I wouldn't go.'

'God provides.'

'I doubt it. You doubt it too or you wouldn't go a-begging.'

'We go because it is His hand that is held out to us from every door. If it weren't for that we would never go "a-begging" as you call it. No, not even if we starved to death.'

'Where do you come from, Kamal Lata?'

'I told you yesterday. The path is my village and my home under the trees.'

'Then why do you stay in the *akhra*?'

'I wandered about for years. I would go away again, this moment, if I found company.'

'That shouldn't be difficult. Anyone would be happy to go with you.'

'Would you?'

'Certainly. As a boy I wasn't afraid of wandering about with a *jatra dal* (an opera troupe). Why should the prospect of going off with a Vaishnavi frighten me, now that I'm an adult?'

'You were with a *jatra dal*? Then you must know how to sing.'

'No. The manager threw me out long before I reached that stage. Who knows what would have happened if you were in his place!'

The Vaishnavi laughed. 'I would have thrown you out too.' Then, sobering down, she said, 'You've never been to Sri Vrindavan Dham, you said. Why don't we go together? I'll show you everything. We will beg as we walk. I can sing and you—you may take God's name as you will. People give alms easily. The truth is that I feel cooped up here in the *akhra*. I long to set foot on the path again—the path to Vrindavan. Come with me, Natun *gosain*.'

I looked up at her, amazed. 'Kamal Lata,' I said, 'You've known me for less than twenty-four hours. What makes you trust me so implicitly?'

'Trust is not a one-way affair, *gosain*. You must trust me too or you'll be in trouble in strange lands and climes. But I know we won't let each other down. Shall we leave tomorrow? It is the fifth day of the new moon—a very auspicious day. And if you get tired and wish to return, you may take a train back. I won't stop you.'

I scrutinized her face. I had not a doubt that she meant every word she said. For some reason or the other she wanted to leave the *akhra* and go off on a pilgrimage and she would do it with or without me. It was obvious that her links with the *akhra* were crumbling. Its air had grown oppressive to her and she was anxious to escape. At this moment, a Vaishnavi came in and announced that prasad had been served.

'Let's go to your room,' Kamal Lata said.

'My room! That's a joke.'

I entered it, however, and found a sumptuous meal of prasad laid ready on the floor. I would have enjoyed discussing the details of our flight while I ate, but no sooner did I sit down to do so than a Vaishnavi came and took Kamal Lata away. I finished my meal and came out into the yard. But there was no sign of Kamal Lata or of Dwarika Das Babaji. A cluster of ancient Vaishnavis with dour faces went about their tasks. I recalled that these very faces had appeared angelic to my eyes last evening in the dim light of the shrine. But daylight dispelled the illusion with a ruthlessness I couldn't bear. Sickened, I walked out of the *akhra* as rapidly as my legs could carry me till I came to the faint trickle, choked with sedge and hyacinth, that was the river. Around me, on all sides, were dark, thorny woods, thick with reeds and bamboo clumps. A shiver ran down my spine for I hadn't been in these woods for many years.

As I turned to retrace my steps, a man moved from behind a tree and stood before me. I jumped, for I hadn't expected anyone to come creeping out of the jungle. I judged the man to be about my age or some ten years older. His body was thin and worn away; his complexion was sallow, and there was something odd about his face for the lower part was disproportionately small and the upper adorned with a pair of eyebrows of astonishing length, breadth and thickness. It seemed as if Nature, in a whimsical mood, had planted a pair of fierce moustaches on his brow. He was dressed like a Vaishnav with thick ropes of basil knotted about his throat but his clothes were soiled and torn and his general appearance was wild and dishevelled.

'*Moshai!*' he said, blocking my path.

'Command me.'

'May I ask when you came here, without giving offence?'

'You may. I came last evening.'

'Did you spend the night at the *akhra*?'

'I did.'

'Oh!'

A brief silence followed. As I took a step forward he stopped me again. 'It is obvious, from your appearance, that you are a gentleman—not a Vaishnav. How did they let you stay?'

'You had better put the question to the inmates of the *akhra*.'

'Was it Kamal Lata who asked you to spend the night?'

'Yes.'

'Do you know her real name? It is Ushangini. She is from Sylhet though she pretends she's a Calcutta woman. We both come from a village called Mahmudpur. Would you like to hear the truth about her morals and character?'

'No,' I said, shortly. But, overcome with curiosity, I added, 'Are you related to Kamal Lata?'

'Am I not?'

'How?'

The man hesitated a little then, working himself up, roared in a menacing voice, 'I'm her husband. That's who I am. A *kanthi badal** took place between us with her father as witness. He's dead now but there are other witnesses.'

I didn't believe him—why, I do not know. 'What caste are you?' I probed.

'We are Tilis.'

'And Kamal Lata's family?'

'They are Sunris.' The eyebrows shrank with distaste. 'We don't even wash our feet in their water. Can you send her to me?'

'No I can't. You many go in and speak to her yourself, if you wish. Everyone is welcome in the *akhra*.'

'I *will* do that,' the man said angrily. 'I'm not afraid. I've bribed the constable and he has promised me a couple of men. I'll go in one of these days and drag her out by the hair. That rascal of a Babaji wouldn't dare stop me.'

---

* The Vaishnavite ritual of exchanging basil garlands to signify marriage.

I walked away in disgust. His voice came from behind, harsh and grating, 'What sort of a gentleman are you? Why can't you send her to me? What harm will it do you?' He spat out the word *gentleman* with a venom that made me walk rapidly away. I feared that if I turned back, I'd thrash the puny fellow till his bones rattled. At last I understood or thought I understood Kamal Lata's need to escape.

On reaching the *akhra* I went straight to my room and shut the door. Then, carrying the lamp to the head of the bed, I picked up a volume of Vaishnav philosophy from the pile on the table and lay down on the bed. As I turned the pages (books of Vaishnav philosophy are not meant to be read) I went over the afternoon's encounter. Needless to say, it had disturbed me considerably. And the disturbance was compounded further by the fact that Kamal Lata kept assiduously away. Dusk fell and the sweet sounds of cymbals and kirtan-singing wafted in through the window. The evening arati had begun, but no one came to call me and take me to the shrine. I wondered where Gahar was. I hadn't seen him all day and the fact puzzled me. I had planned to spend a few days at the *akhra* but, as matters stood, I thought the better of it. I decided to leave for Calcutta the next morning.

Late that night, there was a tap on the door accompanied by a voice calling, 'Natun *gosain*!' I sat up on the bed.

Kamal Lata stood in the doorway, her form dim and shadowy in the dark. 'You are sad, Natun *gosain*,' she said softly. 'Is it because I didn't come to you?'

'Yes.'

The Vaishnavi hesitated a little and asked, 'What was that man saying to you—in the woods?'

'Did you see him?'

'Yes.'

'He said he was your husband.'

'Did you believe him?'

'No, I didn't.'

The Vaishnavi sighed softly and asked, 'Did he hint that I was a woman of loose morals.'

'Yes.'

'And my caste—'

'He said you came from a family of Sunris.'

There was a long silence. Then a voice, seemingly disembodied, spoke from out of the dark. 'Shall I tell you my story, Natun *gosain*? My childhood and youth—but no, you will despise me if I do.'

'Then, I'd rather you didn't tell me. I'm leaving tomorrow and I would like to remember you as I see you now. Knowing you has been a beautiful experience. Why spoil it, Kamal Lata?'

Another long silence. I wondered what she thought and felt as she stood there in the dark. 'What are you thinking of, Kamal Lata?'

'I'm thinking,' she said clearing her throat, 'that I won't let you go tomorrow.'

'When will you let me go?'

Her answer took me by surprise. 'Never,' she said firmly, adding, 'It is very late. You had better go back to sleep. Is the mosquito net properly tucked in?'

'I've no idea. It must be.'

The Vaishnavi laughed. 'You are a strange man, *gosain*.' Then, moving forward, she ran her hands deftly around the bed and said, 'I'm going now. Try and get some sleep.'

She tiptoed away, shutting the door gently behind her.

Seven

ONE DAY, THE VAISHNAVI MADE ME SWEAR A SOLEMN OATH THAT I would listen to the story of her life even if it meant abhorring her ever afterwards.

'I don't wish to hear it,' I said, 'though I will if you insist. But I won't hold you in abhorrence—ever.'

'Why not? Everyone does. Men and women equally.'

'Women are less forgiving than men when one of their own sex goes astray. I know the reason for it though I shan't tell you. When men condemn women—it is mostly a pose. I may tell you straight away that I've heard of worse crimes than the one you are about to charge yourself with. Yet, I've never found myself hating or despising anyone.'

'Why not?'

'I don't know. I'm made that way, I suppose.'

Kamal Lata was silent for a minute or two. Then she said, quite out of context, 'Do you believe in reincarnation, Natun *gosain*?'

'No. I have better things to believe in.'

The Vaishnavi fixed her eyes, dark and sombre, on my face. 'I'll tell you something,' she said. 'Look, I have my face turned towards the shrine. I shall not lie.'

'I know you won't, Kamal Lata.'

'Then listen carefully. About a month ago, Gahar *gosain* came to the *akhra* after a week's absence. He said that a childhood friend had come to visit him. I wondered who it was who had the power to keep Gahar *gosain* away from the *akhra* for six whole days. I also marvelled at the fact that a Brahmin thought nothing of spending a week in a Mussalman household. When I put the question to Gahar *gosain*, he answered, "He is alone in the world and a law unto himself. He fears no one." "What is your friend's name, *gosain*?" I asked. When he told me your name I was startled. You know, don't you, that I mustn't utter that name?'

I smiled. 'I've heard you mention the fact.'

'I asked him a lot of questions about you—your age, your looks and he answered them faithfully. But my head was in a whirl and my heart beat loud and fast and I saw nothing and heard nothing. You must be laughing at me, *gosain*! You must think me insane to react so over a name. But it is true. Utterly and absolutely true! I'm not the first woman in the world to be driven to madness by a name.'

'And then—' I prompted, smiling.

'After a while I became myself again. I even laughed at my foolishness. But, try as I would, I couldn't drive you out of my thoughts. "He'll come to me," my heart sang. "I'll see him with my own eyes."'

The smile left my face. There was something in her eyes that I couldn't fathom.

'I saw you for the first time only yesterday. But, today, no one in the world loves you more than I do. Isn't that proof enough that we were very close in a previous incarnation?' The Vaishnavi paused for a few moments and added, 'I know you haven't come to stay and stay you won't however hard I beg. You will go away from me in a day or two. How shall I bear the pain of parting?' And she raised the edge of her sari and wiped her streaming eyes.

I was so shocked that I didn't know how to react. Here was a young woman declaring her love for me as openly and unashamedly as the sun was shining in the sky. Far from having encountered anything like it in my life, I hadn't even read about it in books. Yet, I could swear that this was no play-acting. I felt dazed and acutely depressed. I wondered if I had done anything to deserve the situation. It was perfectly true that Kamal Lata's beauty and sweet singing voice had attracted me and I had told her so out of a sense of indulging in a mild flirtation. She had looked after my comforts with genuine concern and, in return, I had paid her lavish compliments and sought her company. But the fact that she was nurturing a secret passion for me was beyond my wildest dreams.

My face burned with shame and my heart beat thick and fast. I sensed danger around me. I had no idea that a beautiful woman's love could convey such unpleasant sensations. It was indeed an ill wind that blew from Kashi, I thought. First Putu, then Kamal Lata. And, all the while, Rajlakshmi held me in the hollow of her hand refusing to relax her grip even infinitesimally. I wondered why such a flood of feminine passion was engulfing me at my time of life when youth and health were things of the past. The need to escape was urgent. 'To hell with Vaishnav philosophy, Putu's wedding and the rest,' I thought, and decided, there and then, to leave for Calcutta the next day.

'Oh! My goodness. I nearly forgot. I must fetch you your tea.' The Vaishnavi rose.

'Tea? Is there such a thing in the *akhra*?'

'There isn't—usually. I sent someone to the village to buy the leaves. I'll make it in a minute. Don't run away.'

'I won't—but do you know how to make tea?'

In answer, Kamal Lata smiled and left the room. I looked at her departing figure and something clutched at my heart. I knew that tea-drinking was not part of the *akhra* routine. It may even have been forbidden. But Kamal Lata had discovered my preference for it and taken the trouble to procure the leaves and make it herself. I knew nothing of her past or present and what had been hinted at by the man in the woods was unsavoury enough. She, herself, believed that I would despise her if I knew the truth about her. Yet, she had wanted to tell me! I had refused to listen but she had insisted. I could see that her need to unburden herself was great. And, till she did so, she would know no peace.

One thing puzzled me—her statement that if she uttered my name she would be guilty of misconduct. I wondered who this other Srikanta was in her life. He was, undoubtedly, at the root of my present troubles. A chance meeting, a common name and the Vaishnavi had escaped into an imaginary world. She had created a myth of love through many incarnations and had drowned herself in it. The real world and its claims meant nothing to her now. My feelings changed. I experienced a flash of intuitive understanding. I realized that she, who had submerged herself in the religion of love, had never known love in the flesh! Her unfulfilled body and soul were weary with years of whipping up emotions that did not spring from the heart. The fount was running dry. Hence her bewilderment. Hence her fear and pain. Her unsatisfied cravings sought a path of escape but she knew not where it lay. I was her only hope. If I understood her, if I admitted her—her life would have a direction and a meaning. My name, *Srikanta*, would be her password. Clutching it tightly in her hands she would set sail for an unknown destination.

The Vaishnavi brought me my tea and I drank it with pleasure. The depression and distaste of a little while ago vanished and my heart was light.

'Kamal Lata,' I asked, 'Are you a Sunri?'

'No.' She smiled. 'We are Sonar Bene. But surely that is unimportant. It is all the same—to you.'

'True. I don't believe in caste.'

'So I gathered. I've heard you've even eaten food served by Gahar's mother.'

'She—she was a wonderful woman, Kamal Lata. Gahar is exactly like her. Have you ever seen anyone with a sweeter, gentler disposition than Gahar? He got it from his mother. I'll tell you of an incident I remember from my childhood. Gahar's mother had given away some money to someone—I don't remember who—and his father had discovered it. He was a hot-tempered man and very worldly. There was a violent quarrel and I ran away, frightened. When I returned, a few hours later, I found her sitting, downcast, in a corner. I asked where Gahar's father was. She sat, glum and silent, for a few minutes. Then, suddenly, she burst out laughing. Tears rolled down her cheeks but she couldn't stop laughing—'

'Why? What was there to laugh at?' Kamal Lata looked puzzled.

'That is exactly what I asked her. When she had collected herself she wiped her eyes and said, "I'm laughing at my own foolishness, Srikanta. Your uncle has had a good lunch and is snoring away happily in his bed. And here I am—sitting and sulking. What have I gained but an empty stomach and a host of bitter feelings?" And, with that, her troubles were over! It is a great quality in a woman—this ability to make light of a quarrel. Only those who have experienced the opposite can appreciate it.'

'Are you among them?'

I was taken aback for I hadn't expected the question to rebound on me. 'Everything needn't be experienced personally,' I said. 'Many things are learned from strangers. What about the man with the eyebrows? Have you learned nothing from him?'

'He is no stranger.'

I stared at her, incapable of uttering another word. The Vaishnavi, too, was silent for a long time, then clasping her hands before me, she said, 'I beg you, *gosain*. Allow me to tell you the story of my life.'

'Well—do so, if you must.'

But, in attempting to, she found it difficult. Her lips trembled and she sat with her head bowed, struggling with her feelings. Only for a few seconds, however. Then she raised her head. There was a glow on her face I had never seen before. She said firmly, 'One's ego stands between oneself and the truth, Natun *gosain*. It is like a fire of chaff that burns unseen. "Blow away the ashes," Bara *gosain* says, "and you'll see it smouldering in spasms." But I dare not fan it into a flame, either. I must put it out or else the vows I took on my initiation will be rendered meaningless. I'll tell you the truth. I may gloss over some details—I'm a woman, after all.'

I felt embarrassed. I begged her, once more, not to tell me anything. 'Forgive me, Kamal Lata,' I said. 'I have never been interested in female immorality. I feel no curiosity—in fact it distresses me terribly. I don't know if your insistence on telling me about your past arises out of any desire for penitence. If that is so, if you Vaishnavis believe that to reveal one's secret sins is equal to wiping them away, I request you to take your story to people who'll enjoy listening to it. I'm leaving the *akhra* tomorrow and we may never see each other again.'

'My insistence on telling you the truth about myself arises out of my needs—not yours. I thought I had made that clear. But I cannot accept your statement that we may never see each other again. My heart tells me otherwise. And I will live out my life with that hope burning in my breast. But tell me—are you really averse to hearing the truth? Rumours, doubts, speculations—will they always be enough for you?'

'Then tell me, first, about the man I met today in the woods, the one you don't allow into the *akhra* and from whom you are anxious to escape?'

'So you guessed—'

'It's obvious isn't it? But who is the man?'

'If the agony and torment of hell can be personified—he is that. He hounds me and will continue to hound me from this life to the life hereafter. Do you know what my only prayer is these days? "Oh Lord, take pity on me. Remove this venom from my breast. My years of dedicated service, at your feet, are being wiped away by my hatred of Man. It chokes and pollutes me. Save me. Give me a breath of fresh air to breathe."Yet, there was a time when no one was closer to me in the world—no one I loved more dearly.'

I stared at Kamal Lata's tormented eyes. I recalled the man's cadaverous face and crude manners and marvelled that a lovely woman like her could ever have loved him.

My disgust must have shown on my face for the Vaishnavi smiled. 'What you saw was only the outside. You know nothing of him. Allow me to tell you.'

'Go on,' I said.

The Vaishnavi drew a deep breath and began, 'I am the eldest of my parents' children and the only daughter. We come from a village in Sylhet but my father had a flourishing business in Calcutta and that is where I lived from childhood onwards. My mother lived in the ancestral house with my two younger brothers. I used to visit her, from time to time, but I didn't like it there and would come away as soon as I could. I was married at seventeen and widowed almost immediately afterwards. My husband's name was the same as yours. That is why I call you Natun *gosain*.'

'Go on.'

'The man you saw today was a steward in our household. His name is Manmatha—' She paused, then went on with a kind of desperation, 'When I was twenty-one I discovered I was pregnant. Manmatha had an orphaned nephew called Jatin. He lived with us and Baba paid for his education. He was younger than I and loved me more dearly than anyone else in the world. I had no one to turn to so, in my desperation, I sent for him. "Jatin," I said, "I have never asked anything of you before. Don't refuse me what I ask now. Get me some poison that I may kill myself before anyone discovers my shame." He didn't understand, at first, but when he did his face turned as white as a sheet. "Don't delay, bhai," I begged, "Get it as soon as you can. I haven't much time." Jatin wept as if his heart would break. How bitterly disillusioned he was in me—only I could tell. "Usha Didi," he said, "taking one's life is a grievous sin—even more grievous than the one you are guilty of. The first will not wipe out the second. I will obey you in everything, but not this. If you truly believe death to be the only path left to you—you must seek it alone. I cannot help you." So I had to go on living.

'The news reached my father's ears. He was an upright, honourable man and a true Vaishnav at heart. He didn't say a word to me though the shock half killed him. Yet, overwhelmed with shame and grief though he was, he collected himself and, taking me with him, left for Nabadweep where his gurudev lived. On gurudev's advice, it was decided that Manmatha would be sent for; that we would be initiated into the Vaishnav cult and then married, according to custom, by an exchange of basil strings. I felt a tremendous relief, not at the thought of becoming respectable again but because marriage would allow me to keep the child that had come unbidden into my womb. The initiation took place. I was given a new identity and a new name. I became the Vaishnavi—Kamal Lata. I didn't know, then, that Manmatha had agreed to marry me on the promise of a payment of ten thousand rupees. I only knew that the marriage had been postponed for about a week. Why—no one cared to tell me.

'I spent the days by myself in the house at Nabadweep. Manmatha was hardly to be seen. Then the auspicious day came. I rose early, bathed and entered the prayer room. I felt pure in body and my heart was light. My father came in for a moment. I noticed that his face was pale and careworn. And then I caught a glimpse of Manmatha in the garb of a new initiate. A tremor ran through my frame—whether of joy or sorrow I could not tell. I wanted to run to him and lay my head on his feet—so humble, so truly grateful did I feel. As I sat waiting, an old maidservant—she had nursed me in childhood—entered the room. And it was from her lips that I heard the reason for the postponement.'

The Vaishnavi's voice grew heavy with tears. What she was speaking of had taken place years ago but it still had the power to make her suffer. She turned her face away from me and wiped her eyes.

I waited a little and asked, 'What did she say was the cause?'

'She said,' the Vaishnavi went on, 'that a day before the date fixed for the *kanthi badal*, Manmatha had declared that ten thousand rupees was too small a sum for what he was about to undertake and had demanded twenty thousand from my father.'

"You mean Manmatha agreed to marry me on the payment of money? And Baba agreed?" I asked, amazed.

"What else could he do, *didimoni*?"* the maid answered. "He would lose everything if the truth came out—caste, position, prestige—"

'Then she went on to tell me that Manmatha had disclaimed responsibility for my condition and accused his nephew—Jatin. He had said that accepting the paternity of another man's child was not such a trifle that he would do it for the paltry sum of ten thousand rupees. Jatin was sent for and charged with the offence. He was too shocked to react at first, then he said in a trembling voice, "That is a lie."

"You worthless rascal!" Manmatha roared, "I took pity on your orphaned state and brought you over from the village. The master took you in, at my request, fed you, clothed you and educated you. Is this how you repay his kindness?" And the disgraced uncle beat his head and chest and shouted, "Don't you dare deny it! Usha has admitted that you are the father."

"Usha Didi has admitted—" Jatin's voice was a whisper, "but that's impossible. She has never told a lie in her life."

"You dare open your vile mouth and deny it? Ask the master. Hear what he has to say."

'The master nodded his head.

"Didi said that? You heard her say it?" Jatin asked, again and again.

'The master said, "Yes."

'Jatin didn't utter another word. He revered my father like a god. He stood silent for a while, then left the room. Nobody knows what he thought or felt. The next morning, his body was discovered hanging from a beam in the stable.

'I don't know what purificatory rites are laid down in the Shastras for a man whose brother's son has taken his own life.

* A term of respect used for the young mistress of the house.

Perhaps none at all. Perhaps a dip in the river—nothing more. Whatever it may be, Manmatha was back in Nabadweep in a few days, all set and ready to do his duty by a wronged woman—'

The Vaishnavi's lips twisted into a smile as she went on. 'The garland I was to hang on his neck was in my hands as I heard the story. I tore it to shreds and flung it at God's feet then rose and left the room. Manmatha's purification was complete. But mine had yet to begin. The man was clean and whole but the adulterous woman had to burn for her sins till she was reduced to ashes. The burning goes on to this day, Natun *gosain*.'

'What happened then?' I asked.

The Vaishnavi's face was turned away from me. I could see that she was struggling for self-control. In a little while she said, 'Do you see, *gosain*, why sin should be so dreaded in the world?'

'Well, yes. In a sense—though I'm not sure I understand what you mean.'

'From that day onwards I saw the effects of sin as I never had before. The powerful and vicious commit evil and the innocent and weak pay for it. Manmatha and I lived on and still do, but little Jatin, who feared the taking of life above all else in the world, had to die by his own hands. He paid for his didi's sin with his life. Such is God's justice!'

I had no wish to argue. Her reasoning was neither clear nor convincing but if it gave her the strength to overcome the pain and humiliation of the past—who was I to interfere?

'What happened then?'

Kamal Lata looked up. Her eyes were wild and tormented. 'Tell me, honestly. Do you still wish to hear the rest of my story?'

'I do. Believe me, I do, Kamal Lata.'

The Vaishnavi wiped her eyes and said, 'Four days later, I delivered a stillborn child. I took him in my arms and walked down to the river. I laid him on the waves and watched him float away. Then I bathed in the Ganga and came home.

"I must go back to Calcutta, beti," my father said, his voice heavy with tears. "I can't stay here any longer."

"Yes. You must go back."

"You'll send me your news from time to time?"

"No. You mustn't seek it either."

"Your mother—what shall I tell her?"

"Tell her I'm dead. She will grieve for me but it is better so. If my chaste and noble mother hears the truth she'll never survive it." My father wiped his eyes. Next morning he left for Calcutta.'

The Vaishnavi paused. I waited for what was still to come.

'I had some money with me,' she continued. 'I paid the rent, wound up everything and left Nabadweep. I joined a group of pilgrims and went with them to Sri Vrindavan Dham. And after that—it was one pilgrimage after another. I walked the roads from dawn till dusk. At night I sheltered under the trees.'

'What about the thousands of Babajis that lurk in those places? Didn't any of them cast loving glances at you? Tell me the truth, Kamal Lata.'

The Vaishnavi laughed and said, 'Their glances were all pure and holy. You mustn't make fun of them, Natun *gosain*.'

'I'm not making fun. I respect them highly. I'm curious to know the truth. That's all.'

'Our Shastras command us to hide the truth from those who love us.' There was a hint of laughter in her voice.

'So be it. Obey your Shastras. Tell me about Dwarika Das Babaji. From where did you pick him up?'

Kamal Lata bit her tongue and shook her head. 'You mustn't say things like that, *gosain*. He is my gurudev.'

'Gurudev! Was it he who initiated you?'

'No. But I revere him nonetheless.'

'And all these other Vaishnavis? What are they? Handmaidens of the Lord?'

Kamal Lata bit her tongue again and said, 'They are his disciples—the same as I am. He has redeemed them as he has redeemed me.'

'I'm sure he has. But how? By making them his concubines? Isn't there some such custom amongst you? I've heard Vaishnavs refer to it as the *Parakiya*[*] philosophy.'

The Vaishnavi's face reddened. 'You only betray your ignorance when you say things like that. You have never lived among us and know nothing of our philosophy. All you can do is jeer from a distance. Don't ever say such things about Bara *gosain* again. He is an ascetic in every sense of the word.'

Her words and manner shamed me. She noticed it, smiled and

---

[*] The philosophy of love.

said, 'Why don't you stay with us for a while? I don't ask it for Bara *gosain's* sake but for my own. You love me. Wouldn't you like to know how I live? What I think and feel? We may never see each other again. I want you to go away knowing that I haven't forgotten Jatin.'

I was silent. I didn't accept her statement that I knew nothing of Vaishnavs and their ways. I remembered the pure Vaishnav-born Tagar, but I didn't have the heart to tell Kamal Lata about her. Her mention of Jatin saddened me.

'Tell me, *gosain,*' she continued. 'Have you ever been in love?'

'What do you think, Kamal Lata?'

'I think—not. Yours is the nature of a true *bairagi*. You flit like a butterfly from flower to flower. Nothing and nobody can bind you.'

'That's a good comparison,' I laughed. 'Calculated to drive the woman I love to a fine fury—if there is such a woman.'

The Vaishnavi laughed too. 'Never fear, Natun *gosain*. If there is such a woman she won't believe a word I say. And she'll never guess that your love is no more than a bubble of sweet nothings.'

'Why worry about her then? Let her remain happy in her illusions.'

'No,' the Vaishnavi shook her head sagely. 'A lie cannot pass for the truth—for any length of time. She may not know what makes her weep but weep she will. I've seen the effects of deceit, over and over again, in my own life. Self-deception is the worst. So many people dedicate their lives to the service of Govindaji but their dedication is a lie. So all their fasts and prayers and abstinences are like scatterings of sand on the sea. The waves engulf them in seconds—' She paused to take a breath and went on, 'Such people know nothing of true faith and true surrender. They waste their time in the futile service of a stone image. They torture and punish themselves. And, wearying of it all in a few days, they turn their thoughts elsewhere. It is these amongst us who deserve your taunts. But I wander from the point. What I'm trying to tell you is that the woman who loves you truly will have to weep for you all her days. You'll forget her in a trice but she cannot forget you—ever.'

'Are you trying to tell me that any woman who loves me is destined to be unhappy?'

'I didn't say anything about unhappiness. I only spoke of tears.'

'Isn't it the same thing?'

'No, *gosain*. They are different. Women are not afraid of either. But you, of course, do not understand—'

'I confess I don't. Why speak to me of things I do not understand?'

'I can't help it. When you men declare you know all there is to know about love—I can't resist a smile. You don't know, nor do you care to know, that women love differently from men. In love men seek expansion, women—depth; men seek excitement, women—peace. Did you know, *gosain*, that we women are afraid of excessive love? That its passion and intoxication make our hearts quake?'

I was about to say something but the Vaishnavi swept on, 'We accept them but never make them our own and we heave a sigh of relief when they are spent. What we truly yearn for in love is security. But you won't give anyone that—'

'You know it for certain?'

'I *do* know it for certain. That is why I can't abide your boasting.'

'I've never boasted in my life, Kamal Lata. Not before you at any rate,' I cried, stung by her words.

'Not in words perhaps but that superior, withdrawn, roving mind of yours is a piece of arrogance—the likes of which I've never seen.'

'We only met two days ago. You think you know all there is to know about me?'

'I do. But that, you see, is because I love you.'

'I know you too, Kamal Lata,' I said to myself, a vague idea of the difference between tears and unhappiness dawning on me. I realized that what she was saying was the consequence of her years of wallowing in the sentiments of a religion of love.

'Do you mean it, Kamal Lata?' I said, aloud. 'Do you truly love me?'

'Yes.'

'But you have dedicated yourself to Govindaji's service. What will become of that?'

'With you by my side my service to Him will grow in strength and meaning. Come, Natun *gosain*. Let us leave everything behind us and walk out into the world.'

I shook my head. 'I'm leaving the *akhra* tomorrow. But before I go I'd like to hear the truth about Gahar.'

The Vaishnavi sighed. 'It's no use. You won't understand. Are you really going away?'

'I am.'

She was silent for a minute or two, then fixing her eyes on mine, she said, 'You'll come back, again, one day but you won't find Kamal Lata.'

Eight

I KNEW I SHOULDN'T STAY A MOMENT LONGER BUT, EVEN AS I TOOK the decision to leave, a voice whispered within me, 'Don't go. You wanted to stay a week. Why don't you stay? There's no lack of comfort here.' That night, I lay on my bed thinking, 'What are these beings that lurk within us and drive us mad with their secret promptings? Are they strangers or are they closer kin than reason, intelligence, thought and logic? Why are we swayed more by what they say than by what we recognize as the truth? This incessant conflict—will it never cease? Logic and reason tell me I must leave—for my own good. Why, then, do tears gush into my eyes at the thought? Why am I denied all peace and tranquillity.'

I hardened myself. Go I must. But how? There was a way I remembered from my childhood. I had used it often and could do so again. Tomorrow morning, at crack of dawn, even before Govindaji's mangal arati began, I would rise from my bed and walk out of the *akhra* without a word of farewell or explanation or promise of return. I was here once, I was here no more. That was to be the final, the ultimate reality. I would leave that burden to be borne by those who discovered my absence. My plans were made. But there was one hitch. I had left my bag, with Putu's dowry money in it, in Kamal Lata's care. I decided to go without it. I had a few rupees in my pocket. It would suffice for the train journey to Calcutta. I would write to her from there or from Burma. Leaving my bag behind would ensure her continued presence in the *akhra*. She wouldn't leave it before I reclaimed my money.

These thoughts ran frantically round in my tired brain till sleep overtook me. I don't know how long I slept but it seemed only a few minutes before I woke to the sound of a woman's voice singing a morning raga, caressing and sweet. I thought, at first, that I was dreaming. Then, still in the twilight zone between sleeping and waking, I thought that the night had just begun and the evening arati not yet concluded. But the familiar thudding of drums and clashing of cymbals were missing. The sound came closer, became words:

> *Rai jago, Rai jago*
> *Suk sari bale*
> *Kata nidra jao lo*
> *Kalo maniker kole....*

(The love birds call out to Rai
'Awake, Radha, awake'
How much longer will you sleep,
In the lap of the dark jewel—Krishna?)

'Wake up, *gosainji*. The night is over. How can you go on sleeping?'

I sat up and rubbed my eyes. The mosquito net had been lifted and the window was open. Through it, I caught a glimpse of the sky. It was dark but the east was streaked with dawn like a distant fire. A cloud of bats wheeled by. The rush of their wings came to my ears and my heart felt heavy. Faint stirrings came from the bakul tree beyond my window. Throngs of robins, nightingales and thrushes nested among its branches. Bengal was their country, I thought whimsically, and Calcutta their capital city. And the bakul tree must be their stock exchange. The business of the day had begun for them—the business of singing and dancing. They were all skilled professionals, no less untiring in their efforts than the famous ustads of Lucknow. The *akhra* was surrounded by woods in which they flew and sang. The inmates were drowned in music. If the one within ceased for a while the one without didn't—ever. It went on relentless and overpowering. I remembered with what persistence a pair of hawk cuckoos had disturbed my afternoon siesta of the day before. I was not the only one they offended, for an egret, perched precariously on a hyacinth leaf, had scolded them heartily in a grating voice. I thanked heaven there were no peacocks in the woods. They would have compounded the confusion further.

I remembered my decision of the previous night. I had planned to escape before anyone was up. But Kamal Lata had been a step ahead. Like a careful gaoler she had taken up her position by my side even before the night was over.

'I'm not Rai,' I said angrily. 'And I have no Shyam hidden in my bed. Why do you wake me up in the middle of the night?'

'The night is over, *gosain*. It is dawn and you have a train to catch. Don't you remember? Go have a quick wash while I make the tea. But don't bathe. You're not used to bathing at this hour. You may catch a chill.'

'I could have caught a later train. Why are you trying to pack me off at crack of dawn?'

'I would like to walk with you as far as the highway. We must leave before anyone awakes.'

Her face was not clearly visible in the dim light. But I could see that the long hair streaming down her back was damp and dinging. She had had her bath and was ready to leave.

'Will you return to the *akhra* after we part?' I asked.

'Yes.' She put down my bag on the bed with the words, 'Keep it carefully. Count the money first.'

I was struck dumb for a minute. Then I said, 'You are no Vaishnavi, Kamal Lata. You were born Usha and Usha you have remained.'

'Why do you say that?'

'Why did you ask me to count the money? Do you really believe me capable of it? There is a name for people who say one thing and mean another. It is *hypocrite*. And that's what you are—a hypocrite. Before I leave the *akhra* I'll tell Bara *gosain* to strike your name from the *akhra* register. You are in the wrong place.'

The Vaishnavi didn't say a word and I didn't press her. I said instead, 'I have no desire to leave the *akhra*. Not today, at any rate.'

'Then sleep a while longer. Send word to me when you wake up.'

'What will you do now?'

'I'll go out and pick flowers.'

'So early? You won't be afraid to enter the forest at this hour?'

'Why should I be afraid? I always pick the flowers for the morning puja.'

I had noticed, in my two days in the *akhra*, that Kamal Lata always took upon herself the duties that were most difficult and demanding. It was she who arranged everything and looked after everyone's comfort. The Vaishnavis worked under her direction and the *akhra* ran on oiled wheels. No feuds or tensions marred the routine. It saddened me to think that she was being compelled to leave the place she loved because her past had caught up with her. As for the *akhra*, her absence would plunge its inmates into confusion and despair. Like a satellite that had lost sight of its sun, it would spin crazily in a million different orbits till it was shattered into fragments.

'Come, Kamal Lata,' I said. 'Let us pick flowers together.'

'You haven't bathed or changed. Your flowers will not be acceptable to God.'

'I needn't touch them. I'll pull the branches down for you. That will be a help, will it not?'

'The trees are not too high. I can reach them by myself.'

'We can chat as we go along. It will keep you entertained.'

'You show a lot of concern for me—all of a sudden. Come along then. Wash your face and hands and change your clothes. I'll fetch the basket in the meantime.'

The flower garden was situated a little distance away from the *akhra*. We walked through a mango grove, dark and shadowy, the Vaishnavi leading—I following in her footsteps. Piles of dry leaves crackled beneath my feet. As far as I could see, there was no trail.

'I hope you won't lose your way, Kamal Lata.'

'I can't afford to, now that you're with me.'

'Will you say "yes" to a request of mine.'

'What is it?'

'Don't leave the *akhra*.'

'How does my leaving or staying back affect you?'

I had no answer. The Vaishnavi went on, 'There's a verse by Murari Thakur. Have you heard it?

Sakhi hé, phiriya apan ghare jao
Jiyanti maria je apna khaiyachhe
Tara tumi ki ar bujhao….

(Go back home, dear friend
What do you hope to teach one
Who has lost herself in a
life-in-death.)

'You leave this evening, don't you, *gosain*?'

'I haven't made up my mind. Let's see what the morning brings.'

The Vaishnavi made no further comment. After a while she started humming under her breath:

Kahe Chandidas shuno Binodini
Sukho dukho duti bhai
Sukher lagiya je kare piriti
Dukho jai tari thain….

('Listen Binodini—' says Chandidas,
'Happiness and sorrow are twin brothers
If your love is a quest for happiness
Sorrow will follow you for ever.')

'And then?' I prompted.

'Then—nothing.'

'Sing something else.'

The Vaishnavi sang softly:

Chandidas bani, shuno Binodini
Piriti na kahe katha
Piriti lagiya paran chharile
Piriti milaye tatha….

('Listen Binodini—' says Chandidas,
'Love is dumb and bereft of words
If you lose your soul in your quest for love
Love will find her way to you.')

'And then?'

'Then—nothing. This is the end.'

It was the end. Silence fell between us. A madness came upon me all of a sudden. I wanted to rush up to her and seize her hand and walk the path holding it in mine. I knew she wouldn't reject me, she wouldn't pull her hand away. Yet, I could neither move nor speak. I followed her, dragging my feet, till we came to the edge of the wood. In front of us, under a patch of open sky, was a garden full of flowers. It was neatly fenced on all sides and had a bamboo gate.

We had come out of the shadows but the light was still faint. I could discern the shapes of jasmine bushes glimmering white and pure and knew that they were covered with flowers. A champa tree, just within the gate, stood stark and leafless with not a bloom on it, but a sheaf of tube roses, somewhere near at hand, made up the deficiency with its overpowering scent. In the centre was a little cluster of sthal-padma—some five or six trees growing thick and intimate, their leaves and branches entwining and their innumerable, crimson buds gleaming like eyes in the dim light. I had never left my bed so early before. Like a hibernating animal, I had slept off the best hours of the day. I realized what I had missed. The sights and scents of dawn overwhelmed me. I felt uplifted, pure.

'Kamal Lata,' I said in a gush of sentiment. 'Life has treated you cruelly. I pray that your sufferings cease and some happiness falls to your lot.'

The Vaishnavi had hung her basket on the champa tree and was opening the gate. She turned around and asked, 'Is anything wrong, *gosain*?'

My own words had taken me by surprise and her startled question embarrassed me. I had no answer. We stepped into the garden and she commenced her work. After a few minutes she said gently, 'I'm quite happy, *gosain*. I have dedicated myself to one who will never reject me.'

I was not sure of her meaning but I dared not ask. The Vaishnavi swayed her head and sang:

Kalo maniker mala ganthi nibo gale
Kanu guno jash kane paribo kundale
Kanu anurage ranga basan pariya
Deshe deshe bhoromibo jogini hoiya
Jadunath das kahe—

(The dark jewel's garland will I string around my neck
Kanu's fair name will hang in rings from my ears
Crimson robes will I wear for love of my Kanu
And like a wandering mendicant,
    roam from land to land.
Jadunath Das says—)

I stopped her in the middle of her song. 'Leave Jadunath Das for the present. Can't you hear the cymbals? It is time we returned.'
Kamal Lata smiled archly at me and went on singing:

Dharam karam jauk tahe na darai
Maner bharame pachhe bandhu re harai:....

(I care not for piety, service or creed
For losing myself in thee
I might forget my beloved one.)

'Respectable men find the singing of women offensive to their ears. Do you know that, Natun *gosain*?'
'I do. But I don't belong to that class of respectable barbarians.'
'Then why did you stop me in the middle of my song?'
'Because the arati has begun. And without your presence the ritual will be marred.'
'This is a fine bit of deceit, Natun *gosain*.'
'Why should I deceive you?'
'That—only you can tell. Anyway, what makes you think that my absence from the shrine affects the worship of the Lord in any way?'
'I have eyes to see.'
She threw me a strange glance, then went on filling her basket with the freshest of blooms. At last she turned. 'That's enough. Let's go.'
'You didn't pluck any sthal-padma blooms?'
'No. We dedicate those to the Lord from the trees. We don't touch the blooms.'
The sky was filling with light but the woods were still dark and lonesome. As we walked along, I asked, 'Are you really leaving the *akhra*, Kamal Lata?'
'Why do you ask me the same question over and over again? What is it to you?'

Once again I had no answer. I wondered why I felt this compelling urge to stop her from going. What would I gain by her staying on?

On entering the *math* we found everyone awake and going about their tasks. The mangal arati had not yet begun. The cymbals I had heard were part of the 'Waking the Lord' ceremony. Several pairs of eyes looked up at us as we walked in together but there was no curiosity in them. Only young Padma giggled a little as Kamal Lata put down the basket by her side. 'How dare you laugh, you wicked girl!' Kamal Lata rolled her eyes at her in a mock threatening manner. Padma giggled some more but didn't lift her head. Kamal Lata went into the shrine and I entered my room.

I was to catch the evening train to Calcutta. Before leaving for the station I went to say goodbye to Kamal Lata. I found her in the shrine dressing the Lord. She looked up as I entered and said urgently, 'Padma has a headache and Lakshmi and Saraswati are both down with fever. I can't manage all this by myself. I need your help, Natun *gosain*. Do sit down and crimp this yellow material for me.'

I obeyed her command and missed my train. I stayed on the next day and the day after. Early dawn saw me out in the garden picking flowers with the Vaishnavi. Afternoons and evenings were spent in her company helping her in her innumerable tasks. The days passed, one by one, in a dream of contentment. Bird-song and evensong; laughter and prayer; the perfume of incense and flowers became a part of my life. I floated on a sea of love and tender care. Sometimes I asked myself what I was doing, why I was shutting out the real world and wasting my time in the service of a graven image. But try, as I would, I couldn't break away.

One morning I awoke by myself. Kamal Lata had not come into my room singing her song of awakening as she always did. At first I thought it was still night but when I opened my door I found the courtyard bathed in pure, clear light. Kamal Lata stood before me, unbathed and dishevelled. I had never seen her like that before.

'What is it?' I asked anxiously. 'Are you all right?'

A smile flickered on the pale face. 'I don't feel too well this morning. I couldn't rise at dawn.'

'Who is picking the flowers?'

She pointed to a straggling oleander growing in the yard. It had a few blooms on it. 'We'll make do with those for the morning puja.'

'And the garlands for Radha Govinda?'

She shook her head. I felt my heart go out to those stone images. I couldn't deprive them of their garlands.

'I'll have a quick bath and pick your flowers for you,' I offered.

'Do that,' she answered. 'But don't bathe at this hour. You'll catch a chill.'

'I don't see Bara *gosain*. Where is he?'

'He left for Nabadweep the day before yesterday. He is visiting his gurudev.'

'When does he return?'

'I haven't the faintest idea, *gosain*.'

Despite my prolonged stay in the *math*, I had not come any closer to Dwarika Das Babaji. This was partly owing to my own lack of initiative and partly to his temperament which was austere and aloof. But I had noticed several traits in him that interested me for they didn't fit with my preconceptions of the head of an *akhra*. He was a man of very strong morals. He was not a hypocrite and he didn't bore his audience with long recitations and analyses of Vaishnav texts. Although I didn't share his religion or philosophy of life I found much in him that was admirable. His voice was gentle, his looks frank and honest and his living clean and disciplined. He commanded respect and, barring one occasion when he shamed me by fixing his benevolent gaze on me for a long while, I never entered into any argument with him. In fact, I avoided him as best as I could.

However, something continued to intrigue me. He was the only man in the *akhra*. He was surrounded by females eager to serve him. He practiced a religion that placed human love above all things in the world. Yet he succeeded in living the life of an ascetic. I had planned to ask him the secret of his strength the day I left the *akhra*. But that, evidently, was not to be. I decided that if I ever returned, I would put the question to him.

A couple of days went by. I pulled myself together and took a decision. Now was the time to leave. If I didn't go today I would never go. Kamal Lata had recovered from her illness. Padma and the two sisters, Lakshmi and Saraswati, had taken up their duties. There was no excuse for tarrying. Bara *gosain* had returned the night before. I went to take leave of him.

Babaji said, 'You leave today. When do you return?'

'I can't say, for sure, *gosainji*.'

'Kamal Lata will weep her eyes out.'

I was annoyed at the insinuation. I said, a little roughly, 'Why should *she* weep?'

'Don't you know, *gosain*?'

'Indeed I don't.'

'It is her nature. She can't bear to see anyone leave the *akhra*.'

That annoyed me even more. 'If that is so,' I said, 'who can help her?' I caught Dwarika Das Babaji's glance and turned around. Kamal Lata stood behind me.

Dwarika Das hastened to say, 'Don't be angry with her, *gosain*. I hear she made you work very hard when some of the Vaishnavis were ill. It was wrong of her and she admits it. We are humble folk who beg for a living. You have been uncomfortable living among us but we love you and wish you well. When you are in these parts again do not forget to visit us.'

I nodded my head and came out of the room, my heart heavy and dull. I had anticipated the tenderest of leave takings from Kamal Lata. I had wanted to hear so much from her and say so much. But it was all ruined by my own foolishness. My weakness was feeding inwards, turning me harsh and bitter. That I knew. But I never dreamed that it would burst out into the open with such shameless hostility against the woman who loved me. I was filled with self-loathing.

Nabin came to the *akhra* looking for Gahar. His master hadn't come home for two days, he said.

'That's impossible!' I cried. 'He hasn't been here either.'

Nabin didn't seem unduly alarmed. 'He must be roaming about in the woods, then,' he said stoically. 'All we need now is the news that he's been bitten by a snake. Then we can all sit back and relax.'

'We must look for him, Nabin.'

'Where? I have no intention of losing my life chasing him about in the woods. But where is *she*?'

'Who?'

'Kamal Lata.'

'How is she to know where Gahar is?'

'She knows everything. If she doesn't, who does?'

I didn't want to get into an argument with Nabin so I steered him gently out of the *akhra* with the words, 'Believe me, Nabin,

Kamal Lata knows nothing of Gahar's whereabouts. She has been ill for the last three days and hasn't stepped out of the *akhra*.'

Nabin didn't believe me. He said angrily, 'She knows everything. Heaven knows what charms she practices on the wretched boy—she's enslaved him completely. All the money his father left him has disappeared as if by magic.'

'Kamal Lata hasn't taken his money, Nabin.' I tried to calm him down. 'She's a Vaishnavi and her habits are simple. She sings the name of the Lord and lives on what people give her. She's not greedy or acquisitive.'

'I didn't say she has taken it for herself,' Nabin said in a softened tone. 'She's a gentlewoman—anyone can see that. And the Babaji is a decent soul. But they need money to feed all the women who crowd into the *akhra*. And that too on fine foods—*luchi* and sweetmeats and milk and butter—in the name of the Lord. Nayan Chakravarty says that my master has signed away twenty bighas of land in Kamal Lata's name.'

'That may only be a piece of malicious gossip. Nayan Chakravarty is no angel. Hasn't he wangled quite a bit of property for himself?'

'You are right, Babu,' Nabin admitted. 'That rascally Brahmin is as cunning as a fox. But I can't help believing him. I know my master, you see. Only the other day he signed away ten bighas of land in favour of my sons. I begged him not to but would he listen? "I know your father left you a lot of land," I said, "but if you give it all away, how will you live?" "I come from a line of fakirs, Nabin," he replied. "I can take up my ancestral vocation whenever I need to. No one can cheat me out of that." This is the way he talks, Babu.'

Nabin went away. I noticed that he didn't ask me what I was doing in the *akhra*. I'm glad he didn't, for the question would have embarrassed me. Just before leaving he gave me the news that Kalidas Babu's son's wedding had taken place the day before with much pomp and ceremony. The date—the twenty-seventh—had slipped my mind.

I kept worrying about Gahar's disappearance till the truth dawned on me, suddenly, like a bolt of lightning. Why was the Vaishnavi so eager to leave the ashram? And why was she hiding the reason from me? I was convinced that it was not the Vaishnav in the woods and his demand for the restitution of his conjugal rights that was worrying Kamal Lata. It was Gahar's love for her. I remembered Kamal Lata saying, on my first day in the *akhra*, that Gahar would not mind my staying the night if he knew I had done so at her request. Gahar was a mild, gentle soul. He had nobody in the world and he cared for nothing—neither land and money, nor public disapproval. What was it that was keeping him away from the *akhra* he loved? The Vaishnavi knew the reason—I was sure of it. And it was out of a desire to release him from the pangs of an unrequited love that she had decided to go away.

I sat on the bench beneath the bakul tree for a long time after Nabin left, these thoughts and many others flitting through my head. Then I took out my watch and looked at the time. If I meant to catch the five o'clock train I should start getting ready, I told myself. But planning to leave and staying behind had become a habit. A tremendous lassitude overtook me and I could not move. I told myself that it was my duty to look for the missing Gahar and that I had promised to attend Putu's wedding reception. But I had no one barring myself, to remind me of my obligations. After a while Padma came with a message from Kamal Lata. Following her into the yard I came face to face with the Vaishnavi.

She said, 'The train won't reach Calcutta before midnight. You'd better have something to eat before you go. I've got some prasad laid out in your room.' There was not the faintest change in her voice or manner. She was the same Kamal Lata—warm and tender and loving.

'You'll come again, won't you, Natun *gosain*?' she said just before I left.

'If you promise not to leave the *akhra*.'

'How long must I stay?'

'You tell me when you want me back.'

'No, I can't do that.'

'Then tell me something else—'

'I can't tell you that either. You must work out the answers for yourself.'

I wanted, desperately, to stay. 'I'll go tomorrow,' I wanted to say. But I couldn't bring myself to say it. As I rose to leave I saw that Kamal Lata had turned her face away. The gesture went straight to my heart. I walked out of the *akhra* without a word.

Nine

A BANDONING THE HIGHWAY, I WALKED THROUGH THE WOODS
trying out one trail after another. I knew I would get a train,
whenever that might be, and I was in no hurry. As I walked on,
the unfamiliar woods became familiar. I remembered the trails
from my childhood. Only what had seemed wide and clear then
was cramped and confined now. Why, wasn't that the garden with
the haunted tree? It had belonged to the Khans if I remembered
right. That meant I was walking along the southernmost fringe
of my own village. I came up to the tree and stood below it.
It was rumoured that a man had hanged himself from the
topmost branch and had haunted the garden ever afterwards. I
remembered how terrified I was of the tree, as a child. If I came
upon it, unawares, I would run away, trembling. But now the tree
was old and gnarled. It had fared no better nor worse than other
tamarind trees of its years. It was bent over double and its roots
stood out, monstrous and black. It wrinkled its old face into a
smile and said, 'How are you, friend? You haven't passed by in
many years. Are you still afraid of me?'

I put out a hand and stroked the rough bark. 'I'm well, bhai,'
I said. 'I'm not afraid. Why should I be? You are my childhood
friend—dearer to me than the closest of relations.' The shadows
of twilight gathered slowly around me. I turned reluctantly.
'Farewell, my friend,' I said. 'It was my great good fortune that we
could meet again.'

I passed garden after garden on my way to the station. Then came a little clearing among the trees. Overwhelmed by childhood memories, I would have walked through it but there suddenly came, wafting on the air, a rich scent, long forgotten yet maddeningly familiar. I looked around and saw that I stood on Jashoda Vaishnavi's land. And, sure enough, there was her aush tree standing in its corner, gnarled and mossy with age. It was a dead tree but one branch still lived and breathed, and on it, tucked away in a nest of green leaves, were the tiny white flowers that gave out such a heady perfume. I remembered how I had loved those flowers as a child; how I had pestered the Vaishnavi to give me some, for this tree was the only one of its kind in these parts. The Vaishnavi's Vaishnav was buried beneath it. Gahar and I had never seen him—he had left the world before we came into it—but his presence was made real to us by the mound of earth on which the Vaishnavi lit her lamp each evening. Whenever we worried her for aush flowers she would point to the mound and shake her head. 'No, Baba Thakur. Those flowers are for my puja. My Lord will be offended if I let you touch them.'

Jashoda made a living out of selling combs, ribbons, spools of thread, glass dolls, tin whistles, hair oil, vermilion, fishing-rods and tackle. It was her husband's business but she had carried it on after his death. All her wares were contained in one barrel yet not a week went by without one or the other of us knocking on her door to buy something from her.

I could see that Jashoda had found a place beside her husband, for now there were two mounds beneath the aush tree. But they were not clean and smooth as of old. Weeds and creepers grew on them, thick and lush with many rains and, coming closer, I found the lamp, rusty and blackened with age, lying face downwards on a bed of nettles. The hut still stood though the thatch had come down in several places and many of the posts were missing. I remembered Jashoda's dwelling as I had seen it in my childhood, a neat, strong hut with an earthen yard, smooth and gleaming with cow-dung, behind it and a little garden with the aush tree in it, in front. A secure fence of bamboo rails had surrounded it on all sides. My heart was heavy as I surveyed the havoc wrought by time. But worse was to follow. A starved, mangy skeleton of a dog came creeping out of the shambles and, looking at my face with hollow eyes, tried to wag a feeble tail. This was Jashoda's dog. The red flowered collar that she had made for him out of a sari border was still around his neck. The childless widow had reared him with all the tender care she would have lavished on a child. But now he was old and gaunt and left to fend for himself and he neither had the training for it nor the capacity. He stayed on in the only place he knew, waiting for the only person he knew to return. And all the while he was dying a slow death.

I entered the hut and threw a quick glance around. I couldn't see much in the dark but I noticed that the pictures on the walls were still intact. Jashoda had a craze for collecting pictures and pasting them on her walls. Mouldy and blurred with age and the lashings of many monsoons, her gods and goddesses and kings and queens still clung to the mud walls with desperate life. And the gaily daubed claypot in which she kept her vermilion stood, as it had always done, in a little niche on the wall. A few other things lay scattered about. I had the strangest feeling that they recognized me and tried to reach out to me. But they spoke a language I did not know.

The dog followed me a little way. Then, overcome by fatigue, he stood gazing on my departing back with soulful eyes. We were of a kind, I thought sadly. I was on my way to an alien country and an unknown future, and he had no option but to return to an environment which, though familiar from infancy, was now strange and friendless.

The trail turned and I lost sight of him. My heart twisted with pain and tears gushed to my eyes. 'Why do these things happen?' I asked myself over and over again. The agony of a dying dog may not have moved me, to any great extent, at any other time. But, today, my heart was heavy with clouds of misery and despair and a little waft of breeze was sufficient to set a fierce storm raging in my breast.

I was lucky, for on reaching the station, I found the train to Calcutta standing on the platform. I bought my ticket and boarded it. The guard blew the whistle and the train moved away without a backward glance. It had no nostalgic memories. It didn't bid any tearful farewells. 'Ten days are so few in a man's life and yet so many,' I thought for the hundredth time that day. 'Kamal Lata will pick her morning flowers without me. She will perform her innumerable duties, but her Natun *gosain* will not be by her side.'

I wondered how long it would take her to forget her friend of ten days. She had said that she was happy, that she had dedicated herself to one who would never reject her. 'So be it,' I said to myself. 'May she find peace and fulfilment in the service of her Lord.'

*

I have never had a goal before me for as long as I can remember. Nor have I desired anything with passion or conviction. Consequently, I have lived my life in another's shadow. Conditioned by her needs and desires I have gradually lost the little capacity I was born with for independent thought and action. My acquaintances believe me to be weak and worthless but the truth is that a part of me does not belong to the ordinary world. I have resented that aspect of my being all my life; I have tried to disown it. Then, in a *bairagi's akhra*, tucked away in the remote wilds of a Bengal village, it met me—not glaringly, not face to face, but in the form of a shadow, elusive and insubstantial. I have been compelled to acknowledge its presence ever since. I have seen its beckoning fingers and been haunted by its timid smile.

And the Vaishnavi, Kamal Lata! Her life was a re-enactment of an ancient myth cast into verse and song by poets of old. One could fault the metre or look askance at the imagery but the tune went straight to the heart. She was like the sky at twilight, changing colour every moment. She defied description. 'Come, Natun *gosain*,' she had said. 'Let's roam the world together, singing for a living as we go along.' She wouldn't utter my name for she believed me to be the companion she had lost, over and over again, through many incarnations. She had no fears of me, no doubts. I was awed by the strength of the mantra her guru, Bara *gosain*, had given her.

Suddenly, I remembered Rajlakshmi and the letter she had written. Its tone was harsh but it did not offend, for mixed with her selfish preoccupations was a strain of true and tender concern. I smiled to myself. I realized now, as never before, that my life was drawing to a dose and that my need of her was over. The place she occupied was a blank. I wondered if there was anyone in the world who could fill it.

As I stared out of the window at the darkening expanse, I was overwhelmed by memories … that first meeting in Kumar Saheb's tent … those bright, dark eyes fixed on my face in fascinated wonder. I had not recognized her—believing her to be dead. Then, her impassioned appeal when I declared my resolve to go to the burning-ghat at dead of night, and her anger, desperation and hurt bewilderment at my rejection. She had stood at the door of the tent blocking my path. 'Do what you will, I shan't let you go,' she had said. 'Who will look after you if anything happens? Your friends or I?' It was then that I had recognized her.

Her strength had been her most significant attribute and it had remained with her through all the upheavals of her life. I had lain unconscious in Ara station and when I opened my eyes I had seen her sitting by my bed. It was from that moment onwards that I had entrusted myself to her keeping. I had surrendered body and soul. Then, again, when I lay sick with fever in our ancestral village—she had not hesitated to come to me. She had no place there. She was dead to its inhabitants. But she had braved everyone's scorn for my sake. In her letter she had written, 'Who will nurse you in your illness? Putu?' I had not replied. I had not had the courage.

My mind wandered over her many attributes—her beauty, her intelligence, her rigorous self-control and her ability to command. How little was the tender, humble flower, Kamal Lata, hidden away in a remote ashram, in comparison! Yet, it was in Kamal Lata's gentle obscurity that my soul had found true affinity. I had had a taste of freedom. I had found space to breathe. I had value in her eyes. She would never take me in hand, as Rajlakshmi had done, and overwhelm me with her presence. What would I do in Burma? Why was I going? I had been there once. Had I come back enriched in any way? It wasn't Kamal Lata alone who had welcomed my presence in the ashram. Bara *gosain* had begged me to return. Was that only a ploy to get at my money? I had discredited people like them all my life. I had believed them all to be hypocrites and charlatans. But my life wasn't over yet. It might be that I still had a lot to learn. Was faith always to be scoffed at and scepticism to be idealized? I did not know.

By the time the train entered Howrah station, I had arrived at a decision. I didn't need a job and I didn't want to go to Burma. I would spend the night in Calcutta but first thing, tomorrow morning, I would wind up my affairs, pay my creditors and leave for the *akhra*. On reaching my lodgings I washed, changed and was preparing to go to bed when a well remembered voice murmured behind me, 'You've come back, Babu!'

'Ratan!' I turned round, dismayed. 'Since when have you been here?'

'I came just before dusk. I fell asleep on the veranda and didn't hear you come in. There's a fine breeze outside.'

'Have you had your dinner?'

'No, Babu. What about you?'

I shook my head. I was hungry but there being nothing to eat I had decided to ignore the pangs.

'All the better!' Ratan said happily. 'I'll have the privilege of partaking of your prasad.*'

'In that case,' I said drily, cursing his self-possession, 'you'd better go out and see if any prasad is to be bought at this hour. But what brings you here? Is there another letter?'

'No, Babu. Letters are useless. She will say what she wishes to say with her own lips.'

'Does that mean I'm to follow you to Kashi?'

'Oh no! Ma is here.'

'Here!' I exclaimed, agitatedly. 'Has she been sitting in the carriage all this while?'

'No, Babu, though she is quite capable of it,' Ratan smiled. 'We've been in Calcutta for the last four days. I've been stationed here with instructions to catch you the minute you return and take you to her.'

'Where is she? How far away?'

'We've taken a house at a little distance from here but I have a carriage waiting. Let's go.'

There was nothing for me to do but put on my clothes, lock the door and follow Ratan into the carriage. We drove through half the city, then stopped before a handsome mansion with high walls enclosing a garden. Rajlakshmi's old durwan, a man from Munger and a Kurmi by caste, opened the gate with a great salute of welcome.

'How are you, Babuji?'

'I am well, Tulsidas. And you?'

He bent down and touched my feet. He had always stood in

---

* Ratan uses the word prasad to imply the leftovers from Srikanta's meal.

tremendous awe of me because I was a Brahmin. Another servant, a new one, came running out of the house at the sound of our arrival. He looked dazed and stupid with sleep and was roundly abused by the superior Ratan. 'Why do you think you're here? To eat and sleep? Go, get the hookahs ready at once.' Bullying the other servants, shamelessly, was Ratan's way of showing the special position he enjoyed in the household. This man, being new, was suitably impressed and darted back the way he had come.

We went up a flight of steps and, crossing a veranda walked into a huge, beautiful room, lavishly spread with carpets and bolsters and bright with gas light. My favourite hookah—dear and familiar with years of use—stood in a corner and by it were my gold embroidered velvet slippers. Rajlakshmi had made these herself and given them to me as a birthday present some years ago. There was another room leading from it with a connecting door. This being open, I caught a glimpse of the interior. There was a neatly made up bed and a clothes-horse with some clothes on it that I recognized as mine. They had been bought just before we left for Gangamati but I had never worn them and had consequently forgotten that they existed. All the furniture was new and bright with polish but both rooms were empty.

'Ma!' Ratan called and the next moment Rajlakshmi stood in the room. She bent down to touch my feet then, turning to Ratan, said, 'Bring up some tobacco, Ratan, then go and rest. You've had a hard time these four days.'

'I don't worry about myself, Ma,' Ratan replied. 'I'm thankful I could bring him to you safe and sound.'

I looked at Rajlakshmi with new eyes. This was the old Pyari—but not quite. Bathed in the tears and suffering of the last few years she had emerged in a new form, —infinitely brighter and incredibly beautiful. Her jewels, few but choice and expensive, dazzled the eyes. Yet her sari was a simple one of ordinary cotton. Its finely worked border encircled the lovely face and little tendrils of silky, black hair peeped out from under it and rested on her glowing cheek and brow. I stared at her, fascinated.

'Why do you stare at me? Am I a stranger?'

'That is what it seems.'

'Do you know what I feel like doing?'

'No!'

'I feel like putting my arms around your neck.' Rajlakshmi

laughed, peal after peal of delighted laughter. 'Will you push me away if I do?'

'Try me,' I laughed with her. 'You seem intoxicated. Have you had *shiddhi*?'

The sound of approaching footsteps (the intelligent Ratan always made a great clatter as he approached us) forced her to control herself. She whispered threateningly, 'I'll show you what I've had in a minute. Wait till Ratan leaves.' Then, suddenly her voice became heavy and tearful. 'It is just like you to leave me alone in a strange city and go off to attend Putu's wedding. Do you have any idea of how I've spent my time?'

'How was I to know you were here?'

'You knew it well enough. You wanted to punish me and that's why you disappeared.'

At this point, Ratan entered with the tobacco and, turning to Rajlakshmi, said, 'Shall I tell the cook to serve Babu's meal? I'm to get some prasad and it is past midnight.'

'I'll bring it up myself.' Rajlakshmi rose hurriedly. 'Spread an asan on the floor of my bedroom, Ratan.'

I remembered my last days in Gangamati when the cook and Ratan were the custodians of my welfare, when Rajlakshmi had had no time for me. Today, she would do everything for me with her own hands. She could trust no one. I heaved a sigh of relief for this was the old, the true Rajlakshmi. The other was an aberration.

'What was the wedding like?' Rajlakshmi asked after I had eaten.

'I didn't attend it but I've heard it went off very well.'

'You didn't attend it? Then, where were you all these days?'

I told her of my meeting with Kalidas Babu and its consequences and she was suitably impressed.

'It's a strange world,' she said, her eyes wide. 'You should have gone to the wedding and given the girl a present.'

'You can do that for me.'

'I *will* do that but not on your behalf. You still haven't told me where you were.'

'Do you remember the Babaji's *akhra* at Muraripur?'

'Of course. The Vaishnavis used to come singing to our door I remember my childhood very well.'

'That's where I was.'

Rajlakshmi shuddered from head to foot. 'In the Babaji's *akhra*!' she exclaimed. '*Ma go Ma!* I've heard they lead lives as filthy as hell!' Then, quite unaccountably, she burst out laughing. 'You are the limit. You really are. Remember the sanyasi at Ara? The matted hair and brass bangles and rudraksha beads? What a beauty—' she could say no more for, overcome with laughter, she rolled all over the bed. I took her by the shoulders and made her sit up. She went on laughing, then controlling herself with a great effort, she said, 'What did the Vaishnavis say to you? There are lots of them there—all flat-nosed and tattooed ….' She burst into another fit of laughter.

'You'd better stop laughing at once,' I said sternly, 'or I'll teach you such a lesson you'll be ashamed to show your face to the servants.' Rajlakshmi sat up quickly and drew herself away, out of my reach. However, that didn't prevent her from saying witheringly, 'You'll never have the guts. You are the biggest coward the world has ever known.'

'You know nothing of me, Lakshmi. You call me a coward but there was a Vaishnavi in the *akhra* who said I was arrogant and superior.'

'Why? What had you done to her?'

'Nothing. She called me Natun *gosain* and said that my withdrawn, roving mind was a piece of arrogance—the like of which she had never seen. So you see, I'm a strong man and a hero—not a coward at all.'

'From where did the Vaishnavi slut get the key to your roving mind?'

'Mind your language, Lakshmi. Remember that Vaishnavis are women of God.'

Rajlakshmi swept my admonition aside with a wave of her hand. 'She called you Natun *gosain*. What did you call her?'

'Her name is Kamal Lata. Some call her Kamli Lata and swear she's a sorceresws. Her singing drives men mad and they lay their souls down at her feet.'

'Have you heard her sing?'

'Yes. Her voice is beautiful.'

'How old is she?'

'About your age. A little older, perhaps.'

'What does she look like?'

'She's attractive enough. Not ugly at any rate—certainly not flat-nosed and tattooed. She comes from a good family.'

'I knew that the moment I heard what she had said. Did she look after you while you were in the *akhra*!'

'Yes, very well.'

Rajlakshmi suppressed a sigh and rose. 'She has no idea of what she has undertaken. It is easier to realize God—she'll learn that soon enough. Why should I feel threatened?' And she swept out of the room. I lay back on my pillows and pulled deeply on my hookah. As the rich, scented smoke curled into my lungs my eyes fell on a corner of the ceiling where a tiny spider ran around in circles, weaving a web. In the dim light its shadow took on immense proportions and hung from the beam like some gigantic animal—grotesque and frightening. I thought of how the shadow overcomes the substance in the absence of true light, and a sigh escaped me.

Rajlakshmi returned a few minutes later and lay down beside me—her elbow resting on my pillow. I put out a hand and stroked her face. It was damp. 'What made you decide to come to Calcutta all of a sudden?' I asked.

'It wasn't sudden. I've been wanting to come to you ever since the day you left Kashi. I've been so unhappy—I was afraid I'd die without ever seeing you again.' She put out a hand and pushed the pipe away. 'Give over puffing for a moment and listen to me. I can't see your face for the smoke.'

I let go of the hookah and took her hand instead. 'How is Banku behaving?' I enquired.

'The way sons behave when daughters-in-law take over.'

'Just that much and no more?'

'I can't specify the quantity. Anyway, Banku's behaviour does not worry me in the least. How much pain can he inflict? True affliction, for a woman, can only come from the man she loves—as mine does.'

'Have I ever hurt you in any way, Lakshmi?' I asked, gently.

'No,' she said instantly, stroking my brow with a gentle hand. 'On the contrary, it is I who have hurt you over and over again. I reduced you in the eyes of the world out of my selfish love, and, having entangled you in my life, I neglected you upon a whim. I'm being punished for it—can't you see?'

'I'm afraid I can't,' I said, smiling.

'You must be wearing blinkers, then,' she said with a flash of her old spirit. Then her voice softened and her eyes grew dim. 'I was the lowliest of sinners but God didn't forsake me. He gave you to me out of his great goodness. And what did I do? I threw away his gift in the belief that, in rejecting it, I was being purified. Not content with abandoning you, I turned you away from my door when you came again to me.' Tears rolled down her cheeks. She put up a hand to wipe them away and continued, 'I planted the poison tree with my own hands and the fruit was too bitter to swallow. I couldn't eat, I couldn't sleep. Doubts and fears beset me from all sides. Gurudev tied an amulet on my arm and commanded me to chant the name of God ten thousand times a day. I sat in my prayer room for hours on end but God was not with me. Then your letter arrived and the disease was diagnosed.'

'Who diagnosed it? Gurudev? Did he give you another amulet?'

'Yes. But that was for tying around your neck.'

'Tie it by all means if it cures your disease.'

'I read the letter over and over again for two days. Then I wrote my reply and gave it to Ratan. After he left, I bathed in the Ganga and, standing in the temple of Annapurna, I prayed that the letter would reach you in time. "Save me, Ma, from destroying myself," I wept.' Rajlakshmi fixed her full, dark eyes on my face and asked, 'Why do you bind me so ruthlessly?'

I couldn't answer for a moment. Then I said, 'Women allow themselves to be bound in a way men can't dream of.'

'You admit it?'

'I do.'

'Coming out of the temple,' Rajlakshmi continued, 'the first person I saw was a silk merchant called Lakshman Sahu. The old man used to sell me Varanasi saris and was very fond of me. "I wish to go to Calcutta, Sahuji," I said. "I know you do business there. Can you arrange a house for me?" He said I could have a house he owned in Bangali Tola at the price of construction. I agreed instantly for I knew him to be a good and pious man. I brought him the money. He made all the arrangements.' She paused for breath and continued, 'A week later, I left Kashi and took up residence here. Ma Annapurna must have heard my prayers for without her intervention none of this would have been possible. I wanted to see you so desperately and here you are.'

'I won't be here long. I'm going to Burma.'

'We'll go together,' she said instantly. 'I hear there are Buddhist temples all over the country. I can see them. And Abhaya is there!'

'It is a filthy country, Lakshmi. You'll lose your caste.'

Rajlakshmi brought her lips close to my ear and whispered something I couldn't catch.

'Speak a little louder,' I said.

'No,' she said decidedly, then resting her head against my chest, she lay silent for a long while. Her warm breath floated over my neck and face.

Ten

'WAKE UP. RATAN IS WAITING WITH YOUR TEA.'

Not receiving a reply, Rajlakshmi went on, 'The sun has been up for hours. How can you go on sleeping?'

I snuggled into the pillow and murmured drowsily, 'I've only just dropped off. You kept me awake all night—' The bang of a teacup on the table told me that the embarrassed Ratan had made his escape.

'What a shameless creature you are!' Rajlakshmi cried. 'And what lies you tell! I sat up all night fanning you while you snored like Kumbhakarna* and now you accuse me of keeping you awake. Get up this instant or I'll throw a bucket of water on you.'

I sat up in bed and rubbed my eyes. The windows were wide open and the morning light streamed in. Rajlakshmi stood in the middle of the room. The rich folds of a vermilion Varanasi sari glowed like flames around her freshly bathed body and the red and white sandal paste on her brow (put there by the Oriya *panda*** at the bathing-ghat) gave her face an unearthly beauty. A beam of golden light, slanting in from the eastern window, fell on her face and neck. Her cheeks glowed with embarrassment but the familiar

---

*   See Glossary.

**   A Brahmin priest who acts as a guide to pilgrims.

dimple twinkled mischievously and the rosy mouth curved upwards in a saucy smile. Her eyes, too, were bright with laughter as she said, 'Why do you stare at me? You've been doing so all evening.'

'Why don't you tell me why?'

'You're comparing me with Putu and Kamal Lata and trying to decide which of us is the prettiest.'

'Wrong. Putu and Kamal Lata are not a patch on you where looks are in question. A glance at you is enough to tell me that. I don't have to stare.'

'What about accomplishments?'

'That is a question that needs serious consideration.'

'Indeed!' Her lovely lip curled in derision. 'All she can do is sing kirtans.'

'Yes and very well too.'

'How do you know?'

'Well! Her sur and laya are perfect. And her tal—'

'What is tal?'

'Tal is that which used to fall on your back when you were a scrawny kid with a stomach like a drum. Don't you remember?'

'Of course I remember. Kamal Lata has found out all about your roving mind. Haven't you told her what a man of action you were?'

'No. Self-advertisement is not a good thing. You can do that for me. But, believe me, she has a beautiful voice and sings truly well.'

'You, of course, are the best judge. Do you remember the song you used to sing when we were together in the pathshala? The one that had us all enthralled?' Her eyes twinkled with merriment. 'It went something like this—*Kotha geli praner pran bap Duryodhan re-e-e*! (Where are you lost, life of my life, son Duryodhan). It was a truly touching song. Even the cows and goats had tears in their eyes!' And she stuffed her sari into her mouth and doubled up with laughter.

Footsteps were heard on the stairs and within seconds Ratan was at the door. 'I've put the kettle on for fresh tea. It'll be ready in a minute.' And, picking up the cup of stone-cold tea, he was preparing to depart, when Rajlakshmi said, 'If you don't get out of bed at once the second cup will also go waste. And Ratan can't stand waste, can you, Ratan?'

'I don't know about you, Ma, but I can stand a good deal, particularly from Srikanta Babu.'

Rajlakshmi looked at his departing back with a tender smile and said, 'Ratan loves you very much.'

'Yes,' I said.

'He threatened to leave my service the day you came away from Kashi. "Ratan!" I said to him, "Have you forgotten all I've done for you?" "No," he said. "I haven't forgotten. I'm not an ingrate. I'm going to Burma to serve Srikanta Babu. That's the best way I know of repaying you." It took a lot of persuasion to make him change his mind. And then—your wedding invitation arrived.'

'Don't talk nonsense,' I interrupted. 'I only asked for your opinion—'

'Oh yes? And what if I'd said "go ahead"? You would have married her, wouldn't you?'

'No.'

'Of course you would. You men are capable of anything.'

'That's not true. Everyone is not capable of everything.'

'I don't know what Ratan thought or felt,' she continued, cutting me short. 'I noticed him giving me strange glances and several times I saw tears in his eyes. Then, when I gave him the letter to post, he said, "I'll go to Calcutta and deliver it myself." "Why waste all that money, Ratan?" I asked and his answer was, "I don't know why but, looking at you, I get the feeling that the ground is being cut from under your feet and that the tide will sweep you out to sea in a matter of moments. I won't take the fare from you even if you offer it, for all I have today is through your kindness. However, if Lord Vishwanath hears our prayers and all goes well you may send a little something to my woman in the village."'

'That son of a barber is as shrewd as a fox,' I remarked with a wry smile. Rajlakshmi smiled too but did not comment. She urged me, once again, to get up and get ready before Ratan arrived with the second cup of tea.

Sitting down to my midday meal, I asked Rajlakshmi why she was dressed in Varanasi silk.

'You tell me the reason,' she said, smiling.

'How would I know?'

'Don't you recognize the sari?'

'Yes. It is the one I sent to you from Burma.'

'The moment it came I decided to wear it on the most important day of my life. Neither before nor after.'

'Is that why you are wearing it today?'

'Yes.'

After a while I said, 'I hear you're leaving for Kalighat in a few minutes.'

'How can I? I must feed you first and put you to sleep. Only then I'll be free.'

'No, you won't be free even then. Ratan tells me that your fasts have doubled in number and you eat practically nothing these days. You must give up your wilful ways. I've decided to be very strict with you and I'm beginning now. You're not going to Kalighat today.'

Rajlakshmi folded her hands in entreaty. 'Grant me this one day for my own. Keep me as your humble slave from tomorrow onwards.'

'What utter and abject servility!' I sneered.

Rajlakshmi's face grew solemn. 'That is how I should be. I became so proud and insolent that I forgot what I owed to you. I don't deserve your love and tenderness. I've lost my right to them through my own fault.'

I looked up and saw that her eyes were wet. 'Go tomorrow,' I said gently. 'You stayed awake all night fanning me. You must be tired.'

'Serving you doesn't tire me. I've stayed up night after night nursing you in illness and never felt anything at all. Something—I don't know what—soothes all my weariness away. I've lost sight of God for so long now. Today, on my day of happiness, I want to find him again. Don't stop me, dearest. Let me go.'

'Then let's go together.'

Rajlakshmi's eyes brightened. 'Come then,' she cried joyfully. 'But promise not to think any blasphemous thoughts.'

'I can't guarantee that. I'll tell you what. I'll wait for you at the temple gate. You may say a prayer on my behalf and ask for a boon.'

'What boon?'

I thought for a while but could come up with nothing. 'Lakshmi,' I asked, 'What would you wish for me?'

'A long life,' she said promptly. 'And health and strength. And the capacity to be stern with me. I was on the point of being destroyed by your indulgence.'

'This is gross self-pity, Lakshmi.'

'It is. Can I ever forget your letter?'

I sat silent, my face downcast. She put out a hand and raised it, smiling. 'I can't bear this either,' she said, shaking her head. 'But sternness is not part of your nature so I shouldn't expect it of you. I must undertake it myself.'

'What will you do? Fast some more?'

'No. Fasting is no punishment for me. If anything, it makes me more arrogant. That won't be my way.'

'What is your way as you see it now?'

'I don't see anything. I'm groping in the dark.'

'Tell me, Rajlakshmi—do you think I'm capable of harshness and cruelty?'

'I do, my love, I do.'

'That's a lie.'

'It *is* a lie but it is also at the root of all my troubles, *gosain*. A fine name your Kamal Lata has found for you. I shall call you Narun *gosain* too, from now on.'

'Do so—by all means.'

'The name has many advantages. You may, occasionally, mistake me for Kamal Lata and heave a sigh of relief. Am I right?'

'This is the language of slaves indeed!' I laughed. 'You haven't changed one bit, Lakshmi, for all your talk. If you were a real slave your master would have punished you for your impertinence by sending you to the gallows.'

'Perhaps. But I've put the noose round my neck and my fate in a hangman's hands from childhood onwards.'

'You're a very naughty girl and have been so from childhood onwards. No hangman has ever had the power to keep you under control.'

Rajlakshmi was about to make a laughing rejoinder when she glanced at my *thala* and stood up. 'Good Heavens! You've finished. Where's the milk? Promise me you won't get up. I'll fetch it in a minute.' And she hurried out of the room.

A sigh escaped me. 'Rajlakshmi and Kamal Lata!' I thought.

She came in a few minutes later and put down a bowl of milk, then, picking up the fan, waved it gently and said, 'I used to think there was something wrong, something sinful in all this. That is why I left Gangamati and went to Kashidham. I cut off my hair, wore widow's weeds and started a course of rigorous penance under Gurudev's guidance. I was sure I was on the right path and the golden gates of heaven almost within reach. You were the one obstacle in my path and I swept you away harshly, ruthlessly. But ever since that day my tears have not ceased. I forgot my mantra and lost sight of God. My soul was parched as if with years of drought and I thought, "If this is the path to God, why do I suffer so?"'

I looked at her and smiled. 'God wishes to test the faith of his devotees. Had you been a little patient, a little more firm of faith, you would have realized God.'

'I don't wish to realize God. I've found what I wanted.'

'Where did you find it?'

'Here. In this house.'

'Impossible! Prove it.'

'Why should I prove it to you? Have I nothing better to do?'

'Slave girls don't talk like that!'

'Don't keep calling me a slave girl. I don't like it.'

'Very well, then. You aren't a slave girl. I give you your freedom.'

'Oh! You do, do you? Last night you fell asleep with your arms around my neck. I removed them gently and sat up. I saw that your brow was drenched with sweat. I wiped it with the end of my sari and took up the fan. Your face looked so beautiful in the lamplight—I sat gazing on it for hours. "If this is immoral," I thought, "who cares for morality? If this is vice—to hell with virtue. My soul recognized him for my own even before it awoke to full consciousness. If this is a lie—what and where is the truth?" You haven't had your milk. Shall I bring some fruit?'

'I can't eat any more, Lakshmi.'

'But you must. You've become very thin.'

'If I have, it is from months of neglect. Don't try to remedy it in one day. I'll die in the attempt.'

Rajlakshmi's face grew pale. 'It won't happen again. I've learnt my lesson.' Then, after a few minutes' silence, she continued, 'And so the night went by. I woke with the first glimmer of dawn and taking the durwan with me, went down to the river. As I sank into the water I felt my pain and guilt flow out of me. Ma Ganga took me to her bosom and made me whole again. I came home and entered my prayer-room. I found that my mantra had come back to me and I could pray. My God had come back to me. I felt his presence blotting out the glaring light of my sky like masses of shadowy cloud and my shrivelled up soul, smouldering with years of aridity, grew moist and green again. Tears poured out of my eyes but they were not wrung out of a heart burning with pain. They ran down like cascades of silvery light. They drenched me in their sweetness, they drowned me in their joy…. Let me bring some fruit and feed you with my own hands. Shall I?'

I nodded. As she left the room I sighed, once again. 'Rajlakshmi and Kamal Lata!' I thought. I wondered who had presided over her birth and thought of naming her Rajlakshmi. After all, there were thousands of other names.

It was nine o'clock at night when we returned from Kalighat. Rajlakshmi had a bath, changed into a simple sari and came and sat by me.

'I see that you've shed your regal apparel,' I remarked. 'It's a relief to see you as your normal self.'

'It was given by my king—so it had to be regal. I want that sari put on me when I am dead.'

'I'll remember your command. But you've lived on dreams all day. Aren't you ever going to eat? Shall I ask Ratan to bring up your meal?'

'Here? Have you ever seen me eat in your presence?'

'I haven't, yet. But what if I do?'

'Women eat like monsters. They prefer to eat in private.'

'You can't fool me with your tricks, Lakshmi. I'm not letting you starve anymore. If you don't do as I say, I shall stop talking to you.'

'Go ahead. See if I care.'

'I won't eat, either.'

'You win,' she laughed. 'I couldn't stand that.'

The cook brought up her meal—a simple one of fruit and sweetmeats. She ate a little and said, 'Ratan has complained to you that I don't eat enough. Would you be able to eat if you were in my place? My case was lost irretrievably, I thought, yet I came to

Calcutta to seek a fresh court of appeal. Every day I sent Ratan to your lodgings and sat here tense with fear that you would refuse to come. What could I expect after treating you the way I did?'

'You could have come to my lodgings yourself and pounced on me the way a green beetle pounces on a cockroach.'

'Who's the cockroach? You?'

'Who else? There isn't a meeker and humbler insect in the world.'

Rajlakshmi thought for a moment and said, 'Yet I fear you more than anyone else in the world.'

'That's a joke.'

'It isn't. I know you better than you know yourself. You care very little for the opposite sex. You don't desire women or really need them though you feign an interest, sometimes, out of consideration for their feelings. If you had refused to come to me I would have been powerless to make you do so.'

'You're wrong. If I desire anything at all in the world, to this day, it is you, Lakshmi. I can refuse anyone anything—but not you. You say you know me better than I do myself. And you don't know this?'

'I'll go and wash my hands,' Lakshmi rose and left the room.

The following evening, her daily duties concluded, Rajlakshmi came and sat by me. 'I want to hear all about Kamal Lata,' she said. 'Tell me.'

I told her all I knew but, fearing a misunderstanding, left out those bits that concerned just the two of us. She heard Kamal Lata's story with great concentration and commented, 'It was Jatin's death that broke her. After all, she was responsible.'

'How was she responsible?'

'Wasn't she? Had she not sought his help in taking her life, it would never have occurred to him to do the same. It was inevitable. That is why one must never ask a friend to be a partner in one's sin. The scales overbalance and one has to pay for the other's crime. She lives on but the boy she loved so dearly had to die.'

'Your reasoning is a bit obscure, Lakshmi.'

'It may be to you. It isn't to me or to Kamal Lata!'

'Is that so?'

'Of course it is. I'm ashamed to go on living when I look at you.'

'You said, yesterday, that all your guilt and pain had been washed away. Was that a lie?'

'Of course it was. They are my constant companions and will remain with me till the hour of my death. I've tried to die but I couldn't—because of you.'

'I know that, Lakshmi. But if you keep hurting me like this, over and over again, I'll go away—so far away that you'll never find me again.'

Rajlakshmi shivered and, clutching my hand, laid it on her breast. 'You are too cruel,' she said. 'Don't ever speak those words again.'

'I won't.'

'You mustn't even think them. And promise me you'll never leave me—'

'I didn't leave you because I wanted do. You asked me to go.'

'That wasn't your Lakshmi. That was someone else.'

'But I'm still afraid of that someone else.'

'You needn't be, anymore. She's dead—the wicked ogress.' And she gripped my hand with all the force of her delicate flower-like one. We sat, silent, for a few minutes, then she asked, 'Are you really going to Burma?'

'Yes.'

'Why are you going? We are just the two of us. How much do we need?'

'However little we need—it must be earned.'

'God will provide. I won't let you take up a job. You're not strong enough.'

'If my health breaks down, I'll come back. What else can I do?'

'You *will* come back. I know it. But must you torture me by dragging me away to the end of the world?'

'You don't have to be tortured. You needn't go.'

'Don't joke—for God's sake.' Rajlakshmi's eyes flashed fire.

'I'm not joking. It will be a hard life. You'll have to cook, clean, sweep and swab, make beds—'

'What will the servants do then?'

'There won't be any servants. I won't be rich enough to afford them.'

'I don't care. I *will* go with you no matter how hard you try to dissuade me.'

'Come then. We'll go together—you and I. There'll be so much to do that you'll have no time for your innumerable prayers and fasts or for quarrelling with me.'

'I'm not afraid of work.'

'Very true. But it will be a different kind of work. I doubt if you'll stay even a week.'

'I'll go with you and come back with you—if I don't like it there. I don't have to leave you behind.' She thought for a minute and said, 'As a matter of fact, it might be rather nice. Just the two of us in a little house with no servants to disturb us. Keep me as you will. I won't complain. And I won't want to come back either.' She put her head down on my lap and shut her eyes.

'You seem deep in thought,' I remarked after a while.

She opened her eyes and smiled. 'When do we go?'

'You'll have to make arrangements for your house and servants. We'll go as soon as you are ready.'

She nodded and closed her eyes, then opened them again. 'Let's go to Muraripur before that, and spend some time in the *akhra*.'

'I did promise to do so before leaving the country—'

'Then, let's go tomorrow.'

'Will you come?'

'Why not? Kamal Lata loves you and Gahar Dada loves her. This is a fine state of affairs.'

'Who told you all this?'

'You told me.'

'I did nothing of the sort.'

'Oh yes, you did. Only—you don't know when.'

I was alarmed and tried to retrieve the situation. 'I'd rather you didn't go.'

'Why?'

'You'll make fun of the poor girl and worry the life out of her.'

Rajlakshmi drew her brows together. 'Is that your reading of my character? After all these years? Am I likely to make fun of Kamal Lata because she loves you? Am I not a woman? Is loving you a crime? It is quite possible that I may grow to love her myself.'

'Nothing is impossible for you. Come along, then.'

'We'll go by the morning train tomorrow. Don't worry, dearest. I won't give you cause for a moment's unhappiness. Not anymore. I promise.' She lay down again and shut her eyes. Her breathing grew slow and measured; her breast heaved gently. She seemed to have gone far away—very far. I was frightened and gave her a little shake. 'Is anything wrong?'

'No, nothing.' Rajlakshmi opened her eyes and smiled. But even her smile seemed strange, for some reason.

Eleven

$\mathcal{W}$E DIDN'T LEAVE THE NEXT DAY—I DIDN'T FEEL UP TO IT—BUT THE day after saw us on our way to Muraripur. Rajlakshmi's faithful retainer, Ratan, without whom she wouldn't stir a yard, left by the morning train with a vast quantity of luggage and Rajlakshmi and I followed with another lot of bundles and baskets and the kitchen maid, Lalur Ma, in attendance.

'Are you planning to settle down in Muraripur?' I asked Rajlakshmi.

'I'll stay for a while. You went and saw the woods and fields and river of our childhood all by yourself like the selfish creature you are. Don't they belong to me too? And don't I yearn for them the same as you do?'

'That's understandable enough. But do we need so many things? And so much food?'

'We can't go empty-handed to a place of God. Besides, you haven't been asked to carry anything. Why do you worry?'

As a matter of fact, that was the least of my worries. What I feared most was Rajlakshmi's reception of Govindaji's prasad and the effect it would have on Kamal Lata. Rajlakshmi would treat it with the utmost reverence but not a morsel of it would pass through her lips for it would be touched by *bairagis* and Vaishnavs. She might start fasting all over again or she might, just possibly, set up a kitchen of her own. Both would be acutely embarrassing for me. But I knew that she would do whatever she did gracefully and courteously. She would be so charming and vivacious that the inmates of the *akhra* wouldn't dream of taking offence. That was the only thought that comforted me.

I watched her as she put away a variety of things in two tall almirahs that had been brought in the day before. Her body had always been light and slim and supple of movement. And the prolonged fasts and deprivations of the last few years had given it a glow that nearly dazzled the eyes. She had bathed early this morning and draped a Vrindavani sari about her form. It was of catechu brown silk woven over with fruits and flowers and leaves and buds whose colours matched the streaks of sandal, vermilion and saffron that the Oriya *panda* at the bathing-ghat had marked, carefully and tastefully, upon her brow. The jewelled eyes of her shark-headed bangles flashed fire with every movement of her hands and the diamonds and emeralds around her neck glittered and sparkled between the borders of her sari. A blue flame darted from the jewels in her ears. She wore no blouse—she rarely did, in the house—(she always said that, being a simple village girl, she found these newfangled articles of clothing constricting and irksome) and her neck and arms and part of her breast were bare. I couldn't take my eyes off her.

She shut the door of the almirah and locked it. Then, turning around, she caught my eye and, drawing her sari quickly about her shoulders, laughed ruefully. 'Why do you stare at me so? Do you see anything special?'

'I see God's handiwork. I wonder who gave him the assignment.'

'You. Who else has such perverted taste? You came into the world some five or six years before me. You told Him to make me for you just before you came. Don't you remember?'

'No. But how do *you* know all this?'

'Because God whispered it in my ear just before packing me off. Have you finished your tea? We'll miss the train if you don't hurry.'

'What if we do?'

'You don't seem very enthusiastic about going. Tell me why.'

'Because I'm afraid of losing you in the crowd.'

'You won't lose me. On the contrary, I may lose you.'

'That isn't desirable either.'

'Don't put me off, please. Let's go. I hear Natun *gosainji* has a room of his own in the *akhra*. The first thing I'll do when I'm there is to break the bolts of the door. As for me—your slave girl will be there for you whenever you want her.'

'Let's go then.'

It was mid-afternoon by the time we reached the *akhra*. Govindaji's *bhog* had just been concluded. We had arrived without any intimation and there were so many of us but the inmates of the *akhra* were delighted to see us. Bara *gosain* was away, I was told, on a visit to his gurudev in Nabadweep and a couple of *bairagis* had taken possession of my room.

'I never dreamed you would come back to us so soon, Natun *gosain*,' Kamal Lata said in a voice thick with emotion.

'He would have come sooner, Kamal Lata Didi,' Rajlakshmi replied for me. From the way she spoke, one might think she had known Kamal Lata all her life. 'I am responsible for the delay. Blame me, if you will.'

Kamal Lata's face reddened at these words and Padma let out a squeal of laughter. From Rajlakshmi's appearance and manner, it was obvious that she was a gentlewoman of good birth and breeding. What the Vaishnavis wanted to know was her connection with me. The intelligent Rajlakshmi perceived this in a moment and proceeded to satisfy their curiosity. 'Do you recognize me, Kamal Lata Didi?' she asked brightly. 'Have you never seen me in Vrindavan?'

The joke was not lost on Kamal Lata. She smiled and answered, 'I don't seem to remember, *bon*.'

'That's just as well, Didi, because I've never been to Vrindavan in all my life. I lived here, in these parts, as a child.' Pointing to me she continued, 'We went to the pathshala together. We were so fond of one another—we were like brother and sister. I called him Dada and he loved me as tenderly as a little sister. He never laid a finger on me!' And, turning to me, she asked, 'Isn't that true?'

'I knew it,' Padma said with her customary giggle. 'That's why you look alike—both tall and slim. Only you are fair and Natun *gosain* is dark. I knew it the minute I saw you.'

'Yes, Padma,' Rajlakshmi replied gravely. 'We have to be alike. There's no other way for us.'

'You know my name?' Padma cried out in wonder. 'Who told you? Natun *gosain*?'

'Yes. That is why I've come to see you. "Take me with you to the *akhra*," I said to your Natun *gosain*. "Your reputation won't suffer with me by your side. And, even if it does, no harm will come to you. The poison will stick in your throat as it did for Neelkanth.[*] It won't spread to the rest of your body."'

'Why do you talk such nonsense?' I asked angrily. 'That too before a child.'

'It isn't nonsense. I'm absolutely serious.'

'Don't believe her, Kamal Lata,' I said. 'She's eternally plotting and planning mischief.'

'Oh I am, am I? Why do you malign me, *gosain*? It must be you who is plotting something—in connection with me.'

'I don't deny it.'

'But I have nothing to do with it. I'm as innocent as a new blown flower.'

Kamal Lata laughed at her manner but I could see that she was bewildered and didn't know what to make of this exchange. I hadn't told her about Rajlakshmi. After all, what had been there to say, then?

'What is your name, *bon*?' she asked after a while.

'My name is Rajlakshmi. Your *gosainji* has dropped the first syllable and shortened it to Lakshmi. I had no name for him till you gave him one. He tells me to call him Natun *gosain* these days. "I'll feel better if you do," he says.'

Padma laughed and clapped her hands. 'I know what that means,' she said happily.

Kamal Lata glared at her. 'What do you know, you nitwit?'

'I know. I know. Shall I tell?'

'There's no need. Run along now.' Then, taking Rajlakshmi's hand, she said, 'It is very late, *bon*, and you look tired and hungry. Wash your hands and feet and come to the shrine. Then we'll partake of prasad together. You, too, Natun *gosain*.'

The crucial moment was upon us and I waited, tense with inner conflict. Rajlakshmi's mania for purity and sanctity, particularly where food was in question, had become so much a part of her that logic and reason held no ground before it. It wasn't a question of belief—it was habit, pure and simple. Her set of

---

[*]   See Glossary.

standards was for herself alone. She didn't expect it of others, least of all, me. Whenever I reported some particularly unholy or unscriptural conduct of mine (as I enjoyed doing) she would cover her ears and pretend not to hear, or laugh and shake her head. 'Honestly! I don't know what I've done to deserve you. You'll drag me to hell at this rate.'

But the situation here was different. Here she was up against a group of intensely religious beings who had given up the world and embraced a doctrine of love and brotherhood. Caste and its hierarchy meant nothing to them for, in their code, birth was an accident and the past insignificant. What mattered was the present—the association of a group of people drawn together by a religion of love. No one had, to this day, insulted them by refusing to partake of Govindaji's prasad. If such a thing happened, and through me, I could never hold my head up again. I knew Kamal Lata. She would not utter a word of reproach. Nor would she allow me to explain. She would hold my eyes with her own for a brief moment before walking away. And her unspoken comment would sear my soul!

'Come, Natun *gosain*,' Padma came to call me. 'Have you had your wash? They're all waiting for you. Prasad is being served.'

'What is the prasad today, Padma?'

'Today is Govindaji's *anna bhog*.*'

'Worse and worse,' I thought. Aloud I said, 'Where are you taking me?'

'To the eastern veranda. Your *thala* has been laid beside Babaji *moshai*'s. We women will eat later. Rajlakshmi Didi is to serve us.'

'Isn't she going to eat with you?'

'No. She's a Brahmin. She'll lose caste if she eats anything touched by Boshtoms like us.'

'Did she tell you that?'

'Yes.'

'Wasn't your Kamal Lata Didi offended?'

'No. Why should she be? She laughed and said,"In our next birth we'll be born sisters and we'll eat together from the same *thala*. And if you brag about your caste, then, and try to be saucy, Ma will box your ears."'

---

* A rice offering.

I was pleased at Rajlakshmi's discomfiture. She had met her match at last.

'What was her reply?' I asked Padma.

'Rajlakshmi Didi laughed too. "Why should Ma box my ears, Didi?" she said. "You'll be the older sister. You may punish me as you will."'

On seeing them together I found that this little exchange hadn't soured their relationship. If anything, it had helped to forge a mutual bond that was pleasing to behold. Bara *gosain* arrived by the evening train, a group of babajis with him. Bara *gosain* was pleased to see me but not the others. One couldn't blame them for they were all, without exception, wholeheartedly, even ostentatiously, Vaishnav, with intricately marked noses and foreheads. One was a famous kirtaniya (so I was told) and another—an expert on the mridanga.

The meal over, I walked down to my favourite haunt in the woods. Pushing my way across great stretches of reeds and brambles that tore at my skin, I came upon the sun setting over the dying river. I sat on the bank watching the scene but not for long for somewhere, near at hand, a clump of the bulbous *andhar manik** was opening its petals and the stench of putrid flesh came to my nostrils with every gust of wind. I returned to the *akhra* wondering why poets rated flowers so highly. If someone were to send them a bunch of *andhar manik* as a gift, what would they feel?

Padma met me as I entered and said, 'You love to hear kirtans, don't you, *gosain*? Manohar Das Babaji will sing to us tonight after Govindaji's arati. He has a wonderful voice. You've never heard anything like it before.'

'I've loved the *padavalis*** of Vaishnav poets from my childhood, Padma. I find them more melodious than any other music in the world. As a child I would walk miles and brave every kind of punishment to hear the songs of kirtaniyas. Won't you be singing tonight, Kamal Lata?'

'No, *gosain*. I have hardly any training. Singing before a great

---

* A wild flower with a foul smell.
** Religious verses—usually sung.

master like Manohar Das Babaji would be impertinent of me. Besides, my voice is not what it used to be. My throat was affected by the fever and is still heavy and hoarse.'

'But Lakshmi must hear you sing. She thinks I exaggerate—'

'I'm sure you do, *gosain,*' Kamal Lata blushed and turned to Rajlakshmi. 'I'll sing, whatever little I know, some other time, *bon.*'

'Do that,' Rajlakshmi smiled. 'Just send me word when you are ready and I'll come to you myself. One other thing. Tell Bara *gosain* that I would like to sing tonight—after Babaji *moshai's* kirtan—'

Kamal Lata shook her head doubtfully and said, 'I wonder if that would be wise. The Babajis are very particular—'

'There's no harm in taking the name of God—surely. No one could be more particular than my Durbasha muni* here,' she laughed, pointing at me. 'I'm not nervous of Radha Govinda or of the Babajis but I am of him.'

'You'll get a reward from me if you pass the test,' I said.

'*Ma go*! Don't give me any rewards please. Not in front of all these people. I don't trust you. You're capable of anything.'

The Vaishnavis giggled at her words and little Padma clapped her hands and sang joyfully, 'I know what that means.'

'Be quiet, you silly girl,' Kamal Lata scolded her tenderly. 'Take her away. One never knows what she'll say next.'

The singing commenced at dusk. The open space outside the shrine was packed with people from the neighbouring villages: *bairagis* and Vaishnavs for the most part. The inmates of the *akhra* sat at one end, guests and outsiders at the other. In the centre, under a blaze of hanging lamps, Manohar Das Babaji and his musicians sat, ready for their performance. The young Vaishnav who had dislodged me was to play the harmonium. The harmonium and mridanga belonged to the *akhra,* and were brought out on occasions like this one. Word had gone around that a young woman of high birth and surpassing beauty had arrived from Calcutta and that she would be singing devotional songs in praise of Radha Govinda. People whispered to one another about her wealth, the servants she had brought with her, the goods she had donated to the *akhra*

---

*   See Glossary.

and the young man who was her companion, one Natun *gosain*—a compulsive rover, born and bred in these parts.

Babaji had not yet concluded his prefatory verses in praise of Lord Chaitanya when Rajlakshmi made an appearance. There was a hum of awed whispers from the crowd. Babaji's voice shook a little and the mridanga player nearly missed a beat. Only Dwarika Das Babaji sat, immobile as a statue, eyes closed, back resting against a pillar. Rajlakshmi wore a sari of midnight blue whose intricately woven border of silver threads blended and became one with her powder blue blouse of fine silk. The same choice jewels hung upon her person but the sandal and saffron of her forehead had got rubbed off. Only the faintest traces remained, pale and glimmering like the mist on an autumn morn. She walked straight past me without deigning to throw a glance in my direction but her lips were curved in a smile—or so I imagined.

That evening, Manohar Das Babaji failed to command the attention he usually did. The fault did not lie in his singing but in the audience, who were all eagerness to hear Rajlakshmi. Dwarika Das Babaji turned to her and said, 'Come, Didi, sing something for my Radha Govinda,' then, pointing to the *khol* (drum), he asked, 'That won't be in the way, will it?'

'No.' Rajlakshmi took her place composedly, facing the shrine. Her answer took the Babajis by surprise for they hadn't expected such a degree of skill from a mere woman. But there was a greater surprise in store for them. A gasp rose from the audience as the rich, pure tones of a Vaishnav *padavali* cascaded from her throat with the force and clarity of a mountain stream. She had a naturally melodious voice and was rigorously trained in the classical music of the north. But I never knew that she had mastered this particular tradition of the devotional music of Bengal. Her intonation was perfect, her rhythm masterly and her diction unflawed. But there was more—much more. She sang, not with her voice alone, but with every fibre of her being. Her Radha Govinda were in front of her, her Durbasha muni behind her and I knew not for whom she sang these lines:

E ke pada pankaja, panke bibhushita
Kantake jara jara bhel
Tua darashana asi kachhu nahi janulu

Chira dukho aba dure gel
Tohari murali jaha shravane prabeshilo
Chhorunu griha sukho as
Panthaka dukho tunhu kari na ganunu
Kahe tahin Govinda Das....

(Earth and slime adorn my lotus feet
Thorns tear them to shreds
At the hope of a glimpse of your wondrous form
All pain is gone; all sorrow's spent
I left my home and kin for ever
The day your flute's melodious strain
Entered my ears, my long dark path
Is naught to me, so says Govinda Das.)

Tears of ecstasy rolled down Dwarika Das Babaji's cheeks. He stood up, swaying on his feet and, walking over to the shrine, took the thick garland of mallika flowers from Govindaji's neck and put it around Rajlakshmi's. 'May all that is dark in your life be wiped away,' he said. 'May only truth and light guide you on your way.'

Rajlakshmi bent her head in acceptance of his blessing then, rising, she came to me and touched the dust of my feet to her brow in everyone's presence. Lowering her head she whispered, 'This garland is yours. If you hadn't threatened me with a reward, I would have put in round your neck, here and now.'

While prasad was being distributed, I took her aside and said, 'Keep the garland carefully. I won't wear it here. Put it around my neck when we get home.'

'Are you afraid of wearing it here because this is a place of God? Are you afraid that it will bind you in some way?'

'No. I have no fears left. They've all been wiped away. If I had the world in my possession I would have laid it at your feet, tonight, Lakshmi.'

'How generous of you! You know very well that whatever you give me will remain yours.'

'Thank you a million times for this day, Lakshmi.'

'Why do you say that?'

'Because today I know for certain how little I deserve you. I'm no match for you in anything—beauty, brains, accomplishments, love, passion, tenderness. What God has given me, he has given no one in the world. I'm humbly and truly grateful to you, Lakshmi.'

'I don't like such talk—'

'You've thrown yourself away on an unworthy person. I don't know where to keep this priceless treasure.'

'Are you afraid someone will steal it if you're not careful.'

'No, Lakshmi. No one would dare do that. Where would the thief, poor fellow, find a storehouse large enough to contain you?'

Rajlakshmi took my hand and laid it on her breast without a word. Then she said, 'The Vaishnavis will laugh if they see us whispering together in the dark. But I'm worried about something. Where will you sleep tonight?'

'They'll make some arrangement. You needn't worry.'

'I wonder what arrangement they'll make. Everything is so disorganized here.'

Things were disorganized with the sudden arrival of so many people. A bed was made for me in the veranda. Rajlakshmi grumbled about it but could do nothing. I'm sure she checked on me several times during the night but, tired with the journey and the varied events of the day, I slept like a log and knew nothing.

On waking up the next morning, I saw Rajlakshmi and Kamal Lata enter the *akhra* with baskets heaped with flowers. I don't know what passed between them in the privacy of the flower garden but the look on their faces removed the last of my fears. Peace flooded my soul. They had slept together the night before (the difference in their castes had not presented itself as an obstacle) and today they behaved as though they had known each other all their lives. Referring to yesterday's incident, when Rajlakshmi had refused to eat anything touched by her, Kamal Lata laughed and said, 'Don't let that worry you, *gosain*. I've found a way to punish her. I'll box her ears soundly in our next birth for I'll be the older sister.'

'I've agreed to that on one condition, *gosain*,' Rajlakshmi retaliated. 'If I die first she'll have to leave the *akhra* and come and look after you. I know I'll have no peace, even in heaven, worrying about you. Like the old demon in Sindbad's story, I'll sit on her back and make her do whatever I want.'

'*Ma go*! I can't carry you on my back, *bon*. So you'd better not think of dying first.'

After drinking my tea I went out to look for Gahar. 'Come back as soon as you can and bring Gahar *gosain* with you,' Kamal Lata said. 'I've got hold of a Brahmin cook, this morning, to prepare the *bhog*. Rajlakshmi is helping him. She'll have a hard time for he is as dirty as he is lazy.'

'You've made this hew arrangement for Rajlakshmi's sake. But I doubt if Govindaji will approve—'

'Don't say that,' Kamal Lata bit her tongue and shook her head. 'If Rajlakshmi hears it she won't let a drop of water pass through her lips.'

'You met her only yesterday. Yet you understand her perfectly,' I smiled.

'Yes. I do understand her. She is one in a million. You are a lucky man, *gosain*.'

Gahar was not at home. I was informed by Nabin that he had gone over to Sunam village where his maternal cousin—a widowed woman with many children—lived. A strange, new fever had appeared in those parts and was devastating the villages. Some of her children had been afflicted and Gahar had gone over to help her out. It was over a fortnight now but not a word had come from him. Nabin was distracted with worry but hadn't a clue to where the village was. Suddenly, he burst out weeping—great, racking sobs shaking his chest. 'He may be dying, Babu, and I'm sitting here doing nothing. I'm an ignorant, unlettered peasant. I don't know where to go or what to do. I keep begging Chakravarty *moshai* to accompany me to Sunam village—I even offered him a hundred rupees—but the rascally Brahmin refuses to budge an inch. But I tell you this, Babu. If my master dies I'll set fire to his house and burn him alive even if I have to jump into the flames myself. Such a base ingrate should not be allowed to live.'

'Do you know the name of the zila, Nabin?'

Nabin shook his head. 'All I know is that it is somewhere near Nadia and that the village is situated several kos away from the railway station. One has to reach it by bullock-cart. The old man knows but he refuses to tell.'

I told Nabin to bring me all the old letters and papers he could lay his hands upon but the examination yielded no result. Only one significant fact came to light. Nayan Chand Chakravarty had borrowed two hundred rupees from Gahar to get his widowed daughter remarried, two months ago. Gahar was a simpleton with a lot of money. Such people are the natural prey of cheats and swindlers. Resentment was useless. But I had to agree with Nabin that the extent of the old man's villainy was rarely to be seen.

'He wants my master to die,' Nabin said. 'Then he won't have to pay back a paisa.'

I couldn't deny his logic but, there being nothing else to do, I took him along with me to Chakravarty *moshai's* house. Such a kindly, humble, sympathetic, decent old soul was never to be found! But old age had afflicted him so grievously, had robbed him of his memory so ruthlessly that he could remember nothing—not the name of the zila nor the direction nor the name of the station.

I got hold of a railway guide and read out the names of all the stations in North and East Bengal but not one of them rang a bell. It grieved him excessively and he shook his head in self-pity. 'I'm an old man, Baba, and my powers are failing me. People cheat me in so many ways. They borrow money and household articles but nothing is returned. I can't recall who took what. I'm resigned to my fate. "God is watching everybody," I say to myself, "and He will dispense justice. He will give the righteous their due.'

Nabin could bear it no longer. 'Yes,' he roared, 'He will dispense justice. If He doesn't, I will.'

Chakravarty clicked his tongue gently and shook his head. 'Don't distrust me, Nabin. I'm an old man with a foot already on the road to heaven. Am I likely to tell a lie? Besides, don't I love Gahar as my own son?'

'I don't know all that. I'm asking you for the last time. Will you or will you not take me to my master? If you don't and anything happens to him—remember that you have me to reckon with.'

Chakravarty *moshai* tapped his forehead with a shaking hand. 'Destiny,' he moaned. 'All is preordained. If it were not so would you be standing here talking to me in that tone of voice?'

We returned—defeated. I waited outside his door for a while in the hope that he might, in a moment of repentance, come out and tell us what we wanted to know. But nothing of the kind happened. I glanced within, for the door was ajar, and saw him pick up his discarded hookah and proceed to pack it with tobacco, his countenance as calm and benign as it always was.

It was three o'clock in the afternoon when I returned to the *akhra*. The Babajis were not to be seen. I guessed that, worn out with the effort of swallowing the enormous meal of prasad that was habitual with them, they were enjoying a prolonged siesta with true ascetic fervour. The same amount of time and energy would be required at night. No wonder they needed to recharge themselves. A little knot of women huddled around someone on the veranda. Looking over their shoulders, I saw that it was an astrologer complete with almanac, slate, pencils, chalk and other essentials of his trade.

Padma was the first to see me. 'There's Natun *gosain*,' she cried.

Kamal Lata looked up eagerly. 'I knew Gahar *gosain* wouldn't let you come away without a meal. What did you have?'

Rajlakshmi clapped her hand on the Vaishnavi's mouth. 'Don't, Didi,' she begged, 'don't ask him that—for God's sake.'

Kamal Lata removed the restraining hand gently but firmly and said, 'You look hot and tired and your hair is full of dust. Have you had a bath?'

Nabin had begged me, many times, to have a bath and a meal in the house but, needless to say, I had refused.

'Ganak Thakur tells me that I have a great future. I shall be a queen some day,' Lakshmi informed me, mightily pleased.

'How much did you give him?'

'Five rupees,' Padma answered for her.

'If you had given them to me I would have predicted something better for you.'

The astrologer was an Oriya Brahmin but he knew Bengali and spoke it well. He smiled at my words and said, 'No, *moshai*! It wasn't the money. I earn enough, in my profession, to keep me in comfort. Her hand is unique. I haven't seen one like it in all my years of fortune-telling. Mark my words, I won't be proved wrong.'

'Can you tell me something I want to know without looking at my palm?'

'I can. Take the name of a flower.'

'*Simul* (silk-cotton).'

The astrologer laughed. 'So be it,' he said, and proceeded to draw a number of lines and figures on his slate. Then he looked up and said, 'You are worried about something. You are looking for information.'

'What kind of information?'

He looked me in the eye and said, 'No. It has nothing to do

with a court case. You want to know the whereabouts of a certain person.'

'Can you tell me, Thakur?'

'I can tell you that he is alive and will return home in a couple of days. There's no cause for worry.'

I must admit that his answer startled me. It must have shown in my face for Rajlakshmi exclaimed triumphantly, 'I told you, he is a very good astrologer. But you are such a sceptic.'

Kamal Lata rushed to my defence. 'He's not,' she said. 'Show your palm to Ganak Thakur, *gosain*.'

I stretched out my hand. The astrologer took it in his and studied it carefully. Then, making his calculations, he looked up gravely. 'You have a bad time ahead of you, *moshai*.'

'A bad time? When?'

'Very soon now. It's a question of life and death.'

I looked at Rajlakshmi. She was as white as a sheet. The astrologer turned to her and said, 'Let me have another look at your palm, Ma.'

But, this time, Rajlakshmi turned on him and snapped, 'No. I've no need of your predictions.' Her sudden, violent change of mood was obvious and the wily astrologer knew that his shaft had gone home.

'I'm only a mirror, Ma,' he said humbly. 'The future is reflected in me and my mouth utters what the inner eye sees. That's all. But it is possible to dilute the influence of evil planets. There are certain rituals for which a little money is required. A paltry ten or twenty rupees.' Rajlakshmi did not reply. It was obvious that though she had full faith in the man's prediction, she had grave doubts about his ability to get around the planets.

'Come, Natun *gosain*,' Kamal Lata said. 'It is time you had your tea.'

'I'll make it,' Rajlakshmi rose hastily. 'Where is Ratan? I haven't seen a hair of his head since yesterday. Ask him to prepare a hookah, Didi.'

Ratan dusted the string-cot on the southern veranda, brought me water to wash and prepared a hookah, his face red and indignant. He hadn't had a moment's rest since yesterday and his mistress complained that she hadn't seen a hair of his head! If I were to tell him of the Rahu that threatened to swallow me up in the near future he would, I'm convinced, have answered, 'No, Babu. Not you. It is I who am about to be swallowed up and I know by whom.'

I was telling Kamal Lata about Gahar's disappearance when Rajlakshmi came in with the tea. She put the cup down on a stool and said, 'I've told you, again and again, not to wander about in the woods alone. Who knows what might happen? I beg you with folded hands—listen to me, please.' She must have thought this up while making the tea. For, what else could happen 'very soon'?

Kamal Lata looked up, surprised. 'When has *gosain* been wandering about in the woods?'

'How do I know? Is it possible for me to keep a watch on him every minute of the day? Have I nothing else to do?'

'She hasn't seen anything. She only assumes it,' I said, irritably. 'That son of an astrologer has made life hell for me.'

Ratan smirked and walked away hastily and Rajlakshmi turned on me. 'Why do you blame the astrologer? He only told us what he saw on your palm. Haven't you heard of such things before? Have you never seen anyone going through a bad phase?'

There was no point in arguing with her, so I didn't. Neither did Kamal Lata. Rajlakshmi looked sharply at me for a minute and asked, 'Why are your eyes so red? Have you been bathing in the river?'

'No. I haven't bathed at all today.'

'Have you been eating anything you shouldn't?'

'I haven't eaten anything at all. I wasn't hungry.'

Rajlakshmi hurried to my side and laid a hand on my brow. Then, feeling my chest under the shirt, she exclaimed, 'Just what I thought! Touch him and see, Kamal Didi. He's very warm—'

Kamal Lata stayed where she was and answered composedly, 'What if he is? Why do you worry?'

'He has fever—'

'If he has fever we'll do something about it. You have come to us. You are our responsibility.'

Her cool measured tones and matter-of-fact manner shamed Rajlakshmi into exercising a measure of self-control. 'I know that,' she said awkwardly. 'Only there are no doctors and I've noticed that his fevers always turn serious at some stage. Besides, that sour-faced astrologer has frightened me so—'

'You shouldn't allow anyone to frighten you.'

'You're right, Kamal Didi. But I've noticed something about astrologers. When their predictions are good they never come true but when they are bad—God help us!'

'Don't be afraid, Raju.' Kamal Lata smiled kindly at her. 'It won't come true this time. *Gosain* has been out all afternoon and has got a touch of the sun. That's all. He'll be as fit as any of us by tomorrow morning.'

At this moment Lalur Ma appeared with the message that Rajlakshmi's presence was urgently required in the kitchen. Rajlakshmi hastened away but not before throwing a grateful glance towards Kamal Lata.

Kamal Lata was right. The fever left me, not the next morning but in a couple of days. But our secret was out. Kamal Lata understood how things were between us and so did Bara *gosain*.

Kamal Lata sent for us the day we were to leave the *akhra*. There was a *thala* by her side with a pair of garlands and bowl of sandal paste on it which, I guessed rightly, had been brought in from the shrine.

'Do you remember the year you got married, *gosain*?' she asked.

'He remembers nothing,' Rajlakshmi answered for me. 'Ask me.'

'Isn't it strange that one should remember and the other forget?'

'It happened in our childhood. He was very young—'

'But he is older than you, Raju.'

'Only five or six years older,' Rajlakshmi said carelessly. 'I was eight or nine then. One day, I put a garland around his neck and said to myself, "From this day onwards you are my husband." I said it three times. But this monster stood right where he was and ate up my garland.'

'Ate up your garland? Did you eat flowers in your childhood, *gosain*?' the Vaishnavi laughed, unbelieving.

'It was a garland of ripe *bainchis*,' I answered. 'Anyone would've eaten it.'

'From that moment onwards my troubles started,' Rajlakshmi took up her tale again. 'I lost sight of him and—don't ask me the rest, Didi. People say so many things and think so many things.

None of them are true. I only know that I wept and prayed day and night and, at last, God took pity on me. He gave back to me what He had taken.' She turned her face in the direction of the shrine and shut her eyes. Her lips moved as though she uttered a prayer of thanksgiving.

'His garlands and sandal are before you, *bon*. Put them on one another before you leave the *akhra*.'

But Rajlakshmi shook her head and folded her hands in supplication. 'I don't know about him,' she said, 'but I can't obey you in this, Kamal Didi. Whenever I close my eyes I see my red garland swaying on his youthful breast. I want that image to remain the eternal one.'

'But I ate up that garland,' I said.

'Yes, Mr Monster, you did. Now eat *me* up if that will fill your stomach.' And, laughing, she dipped her fingers in the bowl of sandal paste and smeared it all over my face.

We went to take leave of Bara *gosain*. He looked up from the book he was reading and welcomed us warmly.

'We have very little time, *gosain*,' Rajlakshmi said, dropping down on the floor. 'We've come to say goodbye and to beg forgiveness for all the trouble we've caused you.'

'We are *bairagis, bon*. We are not used to others begging from us. But when do you propose to trouble us again? Let it be soon for the *akhra* will become dark and lonesome without you.' Kamal Lata smiled and nodded her head in agreement and Bara *gosain* went on, 'The last few days were some of the happiest days of my life, *bon*. You are a veritable spirit of joy. You shower love, happiness, song and laughter wherever you go. Your presence illumined our little hermitage with the power and force of lightning.' He stopped, then pointed to me and said, 'Kamal Lata calls him, Natun *gosain*. I shall call you Anandamayee.'

I had to interrupt this flow of rhetoric. 'You've only seen the lightning of your Anandamayee's eyes. You haven't heard the thunder of her voice as I do all day long Ratan is here before us. Ask him, if you don't believe me.'

Ratan fled in embarrassment and Rajlakshmi said coolly, 'Don't believe a word of what he is saying, *gosain*. He's jealous of me—that's all.' She glanced witheringly in my direction and went on, 'I don't get a moment's peace with this sickly, boring creature hanging around me day and night. I shall keep him locked up at home when I come next.'

'You'll never do that, Anandamayee. You won't be able to.'

'I will. I get so exasperated sometimes—I wish I could die.'

'Such a wish was expressed by Radha Rani in Vrindavan, many a time. But she couldn't die for who would look after her Kanu? Don't you remember the song:

Sakhi kare diye jabo?
Tara Kanu sebar ki ba jane?

(Friend! In whose care shall I leave my Kanu?
Can anyone serve him the way I do?)

'How little we know of love! Most of the time we only delude ourselves. But you are different. You have known true love. You have felt it in your heart. If only you could surrender what you have at Sri Krishna's feet—'

'Don't wish that for me, *gosain*!' Rajlakshmi shuddered. 'Pray, rather, that I live out my life as ordinary people do and leave him alive and well when I go.'

I understood Rajlakshmi! I knew that the guilt and pain of casting me off still lay on her heart like a weary burden and that she lived, from moment to moment, in fear of a terrible retribution. I wanted to soothe her fears away so I said, lightly, 'Taunt my poor, sickly body all you can. You haven't a clue to its hidden powers. It is indestructible. I'm certainly not going to die before you.'

Rajlakshmi gripped my hand and cried feverishly, 'Swear before all these people that what you said is true. Swear it thrice.' Her eyes swam and large tears rolled down her cheeks. Everyone stared at her—shocked at her vehemence. She released my hand, quickly, and laughed awkwardly. 'That old fraud of an astrologer has made me so nervous—' She dabbed at her eyes and laughed, unable to complete her sentence.

We took leave of everyone in the *akhra*. Bara *gosain* promised to visit us and to bring Padma, who had never seen the city, with him. On reaching the station, the first person we set eyes on was the 'sour-faced astrologer' of Rajlakshmi's description. He sat on a piece of blanket in the centre of the platform, a group of people around him.

'Is he to go with us?' I asked Rajlakshmi.

She nodded but averted her face to hide her embarrassment.

'No, he is not,' I said, firmly.

'Why not? He won't do any harm even if he can't do any good.'

'I don't care about what he can do—good or bad. Give him whatever you promised and get rid of him. If he really has the power to appease the planets he can do it here, where we won't see him.'

'I'll tell him that.' Rajlakshmi commanded Ratan to bring the man to her. I don't know what she gave him or what she said but he nodded his head many times and looked pleased. The train arrived in a few minutes and we set off on our journey back to the city.

Twelve

RAJLAKSHMI'S CROSS-QUESTIONING FORCED ME TO REVEAL THE source of my new found wealth. The facts of the case were as follows. While in Burma, a racing enthusiast who was an officer of mine had borrowed my savings, on the promise that I would get fifty per cent of his gains, if any, over and above the interest accrued thereon. On my return to Calcutta I found a registered parcel containing four times the amount I had loaned out, waiting for me.

'What is the amount?' Rajlakshmi probed.

'A fortune to me but a mere trifle to you.'

'Still, how much is it?'

'Eight thousand.'

'You must give it to me.'

'Aré! I thought Lakshmi was a giver—not a taker.'

'Lakshmi doesn't approve of squandering money. She doesn't trust fakirs and sanyasis. They are worthless wastrels, in her opinion. Bring me the money.'

'What will you do with it?'

'I'll spend it on myself. From this day onwards it will be the sole means of my support.'

'The sum is too small. You can't even pay your servants' salaries out of it—let alone Gurudev, your widows in Benaras and your hundred and one charities.'

'I'm not speaking of them. I'm speaking of my own day-to-day living.'

'This is another of your self-delusions, Lakshmi.'

'It isn't. I'm not giving up my own money. That will be used for all my other expenditure. But I will live on what you give me. If it is enough, well and good. If not—I'll starve.'

'Then you'd better make up your mind to starve.'

Rajlakshmi laughed. 'You think it is a small amount. But I know the secret of making a little go a long way. I've often wanted to tell you how I made my money but I couldn't because of the way you clam up the moment I mention my past. But, one day, you'll realize that your preconceptions are totally without foundation.'

'Why didn't you tell me that before?'

'Because you wouldn't have believed me. You won't touch my money because you think it is tainted. Yet you've never asked me for the truth.'

'Then why do you talk of it today, all of a sudden?' I cried, hurt by her allegation.

'It may be sudden to you. It isn't to me. It is a thought that torments me day and night. Do you really believe me capable of using money earned in sin in the service of my gods? Or for your welfare? Could I have saved your life, over and over again, if I had done anything so vile? God would have taken you away again, I'm convinced of it. But you don't trust me. You don't believe me to be truly yours.'

'I do.'

'No, you don't. You had barely met Kamal Lata, yet you gave her a patient hearing. You allowed her to share the most intimate details of her shameful past with you and, in doing so, relieved her of the burden she had carried for years. You released her from the pain of memory. But I, whom you've known from childhood, what have you ever done for me? Have you ever asked me for the truth about myself? You haven't. Why? Because you distrust and fear me. Because you distrust yourself.'

'I didn't ask her to tell me anything. She compelled me to listen.'

'You didn't ask her because she was a stranger. Her life was not tied up with yours in any way. Would you say the same of me?'

'No, I wouldn't. But are you Kamal Lata's disciple? Do you have to pour out your woes before me simply because she did?'

'Don't try to put me off. I insist on telling you.'

'Was ever a man plagued so? I don't want to hear—yet I must.'

'You may stop loving me. You may even cast me off but hear me you must.'

'Why do you force me to take these difficult decisions?'

'You are a man,' Rajlakshmi laughed. 'Don't you have the strength of mind to cast me off if you think it right?'

I confessed my lack of strength with a humility that would have melted any woman's heart. 'Lakshmi,' I said, 'don't make the mistake of counting me among the men of your acquaintance. They are iron men with hearts of steel and I esteem them highly. But I am human and weak. I dare not cast you off for fear that you'll really go away. And then, what will become of me? Is it not better to leave things as they are?'

'You may have heard,' Rajlakshmi went on inexorably, 'that my mother sold me in childhood to a Maithili prince.'

'Yes. I heard another prince mention the fact many years later. He was my friend.'

'One day I lost my temper and threw her out. She went back to the village and spread the news of my death. You must have heard of my death in Kashi.'

'Yes I did.'

'What did you feel?'

'I felt—sad. "Poor Lakshmi!" I said to myself. "She died young."'

'Just that and nothing more?'

'Not just that. "She's fortunate to have died in Kashi," I thought. "Her soul is already on its way to heaven. Poor Lakshmi!"'

'I don't believe a word. "Poor Lakshmi" indeed! I'm sure you didn't waste a moment's thought on me. Swear on my head that you did.'

'It was so long ago,' I said hastily. 'I don't remember exactly. That is what I must have felt.'

'You felt nothing of the sort. You don't have to reconstruct the past for my benefit. I know what you felt well enough.' She paused for a moment and continued, 'And I? I wept day and night and prayed unceasingly to Lord Vishwanath. "Why do you punish me so cruelly?" I cried, over and over again. "Am I to live this life of shame to the end of my days? Am I to lose him whom I took for my husband even before my heart and soul were fully awakened?"'

I can't bear to think of those days, even now. Memory is so painful! 'I'd die, willingly, if death would blot it out.'

I glanced at the tense, pale face and felt my heart constrict with pain. I wanted to stop her from undertaking the nightmarish journey into the past, but I lacked the power. I understood her completely. Her memories had tormented her night and day but she hadn't dared to share them with me for fear of losing the little she had gained. But her association with Kamal Lata had strengthened her. She was determined, today, to lay down her burden of memories, as Kamal Lata had done, and so win her release. She would burst the shackles of fear that bound her and stand revealed before me even if it cost her her love. Kamal Lata was the only one before whom this proud, arrogant woman had bowed her head and begged humbly for a way out of the darkness that stifled her soul. I saw this in my mind's eye as clearly as in the clear light of day and peace and contentment filled my heart at the thought.

After a brief silence, Rajlakshmi took up her tale again. 'After the prince's death—he died suddenly—Ma secretly conspired to sell me again.'

'To whom?'

'To another prince. That gem of a friend of yours—don't you remember?'

'Not very well. It was so long ago. What happened then?'

'The plot was discovered. I told Ma to go back home. "I've taken a thousand rupees as an advance," she cried. "You may keep the touting fee," I told her. "I'll repay it to the last paisa. But if you don't leave by the night train I'll sell myself to Ma Ganga. By daybreak, tomorrow, you'll only have my corpse left to do what you like with. You know me, Ma. I don't make idle threats." Ma went back to the village and spread the news of my death, on hearing which you sighed and said, "Poor Lakshmi! She died young."' She laughed a little and continued, Had your sigh come from the heart it would have been enough for me, then. But today, I want more from you. I want you to shed a few tears for me when I'm really and truly dead. I want you to say to yourself, "Everyday, since the world began, thousands of lovers exchange garlands and vows of constancy. But no love in the past, present or future can compare with my poor, unchaste, unfulfilled Lakshmi's love. Not one heart in the world can match the constancy of the nine-year-old one that beat for me alone to the day of her death." Will you whisper these words in my ear? I'll hear them even after I'm gone.'

'Why, Lakshmi! You're crying.'

She wiped her streaming eyes with the end of her sari and continued, 'Do you think God didn't see how a helpless child was tormented by her own mother? Will he not dispense justice?'

'He should. But religious people like you understand God and his ways better than I do. In any case, He is not likely to listen to a heretic like me even if I request Him to do so.'

'You must joke about everything!' She thought for a minute and said, 'People say that a man and a woman cannot live together unless they share a common faith. We share nothing yet we manage to live together. How?'

'We live a snake-and-mongoose life, threatening to kill one another every minute. But since killing is punishable by law we torture each other in so many different ways. One banishes the other out of a fear that he will become a hurdle on her path to heaven.'

'What happens then?'

'Then she realizes that she's made a terrible mistake. She weeps and beats her breast and begs forgiveness.'

'Is she forgiven?'

'Yes. But go on with your story.'

'An old Bengali ustad of Kashi—I called him Dada Moshai— used to come to the house to give me singing lessons. He had been a sanyasi once but had abandoned the saffron robes many years ago and married a Mussalman woman. This lady was a celebrated dancer and taught me all I know about dance. They loved me as tenderly as if I was their own daughter and I trusted them implicitly. "Dada Moshai!" I begged. "Let us run away from here. I can't live this kind of life anymore." He was a poor man and was reluctant to take the risk. "I have a lot of money with me," I said. "It will last us a long time. After that—He will provide. We must put our faith in Him." We wandered all over the country. We went to Allahabad, Lucknow, Delhi, Agra, Jaipur, Mathura and finally settled down in Patna. Half the money I loaned out, at a high rate of interest, to a usurer and the other half I invested in a cloth and cosmetics business. I bought a house and had Banku brought over from the village. And how I earned my living—you've seen with your own eyes.'

I was silent for a long while. Then I said, 'I believe this story because *you* are telling it. If it were anyone else I would have dismissed it as fiction.'

'Can't I cook up a story?'

'You can, I suppose. Only I don't believe that you are capable of deceiving me.'

'Why do you trust me so implicitly?'

'Because I know you, Lakshmi. You would live in mortal fear of some harm coming to me had you deceived me. You wouldn't be worried for yourself—only for me.'

'How do you know that? This fear haunts me day and night—it doesn't haunt you.'

'Would you be happy if it did?'

'No. I wouldn't ever want you to share my pain. I'm your slave. Don't think of me as anything else.'

'Hopeless!' I exclaimed in exasperation. 'You should have been born a thousand years ago—in the age of Sita and Savitri and the other chaste women of our myths.'

'Yes. I should have. I feel closer to them than to the women of today. You admire modern women and think you understand them but I know them better than you do. Try exchanging me with one of them. You'll come back in a week, weeping and beating your breast—as you accused me of doing a little while ago.'

'The argument is purely hypothetical. You know, very well, that I won't exchange you with anybody. But you're being excessively unjust to the modern woman, Lakshmi!'

'Even if I'm being unjust, it's not excessively so. I'm not blind, *gosain*, and I haven't lived in a well. I've travelled a lot, seen a lot. In fact, if you have one pair of eyes, I have ten.'

'Maybe, but since they're all fitted with coloured glasses, none of them are to be trusted.'

'If I wasn't so stupidly bound to you, I would have taught you the lesson of a lifetime. But, shame me all you can, I *will* follow in the footsteps of the "chaste women of our myths" as you call them. Serving you will be my highest duty. You've wasted a lot of your time and energy on this worthless slave. You shan't any more. You are a man. There is a great deal for you to do, to achieve.'

'That is why I wish to get back to my job as soon as possible.'

'I won't let you take up a job.'

'Then what'll I do? I can't run a cosmetics business!'

'Why not?'

'I'm hopeless at figures. I can't remember the prices of things and I can't make quick calculations. Your business will collapse if I am in charge. I may even get into a fight with your customers.'

'Open a cloth shop, then.'

'I'd rather open a shop of wild animals. I'd get along better with lions and tigers.'

Rajlakshmi burst out laughing. 'What a lazy good-for-nothing God gave me—after all my prayers and entreaties. What use are you to me?'

'Your prayers couldn't have come from the heart or they wouldn't have rebounded on you as they have done. However, nothing is lost. There is plenty of time for another try. You may get the man you deserve, yet. A strong man—tough as a betelnut; a man no one can get the better of; a yes-man who never learned the word 'no'; a man who can look after himself and you and your money; a man who never falls sick, never gets lost, never—'

'Stop! Stop!' Rajlakshmi cried, shuddering and covering up her ears.

'Why? What's the matter?'

'The picture you drew terrified me so! I'd die of fear if even half of what you said came true.'

'But what will you do with me?'

'What can I do but curse God and die a million deaths? What else have I done with you all these years?'

'Why don't you send me to the *akhra* at Muraripur?'

'The Vaishnavis will have no use for you either.'

'I'll pick flowers for them at dawn. I'll weave garlands for Radha Govinda and live on their prasad. And, when I die, they'll bury me under the bakul tree. Every evening, at dusk, Padma will light a lamp over my grave but, being young and playful, she will forget—sometimes. On those nights I shall lie in the dark feeling lonesome and unloved. But every dawn, on her way back from the flower garden, Kamal Lata will stop by and throw a handful of flowers over me—mallika sometimes and sometimes kunda. And if someone I know stops by at the *akhra* on her way to some other place, Kamal Lata will show her my grave. "There!" She'll point out. "That's where our Natun *gosain* lies. Can't you see a little mound under the bakul tree? There, where heaps of flowers lie strewn—champa and mallika and rain-washed bakul? There—"'

Rajlakshmi's eyes swam with tears. 'What will she do then? The someone you know?'

'I have no idea. She may spend a lot of money and build a shrine.'

'You're wrong. She won't build a shrine. She'll build a little hut for herself under the bakul tree. Birds will flutter and sing among the branches, nest and make love, and flowers will drop on her head, pitter-patter, like starry raindrops. She'll spend her mornings sweeping the little grave clean of fallen leaves and weaving garlands of bakul. And, at night, when all the world is asleep, she'll sit under the moon and stars and sing the old *padavalis* of Vaishnav masters—the songs he had said he loved. And when her time comes she'll send for her Kamal Lata Didi and say, "Bury me close, so close that our mounds become one. Leave no gap between us. And—here is the money. Build a shrine over us for the worship of Radha Govinda. But carve no names on the lintel. Leave not a trace of our identities. Let no one who comes here know who we were or from where we came."'

'Lakshmi!' I murmured. 'The picture you present is beautiful, infinitely more beautiful than mine.'

'Yes, because mine is real, *gosain*. It is woven out of age-old feelings that time cannot erode or circumstances dim. Yours is made up of hollow words. That is why, while mine will be transmuted into reality, yours will remain what it was.'

'How do you know?'

'Because I know *you*. Better than you know yourself! Who has occupied the thoughts of my days and the dreams of my nights for as far back as memory can go? Whose face comes before me as I pray? Whose—'

'Ma,' the *maharaj* called from below. 'Ratan is out and Babu's tea is ready.'

'I'm coming, Baba,' Rajlakshmi wiped her eyes and hurried downstairs. She came back a little later, a cup of tea in her hands. Setting it down on the table, she said, 'You love reading books. Why don't you do just that from now on?'

'That won't bring in any money.'

'We don't need more money. We have enough.' She paused for a moment and continued, 'Ananda Thakurpo will buy the books. The south-facing room upstairs will be your study. I'll dust and clean it myself and make it the loveliest room in the house. The room next to it will be my bedroom and the one adjacent— my prayer-room. This little area will be the three worlds for me. May I never wish to venture beyond it.'

'If the sanyasi is to buy my books, the kitchen will become your three worlds. Have you had news of him?'

'Yes, from Kushari *moshai*. Ananda will be coming in a few days and then we'll all go together to Gangamati. We'll stay there for a while.'

'Won't that be embarrassing for you?'

Rajlakshmi laughed ruefully and shook her head. 'They don't know that I cut off my hair and nose and turned myself into a clown. My hair has grown quite long and I've managed to stick my nose on with glue. Besides, you'll be with me.' She paused for a moment and continued, 'I hear Malati is back in Gangamati with her new husband. I'll give her a gold necklace as a wedding present.'

'That's a good idea. But if Sunanda catches you again—what then?'

'There's no fear of that. I've come out of her spell. That girl and her religion, *Ma go Ma*! I caught the infection so badly that I nearly died of it. I couldn't eat. I couldn't sleep. It's a blessing I didn't go mad.' She laughed and went on, 'Your Lakshmi is not as soft and gullible as you think. Once she sees a thing is wrong, she can stand firm against it. No power on earth can sway her. Not even Sunanda.' She thought for a while and continued, 'I feel as if I've come home after a long and perilous journey. My body and soul are at rest. If this isn't God's will why do I feel engulfed in a sea of bliss and wish the same for everyone in the world? I wish it so intensely that I pray for it day and night. That is why I've sent for Ananda Thakurpo. I'm going to help him in his work from now on.'

'Do that,' I said softly.

A long silence followed. Rajlakshmi was trying to work out something in her mind. I saw that clearly. Suddenly she said, 'I often think of Sunanda! I've never met anyone as straightforward, honest and truly austere in temperament as her. But she rates herself too high on account of her learning. It has become useless to her and to everyone else, in consequence. She needs to tone down her ego a little.'

'Sunanda isn't proud and egoistic.'

'Not as the vulgar masses are—not in the least. She is truly educated in the best sense of the word. Yet there is a deficiency somewhere. There must be, otherwise all that she taught me couldn't have proved such a failure. Have you noticed that everyone who comes in contact with her is made unhappy in some way or another? Compare her with her sister-in-law. She's a simple, unlettered woman but her heart is full of love and pity for everyone around her. So many families depend on her for their day-to-day living. But no one knows of it—not even her husband. It was she who wept and implored till her husband agreed to give the weaver's widow her due. Sunanda could never have achieved what her sister-in-law did because her learning has taught her the art of shattering relationships— not mending them. Every crack in her life becomes a chasm. She hasn't learned the wisdom of bridging. She didn't hesitate one moment before defaming the brother-in-law who had been a father to her husband, before calling him a liar and a cheat to his face. Is this the true teaching of the Shastras? I'm a simple, uneducated village woman but I'm convinced that until she learns to accept a human being as human with human failings—a compound of good and bad, vice and virtue, avarice and generosity—she'll never understand anyone. Her book-learned morality will become a source of pain to everyone around her. It will hurt and oppress—not nurture and cherish.'

Her reasoning took me by surprise. 'Who taught you all this?' I asked.

'I can't tell. You—maybe. You never express a wish, make no demands and never force anyone to do anything against their will. That is why one doesn't learn from you. One receives.' She sat silent for a while, then sighed and said, 'I neglected Kushari *ginni* sadly on my last visit. I must make up for it this time. We'll visit her as soon as we reach Gangamati. Shall we?'

'What about my job in Burma?'

'Didn't I tell you I'm not letting you take up a job?'

'You have a lovely nature, Lakshmi. You never express a wish, make no demands and never force anyone to do anything against their will. You're a model of Vaishnavite tolerance and self-denial. You're incomparable!'

'People can't always be allowed to do as they like. There are others to be considered.'

'What about Abhaya? If she hadn't taken me in when I had every symptom of the plague, would I be here today to consider you? Can't she claim a right to consideration?'

Rajlakshmi's face softened with gratitude and compassion. 'You stay,' she said gently. 'I'll go to Burma myself with Ananda Thakurpo and bring them back with me. Some means of living can surely be found for them, here where they belong.'

'Abhaya is very sensitive. She may not come if I don't go to fetch her.'

'She'll come. She'll know, in her heart, that my going to her is the same as yours.'

'Can you stay away from me that long?'

'I don't think I can. But I'll worry about that later. Let's go to Gangamati first and spend a few days.'

'Do you have some work in Gangamati?'

'Yes. Kushari *moshai* has written to say that the adjacent village, Porhamati, is on sale. I'm thinking of buying it. And I must enlarge and improve the house. You weren't very comfortable last time for lack of space.'

'Any discomfort I may have suffered was not due to lack of space. There were other reasons.'

Rajlakshmi ignored this comment and went on, I've noticed that your health improves in Gangamati. That is why I want to take you there, away from the city, as soon as possible.'

'If you have to worry about my broken health, day in and day out, you'll never get any peace, Lakshmi.'

'That is good advice but if you were to give it to yourself instead of to me, we would both be better off. Learn to look after yourself. I may get some peace if you do.'

This was an oft repeated argument that I didn't care to take up for it would be, as it always was, an exercise in futility. Rajlakshmi would never understand, could never accept the fact that I was sickly by constitution. She herself enjoyed radiant health and thought I would, too, if I didn't neglect myself. I said, instead, 'I don't care about the city. I liked Gangamati and would have liked to stay on. Only—'

'I know, dearest, I know. I'll never forget that phase of my life as long as I live.' She smiled and continued, 'Last time you felt an alien, an intruder in Gangamati. This time it will be different. I'll change everything—not only the house and its furnishings but myself and my ways. I'll change you too. I'll break you into a thousand pieces and build you up again. My Natun *gosain* will be mine alone. Kamal Lata Didi will not dare to claim you as her fellow traveller to Vrindavan.'

'You've been planning and scheming quite a bit, I see.'

'Why not? I'll take you from her but I'll pay the price. Besides I, too, came into the world as other humans do. I wasn't borne in by the tide. Shall I leave no trace, no token of my presence here when I go? Shall I carry the burden of my unfulfilled body and soul with me to the other world? Never.'

I gazed into her face, my heart melting with love. 'Love between man and woman is such an ordinary thing,' I thought. 'It has existed since the beginning of time, and will go on— unchanging, continuous, without pause or rest. Yet the same, sometimes, on rare occasions, becomes a thing of divine beauty— eternal and infinite. It enriches and elevates generations of men but never consumes itself.' Aloud I said, 'What will you do about Banku?'

'He doesn't need me. He would be quite happy to be rid of me.'

'Don't forget that he's a very close relation. You've brought him up as your own son.'

'I have and that is all that will remain between us. He is not a close relation and never will be.'

'You can't deny the relationship.'

'I would never have denied it if—' She thought for a few moments and asked, 'You don't know the true circumstances of my marriage, do you?'

'I was away from the village at the time but I've heard some strange stories.'

'Nothing stranger has ever been heard since God created Man. Nothing as cruel either. My father deserted my mother in my infancy. I have no memories, at all, of that time. My maternal uncle took us in. That is how we came to be living in your village. I was a sickly child. You remember what I looked like?'

'I do.'

'I used to suffer from bouts of malaria that went untreated for years. But I didn't die. Not in the ordinary way at least. News came that the Brahmin cook in the household of the Dattas was a Kulin like my uncle and, therefore, the ideal match for my sister. That he was sixty years old and my sister twelve was, of course, no consideration. The villagers warned Mama that if he missed this opportunity he might never get another and his niece would remain a spinster all her life. Mama offered the groom a deal—my sister and myself for fifty rupees. The groom demanded a hundred. Mama begged and pleaded, arguing that though the man was taking two wives he was doing it at one ceremony—the effort and energy expended being equal to taking one. The groom came down to seventy-five rupees. He wouldn't take a paisa less. "*Moshai,*" he said, "you're getting a Kulin match for two nieces at one go. Won't you give me the price of a pair of rams?" The *sampradan** was to take place just before the onset of dawn. Didi stayed awake but I was carried in, a sleeping bundle, and given over to our future lord and master. The sun rose. Arrangements were made for the *kushandika*** but the groom flatly refused to participate till the twenty-five rupees were handed over. Mama suggested that the *kushandika* be performed on credit but the groom announced that a contract was a contract and he didn't believe in debit and credit. He left the house hoping, no doubt, that Mama would go after him with the money and beg him to complete the rituals. But the days went by. Mama couldn't raise the money. He begged the Dattas to intervene and was told that their cook had left their service. Enquiries were made in his village but he wasn't there, either. Ma wept and cursed us incessantly; the neighbours sniggered and nudged one another whenever they saw us. Some said we were born under an evil star and others that we were doomed to bring ruin to whoever befriended us. Didi huddled in a corner of the house not daring to show her face. Six months later she was

---

* The giving away of a daughter in marriage.
** The ritual of putting sindoor in the parting of the bride's hair.

brought out of it—to be taken to the burning-ghat. And another six months later news came from a Calcutta hotel that the groom had died of a strange fever while cooking in their kitchen. The *kushandika* never took place so the marriage was not valid.'

'Buy a bridegroom for twenty-five rupees and this is what you get,' I declared solemnly.

'What did I buy you for? A string of *bainchi*. Even that wasn't paid for. I picked them off the bushes and put them together.'

'My string of *bainchi* is priceless because it has no price. Show me another man with a treasure like mine.'

'Do you mean it—really and truly?'

'Can't you see it in my face?'

'No, I can't,' she laughed and went on. 'I swear I can't—except at night when you are asleep. But, tell me, has an incident like this ever occurred in any other part of the world? Can you quote a single example? Yet thousands of girls, in our country, suffer the same torture and humiliation day in and day out. We treat our women worse than animals!' She paused to take a breath and continued, 'You may think I'm exaggerating; you may argue that our case is a freak one. I could counter-argue that, even if it is, it is a terrible slur on our people and our culture. But I shan't. I'll say that it isn't a freak case. There are many instances of persecution akin to ours. Would you like to come with me to my widow's home in Kashi? If you were to talk to the women you would find that all of them are victims of gross cruelty and criminal neglect.'

'That explains your concern—'

'You would be concerned too if you saw them from the inside. I'll show you everything, one by one, from now on.'

'I'll keep my eyes shut. I'll refuse to see.'

'You won't succeed. My burdens will fall on your shoulders when I go. You may deny the whole world but you can't deny them.' She was silent for a while then, suddenly, she reverted to her earlier subject. 'Tyranny and oppression!' she exclaimed. 'What else can you expect in a country where a man is robbed of his religion for failing to marry off his daughters? Loss of caste, loss of face, loss of prestige—all because a girl, be she blind, deaf, dumb or orphaned, is unwed! What is a man to do? Didi might have been alive today but for these terrifying options before my uncle. And I? You couldn't have been mine as you are now—not in this life at least. Yet, why not? You would have had to come to me from wherever you were, at whatever point of time, and take me away with you. You couldn't escape me.'

I was contemplating a reply when a voice called, 'Mashima!'

'Who is that?' I exclaimed, startled.

'It's the boy next door. Mejo Bou's son. Come up, Kshitish.'

The next moment a pleasant looking youth of about sixteen or seventeen entered the room. He seemed surprised to see me at first, but collected himself soon enough and brought his hands together in a namaskar. Then, turning to Rajlakshmi, he said, 'We've put down twelve rupees against your name, Mashima.'

'Twelve rupees it shall be. But be careful in the water. There must be no accidents.'

'Don't worry, Mashima. We're all good swimmers.'

Rajlakshmi unlocked her almirah and took out the money. Taking it from her the boy said, 'Ma told me to tell you that Chhoto Mama will come with the estimate the day after tomorrow.'

'What estimate?' I asked as the boy ran nimbly down the stairs.

'The house needs repairs. Besides, the second floor was just begun when I bought the house. I'll have to complete it.'

'How do you know all these people?'

'Why, they're our neighbours! They live next door.' She rose saying, 'It's time I started cooking or your meal will get delayed.' And she hastened down to the kitchen.

Thirteen

S WAMI BAJRANANDA ARRIVED EARLY ONE MORNING. RATAN, WHO had no knowledge of Rajlakshmi's summons, came up to my room and announced glumly, That sadhu from Gangamati is here. God only knows from where he got the address. Now we have him on our hands for heaven knows how long.' Ratan disliked and distrusted ascetics as a rule. He hated Rajlakshmi's gurudev and took no trouble to conceal the fact. 'I wonder what that rogue of a sanyasi is up to this time,' he said after a pause. 'He's after Ma's money, I'll warrant. These holy men have a hundred ways of fleecing women.'

'Ananda is a rich man's son,' I replied. 'He's a qualified doctor. He doesn't need money for himself.'

'Humph! A rich man's son indeed! Why should a man with money turn himself into a sanyasi?' And, with this triumphant conclusion, Ratan walked out of the room, his chest heaving with indignation. Ratan couldn't bear the thought of anyone fleecing his mistress—barring himself, of course.

A minute or two later, Ananda burst into the room with a hearty greeting. 'Namaskar, Dada! Here I am, once again. What's the news? Where's Didi?'

'She's in her prayer-room, I believe. She couldn't have heard of your arrival, yet.'

'I'll go to her myself in a minute and send her down to the kitchen. Her prayers can wait. Where's that son of a barber? Why doesn't he put the kettle on for tea?' He bellowed out Ratan's name a couple of times and walked away in the direction of the prayer-room.

A few minutes later, Rajlakshmi and her sanyasi brother made an appearance. 'Off load some money, Didi,' Ananda said with his usual aplomb. 'Five rupees at the least. A morning stroll through the Sealdah bazaar is indicated.'

'There's a very good bazaar much nearer at hand. Besides, why should you go? I'll send Ratan.'

'Ratan? He'll pick up stale fish and rotting vegetables deliberately to spite—' His sentence was left in mid-air as Ratan entered the room. Ananda's handsome features twisted in comic dismay as he said with exaggerated humility, 'Ratan, don't take offence, my son. I didn't know you were in the house. I thought you were philandering in the neighbourhood. I called several times, you see.'

Rajlakshmi and I burst out laughing but Ratan took no notice. 'Ma,' he said, maintaining an air of stern dignity, 'I'm going to the bazaar. Kishen has put the kettle on for tea.' And with that he walked out of the room.

'Ananda and Ratan aren't the best of friends,' Rajlakshmi commented, the smile still on her lips.

'I don't blame him, Didi. He's a well-wisher of yours. He doesn't like rogues and parasites hanging around you. But I'd better seek his company or my lunch will be ruined. I haven't had a decent meal in months.'

Rajlakshmi hurried to the veranda and called out to the departing Ratan, 'Take a few more rupees with you and buy a big sized *rui*, Ratan. Make sure it's fresh.' Then, addressing herself to Ananda, she said, 'Go wash your face and hands while I make the tea.' And she hurried down to the kitchen.

'Why the urgent summons, Dada?' Ananda asked.

'You expect *me* to provide the answer?'

'You're still nursing your anger,' Ananda smiled. 'I hope you aren't planning to disappear again. Goodness! What a storm you stirred up that time in Gangamati. The whole village invited and the master of the house absconding. Ratan ready to drive out the guests and Didi weeping and beating her breast. And I running from pillar to post like a distracted hen. You're really impossible, Dada!'

I smiled with him. 'I've got over my annoyance. You needn't worry anymore.'

'I can't help worrying. Quiet, seclusion-loving people like you frighten me to death. I often wonder why you allowed yourself to become a family man.'

'Destiny!' I said to myself. Aloud I said, 'That means you think of me sometimes. You haven't forgotten me.'

'It isn't easy to forget you. Or to understand you. And it is impossible not to love you. I had only known you for a day or two but I was ready to weep and beat my breast, like Didi, the day you disappeared. If I weren't a sanyasi, trained in the art of stoic self-control, I would have done just that. Ask Didi if you don't believe me.'

'That must have been out of sympathy for your Didi. You came all the way at her request.'

'That is true. For me a request from her is like a mother's call. I couldn't resist it. My feet started moving in spite of myself. I've sheltered in so many homes, I've seen so many women—but not one like her. You, too, have travelled a lot, seen a lot. Have you seen another like her?'

'Many,' I answered shortly.

'Many? Many what?' Rajlakshmi entered the room with Ananda's tea. Putting it down she looked up enquiringly. Ananda stiffened a little as if anticipating an unpleasant scene.

I answered quickly, 'Your accomplishments. Ananda expressed some doubts regarding their number and I objected indignantly, "They are many," I said.'

The tea spluttered in Ananda's mouth and some of it spilled over on to the floor as he laughed and coughed by turns. 'Dada,' he said as soon as he was able to speak. 'Your presence of mind is admirable. How neatly you turned the tables on me.'

Rajlakshmi laughed too. 'He has made up stories for so long now that he's become a master of deception.'

'You don't trust me?' I asked in mock dismay.

'Not a bit.'

'Then you are no less a mistress of deception!' Ananda exclaimed. 'You said "Not a bit" without batting an eyelid.'

'I've learned a little from him—in self-defence. Drink up your tea and get ready for your bath, Ananda. You must be tired and hungry. You haven't eaten anything on the train. I can see that in your face. And—' Rajlakshmi dimpled and her mouth curved upwards. 'Don't make the mistake of asking him to list my virtues. You'll be stuck here for a week.'

Ananda looked at her retreating back and smiled. 'You're a wonderfully compatible pair. God took a lot of trouble matchmaking for you. I noticed it first under that tree in Sainthia station. After that—I haven't seen another couple like you.'

'Ah! Ananda. Why do you always say these nice things behind her back.'

With Ananda's arrival, Rajlakshmi's excitement knew no bounds. She was busy day and night, cooking for Ananda, chatting with Ananda and planning all the things they would do together in Gangamati. I heard only snatches of their conversation but I gathered that among the projects they would undertake was the opening of two primary schools—one for boys and one for girls. There was some talk, too, of a dispensary for the people of Gangamati.

Ananda was a man of action. He had tremendous enthusiasm and energy and the capacity to carry out whatever he undertook to a successful conclusion. He was, therefore, the ideal man for Rajlakshmi in her present mood. If Ananda ever sought my assistance or advice, Rajlakshmi stopped him with a laugh. 'Don't drag him into it. Your work will be ruined if you depend on him.' She understood my incapacity for action, my retiring nature that shrank from anything positive—however deep my feelings. But I couldn't let her comment pass without contradiction.

'Only the other day you said there was a lot for me to do, to achieve,' I grumbled.

'Forgive me, *gosain*.' She brought her hands together in mock humility. 'I'll never make the mistake of saying anything so foolish again.'

'Does that mean I'm never to do anything?'

'Oh no. Do all you can. Only, don't fall ill and frighten me to death. I'll be obliged to your forever.'

'You mollycoddle him too much, Didi. You're turning him into a weakling,' Ananda said.

'I don't have to turn him into anything, bhai. God has done that for me. Besides,' she laughed embarrassedly, 'that astrologer in Muraripur has made me so nervous, I don't dare let him out of my sight for a minute.'

'Astrologer? What astrologer? What did he say?'

I answered for Rajlakshmi. 'He said I was going through a bad phase, that it was a matter of life and death.'

'Do you believe all this nonsense, Didi?'

'Of course she does,' I answered for her once more. '"Have you never seen anyone going through a bad phase?" she asks me, time and again. "Have you never known accidents to happen?"'

'Anything may happen to anybody at any time,' Ananda said gravely. 'But is it written on one's palm?'

'I can't answer your question, Ananda. I can only say that I quake in terror at the thought. God has given me so much! He won't snatch it all away and drown me in sorrow. That is the only thought that gives me comfort.'

Ananda looked at her, in silence, for a while. Then he changed the subject.

The construction of the second floor was to commence. Cartloads of lime and cement, fancy doors and slatted windows arrived. Rajlakshmi seemed determined to transform the house into a palace. One evening, Ananda said to me, 'Let's go out for a while, Dada.'

'At this hour?' Rajlakshmi exclaimed. 'It will be dark by the time you return and he'll be sure to catch a chill.' The prospect of my venturing out of the house alarmed Rajlakshmi these days.

'People are panting with the heat and you're worried about chills. You're impossible, Didi!'

I wasn't feeling too well that day. I said, 'I won't catch a chill. But I don't feel like going out today, Ananda.'

'That's simple inertia. If you keep sitting at home, evening after evening, you'll become a fossil.'

Rajlakshmi hastened to my rescue. 'Kshitish brought my new harmonium over day before yesterday. I haven't had the time to try it out as yet. Why don't the two of you listen while I take the name of the Lord?'

'What does that mean? Can you sing, Didi?'

'A little.' She waved a hand in my direction and continued, 'I took lessons from him as a child.'

Ananda was thrilled. 'Dada!' he exclaimed. 'You're a genius at hiding your talents. Looking at you no one would dream that you could sing.'

Rajlakshmi laughed merrily at the success of her joke but I couldn't join in with equal abandon. I knew Ananda would insist on my rendering a song and would dismiss my entreaties as the humble self-negation of the true artist. He might even take offence. I knew the song the blind Dhritarashtra had sung over his dead son's body, but Ananda wasn't expecting a comic interlude.

The harmonium arrived. Rajlakshmi sang a few traditional verses in praise of the Lord and then—one Vaishnav *padavali* after another. Ananda was amazed. He asked, during a pause in her singing, 'Have you learned all these songs from Dada?'

'Not all. No one can teach you everything, Ananda.'

'That's true.' Then, turning to me, he said, 'Now you must take over. Didi is tired.'

'No, bhai. I don't feel up to it.'

'You turn down my request? Remember that I'm your guest.'

'I feel really unwell, Ananda.'

Rajlakshmi kept a straight face for as long as she could. Then she burst out laughing. Ananda understood, at last. He turned to her, 'Who was your teacher? You must tell me.' Then, after a pause, he said, 'I know something of music. I learned a little but had to give it up. I got too busy and couldn't find the time. But, now I've found you, I'll take it up again. Won't you sing some more, Didi?'

'Not today, Ananda. It's time I went down to the kitchen. You must both be hungry.'

Ananda said, 'People like you, on whom so many depend, have little time to spare. But I'll claim the privilege of a younger brother and insist that you teach me whatever I'm capable of learning. When I'm weary and lonesome, in strange out-of-the-way places, I'll use your gift to comfort myself.'

Rajlakshmi's face softened with love. 'I'll teach you all I know, Ananda. In return you must promise to keep an eye on this sick brother of yours all your life.'

'Don't you ever think of anything else, Didi?'

There was no answer. Ananda glanced briefly at her bent head and turned to me. 'A fate like yours is to be envied. I haven't seen another like it.'

'You haven't seen weakness and vulnerability as pitiful as mine, either, have you, Ananda? God makes us what we are but he doesn't abandon us. He has, out of His great love, sent someone in my life with an arm strong enough to steer my boat safely to the shore. It would have drifted away otherwise or been shattered by the rocks. God balances the strong and weak, the rich and poor, the good and evil—thus. And so His creation survives.'

Rajlakshmi fixed her eyes on my face for a long while after I said these words. Then she rose and left the room.

The construction work began. Rajlakshmi started her preparations for leaving Calcutta. All the things she wouldn't be taking with her was stowed away in one room. The old durwan, Tulsidas, was to remain and supervise the work. The day we were to leave, Rajlakshmi handed me a postcard with the words, 'This is the answer I get to my eight-page letter. Read it.' I glanced at the two or three lines written in a shaky, female hand.

It was from Kamal Lata. 'I'm well, *bon*,' she wrote. 'My Radha Govinda, to whose service I've dedicated myself, will never abandon me. My welfare is in their hands. I trust you are well and happy. Bara *gosainji* sends his Anandamayee his deepest regards. I end—*Sri Sri Radha Krishna Charanasrita*—Kamal Lata.'

She hadn't mentioned my name even once but, as I sat with the postcard in my hand, all that she had left unwritten was before me in an instant. I scanned the lines, once again, to see if a tear marred their evenness but I couldn't find any. I glanced out of the window at the sunlit sky flashing between the fronds of two tall coconut trees that grew in our neighbour's garden. And, suddenly, out of that hot blue sky, two faces swam to the surface. One was Rajlakshmi's, clear and strong and beautiful. The other was Kamal Lata's, vapoury and blurred, a little strange, a little unreal, like a face seen in a dream.

'It's time for your bath, Babu,' Ratan's voice broke into my reverie. 'Ma sent me to remind you.' Even my bath hour was regulated. There was no escaping Rajlakshmi's vigilance.

We arrived at Gangamati early one morning. Everything was the same as on that earlier visit. Only, this time, Ananda was an invited guest—not a stray passenger picked up from the station. The house was full of people, all smiling, all welcoming us.

Sunanda came out of the kitchen, touched our feet and said, 'You don't look too well, Dada.'

'When has he ever looked well?' Rajlakshmi cried impatiently. 'I've failed miserably with him. I admit it. That's why I've brought him over to Gangamati. Now that you all will have the caring of him—do the best you can.'

'Rest assured, Ma,' Kushari *ginni* answered for her sister-in-law in a voice melting with motherly love. 'The climate here is dry and fine and the air and water pure. He'll get back his health in a few days.' The only person who wasn't worried was myself. I didn't feel very ill and I couldn't understand why the others thought I was.

Rajlakshmi and Ananda took up their tasks with the inexhaustible energy that was characteristic of them. But I grew more and more listless as the days went by. This may have been 'simple inertia' as Ananda had described it or it may have been the first symptom of the disease that was feeding on my life force slowly and imperceptibly. I was grateful for one thing. No one disturbed my peace for no one expected anything of me. There was a tacit understanding among all the people surrounding me that I was weak and sickly, that I hadn't long to live. But I didn't feel ill. I ate and drank and slept and awoke and ate and drank again. Ananda would look sharply at me, sometimes, ask me questions and prescribe diets and medicines. At these times, Rajlakshmi would draw him gently away. 'Leave him alone, Ananda. Who knows what will lead to what? If anything untoward happens we'll all have to suffer.'

'Suffering is inevitable, the way you're going about it. If at all, it might be intensified. I'm warning you, Didi.'

'I know, bhai. God set it down in my fate the moment I was born.'

What argument was possible after that?

I passed my days in reading and gazing out of the window at the hard blue sky and dun-coloured fields. Sometimes, I wandered about by the side of the canal or stood for a moment on the rickety bridge. But, more often, I sat at my table and put down on paper the strange and varied events of my life. I knew myself. I had little drive and less ambition. All the things men hankered after in the world—money, power, status, privileges—all seemed dreamlike and unreal to me. It was enough for me to be allowed to live. Sometimes, shamed by the energy and enthusiasm of the others, I would try to rouse myself, to break out of the inertia that had settled on me like a cloud. But, before I knew it, I was back again within its enveloping folds and was my weary, half-conscious, half-dying self again. Yet those same senses, which not all the shoving and pushing in the world could awaken, would burst into exuberant life whenever I remembered my ten days' stay at the *akhra* in Muraripur. I would hear Kamal Lata's voice, not wraithlike and insubstantial, but living and vibrant, in my ears. 'Natun *gosain*, will you crimp this border for me? *Ma go*, what a mess you've made! I'll never make the mistake of asking you again. Where's that good-for-nothing Padma? Why doesn't she put the kettle on? Doesn't she know it's time for your tea?'

She wanted to leave the ashram and would do so, sooner or later. She would resume the journey that had started from Nabadweep, walking the path on her solitary way, singing as she went, till her journey's end was in sight. Whenever I thought of her like that—alone, unprotected, begging for a living—I couldn't stop the tears from gushing out of my eyes. In my helplessness I turned, more eagerly than ever, to Rajlakshmi—my strong, beautiful Rajlakshmi, my goddess of bounty, ever loving, ever giving. She worked from early dawn till late into the night—her hands busy in the service of others. Compassion rained from her eyes and the smile never left her lips. A flood of love welled up in my heart at every thought of her and my soul floated on a sea of divine content.

She hadn't forgotten that phase of her life when, led astray by Sunanda's irresistible influence, she had driven me away from her. The thought never ceased to torture her. Out of that pain and guilt she had found herself again, had become the old Rajlakshmi she had always been.

Even now, she whispers in my ear, time and again; 'You were cruel, cruel! Whoever dreamed that my heart, my soul and all my senses would rush away from me and follow you on the path you took the moment you were gone? What a terrible affliction that was! I shudder even to think of that time. It's a wonder my heart didn't burst.'

It is impossible, these days, to find fault with Rajlakshmi's treatment of me. Despite the innumerable pressures on her, one eye and one ear are ever alert to my smallest needs. She comes into my room a hundred times a day. Sometimes she pushes my book away and says, 'Lie down and shut your eyes. Let me stroke your forehead for a while. You'll get a headache if you read so much.'

Ananda's voice booms from outside, 'I've something to ask you, Didi. Can I come in?'

'Of course. Since when do *you* have to take permission?'

Ananda walks into the room and, taking in the scene, asks in a surprised voice, 'Are you putting him to sleep? At this hour?'

'What if I am? He's not going to take the cows in your pathshala out grazing even if he stays awake, is he?'

'You'll be the ruin of him.'

'What else can I do. The only alternative is ruining myself and my work.'

'You're both going mad,' Ananda announces dramatically and leaves the room.

One day, a letter arrived for me. It had been redirected from our Calcutta address and had travelled through many post offices, to judge by the number of postmarks on it. It was from Nabin and contained the news that Gahar was dying and wanted to see me. The letter was a week old.

Rajlakshmi looked thoughtful. 'You'll have to go, of course.'

'Yes.'

'I'll come too.'

'Where will you stay? Don't forget, it's a house of mourning.'

Rajlakshmi nodded. I thought she would suggest staying at the *akhra* but she didn't. She said, instead, 'Ratan is down with fever since yesterday. Whom shall I send with you? Shall I ask Ananda?'

'No. He's not a coolie to bear my loads.'

'Take Kishen with you, then.'

'I will, if you insist. But it isn't necessary.'

'You must write to me everyday.'

'If I get the time—'

'No. No excuses. The day I don't get a letter I'll come over to you myself.'

I had to agree. Promising to send her a daily bulletin of my health, I left Gangamati. As I took my place in the bullock-cart, I saw Rajlakshmi standing at the door, her face pale and tense with anxiety. 'Promise me you'll look after yourself,' she said for the last time, wiping her eyes with the end of her sari.

'I promise, dearest.'

'You'll come back as soon as—'

'I will.'

Late one afternoon, in the month of *Asadh*,[*] I stood outside
Gahar's door. Nabin heard me come and, rushing up to me, threw
himself at my feet, his body shaking with sobs. The big, strong
man's unrestrained grief told me all I needed to know. I looked at
Nabin with new eyes. His grief was as vast and deep as it was true
and sincere. I saw, in a flash of intuition, that although no mother
had wept over Gahar's body, no wife or sister either—he had not
left the world unloved, unmourned, in rags like a beggar. He had
travelled like a king to that other world. Nabin had seen to that.

'When did Gahar die?' I asked when, exhausted with
weeping, Nabin sat up and wiped his eyes.

'The day before yesterday. We buried him yesterday, at dawn.'

'Where did you bury him?'

'By the river, under the mango trees. He had wished it so.'
Nabin looked up the sky as if he sought something there and
went on, 'He returned from his cousin's house burning with
fever. It never left him.'

'Did you send for the doctor?'

'We did everything that was possible here. But nothing
worked. He knew he was dying.'

'Didn't Bara *gosain* come over from the *akhra*?'

'Once or twice. His gurudev has arrived from Nabadweep.
So he couldn't come very often.'

I wanted to ask about one other person but couldn't bring
myself to do so at first. Then I said with a kind of desperation,
'Did no one else come over from the *akhra*?'

'Yes. Kamal Lata Didi.'

'When did she come?'

'She came every day. She didn't go back at all the last three
days. She sat by Babu's bedside and didn't leave it even once—not
even to bathe and eat.'

I didn't ask any more questions. I had heard all that I wanted
to hear.

'Are you going to the *akhra*, Babu?'

'Yes, Nabin.'

'Wait a minute.' He went inside and came out with a tin box
in his hands. Giving it to me, he said, 'Babu told me to give you

***

[*] The third month of the Bengali calendar (mid June to mid July).

this.'

'What is in the box, Nabin?'

'Open it and see.' He handed me a key. I opened the box and found a pile of notebooks tied with string. It was Gahar's *Ramayana*. On a piece of paper, on top of the pile were written the words:

Srikanta, I couldn't complete my *Ramayana*. I didn't get the time. Give the manuscript to Bara *gosain* and tell him to keep it in the ashram. It mustn't get lost.

There was another, smaller bundle tied with a red cloth. Opening it I found wads of notes of different denominations. There was another letter for me. It read:

Bhai Srikanta, I think I'm dying. I doubt I'll ever see you again. I'm leaving this money in your care. Give it to Kamal Lata if she ever needs it. If she refuses—do what you like with it. May the blessings of Allah be with you—Gahar.

Not a hint of pride or complacency marred the nobility of his gesture. No flattery or servility, either. He had expressed his dying wish and invoked the blessings of Allah for the childhood friend he loved. He had had no doubts, no fears in the face of death. He had not struggled against it or drowned himself in self-pity. He was a poet, the inheritor of a tradition of Mussalman sufism that his fakir forefathers had carried in their blood. He had taken up his pen with a quiet determination and written his last composition in a few, choice, simple words. My eyes had been dry all this while but now tears sprang up in them and rolled down my cheeks in large drops.

The long day of *Asadh* was on the wane. A mass of jewel-blue clouds loomed over the western horizon, then swept across half the sky. And, from out of a crevice of the cloud cover, the setting sun burst out like a flame. Its beams irradiated the tips of the dying rose-apple tree by the wall—the same rose-apple that had inspired Gahar, and to whose blighted branches the madhavi and the malati vines had clung with desperate life. It had been spring then and the vines newly in bud. Now, nurtured by the new falling rain, they were laden with clusters of flowers. So many had been swept away by the wind, so many had fallen to the ground. I remembered Gahar's desire to give me some flowers and his frustration at the sight of the wood ants that had crawled all over the trunk. I bent down and picked up a handful and felt that it was my friend's last gift—given to me with his own hands.

Nabin said, 'Come, Babu. Let me take you to the *akhra*.'

'Can you open up the room in which I slept when I was here last, Nabin? I wish to see it once before I leave.'

Nabin unlocked the door and I went in. Everything was the same—the wooden cot with bedding rolled up at its head, the holes in the floor, the gaping window. A sheet of paper lay on the table with Gahar's pencil beside it. It was here, in this room, that Gahar had sung verses from his *Ramayana*—the tragic episode of Sita's captivity. I had eaten and slept here so often in my childhood; I had played within these walls. I had fought and sparred with Gahar and heard stories from his mother. No one was left to share those memories. My roots were being cut away from me but there was no one, today, to shed a tear.

On our way to the *akhra*, Nabin gave me the details of Gahar's will. The bulk of his estate was to be divided up among his maternal cousins but a part of it had been put aside, in trust, to pay for the maintenance of a mosque his father had got built. A bundle of notes, similar to the one in the trunk, had been left for Nabin's sons.

On reaching the ashram I found it crammed with people. Bara *gosain's* gurudev sat in state, surrounded by throngs of disciples. Looking at them it was easy to see that every luxury the *akhra* could afford was being lavished on them and that they were not likely to leave in a hurry. Dwarika Das came forward to greet me. He expressed grief at Gahar's death but there was something in his face I had never seen before: a dazed, withdrawn look—as if he was not quite comfortable talking to me. I presumed it was the strain of playing host to so many strangers for such a long period of time at a stretch.

Padma heard of my arrival and came to see me. But her face was unhappy, her eyes furtive. Far from being thrilled at my coming she seemed anxious to escape.

'Your Kamal Lata Didi is very busy. Isn't that so, Padma?'

'No. Shall I send her to you?' Padma hurried away from the room without waiting for an answer. I had never seen her behave so oddly. And Bara *gosain's* manner had been strange, to say the least. I grew alarmed.

Kamal Lata came in after a little while. 'Come to my room, *gosain*,' she said. 'We can talk there.'

I had left my bedding at the station. I only had my bag with me and Gahar's tin box. Handing them to her I said, 'Keep the box carefully. There's a lot of money in it.'

'I know.' She pushed it under the bed and turned to me. 'You haven't had your tea yet, have you?'

'No.'

'When did you arrive?'

'In the afternoon.'

'I'll go and bring it.' She left the room taking the servant with her. Padma brought me water to wash but didn't stop or speak a word. I wondered, again, what the matter was. Kamal Lata brought my tea and some sweets and fruits—Govindaji's morning prasad. I hadn't eaten all day so I fell to with a will. As I ate I heard the blowing of conches and the ringing of bells that signalled the commencement of the evening arati.

'Shouldn't you be at the shrine?' I asked, surprised.

'No. I've been forbidden to enter it.'

'Forbidden to enter it? Why? What does that mean?'

Kamal Lata smiled a wan smile. 'Forbidden means forbidden, *gosain*. I've been commanded to keep away from Govindaji's temple.'

'Who commanded you?'

'Bara *gosain's* gurudev. And all those who've come with him.'

My appetite vanished. I pushed my *thala* away. 'Why?' I asked.

'They think I'm unchaste, impure. They say God will be polluted by my touch.'

'Unchaste! You?' The truth dawned upon me in a flash. 'Is it—was it—anything to do with Gahar?' I asked wonderingly.

'Yes.'

I knew nothing about Gahar and Kamal Lata but a denial, born out of an innate conviction rose swiftly to my lips. 'Impossible!' I exclaimed.

'Why is it impossible, *gosain*?'

'I don't know why. I only know that there's no bigger lie in the world. This is your reward, Kamal Lata, for nursing your dying friend, for making his last moments endurable. The world in which we live values your goodness thus.'

Her eyes swam with tears. 'I have no regrets, *gosain*. Not anymore. I wasn't afraid of God for he can look into my soul. I was only afraid of you. I'm so relieved—I could die, this moment, quite happily, *gosain*.'

'There are so many people in the world, Kamal Lata,' I said in a wondering voice. 'Yet you feared no one—only me?'

'Yes. Only you.'

We sat, as though frozen in our places for a long while. Then I roused myself and asked, 'What does Bara *gosain* say?'

'What can he say? If he allows me into the shrine, no Vaishnav will ever set foot in the *akhra* again.' She thought for a moment or two and murmured to herself, 'I knew I would have to go some day. But I never thought it would be like this.' Then, fixing her dark eyes on mine, she said, 'I'm worried about Padma. The poor child will weep her eyes out for me. She's an orphan. Bara *gosain* picked her up from the streets of Nabadweep. Look after her, *gosain*, if you can. If she doesn't wish to stay on in the *akhra* after I'm gone, take her away with you. Raju will look after her.'

Another silence followed. 'And Gahar's money?' I asked. 'Won't you take it?'

'No. I'm a Vaishnavi. I beg for a living. What would I do with all that money?'

'You may need it someday.'

Kamal Lata laughed. 'I had a lot of money, once. Was it of any use? Still, if I ever need any, I'll take it from you. Why should I take money from strangers?'

I stared at her. I didn't have a word to say.

'No, *gosain*,' she took up the subject again. 'I don't need anyone's money. I've surrendered myself in the hands of one who will never cast me off. All my needs will be fulfilled. Don't worry about me.'

Padma appeared at the door. 'Where shall I serve the prasad?' she asked Kala Lata.

'Bring it here. Have you fed the servant?'

'Yes.' But Padma wouldn't go. She stood at the door, hesitating. 'Won't you eat anything, Didi?' she asked.

'I will, *bon*, I will. You'll push it down my throat, if I don't won't you?'

Padma looked relieved and went off to bring the prasad.

I looked out for Kamal Lata the next morning but she was nowhere to be seen. Padma informed me that she spent her days away from the *akhra* and returned only in the evening. But the news gave me little comfort. I remembered her words of the night before and was tortured by the thought that she may have gone and that I might never see her again.

I took Gahar's *Ramayana* to Bara *gosain* and told him of my friend's last request. Bara *gosain* accepted it with the words, 'His wish shall be respected, Natun *gosain*. I shall keep the manuscript, carefully, with the other books of the *akhra*.'

I waited a few moments before saying, 'This scandal about Kamal Lata and Gahar—do you believe it?'

'No.' Dwarika Das raised his eyes and held mine.

'Yet she's being compelled to leave the *akhra*.'

'I'm leaving too, *gosain*. I can't drive out an innocent woman and stay within these walls myself. I chose this path out of all others so that I may live a life of truth. If I abandon it now, all my years of service to Radha Govinda will cease to have any meaning.'

'You are the master of the *akhra*. You can take your own decisions. You can ask her to stay.'

'*Guru, guru, guru.*' Bara *gosain* hung his head and shut his eyes. I understood that this was his guru's command and he couldn't disobey it.

'I'm leaving today, *gosain*,' I said, rising. He lifted his head. Tears poured down his cheeks. He brought his hands together in a namaskar. I did the same. Then I left the room.

The afternoon melted into evening and then dusk. Night fell but there was no sign of Kamal Lata. Nabin sent a man to take me to the station. Kishen had everything packed and ready and was in a hurry to leave. But Kamal Lata didn't return. Padma insisted that she would come but, as the hours passed, my doubts increased till I knew, for a certainty, that she wouldn't. Avoiding the stress of a last farewell she had run away, without any clothes to change into. She had said that she was a beggar woman, a Vaishnavi who sang for a living. Her words, only words till yesterday, had become an accomplished fact.

Padma came to the door as I was leaving. She burst out weeping in the loud, bewildered voice of a lost child. I gave her my address and said, 'Your Didi left you in my care. You must write to me and ask me for anything you wish.'

'I can't write very well, *gosain.*'

'Write as you can. I promise to read every word.'

'Won't you meet Didi before you go?'

'We'll meet some other time.' And, with these words, I walked out of the *akhra*.

Fourteen

I STRAINED MY EYES IN THE DARK, LOOKING FOR HER, ALL THE WAY to the station. But the moment I stepped on the platform I saw her, standing a little apart from the crowd. She came forward on seeing me, and said in a normal, everyday voice, 'You must buy me a ticket, *gosain*.'

'You're really leaving us all, Kamal Lata?'

'What else can I do?'

'Doesn't it hurt?'

'Why do you ask, *gosain*? You know.'

'Where will you go?'

'To Vrindavan. But you needn't buy a ticket for all the way. I'll get off somewhere and—'

'And beg as you walk till you reach your destination. That's the idea, isn't it? You don't want to be too deeply in debt—even to me.'

'It's not the first time, *gosain*. I've walked—' She glanced up at my face and said simply, 'Buy me a ticket to Vrindavan, then.'

'Let's go together.'

'Are you going the same way?'

'No, but I'll go with you as far as I can.'

We took our places in the train. I dusted the bench and made a bed for her with my own hands.

'What are you doing, *gosain*?' Kamal Lata said agitatedly.

'I'm doing that which I've never done for anyone before. I'm doing it so that I may never forget this journey.'

'Do you really wish to remember it all your life?'

'I do, Kamal Lata. Only, no one will know of it. Only you and I.'

'But it is not right for me—'

'It is. Sit in peace and let me do what I must.'

She obeyed. The train passed through many villages and towns, green fields and stretches of wasteland. They revived many memories which Kamal Lata shared with me in her low, sweet voice. She spoke of her many pilgrimages to Vrindavan, Mathura, Govardhan and Radha Kundu and her experiences with sadhus and Vaishnavs. And, then, her meeting with Dwarika Das which had brought her to the *akhra*. I remembered my conversation of the morning and cried eagerly, 'Do you know, Kamal Lata? Bara *gosainji* believes that you are innocent.'

'He does?'

'Yes. He wept when I took leave of him and said, "I can't drive out an innocent woman and stay within these walls. My years of service to Radha Govinda will cease to have meaning, if I do." He's leaving the *akhra* too. Our little ashram, so simple and sweet, will fall to pieces.'

'No, it won't. God will show a way.'

'If you are ever called back—will you go?'

'No.'

'If they are genuinely repentant? If they truly need you?'

'Not even then.' She thought for a moment and added, 'I'll go back only if you want me to. Not for anyone else in the world.'

'But where can I find you?'

She didn't reply. There was a long silence.

'Kamal Lata!' I called and saw that her eyes were shut and her head rested on the window. 'She's fatigued with the strain of the last few days,' I thought, and let her go on sleeping. Then, I don't know when, I fell asleep myself.

'Natun *gosain*!' Someone was shaking me awake. 'You'll have to get off. The train has arrived at Sainthia station.' I sat up and rubbed my eyes. Kishen came in from the next compartment and took down my bag and bedding. I found the sheet and pillow with which I had made a bed for Kamal Lata, neatly rolled up and put away with the rest of my luggage.

'It was such a small thing, Kamal Lata. Yet you returned it.'

'I'll have to walk mile after mile. I can't carry a load.'

'You don't even have a change of clothing with you. Shall I give you a dhoti?'

'You don't understand, *gosain*. Your dhoti will look strange on a beggar.'

'Perhaps it will,' I sighed. 'But even beggars must eat. You have two days of travel ahead of you. Will you keep the food I brought or shall I throw it away before I go?'

Kamal Lata burst out laughing. '*Ma go*! How angry you are! I'll keep the food and eat a huge hearty meal after you leave.'

The interval between arrival and departure drew to a close. It was time to descend. As I rose to do so, Kamal Lata came up to me and whispered, 'There's no one around. Give me the dust of your feet, quickly, before anyone sees us.' She bent and touched my feet for the first time.

It was still dark when I stepped off the train and stood on the platform. I looked up at the sky. Even as I did, a thin band of pearly light appeared in the middle and spread upwards and outwards, slicing away the darkness in two halves. A crescent moon—pale and worn with thirteen nights of waning—gleamed dully from one end and, from the other, the first haze of dawn appeared, shimmering like a mist. I remembered the time I had gone picking flowers with the Vaishnavi. The hour had been the same but the feelings—how different!

The whistle blew. The guard waved his green light and gave the signal. Kamal Lata put out her hand from the window and, for the first time in our acquaintance, she took mine and held it close. 'I've never asked anything of you, ever, *gosain*,' she said in a voice, humble and pleading. 'Will you do something for me?'

'I will.'

'I know how much you love me! How you suffer for me! Don't—anymore. Put your faith in Him. Surrender me in his hands and be free.'

The train moved with a jerk. Her hand was still in mine. I walked a few paces holding it. 'I surrender you, Kamal Lata,' I said. 'May He have the caring of you and may the path you've chosen be wide and free. I shall not insult you by calling you mine—ever again.'

The train moved away. Our hands fell apart. The lights of the station flashed into her face, one by one, through the window in which it was framed. Then all was dark and empty but I thought I saw her waving her hand in a last farewell.

Glossary

Barui:	Those who grow betel leaves.
Bauri:	A socially backward caste, usually palanquin-bearers.
Bharatvarsha:	This was a journal to which Saratchandra contributed regularly.
Boshtom/ Boshtomi:	Colloquial corruption of Vaishnav and Vaishnavi.
Dom:	A person whose caste duty was to cremate the dead and therefore was considered an "Untouchable".
Durbasha muni:	One of the ancient rishis reputed to have a violent temper.
Gangajal:	Women in Bengal formed lasting friendships by using symbolic names for each other, such as *Sai, Moner Katha, Gangajal,* etc.
Goala:	The cowherd caste order.
Jal Achal:	The caste orders considered to be low, therefore water touched by them was not acceptable to Brahmins.
Kaibarta:	The caste order which consists of peasants.
Kamar:	Colloquial corruption of Karmakar.
Karmakar:	The caste order of blacksmiths.
Kayastha:	A Hindu caste considered lower than the Brahmins in nineteenth century Bengal.

Kulin:	Of the lineage of Brahmins on whom an order of honour was bestowed by King Ballal Sen of ancient Bengal.
Kumahar:	The caste order of potters.
Kumbhakarna:	One of the brothers of King Ravana. His capacity for eating and sleeping are legendary.
Kurmi:	A socially backward caste of rural Bengal.
Nabasakh:	The potter, weaver, milkman, barber, spice dealer, garland-maker, blacksmith, confectioners and those who grow betel leaves collectively make up the Hindu caste order of Nabasakh; literally, 'nine branches'.
Neelkanth:	One of the many names of Shiva. The legend goes that when the asuras and devas were churning the ocean for the life-giving *amrita*, they churned up a very destructive poison. Shiva took in the poison to prevent it from destroying the universe—but instead of swallowing it, held it in his throat. Thus, his throat turned blue, and he was called Neelkanth, i.e. 'blue-necked'.
Sadgope:	The milkman caste order.
Sonar Bene:	A person belonging to the caste order of goldsmiths.
Sunri:	A person belonging to the caste order of wine distillers.
Tili:	A person belonging to the caste order of oil crushers.